E

tienne Cartier

Life of Beato Angelico da Fiesole

E

tienne Cartier

Life of Beato Angelico da Fiesole

ISBN/EAN: 9783337331054

Printed in Europe, USA, Canada, Australia, Japan

Cover: Foto ©Raphael Reischuk / pixelio.de

More available books at **www.hansebooks.com**

LIFE OF

BEATO ANGELICO DA FIESOLE,

OF THE ORDER OF FRIAR-PREACHERS.

TRANSLATED BY A MEMBER OF THE SAME ORDER
FROM THE FRENCH OF

E. CARTIER.

WITH INTRODUCTION ON THE PRINCIPLES OF CHRISTIAN ART,
BY THE SAME AUTHOR.

AND COMMENDATORY LETTER OF

HIS EMINENCE CARDINAL WISEMAN.

"Chi fa cofe di Crifto con Crifto deve ftar fempre."
" Who does the things of Chrift, with Chrift muft always be."—V<small>ASARI</small>.

LONDON:
JOHN PHILP, 7, ORCHARD STREET, PORTMAN SQUARE.
1865.

DALZIEL BROTHERS, CAMDEN PRESS, LONDON.

HIS EMINENCE CARDINAL WISEMAN.

LONDON, JUNE 18, 1864.

DEAR SIR,

 SHOULD have been happy to accede to your requeſt by writing a Preface to the "Life of Beato Angelico da Fieſole." No ſubjeƈt would have been more con-genial to my feelings in every way. An "Artiſt Saint" affords ſcope for much, which ſcarcely any other ſubjeƈt could embrace and combine. It is a delicious theme, and inexhauſtible.

Unfortunately before you ſpoke to me, I had already engaged myſelf to the full extent of my leiſure and my ſtrength. I need not ſpecify what I had undertaken, and have been ſtriving to accompliſh. But I can ſay, with truth, that I would have readily complied with your requeſt, had I been able to ſee my way to the work required, within a reaſonable time.

I can, therefore, only give you this expreſſion of my beſt wiſhes, in the ſincere hope that a work as intereſting as that of M. Cartier will be heartily welcomed by readers of every claſs, without any ſpecial recommendation from me. Standing purely on its own merits, it ought to prove eminently ſucceſsful.

Wiſhing you every bleſſing,

I am ever

Yours very ſincerely in Chriſt,

N. CARD. WISEMAN.

MR. JOHN PHILP, 7, ORCHARD STREET,

PORTMAN SQUARE, LONDON.

TO THE REVEREND FATHER

HENRY DOMINIC LACORDAIRE,

OF THE ORDER OF FRIAR-PREACHERS.

REVEREND FATHER,

I DARE not prefent this book to the public without the addition of your name. Permit me to dedicate it to you. It is a fervice I beg of your benevolent affection.

Beato Angelico da Fiefole is one of your predeceffors, and you were the firft to make me admire his mafterpieces under the confecrated arches of the convent of S. Mark. I have written his Life, with the defire of giving a high and holy idea of Chriftian Art. But my work gives but poorly my thoughts beneath the pulpit of Notre Dame : and I place thefe imperfect pages under your patronage, in order that thofe who heard your words may complete them by their own remembrance.

When God chofe you to re-eftablifh the Order of S. Dominic in France, He gave you, with the zeal of the Apoftle, the power of the Chriftian artift, to guide us to the truth. He now rewards you for the good you have done us : He withdraws you from the fad pageant of the world, and re-gathers around you the youth you have loved fo much. At Sorèze, again, you teach the True and Beautiful ; you exercife *the* great art, " *Ars artium, regimen animarum.*" You fafhion fouls to the image of God, by communicating to them the gifts you have received ; and whatever may be the glory of your bye-gone days, you find one more beautiful and fweet in the affection which furrounds you. Happy are thofe who live near you, and know how to underftand your heart.

May God blefs all your works, my dear Father, and multiply the number of thofe who know and love you.

E. CARTIER.

DEAR SIR AND FRIEND,

O U have dedicated to me your Life of Beato Angelico of Fiefole; and in thus recalling me to the beft days of the Order of S. Dominic, you have taken the opportunity of reminding me of days that are no more. I thank you for it. Like you, I think that God has recompenfed me too much, by withdrawing me from the pageant of the world, and preferving for me in my retreat a pious wreck of the miniftry which He had entrufted to me. I live again amidft youth, and love and ferve them. What more could I wifh in the decline of life; Nothing, if it be not the remembrance of thofe who have formerly known and loved me. You affure me that it is faithful to me, and you give me a proof of it in the dedication of a book, in which I am fure to find again the touch of an artift and the piety of a Chriftian. It is a great deal at once. So I leave it to God to recompenfe you, renewing for my own weak part, the expreffion of my high efteem and hearty affeétion.

FR. HENRY DOMINIC LACORDAIRE,

Of the Friar-Preachers.

[The Very Rev. Fr. H. D. Lacordaire clofed his life at the College of Sorèze, November 22nd, 1861.—*Tranfl.*]

LIFE OF BEATO ANGELICO.

INTRODUCTION.

" Chi fa cofe di Crifto, con Crifto deve ftar fempre."

" *Who does the things of Chrift, with Chrift muft always be*."—VASARI.

H E higheft meaning of Art is the manifeftation of the Beautiful. All its efforts tend towards that end; and the artift refts only when he thinks he has attained it. But what is the Beautiful? What is that power which ravifhes the foul, and wrings from it a cry of admiration? What are its principles, its form, its means, and its end? Profound and myfterious queftions, difficult to determine, above all in an age when pride of reafon feems again

punifhed by confufion of language. Let us feek an anfwer, however, by examining the phenomena which the prefence of the Beautiful produces in ourfelves.

We perceive the Beautiful by the fenfes, but the pleafure which found, fhape and colour caufe in us, does not ftop with fenfation. The animal does not fee nor underftand the Beautiful. Man alone enjoys it in the centre of his being; and if we analyfe what he experiences in thus interiorly perceiving beauty in an object, we fhall recognife that he judges by laws independent of that object : and it is the application of thefe laws that man approves.

His pleafure increafes, when, by a natural motion of his mind, he afcends from effect to caufe, and difcovers the beginning and end of this application ; for thefe laws do not exift by themfelves, but refide in a being that poffeffes and realizes them, and the Beautiful thus manifefted becomes a language which eftablifhes a relation between two intelligences. A work of art is the expreffion of an idea; and he who fees this idea not only perceives if it is well expreffed, but judges alfo if it is expreffed with a fuitable aim.

Hence there are two ways of recognizing beauty in a work of art. If we look at the caufe of its form and the means taken to realife it, we judge it according to the laws of nature ; if we look to the aim of this form, we judge it by the laws of morality.[1] Under thefe two afpects, then, form may reprefent natural and moral beauty. Natural beauty is that which befits the nature of every being, and comprifes intellectual

---

[1] Pulchrum habet rationem caufæ formalis, bonum autem rationem caufæ finalis. (S. Thom., i, q. f, a. 4.)

and phyfical beauty. Intelle&ual beauty is the radiation of the divine Intelligence; phyfical beauty is the
image of it, and can only exift through it as an effect
through caufe. What is called fenfual beauty is
merely a corruption of it, which diverts it from moral
beauty, its true end. Moral beauty flows from the
divine will, and regulates the relations of beings
amongft themfelves, and the correfpondence of the
finite with the infinite. The union of natural and
moral beauty conftitutes the perfect beauty which completely fatisfies the foul; for it prefents to it the True
in its principle, and the Beautiful in its end. The
Beautiful is a mirror which reflects the True and Good
on the intelligence and will.

But what is the Beautiful in itfelf? What is its
effence, its neceffary form ? How does it pleafe the
foul that loves and feeks it? The Beautiful is the
evidence, the light, the fplendour of unity; it is
vifible unity, the unity of being in its fubftance,
principle and relations, in its elements and life. The
elements of unity are, order, harmony and proportions,
and its life is its expanfion, its radiation in variety.
The more objects unity embraces, the more beautiful
it is; and in each vifible unity we perceive through
its relations a ftill greater unity. We afcend from
the unity of a grain of fand to the unity of the
celeftial fpheres; and thus, ftep by ftep, we arrive at
the prefence of God Himfelf.[1] We cannot now contemplate the Firft Unity, face to face; but we perceive
it through fecondary unities, juft as we admire the

[1] A magnitudine enim speciei et creaturæ, cognofcibiliter poterit creator horum
videri. (*Sap.*, xiii. 5.)

brightnefs of daylight in the thicknefs of the diamond ; and this ray of the divinity fet in every
creature is its beauty, becaufe it conftitutes its unity.[1]

The Beautiful, vifible unity, pleafes the foul, becaufe
it finds therein its joy, peace and repofe. The foul
does not exift of itfelf, and its centre and true unity is
without. The intellect feeks unity by knowledge, and
unity it purfues in all its analyfes and claffifications ;
and when it reaches the myfteries of the unknown, it
hails unity again in that Firft Caufe, on which its
weaknefs may repofe. The will alfo requires unity for
love ; it attaches itfelf to the unity difcovered by the
intellect, and all its defires tend to be more united with
it, as with its life and chief good.

The Beautiful then fatisfies the two-fold want of the
foul, becaufe vifible unity is a flafh of the infinite, a
track of light towards the firft and laft unity, which

---

[1] Plato has faid, that the Beautiful is the fplendour of the True. Here are
fome other definitions.

Père André. The Beautiful has order for its foundation, and unity for its
eflence.

Winckelmann. Unity and fimplicity are the two real fources of beauty.

Mengs. The Beautiful is a vifible perfection, an imperfect image of fupreme
perfection.

Tieck. The Beautiful is a fingle and unique ray of heavenly brightnefs ; but in
paffing through the prifm of the imagination, it is decompofed into a thoufand
colours and a thoufand tints.

Mendelffohn. The effence of the Beautiful is unity in variety.

Pere Lacordaire has defined beauty, " The expanfion of being in light, harmony,
grandeur and goodnefs."—*Conférences de Touloufe.* Correfpondant, 25 Feb.,
1857.

S. Thomas of Aquinas fays, " Pulchrum eft cujus apprehenfio placet. (I. q. 5,
a. 4.) Ad pulchritudinem tria requiruntur. 1° Quidem integritas five perfectio ;
quæ enim diminuta funt, hoc ipfo turpia funt. 2° Et debita proportio, five confo-
nantia. 3° Et iterum claritas : unde quæ habent colorem nitidum pulchra effe
dicuntur." (*Id.* q. 39)

muſt be its happineſs; for the ſoul finds in God alone
the True, the Beautiful, the abſolute good.

Unity is the aim of all the efforts of life, knowledge
and love. Order, peace, family, country and happineſs
are nothing elſe but unity; and the beauty which
makes it viſible, gives to the ſoul a foretaſte of heavenly
beatitude. But this joy of the ſoul is fruitful. When
the intellect has ſeen the Beautiful, the will is moved
even to love. This impreſſion it deſires to reproduce
without, and to communicate to other intellects and
wills; it wiſhes alſo itſelf to manifeſt the Beautiful.
Its means is Form: this word expreſſes the appearance
of things, the phenomena that ſtrike our ſenſes. But
external form is the manifeſtation of a ſpiritual one,
the impreſs of an idea, the ſign of an intellect and a
will: thus taken, form is language in its wideſt ſenſe;
and by it art manifeſts the Beautiful.[1]

The power of art is founded on reſemblance to
nature. Intellect and will have the ſame laws, live in
the ſame manner, and can mutually communicate
their life by interchanging their ſcience and love.
God is infinite knowledge and love, as the two great
definitions atteſt which He has given of Himſelf.
Under the law of fear, He ſaid to Moſes proſtrate
before the burning buſh, "I am Who am, *Ego ſum
qui ſum.*" Again, under the law of grace, He ſaid to
S. John, ſupported on His breaſt during the Laſt
Supper, "God is love, *Deus caritas eſt.*" The firſt
act of life is, to know; the ſecond, to love. For us,

---

[1] A formis quæ ſunt ſine materia, veniunt formæ quæ ſunt in materia. (Boɛtius,
in lib. i, *De Trinitate.*)

Omnes formæ et motus in iis inferioribus fluunt à formis quæ ſunt in intellectu
alicujus intelligentiæ. (S. Thom., i. q. 65, 4. c.)

thefe acts have date in time; for God, they have none in eternity. The firft Being poffeffes a knowledge without beginning; and the love refulting from it is as ancient and as great as the being and knowledge He unites.

God and man can communicate by art, fcience and love. Every work of art is a free act proceeding from the will. The will, indeed, requires of the intellect the means of art, which depend on the laws of nature, but thefe means are fubordinate to the aim which the will propofes to itfelf; and this aim muft be fubject to the moral law like the will. What is the moral law of art? What rule muft the artift follow? And how fhall we know whether his work be good or bad?

The Firft Caufe is the fupreme and neceffary law of the vifible and invifible world; and by doing what God Himfelf has done, the artift knows how to unite natural and moral beauty in his work. God has the perfection of art, becaufe He has the perfection of being, intellect and will. Not only does He enjoy this fecundity, this internal activity, of which revelation gives us a glimpfe in its myfterious light, but He fhows Himfelf too outfide His effence, by drawing beings out of nothing, and creating forms ftamped with His own perfections.

Why is God an artift? Why does He not remain alone in the bofom of His immutable eternity? Since He is the beginning of everything, nothing can be wanting to Him and be added to His infinite happinefs in the contemplation of Himfelf. If He has created anything, it is becaufe, through His incomprehenfible goodnefs, He loved thofe poffible beings He faw in His own thought, and willed to communicate to them, along with exiftence, the fight of that beauty which is perfect happinefs. The goodnefs of God determined His power to create fpirits and bodies.[1]

Yes, by tracing back the courfe of ages up to this Firft Caufe, the thought alone of which dazzles the underftanding, we come to the folemn moment and ineffable beginning, wherein we can fay that God made heaven and earth, and eftablifhed relations between Nothing and Being, time and eternity, form and matter. That art of God is the type of the art of man, and if we ftudy its marvellous workings, we fhall find in them the conditions and law of the creative faculty, which is one of the fineft traits of our divine refemblance.

Before the Supreme Artift took the work in hand, the form of what He had to make was in Him; and there it is ftill in all the unity and beauty of its beginning and end, without creation having exhaufted or changed it any more than a mirror impairs the image it reflects. The firft form of a work of art is in the thought of the artift. This form comes to man from without, becaufe he does not derive his own being from himfelf. But in God the form is infeparable from His effence; becaufe nothing exifted before Him, and Nothingnefs is devoid of infpiration and power. This is that eternal form, the manifeftations of which human fcience feeks in nature, fuch as the general

---

[1] Cùm Deus fit primum agens, primus quoque finis omnium neceffariò eft. Omne agens agit propter finem. Primo vero agenti non convenit agere proper acquifitionem alicujus finis, fed intendit folùm communicare fuam perfectionem, quæ ejus bonitas. (S. THOM., i, q. 44, a. 44.)

laws of beings, genera, fpecies, life, motion, powers and numbers, which regulate everything : truth immutable, which our ignorance is dividing *ad infinitum* but which we fhall one day contemplate with a fingle glance at the divine light.

When God willed to reveal Himfelf to us in time and fpace, He created matter by a fimple act which we cannot comprehend. Matter is infeparable from form,' but yet diftinct from it. Form changes in bodies, without deftroying the leaft atom of them. Created form is the outward fign of God, the echo of His Word, the reflection of His fplendour ; and as fign, echo and reflection are more perfect in proportion as they approach their model, fo too the gradations of beings in the vifible and invifible world are regulated by the diftance that feparates them from their Author. God and matter are the extreme limits of form ; and the farther form is removed from matter, the more beautiful it is, and the more it refembles God.²

The Word, that *Art of the wife and Almighty God, in whom are all living and eternal ideas,*³ firft of all created light, the moft perfect fenfible image of Himfelf. For He is the true light which enlighteneth men.⁴ Juft as the Eternal Light is the life of the world of fpirits, fo is created light the life of the world of

---

¹ Deus non poteft facere materiam effe fine forma. (S. Thom., i. q. 66, a. 10.)

² Omnis forma, quanto nobilior, tanto magis dominatur materiæ, et minus ei immergitur, et magis eam fua virtute excedit. (S. Thom., i. q. 76, 1. c.)

³ Dixit Auguftinus quod filius Dei eft ars Patris. (S. Bonaventura, *De Reduct. art. ad Theologiam.* S. August., *De Trinit.*, l. vii, c. 10.) Verbum Dei . . . . eft omnis forma et compago et concordia partium. (S. August., *Tract. in Joan.*)

⁴ In ipfo vita erat, et vita erat lux hominum. Erat lux vera, quæ illuminat omnem hominem venientem in hunc mundum. (S. Joan. I, 4. 9.)

bodies. Who could recount its myfteries in nature? It is the element of form, the mainfpring of motion, the neceffity of all beings. Light is the inftrument of the will for God and man. Invifible as fpirit, quick as thought, it is everywhere potentially, and awaits only an act to manifeft itfelf. Admirable in its external phenomena, it enlightens our eye as God does our intellect.[1] It difcovers objects to us, and diverfi-fies and reflects itfelf in colours, as the infinite in finite things. God has made it vifible in the fun to enlighten the world, as He made Himfelf vifible in a body to difpel our darknefs ; and that immovable focus produces the ineffable harmony of day, the unity and variety of colour, the gradations of tint, the play of light and fhade, and the changing wonders of every hour, which feem to give life and motion to inanimate bodies.

God opened to light the immenfities of space. For its palace, He created the ftars, whofe numbers and diftances our ciphers cannot calculate ; and He traced the paths and curves they have followed with perfect tractability from the beginning of ages.

The Supreme Artift then fafhioned the earth : He ftretched out the fea and main land, modelled the mountains and horizons, drew the courfes of rivers and ocean-fhores, decked them with verdure, flowers and fruits, and everywhere fheds life abundantly. He peopled the air, earth and waters with animated beings, and endowed them with wonderful fecundity: but it

[1] Terra nifi luce illuftrata videri non poteft. Ergo et illa quæ in difciplinis traduntur, quæ quifquis intelligit, veriffima effe nulla dubitatione concedit ; cre-dendum eft ea non poffe intelligi, nifi ab alio quafi fuo fole illuftrentur. (S. Aug., Soliloq., l. I. c. 5, n. I.)

was only a preparation, a domain which awaited its mafter.

At laft, God made man to His own image and like-nefs. He took a little flime to form his body, breathed into his face the breath of life, and man became a living foul,[1] uniting the beauties of the vifible and invifible worlds in his two-fold nature. His body is a mafter-piece, where fcience ftudies, as in their centre, the general laws of the univerfe, and all beings feem faithful and devoted vaffals who recognife his empire. So great is the beauty of the body, that one of the chaftifements of the original fall is, to have loft the calm and pure contemplation of it. But happily this beauty ftill appears upon the face of man. Who can even admire enough thofe harmonious outlines, thofe living traits, thofe fupple endlefs lines, that command-ing brow, thofe eyes, that mouth, thofe very hairs, a fingle one alone of which is able to wound the heart.[2] The face is the throne of life : there repofed the creative breath, which has given man his divine like-nefs ; there the foul manifefts its moft delicate thoughts and moft fleeting emotions, with a finenefs of tone and variety of tint which the moft fkilful pencil cannot render. Man refembles God by his foul. His intellect and will are in relation with the fupreme intelligence and will, by the light of which they may be illumi-nated. The foul knows what God knows, and loves

---

[1] Formavit igitur Dominus Deus hominem de limo terræ, et infpiravit in faciem ejus fpiraculum vitæ, et factus eft homo in animam viventem. (*Gen.* ii. 7.)

[2] Vulnerafti cor meum in uno oculorum tuorum, et in uno crine colli tui. (*Cant.* iv. 9.)

what God loves ; and thus partakes of His life, His knowledge and His love.[1] When the Supreme Artiſt had created the world and man to be its maſter, He contemplated His work, and found it good.[2] Good is the true aim of art ; truth, its principle ; and beauty, its means. Theſe three things are diſtinƈt but inſeparable ; and the Creator has ſtamped them on every creature as the ſignature of His adorable Trinity. It is ſaid that God has done all in number, weight and meaſure.[3] In every being, meaſure repreſents the truth of its ſubſtance, number regulates its beauty, and weight determines the order and aim for which it has been created. Thus everything ſhows forth the divine power, wiſdom and goodneſs.[4] Truth, beauty and goodneſs are the elements of all things ; but in us this impreſs of the Trinity is elevated even to likeneſs and reſemblance.[5]

Creation was good, becauſe it was beautiful and manifeſted truth ; above all, it was good, becauſe it was a means of union between God and man.[6] Thus juſtice and goodneſs is the motive and rule of the art of God. He has been juſt towards Himſelf, for He made heaven and earth to tell His glory, and He has

---

[1] Omnia dicimur in Deo videre . . . in quantum participatione ſui luminis omnia cognoſcimus ; nam et ipſum naturale lumen rationis eſt quædam participatio divini luminis. (S. THOM., I. q. 12. a. 11.)

[2] Viditque Deus cunƈta quæ fecerat, et erant valdè bona. (*Gen.* I. 31.)

[3] Omnia in menſurâ, et numero, et pondere diſpoſuiſti. (*Sap.* xi., 21.)

[4] S. THOM. I. q. 45.—S. BONAVENTURA, *Itinerarium mentis ad Deum,* ch. 2 and 4.

[5] S. THOM., I. q. 45, a. 2.

[6] Inviſibilia enim ipſius à creaturâ mundi, per ea quæ faƈta ſunt, intelleƈta, conſpiciuntur ; ſempiterna quoque ejus virtus ct divinitas, ita ut ſint inexcuſabiles. (*Rom.* I. 20.)

created beings to underſtand their language, and render back to Him an intelligent and free homage.

This external manifeſtation was not neceſſary, ſince the teſtimony He was giving to Himſelf ſufficed for His juſtice; but His goodneſs was not ſatisfied, and He willed through love to communicate His happineſs to us. He has reconciled His juſtice and goodneſs by leaving His predeſtined creature to acquire that happineſs, by a trial in the viſible world. God has veiled His eſſence: creation is a revelation of His hidden preſence, which may lead man, by faith and love, up to the contemplation of supreme beauty.[1]

The real aim of creation, then, is the homage of the creature to the Creator; and in the univerſe, man alone can render Him this homage. Natural beauty is only a means of obtaining it. God is its beginning and end: it comes forth from its Firſt Cauſe clothed in the ſplendour of its beginning; but in order to be crowned with the glories of its end, a free act is needed, and that is moral beauty. God has prepared and revealed it to man: He has enlightened his underſtanding, but has ſtopped before his will, which muſt complete the work, and He awaits its deciſion. The free will accepts or refuſes; if it accept, the work of God has been ſucceſsful; but if it refuſe, it becomes, ſo to ſpeak, uſeleſs, for the end propoſed by divine goodneſs has not been attained, and the Almighty is conſtrained to demand of juſtice the glory He expected of love.

God has made man the artiſt of moral beauty, the intelligent and free voice that conſecrates the world to its

[1] Laudent te opera tua, ut amemus te; et amemus te, ut laudent te opera tua. (S. Aug., Conf., xiii, 33.)

Author; and for this He has created him to His image and likenefs, made him capable of knowing and loving Him, and given him alfo means to make himfelf known to his fellow-creatures. Man poffeffes language, that internal word which makes him know his exiftence: that word which becomes incarnate on his lips, in order to reveal the thoughts of his underftanding and the motions of his will: that unique word which ftrikes on the multitude without dividing or altering itfelf.

The orator is pre-eminently the artift. In every way, he penetrates the very foul of man. His voice modulates the founds which communicate his thoughts with an exactnefs and delicacy of expreffion mufic cannot give, and his action fpeaks to the eye by geftures and attitudes the fculptor will ftrive to copy. His look flafhes back the light, whilft the blood paints all his emotions on the features with the richeft colours. He arranges the architecture of his difcourfe, fets all in order, number, weight and meafure, and the truth which he defires to reveal appears there as in a temple.

Man is not an orator alone, he also fixes his thoughts by figns; he is a writer and literary man. His fpeech frees him from time and fpace, goes without him to the extremities of the world and to the remoteft generations, communicates itfelf to all, and acquires an immortal pofterity in intelligences. Language is the moft powerful means of art, becaufe it is the moft free and faithful image of thought.

Man has other means. God lends him matter, and permits him too to create a world, in which he makes his fky and horizons, and diftributes his light at pleafure. His chifel gives birth to the rich vegetation

of ornament, and his pencil fcatters life by peopling it
with images. But this world of architecture, fculpture
and painting muft be a temple. God does not lend
man His materials and inftruments to profane them;
and it is neceffary, too, that, when the work is done, the
look of the Supreme fhall find it good, that is, full of
love and juftice.

The art of man muft be like the art of God, and its
reflection and faithful echo, in order that this echo may
be repeated and this reflection be reproduced in the
fouls of his fellow-creatures, and that all may acknowledge and praife the Lord. As the beginning of his art,
the artift-man muft acquire the eternal truths expreffed
by creation, and by his intellect and will communicate
with the Creator; and when he has feen and underftood
His glory, he will tell it by his works, and ftrive to
communicate to others the happinefs he experiences in
knowing and loving Him. Imitation of nature is not
the true aim of art, for fuch imitation is always incomplete and rude, and is only the fign or writing of moral
beauty.¹ To be juft and good, the art of man muft
be a prayer and an inftruction.

Has the art of man been juft and good? Has the

---

¹ Moral beauty is the foundation of all true beauty. . . . The aim of art is to
exprefs moral by aid of phyfical beauty. The latter is the mere fymbol of the
former. In nature, this fymbol is often obfcure; and in clearing it, art attains
effects which nature does not always produce. Nature may pleafe more; for,
once for all, fhe poffeffes, in an incomparable degree, what forms the greateft
charm of the imagination and eye,—life. Art is more touching, becaufe, in
expreffing moral beauty efpecially, it addreffes itfelf more directly to the fource of
the deep emotions.

Form cannot be a form alone, it muft be the form of fomething. Phyfical
beauty then is the fign of an interior beauty, which is fpiritual and moral beauty;
and therein the ground, principle and unity of beauty exifts. (COUSIN, *Du Vrai,
du Beau et du Bien*, vii. et viii. laçon.)

pupil remained faithful to the Mafter's leffons ? God
had placed him in a garden of delights, where moral
beauty was to rife towards Him with the perfume of
the flowers and the incenfe of prayer. Adam's firft
life was the union of natural and moral beauty:
natural beauty cheered his intellect, and moral beauty
animated his will. Light and heat penetrated his pure
foul, and the art refulting from this knowledge and
love was but the rebounding of a light back to its
fource. The art of Adam was his fong of adoration,
the echo of harmonies heard within his foul, the ema-
nation of pleafures felt within his heart, the admirable
poem which confecrated creation to its Author: art
juft and fublime, art rich in knowledge and in love,
art blended with the art of God Himfelf.

Unhappily things changed; and natural was feparated from moral beauty. Unfatisfied with the fruit
of the tree of life, which in the terreftrial paradife
fymbolized his union with God, man touched the
tree of the knowledge of good and evil, and made a
difaftrous trial of his liberty. He wronged divine
juftice and goodnefs, and became incapable of reflecting them in his works. Sin ftraightway weakened
man's creative faculties ; and his intellect, blinded by
the fenfes, loft the intuition which without effort penetrated into the nature and relations of things. He
had to feek painfully for truth athwart the doubts of
ignorance and falls of error. The Beautiful was
obfcured to his gaze ; and the will, depraved by
concupifcence, re-afcended no more by vifible forms
to unity and primeval beauty.

By fin, man not only became incapable of feeing

*

and returning the Beautiful, but alfo impaired it in himfelf and in nature. The foul is the form of the body[1] and communicates its beauty to it. This beauty is the divine likenefs which it has received from its Creator, and which it muft increafe by love. The great work of man lies there : and when death raifes the veil that conceals it, the degree of likenefs will be that of recompenfe; for God can love only what refembles Himfelf: the reft is lifelefs and abides in death.

By free will, then, the foul has a plaftic power over the body. It increafes or leffens its beauty; and when fin fets it in oppofition to its auguft model, the body, that mafterpiece of the vifible world, neceffarily felt it deeply. Man's brow loft its radiant crown, and creation fmitten in its centre, was itfelf infected with the phyfical evil which punifhed the fault.

What then became of the art of man? Could it remain true and good? By feparating himfelf from God, man had been fevered from his life. He had weakened the light of his underftanding and the ftrength of his will; in feeing beauty lefs, he was alfo lefs capable of rendering it back. Ignorance led him to confound the creature and the Creator in one rude worfhip. Concupifcence attracted him to the pleafures of the fenfes, and made him confecrate to his vices the temple God had given him means to build. In becoming pagan, art has been neither juft nor true. It has been only a falfe prayer and teaching; and man, without love for his gods and fellow-creatures, was an artift through intereft, in order to acquire riches and glory.

---

[1] Anima eft caufa efficiens, finis et formalis sui corporis. (S. THOM., 1. q. 90, a. 2.)—Anima eft forma corporis. (*Id.*, iii, q. 75, a. 6.)

How is this fallen art to be raiſed up again, and its original juſtice and goodneſs reſtored? The creative Word, who made worlds out of nothing, took ſtill more admirable means for glorifying God. He united Himſelf to human nature, and thus at once re-eſtabliſhed the perfeĉt alliance of natural and moral beauty. Mercy and truth have met each other, juſtice and peace have kiſſed[1] in His perſon, and the new Artiſt gave back the divine likeneſs to man. By His blood, He reſtored to him life of the ſoul, light of underſtanding, and ſtrength of will, and ſhowed him beauty ſupreme even in poverty, ſuffering and death. Never was God more viſible than on the height of Calvary.[2]

In offering Himſelf, Chriſt was infinitely juſt towards God, ſince the Viĉtim was equal to the Majeſty outraged. He was infinitely good towards men, becauſe He voluntarily died for them; and the world, cleanſed and transfigured in His perſon, can now worthily glorify its Author. In Chriſt, the art of man has again found juſtice and goodneſs.

Chriſt is the type and model of the artiſt. Perfeĉt eloquence flowed from His lips; and He has left us by His Evangeliſts a book wherein truth, beauty and goodneſs are ſhown in all their ſplendour. In forming the Church, He gave the new plan of the temple which man muſt raiſe to his Creator; and its form, imitated by all the Saints, will be the eternal maſterpiece of divine art.

---

[1] Miſericordia et veritas obviaverunt ſibi; juſtitia et pax oſculatæ ſunt. (*Pſalm* lxxxiv., 11.)

[2] *Dialogue* of S. Catherine of Sienna, ch. xxvi.

For eighteen centuries, the Church has continued the art of Chrift. She fpeaks, writes, builds monuments, adorns them with fculpture and paintings, and employs every means to manifeft the hidden God upon her altars. Her infpiration, principle and aim are there. To make Him known and loved, fhe difplays all the magnificence of her worfhip. Not only does fhe confecrate her priefts and fend forth her apoftles, but fhe choofes her artifts, too, to enlighten fouls and remove them from the feductions of falfehood.

Chriftian and pagan art are always at ftrife together. He who is not for Chrift is againft Him. The artift who does not raife the foul to God, detains it in matter ; and turns it away from truth, in order to debafe it in the enjoyments of the body ; whilft he who offers it the doctrine of the Gofpel, prepares the likenefs which makes it participate in the divine life and beauty. No one can remain indifferent to thefe two arts, for in their ftruggle man's deftiny is decided.

Pagan and Chriftian art have a hiftory. Their remains cover the earth like bones blanched on a battle-field. But knowledge, like the prophet Ezekiel, can make thofe bones to live again, and give them back their forms and fouls. They fhall be raifed again, and render homage to the Lord.[1]

The broken monuments of nations are witneffes that tell the caufes of their greatnefs and decay. A people's art is the expreffion of a doctrine ; and the relation of this doctrine to truth explains that

---

[1] Et dabo vobis fpiritum, et vivetis, et fcietis quia ego Dominus. (*Ezech.* xxxvii, 6.)

people's lot, and the diverſity between the fetiſh of the ſavage and the ſtatues of Phidias.

Amongſt the ancients, pagan art was inſpired by the remnants of a primitive revelation. God and matter, truth and error, were learnedly mingled together, and preſented to man's adoration in ſumptuous temples and under ſenſible forms. Pagan art would never have developed itſelf without this ſcientific and religious baſis; it could have preſented nothing to the ſenſes but the groſſeſt enjoyments. But man cannot entirely drive God away from his intellect. Whatever his voluntary degradation may be, the idea of a Firſt Cauſe, and the principles flowing from it, are always there, to perpetuate or repair his errors. This moral germ art was able to receive without Chriſtianity ; and ſuch imperfect knowledge of truth ſufficed to develope taſte for the Beautiful amongſt the nations ſeated in the ſhadow of death.

This explains the brilliant deſtinies of pagan art in the Eaſt. There, religion gave men the genius and patience to raiſe the gigantic marvels of India and the granite temples of Egypt, the proportions and details of which ſtill ſurpriſe us by their myſterious beauties. Art there ſhows itſelf in the ſilence of adoration and in the immobility of fear. But beneath the ſweeter ſky of Greece, religion, freed from ſacerdotal autocracy, had poets for apoſtles, and gave riſe to artiſts, of whom Phidias was the king. Athens built her Parthenon, and pagan art produced maſterpieces which it was impoſſible for it to renew.

Why this impoſſibility ? Why had Phidias only degenerate ſucceſſors, ſince progreſs ſeems natural to man? Why this decline, fo evident and fo rapid? The caufe is very fimple. Pagan art owed its wonders to its religious beliefs; thefe beliefs fell before the examination of reafon, and art bent with them. The martyrdom of Socrates was the beginning of this double ruin: Greek religion and art perifhed together, and Plato alone made their noble obfequies.

What became of pagan art when reafon had chafed it from its imaginary Olympus? It went to ferve in the train of Alexander's fucceffors, until a Proconful, meeting it in a croffway of Corinth, led it to Rome, and gave it as a flave to the Emperors. Art had then to knead the bricks, build amphitheatres, raife gilded houfes for Nero, and replace the head of its ancient gods by that of Caligula. But thefe humiliations were not enough. Reafon had impoverifhed it, and faith came to give it incurable wounds. It ftill had enjoyments and honours in the palaces of the Cæfars. But what was left to it when Chriftianity had planted the Crofs of Calvary on the Capitol? Shame became its portion, and it was condemned to the guilty exiftence of thofe who fpeculate in vice and work in the fhade.

After having fignalized the caufes of the greatnefs and fall of pagan art, let us rapidly examine the hiftory of Chriftian art. When the fongs of the earthly paradife had ceafed, and man was doomed to toil and tears, a merciful promife came to mitigate the fentence. It was proclaimed that the woman fhould crufh the ferpent's head, and Chrift be lifted up between heaven and earth, as the fign of the new alliance. The Redeemer of the world marked out for Himfelf through ages a prophetic path, in which the Patriarchs hailed His myfterious paffage, and art, regenerated by His unfeen prefence, was enabled to refume its glorious deftinies.

We fee it, from the very firft, raifing altars to God, and offering facrifices which were to be, among every people, the indelible evidence of the fall, and the univerfal fymbol of the atonement. Art, true and good, under the mild features of Abel, offers the choice of his flocks to his Creator, whilft on its fide egotiftic art, in the perfon of Cain, keeps its beft ears of corn, and becomes unjuft and homicidal. At the coming out from the ark, God chofe adorers for Himfelf: and whilft the pride of man, who would fain raife an everlafting monument of his power, is punifhed by the confufion of languages, and goes carrying afar his errors, faithful art finds an afylum beneath the tent of Abraham, and in traverfing Egypt prepares itfelf for the greatnefs awaiting it in the defert.

To lay hold of Chriftian art aright in its whole, it muft be remembered that the revealed truth is as old as the world. Chrift has not come to change, but to complete it. Juft as Chriftianity dates from the firft man, fo Chriftian art muft find its glorious origin in the Old Teftament. Whether before or after the coming of the Saviour, Chrift has always been its infpiration. Are not the canticles of the Church thofe of the temple of Solomon? We date Chriftian art from the time when it clothed itfelf for us with material forms. But architecture, fculpture and painting are only the means of art; its life and foul is eloquence and poetry, that exuberance of the mind and heart, that richnefs of images and affections,

which overwhelm us with a victorious light and heat.
Let us put the Bible in one fcale of the balance, and
heap into the other the mafterpieces of pagan art, and
we fhall fee on which fide the advantage will remain.
If under the Old Law Chriftian art did not put on all
the ornaments which the chifel and pencil could give it,
it was owing to an order emanating from the wifdom
of God Himfelf. Providence wifhed to feparate and
diftinguifh His people from the nations who had made
idols to themfelves. But Chriftian art did not the lefs
preferve a lawful and indifputable fuperiority.

We have feen Greece giving to pagan art its fineft
developments; but now that the great days of Athens
and of Jerufalem are no more, let us compare them by
what they have left us. Literature is the principal and
fundamental part of art: by it others are infpired and
nurtured. Who would dare to deny a brilliant victory
to the books of the Hebrews? In vain have the
Greek authors preferved their harmonious forms;
their rivals, weakened by tranflators, dread not the
conteft. Behold them in the ode, which is the trueft
and moft lofty ftyle of poetry. Can the factitious
and venal enthufiafm of Pindar, or the voluptuous and
frivolous verfes of Anachreon, be compared with the
songs of David, fo full of fincere adoration and radiant
majefty? Will the diffufenefs of Herodotus be fet
againft the admirable fimplicity of Mofes, the jefts of
Socrates againft the maxims of Solomon, or the
tragedies of Sophocles and Euripides againft the
afflictions of Job and the lamentations of Jeremias?
Is it not juft to give the crown of genius to thofe who
have already that of a divine and royal antiquity?

Yes, under the Old Law, Chriftian art was a magnificent chant, which began with Mofes, the conqueror of Egypt on the fhores of the Red Sea, and was ended by the aged Simeon, when at laft he received into his arms Him who was the infpirer and hero of it. The celeftial harp given to announce the Defired of Nations and to foothe the expectation of Him, paffed from the hands of Aaron's fifter to Judith and Debora; Tobias carried it into exile; Ifrael hung it on the willows of the rivers of Babylon; and Mary, to celebrate her divine maternity, drew a laft harmony from it, before fhe gave it to the Church, to make her feftal praife refound.

We muft not believe, however, that before Chrift Chriftian art had only a literary glory. God willed that it fhould prelude, fo to fpeak, its future magnificence. He chofe fkilful artifts to work the materials, and Himfelf traced out for Mofes the plan of the holy ark which Solomon was to place in his temple.[1] The pages defcribing that monument of Jewifh worfhip, may give fome idea of it; but the facts of profane hiftory prove ftill better its grandeur and beauty. When Alexander, who knew all the wonders of Greece, vifited the fecond temple, which caufed regret and tears in thofe who had feen the ancient one, he was ftruck with aftonifhment and reverence ; and the Ptolemies, his fucceffors, who reigned over the moft civilized city of

---

[1] Locutufque eft Dominus ad Móyfen, dicens: Ecce vocavi ex nomine Befeleel filium Uri, filii Hur de tribu Juda, et implevi eum fpiritu Dei, fapientia, et intelligentia, et fcientia in omni opere, ad excogitandum quidquid fabrefieri poteft ex auro, et argento, et ære, marmore, et gemmis, et diverfitate lignorum. Dedique ei focium Ooliab filium Achifamech de tribu Dan. Et in corde omnis eruditi pofui fapientiam, ut faciant cuncta quæ præcipi tibi. (*Exod.* xxxi.)

the world, continued to honour it with their offerings. Now the temple of Jerufalem is deftroyed, its fpoils have adorned the triumph of Titus, the prophecy of Chrift is accomplifhed, and a new era has begun for man and Chriftian art.

The Church, patient as her eternal Author, did not haftily give art all its development. It was neceffary, firft of all, to communicate to fouls the fcience and love fhe poffeffed; and when man had purified his mind and heart in the martyr's fufferings, fhe reftored to him the ufe of the material forms which Greeks and Romans had fo much profaned. Artifts under the Emperors, not knowing what to make of a divinity difcredited by reafon, had fquandered it on beings the misfortune and fhame of the world: they perfonified power and virtue under the features of Tiberius, Nero and Meffalina!

When contempt had done juftice to thofe infamous apotheofes, and the idols were overthrown and the temples deferted, Chriftian art began its work. The Church had given it the programme: the Bible completed by the Gofpel; God vifible in Chrift, as the fupreme type; His beauty reflected in the Virgin and in the Saints. To this theme of inexhauftible fecundity the Church joined again a fymbolifm which extends the fphere of art, and multiplies its means of celebrating the conflicts and triumphs of Chrift. The teachings of S. Hilary, of S. John Chryfoftom, and of S. Ambrofe fell from the facred pulpit like fruitful feed, and S. Auguftine gave artifts admirable efthetics in his treatife *De Verâ Religione.*

Chriftian art, fetting out from Rome with the

preachers of the gofpel, extended its peaceful conquefts to the Eaft and Weft, making itfelf all to all, and varying its means according to the climate and genius of the people. At Conftantinople, it put on the peculiar form called Byzantine art, which has been too much praifed or depreciated. The artifts of Byzantium neceffarily underwent the fad influence of the corruption of the Lower Empire, and ended, like the Greeks of the decline, by making works more rich than beautiful. It is their glory to have had martyrs. When the painters, mutilated by the iconoclafts, fled into Italy, the West received with reverence the types they brought in their bleeding hands; and thofe images, confecrated by perfecution and placed upon our altars, were naturally often reproduced. There was, befides, in thofe hieratic and fevere lines a true grandeur which we may ftill admire, fince the fchifm of Photius retains Byzantine art fo long a time in an aftonifhing immobility. The Eaft again influenced the Weft by the proceffes which it had preferved better, and which we were obliged to borrow from it.

But at laft our emancipated art correcfed the heavy maffes of its architecfture, lopped off the profufion of ornaments that hindered its flight, and fucceeded, particularly in Germany and France, in producing new works, and the marvels we are beginning to underftand, but are fo far from equalling.

In the thirteenth century, Italian painting developed itfelf, and this is the moft brilliant epifode of Chriftian art. That great epoch owes its rife to one of thofe incidents which God makes fruitful, but the world does not perceive. Two men, whofe birth-places were

very far diſtant, met, one day, in a church of Rome.
One had come from Spain, the other arrived from
Aſſiſi. In this providential meeting, ſcience and love
recognized each other, and earth exulted at the kiſs of
S. Dominic and S. Francis. A long generation of
artiſts ſprang from it. The Dominicans and Franciſ-
cans, like brothers with but one ſame fortune and aim,
travelled over the world, and diffuſed enthuſiaſm and
genius. How reſiſt the contaƈt of their eloquence
and of their voluntary poverty put on as the moſt
touching form of love? Dante celebrated their tri-
· umph; and the great ſchool of Giotto conſecrated its
moſt perfeƈt works to S. Francis, whom it ſeemed to
take as its patron, whilſt the children of S. Dominic
themſelves produced marvels which Michael Angelo
was never weary of admiring. Whether clothed in the
religious habit or not, the artiſt then felt the influence
of the two great Orders that regenerated and quickened
human nature under Innocent III. Thoſe waves of
ſcience and love overſpread all Europe like a majeſtic
river, and thence the nations drew copious inſpirations.
: In Italy, Niccolo of Piſa, Fra Siſto, Fra Riſtoro,
Giotto, Orcagna, Taddeo Gaddi, Beato Angelico,
Perugino, and ſo many others, whatever were their
age and country, formed but one family united by the
ſame faith, and praying at the ſame altars.[1]

---

[1] The ſtatutes of the Corporation of Painters of Sienna, in 1335, begin thus:
—" By the grace of God, we are called to make known to rude men who cannot
read, the miraculous things wrought by the virtue and in virtue of holy faith.
Our faith conſiſts principally in adoring and believing one Eternal God, a God of
infinite power, immenſe wiſdom, love and clemency without bounds; as we are
perſuaded that nothing, however little it may be, can have beginning or end
without three things, that is to ſay, without power, knowledge and will, with
love. (Cantu, *Hiſtoire Univerſelle*, vol. xi, p. 593.)

In fine, when Raphael, the defcendant and heir of thofe great men, came to affift in the battle of giants waged by Leonardo da Vinci and Michael Angelo at Florence, it was in the Dominican convent of S. Mark ftill all trembling with the name of Savonarola, that he received from the hands of Fra Bartolomeo, with his laft inftructions, the deftinies of art.

After having painted his great poems at the Vatican, Raphael went unhappily to inaugurate in the Farnefina the period of the Renaiffance. This era has been thus called, becaufe it faw the re-birth in the focial ftate of that art which reafon had impoverifhed and the gofpel of Chrift folemnly condemned.

Incapable by itfelf of reaching a public life, pagan art traitoroufly watched the material progrefs of Chriftian art, availed itfelf of everything which might ferve it in feducing the fenfes, and, in fhort, made itfelf a party amongft thofe naturaliftic painters, who fought the beauty of the creature rather than that of the Creator. In the name of the external perfection that eftablifhed relations between the Greece of Pericles and the Italy of Leo X., pagan art reclaimed its empire; and genius, deceived by thefe falfe titles, fell into an ungrateful and fatal apoftacy. The pro-grefs which art owed to Chriftianity ceafed all at once, and the fall was as rapid as lightning punifhing a blafphemy.

Art fell fo quick and fo low that, half a century later, the fchool of the Carracci was regarded as a refurrec-tion, and its vulgar types paffed for marvels. Bernini came afterwards, with his infolent fafhion, to mix his works with thofe of Raphael, and Rome was incapable of remarking the difference between them. How, in fact, can beauty be appreciated, when tafte has been corrupted in the difturbance of the fenfes?

Pagan art, in the full funfhine of the gofpel, was never to renew again its ancient glory. The paffions, however, fet up their ftatues again, and found adorers for them in the corruption of courts. There did the Renaiffance prefcribe its formula of laws. The code publifhed by the erudition of the Medici and the money of the Florentine bankers rule us ftill. Since the fixteenth century, Chriftian art has undergone this unjuft oppreffion; and they muft make painful efforts who would reftore its fplendour.

The coarfe doctrines of *art for art* and of *realifm* feem to have prevailed. Pagan antiquity itfelf had recognized as · neceffary the alliance of natural and moral beauty;[1] but now-a-days public favour applauds their feparation, and recompenfes the proftitution of talent. Is it good or evil that art exhibits? Is it vice or virtue that fpeaks in our theatres and books? A fenfual literature is fet off like a courtefan, and comes to feat herfelf at the domeftic hearth with her romances and fly-fheets. There fhe brings in fculpture and painting, which, by their nudities, infult our mothers' and our fifters' modefty. A venal and lying criticifm weaves garlands which this corrupting art afterwards receives in academies and mufeums; and the moral fenfe is perverted by thefe fatal triumphs.

The Church, however, always preferves intact the treafures of Chriftian art; fhe poffeffes in their fulnefs the True, the Beautiful and the Good, and to all

[1] Vir bonus, dicendi peritus.

offers her holy traditions and fublime afpirations. Many, wearied with the debaucheries of pagan art, have returned towards her, and have found purer thoughts and fweeter enjoyments in the ftudy of her monuments. They have underftood that religion is the rule of moral beauty, and that without moral beauty natural beauty is corrupted in vice, and difappears in fhame. Without religion, art is only a frivolous paftime and social danger. Religion alone can reftore to it its original dignity and fublime miffion.[1]

With the defire of working for this frefh union of religion and art, we have written thefe pages. We have chofen in the paft an artift whofe example is a great leffon. Beato Angelico lived at the beginning of the fifteenth century, which feparates the middle ages from the Renaiffance. A faithful difciple of the tradition and laft fcion of the fchool of Giotto, he has not been furpaffed in talent by any of the artifts who prepared the reign of Leo X. He was a great painter and a great faint; and thus in his life and works reproduced the divine likenefs, the eternal object of Chriftian art.

This model of artifts we offer to the public. Although much praifed, Beato Angelico is ftill but little known. We have availed ourfelves of former works, and hope we have added to them fome new facts; the chief, we think, is the feparation of Beato Angelico's paintings from thofe of Fra Benedetto, his

---

[1] Inftaurare omnia in Chrifto, quæ in cœlis, et quæ in terra funt in ipfo; in quo etiam et nos forte vocati fumus, prædeftinati fecundùm propofitum ejus qui operatur omnia fecundùm confilium voluntatis fuæ, ut fimus in laudem gloriæ ejus. (*Ephes.* i, 10.)

brother, the inferiority of which has dimmed his glory. We have alfo ftudied Beato Angelico in his relations with his contemporaries, and have done our utmoft to find ufeful leffons in this ftudy.

Have our efforts been fortunate? Our readers muft be the judges. If we have fallen into fome miftakes, let them reprove us for them as foon as poffible; and if we have fpoken fome truths, let them aid us in thanking God for having infpired us with them.

Feaft of the Purification,
February 2nd, 1857.

LIFE OF BEATO ANGELICO
DA FIESOLE.

Chapter I.

PAINTING IN ITALY BEFORE BEATO ANGELICO.

OUNTRY and age are the firſt ele-
ments of a man's life. Birth aſſigns
us a point in ſpace and time, and to
their influence we are neceſſarily ſub-
jeĉted. In our heavens, there is
only one ſun and one truth; but
their rays are varied according to
the motion impreſſed on the world by the hand of
God. Every country has its horizons, light, and fertility; every era, its civilization, belief, and events:
and they make us what we are. Our body derives
development of the ſenſes from the earth which ſup-
ports it; our ſoul is nouriſhed by ideas ſurrounding it,
and from them compounds its power. No one is
iſolated from his age, and none command it. Great
men themſelves are ſubjeĉt to this law; and when they

B

feem to be leading their contemporaries, they are only preceding them.

It is important, then, when we wifh to underftand the life of a man, to ftudy his genefis, and learn what he has received·from his age and country. The artift, more than any other, is the creature of thefe two circumftances, which alone explain the nature of his infpirations. So we will begin the life of Beato Angelico of Fiefole, by telling at what period of hiftory God gave His well-beloved painter to Italy.

Art, like man, had to be born again of water and of blood. Baptifm and martyrdom were the fources of his new being. Chrift had reconquered the beauty loft by the original fall; and when the Tree of the Crofs had borne its fruit, the breath of the Holy Ghoft caft the divine feed of unity where Roman power had fixed the centre of the world. The germ of Chriftian art was buried in the catacombs with all the principles of civilization, and was there developed with the folemn flownefs with which God fets about His work. Man hurries his, urged by the fhortnefs of his life; but God, rich in His eternity, lavifhes ages as He pleafes, and clothes what He does with the majefty of time.

Archæology fhows us this underground germination, which lafted until the reign of Conftantine. Artifts are born in the damp galleries which fhelter the Chriftian myfteries, and there receive holy initiation by the chanting of the Pfalms and the light of the torches. Moral beauty appears to them in all its brightnefs, on the faces of their brethren at prayer, and on the bleed-ing bodies fent to them by martyrdom. Their hands

trace touching words and fymbolical figures on the
ftone and mortar which feal the tombs.

Soon are the vaults of the catacombs enriched with
paintings and fculptures. Life protefts againft death,
and the hiftory of the paft reaffures the faithful againft
the trials of the prefent. Noe in the ark tells them
to await the dove of fafety; Job on his dunghill
repeats his hopes; the children in the furnace fing
their fong of thankfgiving; Daniel prays peacefully
amidft the lions; Jonas delivered from the waves of
the fea repofes under the fhadow of Providence; Jefus,
the Good Shepherd, brings back the ftrayed fheep,
heals the paralytic, and raifes His friend Lazarus again,
to remind His own that He is rich in power as in love.
All nature is obedient to this new Orpheus. The
earth, flowers, animals, the feafons of the year are
reprefented in the catacombs, and everywhere the
figures of the *orantes* raife their hands to God and
offer Him the firft-fruits of the regenerated world.
What more affecting than thefe paintings, which fpeak
to Chriftians of naught but happinefs and victories
amidft the tombs where their perfecutors have buried
them ![1]

The paintings of the catacombs preferved the outward forms of ancient art; and Chriftianity gathered

---

[1] We cannot poffibly admit the fyftem of M. Raoul Rochette, on the origin of
Chriftian types. The learned Academician thinks that Gnoftic reprefentations
were their firft models. (*Difcours fur l'Art du Chriftianifme.*) Chriftian art
never underwent the influence of that impure fect. The ideal of Chrift was in
the Gofpel, and thence the faithful drew their infpirations. Even were the priority
of the Gnoftic monuments proved, no conclufion could be drawn from them
favourable to the fyftem of M. Raoul Rochette. Doctrine is the true origin of
types; and an art never feeks its point of departure in a doctrine it detefts.

them like withered leaves wherewith the winds of heaven cover the ground, in order to protect from winter the feeds to be developed in the fpring. The univerfal myftery of life by death was flowly accomplifhed for Chriftian art. Painting in particular underwent a long preparation; it had been polluted in the debaucheries of idolatry, and God, before giving it back its power, purified it in the blood of the martyrs and the fire of iconoclafts. It iffued forth radiant at laft, and became one of the glories of the Church. After it had been confecrated beneath the arches of the Roman bafilicas, it went, in the thirteenth century, to take poffeffion of the privileged land which Providence had deftined for it.

In the centre of Italy, along the Mediterranean fhores, vaft plains extend, fheltered from the northern winds by the chain of the Apennines. Thefe mountains pour into them fertilizing ftreams, which bring out luxuriant vegetation in their courfe. The mineral wealth and fertility of the foil invite man to labour, and the clearnefs of the fky promifes him long days to gather in the fruits of it. Thither a colony from the Eaft went to fix their travelling-tents.[1] The Etrufcans were a people of incredible activity: they gave to infant Rome its civilization, induftry, and

---

[1] The learned are divided on the origin of the Etrufcans. Some explain it by Helleniftic emigrations into Italy; others make it come more directly from the cradle of the human race. We cannot here difcufs the particulars of the cafe, but will only fay that Etrufcan monuments fhow us an art quite diftinct from that of the Greeks. Etruria certainly felt Grecian influence through its commerce and contact with Southern Italy; but its artiftic forms have an indifputable originality. Afiatic infpiration is evident, efpecially in the ftyle and figures of its tombs. (See *Manuel d'Archeologie* of Muller, § 169.)

monuments, and built upon the heights of the capitol
the temple of Jupiter, wherein the deftinies of the
world were to be directed. Rivals rather than imitators of the Greeks, they ftamped on their works an
originality, admired by Athens in its greateft days;
and when the old world difappeared, they carried off
their mafterpieces to their tombs, as if there to wait
for the refurrection of art.

Etruria, in fact, has been to Chriftian civilization
what Greece was to heathen antiquity. Athens and
Florence were the capitals of the two nations rendered
moft famous in hiftory by the fine arts. Thofe two
cities chofe virgins for their patroneffes. The olive of
Minerva decorated the pediment of the Parthenon at
Athens, and the lily of Mary became the glorious
device of Florence. Have not fable and truth here
met together, to tell us that virginity is the fifter of
poetry, and purity the moft faithful mirror of beauty?

The rife, progrefs, greatnefs and decline of an art
amongft a people are explained by the relations of the
art with the two fundamental laws of all fociety, authority and liberty. Thefe two laws are to the moral
world what the two forces are to the phyfical world
they govern. Authority without liberty, produces
immobility and fterility; liberty without authority,
leads to ifolation and anarchy; perfection fprings only
from the happy alliance of authority and liberty.
Hence three diftinct periods of art.

The firft is the hieratic period. To fay that art
comes of the wants and caprices of man is to belie
reafon and hiftory. If neceffity is the mother of induftry, religion alone is the mother of the fine arts.

The altar has always been a people's firſt artiſtic work. Architecture afterwards built temples, which ſculpture and painting came to decorate; and from theſe ſacred monuments man borrowed, later on, the luxury of his dwellings. Religious dogma is the authority in art; it gives formulæ to belief, regulates ſymbols, and creates the unity of intelligences without which the artiſt could not make himſelf underſtood.

If it remain under the excluſive direction of religious dogma, and liberty does not bring it the activity of life, art is left in the condition of writing, and is not developed, ſave in the narrow circle of material proceſſes. Such is Egyptian art. It is with difficulty if the eye can diſtinguiſh ſlight differences in monuments ſeparated by ſo many ages. Its ſtatues remain bound under deſpotic rules, like mummies in their bandages; and this immobility cannot be overcome, either by the genius of the Greeks under the ſucceſſors of Alexander, or by Roman power under the rule of Adrian. This ſervitude of art is almoſt univerſal throughout the Eaſt. Religions void of truth cannot ſuffer liberty to approach them; for liberty, by convicting them of error, ſlaughters them.

The ſecond period of art is the learned period. In it man not only accepts belief, but his intellect ſtudies and is at work upon it. His will is enamoured of it, and is not ſatisfied with ſimple forms unreflective of his thoughts; ſo he goes freely forth to ſeek in nature all the beauties with which he can clothe them. He requires from lines their pliancy and proportions; from colour, its variety and richneſs; from light, its gradations and harmonies; and reſts not until he has rendered his work worthy of the truth enlightening his foul. This balance between natural and moral beauty is the perfection of art. But man maintains himfelf with difficulty at this elevation. The natural beauty he has difcovered exercifes a powerful feduction over him, and draws him rapidly away into the third or naturaliftic period of art.

The hieratic or religious element is forgotten, and art lofes its greatnefs and dignity. Every one endeavours to imitate the beauties of nature, according to his own caprice, and the merit of a work is meafured only by the pleafure the fenfes experience in it. Tafte is vitiated by its minute diverfities, talent is enfeebled by ifolation, and foon nothing can ftop the progrefs of decay.

Thefe three periods are diftinct in Greek art. The hieratic period precedes Pericles, the learned is perfonified in Phidias, and the naturaliftic period begins with Alexander's conquefts, and fatisfies all the vices of the Caefars.

In Italy, art has paffed through the fame periods. The firft begins with the mofaics of Rome, and ends with Orcagna; the fecond is inaugurated by Ghiberti, and crowned by Raphael; the third dates from the Renaiffance, and continues to this day. The painter whofe life we are writing was providentially placed between the hieratic and learned periods, fo as to be the fummary of the one and model of the other. Let us fee what his predeceffors were, before we ftudy the examples which his fucceffors received from him.

The origin of painting in Italy remains in obfcurity. The cities of Tufcany contend for the honour of its

cradle, as thofe of Greece did formerly for Homer.
But their titles of artiftic nobility prove nothing. The
names efcaped from oblivion have no relation with
each other ; and in them the hiftorian cannot catch
the unity which is the life of art in the great epochs.
To begin with the fixteenth century, fome local fchools
could be eftablifhed, becaufe herds of imitators were
folded in fome certain territory, there to continue the
defign, colouring, and manner of a mafter. But in
the middle ages, artifts of all countries formed but a
fingle community of brethren, marching together in
fpite of frontiers and battles ; purfuing through political revolutions their peaceful conquefts ; fetting up
their victorious tents at Sienna, Pifa, Florence, and
S. Francis of Affifi's ; and leaving mafterpieces everywhere, which their fucceffors admired and imitated.
Ideas unite men ; faith will do more for focial union
than all our railways ; and againft barbarism or the
defpotifm of the fabre there is again no fafety fave
in the ftandard of the crufades.

One of the hiftorical errors moft difficult to deftroy,
is that which afcribes Italian painting to Byzantine
art. Every work before Cimabue (1240-1300) paffes
for a fervile imitation of the mafters of Conftantinople;
and Giotto is proclaimed the creator of a new and
truly national art. Defpite the great authorities fupporting them, we cannot accept fuch affertions ; for
facts too formally contradict them. In the firft half
of the thirteenth century, a fchool of unqueftionable
originality exifted in Italy. The paintings it has left us
prefent genuine lines, which indicate life and announce
progrefs ; whilft the Greek paintings of the fame epoch

offer nothing but fymptoms of complete decline.
The works of Giunta of Pifa, Guido of Sienna, and
Duccio of Boninfegna, recall thofe of the ancient Etrufcans, by the energy of the movements, the fimplicity
of the drapery, and the arrangement of the figures.
The artifts juft named were the mafters of thofe who
honoured the succeeding centuries. Still, we do not
deny the influence exercifed by Byzantine art on Italy;
but before explaining it, we muft proteft againft the
fingular judgments and unjuft contempt, of which
that art is the object.

Byzantine art, yet fo little known to us, received
Chriftian unction at Rome, and confequently had,
from the very beginning, the fame fymbol and hieratic
element as Weftern art ; and the archæologist, to explain
the iconography of our old cathedrals, may profitably
confult the painters of Mount Athos, who live like
phantoms in the routine of ages. They who defpife
Byzantine art probably know it only by its works of
the decline, hawked about by trade, and multiplied
by bad copyifts. Deeper ftudies will, one day, fhow
that it was one of the glorious phafes of Chriftian art,
and that it alone imparted fome grandeur to the fall
of the empire.

People are particularly taken up with a difpute on
the beauty of Chrift, and imagine that the partizans
of the *unbeautiful* came out victorious. This difcuffion
was a quarrel of rhetoricians, and not of artifts. The
fubtlety of the Greek mind upheld contradictory
thefes on certain texts of Scripture ; but it will never
be proved that the conclufion was hoftile to the rules
of tafte and of good fenfe. The greateft Fathers of the

Eaftern Church proclaimed the Saviour to be the
moft beautiful of the children of men; painters and
fculptors believed them, and it was owing folely to
inability if they did not realize the doctrine in their
works. Their figures of Chrift are perfectly con-
formed with thofe of the Virgin, angels and faints,
whofe beauty was not queftioned; and if they had
wifhed to introduce a fyftematic deformity, nothing
would have been eafier, as it fufficed to break fymmetry. On the contrary, their types have a perfect
regularity. We muft judge them, not in the mourn-
ful fcenes of the Paffion, wherein the artifts have often
fought to exprefs only fuffering and expiation, but in
the glory of triumph, in thofe Chrifts feated upon
thrones, on the arches of the bafilicas, where beauty
is fhown with a clearnefs which difpels prejudices
againft Byzantine art. And to them, again, may be
oppofed the numerous ivory carvings of Chrift blefs-
ing the emperors. The one in the Mufeum of
Antiquities at Paris bears the names and portraits of
Romanus Diogenes and Eudoxia, his wife (1068-
1072), and confequently dates from one of the faddeft
periods of hiftory; but in delicacy of model, pliancy
of drapery, and dignity of form, it furpaffes all the
works of art then executed in Europe.

Byzantine art is diftinguifhed by a dignity of ftyle
and richnefs of acceffories which recall the poetry and
luxury of Oriental countries. Its misfortune is, to
have inhaled the miafma of a corrupt civilization.
The prodigalities of the emperors were more hurtful
to it than their perfecutions, and, when it had to fly
before the followers of Mahomet, it arrived in Italy,

like a traveller who has paffed over diftant countries, and brings back to his native land fome rare objects and the recitals of his mifhaps, as the whole of his fortune.

The influence of Byzantine art on Italy had two caufes. The war of the iconoclafts made thofe pictures holy which efcaped from the fury of herefy. They were placed as relics on the altars, and the veneration of the faithful urged the frequent imitation of them. Afterwards people underwent the feduction which triumphs over national pride. Along with the treafures of the Eaft, Venetian veffels brought artifts, who were preferred to others, becaufe they came from afar, and to them were entrufted the direction of the fchools and the decoration of monuments.

The moft celebrated pupil of the old mafters was Cimabue. On his name principally is made to reft that affiliation of Italian painting which we cannot admit. We have already cited older artifts, whofe ftyle is perfectly diftinct from the Byzantine ; and, if we ftudy the works of Cimabue, we fhall fee that he was, fo to fpeak, an exception amongft his contemporaries.

Towards the middle of the thirteenth century, the Florentine Republic had brought Greek artifts to teach the fine arts ; and, whilft watching them painting in the church of Santa Maria Novella, Cimabue had the revelation of his genius. A fchool had been opened in the convent of Friar-Preachers, and there the boy ufed to go and take leffons of his uncle, who taught grammar. His road was always through the church, and the painter's work made him frequently

forget the profeſſor and his books. His copy-books
were filled more with deſigns than with writing, and
his parents giving up making him a ſcholar, entruſted
him to the artiſts of Santa Maria Novella. The pupil
far ſurpaſſed his maſters. He underſtood their traditions, and diſcerned in them the laſt recollections of
Phidias, which ages and barbariſm had not effaced.
Cimabue's merit is in the dignity of his figures and
the majeſty of his compoſitions. His ſuperiority over
the Greek artiſts will not be diſputed, when we compare the paintings attributed to him in the church of
Aſſiſi with the Byzantine ones executed there at the
ſame period. All thoſe paintings certainly belong to
the ſame ſchool; but in his, Cimabue freed himſelf
from the mechanical detail and the exaggeration of
expreſſion and movement which disfigure the work of
the Greek artiſts. He makes an admirable effort to
bring back all the details to unity, and all the pro-
fuſion of ornaments and draperies to beauty. We
will cite eſpecially the "Benediction of Iſaac," in which
the patriarch is ſo majeſtically enthroned upon his
bed; and the "Burial of Chriſt," the ſcholarly arrangement of which recalls the ſolemnity of ancient tragedy.

The reputation of Giotto has done much harm to
the glory of Cimabue. Some believe that there is
a great diſtance between the pupil and the maſter;
yet they are ſeparated only by the progreſs of a regular
development. Giotto's merit is to have returned into
the national path, from which Greek influence had
cauſed Cimabue to deviate. He was the centre of all
the great artiſtic movement which ſignalizes the beginning of the fourteenth century. Hiſtory follows

him to Florence, Sienna, Pifa, Rome, Naples, Affifi,
and Padua, and carefully records all the mafterpieces
and the pupils he left there. His chief qualities are,
truth of movements, fimplicity of expreffion, and
poetry of bringing on the ftage. The fhepherd picked
up upon a rock of the Apennines remains faithful to
the infpirations of nature, as a child who forgets not
the firft leffons of its mother.

S. Francis is his hero, and the epopee he has traced
of him on the walls of the church of Affifi became the
favourite theme of his talent. The very novelty of
the fubject feparates it from the routine of the Greek
artifts ; and with difficulty fragments of fome Byzantine types are met with here and there in his pictures.
We will cite the Apparition of S. Francis during the
preaching of S. Anthony of Padua, his myftical Marriage with Poverty, and the Glorification of the voluntary mendicant which dazzles the eye in the midft of
the multitude of angels chanting and celebrating his
triumph.

The picture by Giotto, in the Mufeum of the
Louvre, is not to be defpifed. The fcene of the ftigmata is given with a great energy, and the charming
gradino accompanying it has all the grace of the
Francifcan legends.

Many of Giotto's contemporaries, who are often
ranked in the number of his pupils, were only his
fellow-labourers and friends. Pietro Cavellini, for
inftance, who was feventeen years older, remained
faithful to the primitive ftyle of the Italian fchool,
and did not quit the old fubjects, to which he knew
how to give a deeply religious character. At the

fame date, the two brothers, Ambrogio and Pietro Lorenzetti, produced works of remarkable originality. Without fpeaking of their paintings at Sienna and Florence, it is enough to examine the frefcoes in the Campo Santo, in which they have reprefented the life of the Fathers of the Defert. All the poetry .of thefe recitals, fo genuine and fo pure, is there given with a grace and dignity until then unknown. We feel that art is drawing new life in thofe paftoral fcenes, and that there is a decided progrefs in thofe figures of hermits praying amidft the fhade, or at work on the banks of their brooks.

The moft illuftrious rival of Giotto is Simon Memmi, only eight years younger than him. The difference of their talent and fuccefs is explained by their different fympathies. Dante was the friend of Giotto ; Petrarch of Simon Memmi. The ftern form of Beatrice feems to infpire the former ; the fweet face of Laura ferved often as the model of the latter. Giotto made his mafterpiece in the Francifcan church of Affifi ; Simon Memmi painted his in the Dominican church of Santa Maria Novella. The one is greater, the other more graceful ; and, without being unjuft, we can love Memmi moft, whilft admiring Giotto more. It muft not be fuppofed, however, that Simon Memmi lacked elevation. On the contrary, his frefcoes in the Campo Santo of Pifa, and in the chapel of the Spaniards at Florence, prefent great character in ftyle and remarkable dignity in compofition. The legend of S. Ranier is efpecially diftinguifhed for fcientific groupings, variety of heads, elegance of draperies and richnefs of expreffion. Thefe frefcoes, doubtlefs, were the moft ftudied by fucceeding mafters. Simon Memmi died at Avignon in 1344.

Amongft the pupils of Giotto, Tadeo Gaddi was the moft cherifhed by his mafter, and the moft illuf-trious. By his pencil, art acquires more fcience and nobility. The energetic countryman has taken the ufages of high fociety, and now wears the fena-torial toga; but fortune has not corrupted him, and his fine drapery always covers a poetic and honeft heart. The " Life of our Lady," painted by Gaddi, in Santa Croce, at Florence, may give a complete idea of his talent, by the grace of the figures, the dignity of the attire, and the fkill of the compofition. The little gradino in the Mufeum at Paris is not unworthy of his reputation. Some parts of it give prefage to the epoch of Mafaccio.

Tadeo Gaddi perfonifies the progrefs of the fchool of Giotto. He left its traditions efpecially to Giottino and Orcagna. Giottino appears to us with the fweet aureola wherewith pofterity crowns talent furprifed in youth and poverty by death. He was not thirty years old when he difappeared, being carried off by the profound fadnefs which the knowledge of an inaccef-fible perfection often caufes in genius. His titles to glory are the frefcoes in Santa Croce, reprefenting the hiftory of S. Silvefter and Conftantine; but one pic-ture recommends him alfo to our admiration, and it is that charming compofition in the church of Affifi in which he has given proof of moft exquifite fenfi-bility. S. Nicholas is miraculoufly reftoring a young captive to her family who had invoked him. Nothing can be more pure and touching than the fcene in

which the pious joy of the parents is fhown by the
trueft expreffions and moft varied attitudes. We love
even the little houfe-dog which comes under the table,
to recognize and fawn upon its miftrefs.

Andrea Orcagna nobly clofes the firft period of art
in Italy. Painter, architect, and fculptor, he tranf-
ferred into his works the poetry of Dante, of whom
he was the paffionate admirer. His "Triumph of
Death" and "Laft Judgment" are worth the fineft
pages of the Divine Comedy : there is the fame energy
of thought and dignity of ftyle. Orcagna has been
often compared with Michael Angelo; but if we compare the paintings of the Siftine Chapel with thofe of
the Campo Santo, we fhall fee that the latter are
fublime, and the former gigantic. Michael Angelo
is extraordinary, whilft Orcagna is religious. Their
compofitions are fummed up in the two Chrifts pronouncing judgment. The one is an executioner
ftriking with a thunderbolt, the other a King, who
condemns whilft he fhows the facred wound of his
fide to juftify his fentence.

The fculptures attributed to Orcagna clofely refemble his paintings. The "Prefentation in the
Temple" and "Burial of the B. Virgin," in San
Michele, at Florence, call to mind the fevere ftyle
and energetic expreffion fo particularly admired in
his "Triumph of Death."

Thofe who have ftudied the hiftory of art too often
neglect to obferve the influences fculpture and painting exercife upon each other. Sculpture is the firft-
born fifter of painting, becaufe fhe offers the fimpleft
and moft natural means of imitating external forms.

The material fhe models reproduces the reality of them, whilft painting only fimulates it by lines, fore-fhortenings, fhades and colours. Painting, confequently, has more difficulties to overcome, and thefe difficulties require more fcience, time and refearch. The priority of fculpture in antiquity is indifputable; in the middle ages, it is lefs evident, becaufe in the flow preparation Chriftian art underwent, fculpture and painting took an almoft parallel courfe; but in the thirteenth century, the dates are pofitive. Neither to the Greek artifts, nor to Cimabue, or to Giotto, muft the real Italian renaiffance be attributed, but to the fchool of fculpture that appeared at Pifa. It freed painting from the fetters of routine, and imparted to it freedom of movement and aĉtivity of life, by teaching it to ftudy truth of form, delicacy of model, pliancy of drapery and happy combination of lines.[1]

Niccolo of Pifa preceded Cimabue. They fay he received leffons from the Greek fculptors who were at work on the cathedral of the city; but he only learned the proceffes from them. His real mafters were the ancient bas-reliefs he ftudied; and if we had no contemporary evidence to prove it, it would be enough for us to cite the fculptures of San Giovanni, in which the imitation of heathen fubjeĉts is flagrant.

---

[1] In his life of Niccolo of Pifa, Vafari proves the happy influence of fculpture on art in Italy. "At this epoch (1240)," fays he, "many artifts, moved by a praifeworthy emulation, applied themfelves to fculpture with greater zeal than they had hitherto done. At Milan, all the Lombards and Germans who worked at the cathedral, and were difperfed when the war broke out between the Milanefe and the Emperor Frederic, ftrove together, and began to produce fome good refults. The fame progrefs was remarked at Florence, as foon as Niccolo and Arnolfo exhibited their firft worksě'

We find there again, amongſt others, the copy of a
modeſt Venus, and the group of the bearded Bacchus
viſiting Icarus.[1]   The compoſition of his bas-reliefs alſo
recalls that of the ancient farcophagi, by the arrangement and great number of their perſonages.   Still it
muſt not be ſuppoſed that Niccolo of Piſa was an artiſt
without originality; in his works, the Chriſtian thought
rules the imitation.   The ſculptures on the tomb of
S. Dominic, at Bologna, preſent new ſubjects of
remarkable compoſition; but his maſterpiece, in our
opinion, is the pulpit of the cathedral of Sienna, in
which the figures adorning it demonſtrate a ſchool
ſuperior to any preceding or contemporary ſchools.
The ſimultaneous ſtudy of the antique and of nature
opens a new career to art.

The progreſs of Italian ſculpture is particularly
viſible in Andrea of Piſa, the pupil of Niccolo, and
contemporary with Giotto.   Andrea of Piſa, who probably came in contact with French artiſts, is diſtinguiſhed by the purity of lines and ſimplicity of compoſition which architectural bas-relief demands.   His
gates made for the Baptiſtry of Florence remind us
of the Greek works of the great epoch.   Ghiberti
continued what Andrea of Piſa had begun, but he
furpaſſed him only in the richneſs of details and
elegance of proportions, and injured ſculpture by leading it aſtray into the domain of painting.

The name of Ghiberti is a date in the hiſtory of
Italian painting.   We have quoted him as the head
of the learned period.   A pupil of the Piſans and an

---

[1] Cicognara, Storia della Scultura. (Pl. xv.)

inheritor of their paffion for ancient monuments, he inaugurated his talent by a fignal triumph. The Republic of Florence had invited all artifts to a great competition, promifing an impartial judgment and noble rewards. Ghiberti's competitors were Jacobo della Quercia, Niccolo d'Arezzo, Simone da Colle, Francefco di Valdambrina, Filippo Brunellefchi, and Donatello, who had not yet reached his eighteenth year. The judges at once fet the works of Ghiberti, Brunellefchi and Donatello above the mark. But the laft two did not wait for the final decifion, and had the glory of crowning the conqueror themfelves. Ghiberti was at work for twenty years on the gates of the Baptiftry of Florence, which Michael Angelo thought worthy to be the gates of heaven. His influence over his contemporaries was immenfe; and the fchool formed around him, which is fummed up in the two names of Maffolino and Mafaccio, led art into a direction, the advantages and dangers of which we fhall have to ftudy.

Art had now arrived at the fulnefs of life, which brings on, both for man and nations, the conflict between good and evil. Until then, the Church had guided its infancy, and had taught it to praife God and give thanks to Him. Its only bufinefs, in the beautiful words of Buffalmaco, was to reprefent the faintly men and women in Paradife, in order to make men better.[1] But when the hour of manhood came, natural beauty prefented itfelf with all its feductions,

---

[1] Non attendiamo mai ad altro, che a far fanti e fante per le mura et per le tavole, ed a far perciò con difpetto de' demoni gli uomini più divoti o migliori. (VASARI, *Vita di Buonamico Buffalmaco.*)

and it was neceſſary to chooſe between vice and virtue.
God and matter had each their partizans, who formed
two camps oppoſed, like the two cities of which
S. Auguſtine ſpeaks. Beato Angelico was providentially born, with Ghiberti, at the beginning of the
ſtruggle. Their birth-places were nigh each other,
and death led them, the ſame year, into the preſence of
God (1455).

Chapter II.

BIRTH OF BEATO ANGELICO.—HIS ENTRANCE INTO THE ORDER OF S. DOMINIC (1387-1408).

EATO ANGELICO received the light of day in 1387, at Vicchio, one of the fine fortified villages which crown the fummit of the Apennines, in the province of Mugello. A century before, Cimabue had picked up, on a neighbouring hill, the child who was to give fo great an impulfe to Italian painting. Vefpignano, Giotto's native place, is but a few miles diftant from the place which faw the birth of him whofe hiftory we are about to ftudy.

Beato Angelico's early years are unknown; we only know that he was then called Guido or Guidolino, that his father bore the name of Pietro, and that he had a brother, whom we find affociated with his fanctity and mafterpieces. This paffage of Vafari is the moft valuable information about his childhood: "Although he might have lived in the world with

the greateſt eaſe, and, beſides what he poſſeſſed, have
earned all he deſired by the arts he knew ſo well even
in his boyhood, yet being naturally ſteady and good,
he reſolved to become a religious of the Order of Friar-
Preachers, for his own ſatisfaction and quiet, and principally to ſave his ſoul." [1]

Thus Beato Angelico did not offer to God a heart
withered by laſſitude, or ſcared by want. He came
to preſent freely at the altar, youth all adorned with
the joys of fortune and promiſes of renown. When
we have long walked in the paths of the world and
ſuffered its trials, we often turn to our paſt years and
ſee how much happier they would have been had we
given them entirely to God; but to know the truth
before theſe tardy leſſons of experience, and to perceive
it with a prophetic glance athwart the illuſions of
youth and its expected crowns, needs a ſupernatural
light and ſpecial favour from on high. And even
when we do thus know the reality of things, we
frequently ſtifle the aſpirations of a holy ambition,
becauſe our heart is weak againſt the recollections of
our childhood and our mother's tears. To the goodneſs of God calling us to a higher life, we oppoſe the
very gifts He has beſtowed upon us.

We do not know what Beato Angelico gave up to
gain the precious pearl of the Goſpel; but with a
ſoul loving and amiable like his, he muſt have renounced the charm of many an affection, and doubt-

[1] Coſtui ſebbene arebbe potuto comodiſſimamente ſtare al ſecolo, ed oltre quello
che aveva, guadagnarſi ciò che aveſſe voluto con quell' arti che ancor giovinetto
beniſſimo far ſapeva, volle nondimeno per ſua ſodisfazione e quiete, eſſendo di
natura poſato e buono, e per ſalvare l'anima ſua principalmente, farſi religioſo
dell' ordine de' frati Predicatori. *(Vita di Fra Giovanni da Fieſole.)*

lefs to affuage his regrets, Providence willed his elder
brother to follow him to the altar.[1]

The fpiritual family Beato Angelico chofe, was the
Order of S. Dominic. The aim of this Order is the
apoftolate, that is to fay, truth known by fcience and
manifefted by love : and as beauty is the natural
form of truth, all who follow the ftar of the holy
founder are eminently artifts, fince they fpread abroad
the Divine truth, the only objeft of art.

Art has many means of aftion. Speech is the firft,
and the moft efficacious and direft. Truth fprings
from the heart of man and efcapes from his lips, full
of life and heat. It communicates itfelf to and im-
pofes itfelf on the intelleft and fubjugates the will. The
orator affimilates his audience to himfelf, and leads
them where he will; but his viftorious word is fleeting, and would be loft in time as in fpace, if art had
no other refources to make its conquefts firm. Not
only does writing fix the word, but painting, fculpture
and architefture multiply and eternalize its wonders.
All the affirmations and fentiments the difcourfe con-
tained, are fet faft by lines and colours, and man's
aftion thus perpetuated may reach the remoteft generations.

It was natural, then, that the Order of S. Dominic
fhould not negleft any means of making the truth
known. To build churches and adorn them with
paintings and fculpture, was the complement of its

---

[1] We cannot follow the opinion of P. Marchefe, in thinking that Fra Benedetto
was younger than his brother Beato Angelico. The teftimony of Vafari is explicit.
The name of Fra Benedetto muft have followed Beato Angelico's on the regifter
of profeffion, if he had entered the convent after him.

apoftolate.   Thus from the beginning, whilft the moft
learned European univerfities of Paris and Bologna
were liftening with admiration to the eloquence of the
Friar-Preachers, Florence, the Athens of the middle
ages, entrufted the glory of its monuments to the
talent of the Dominicans of Santa Maria Novella.

The eftablishment of S. Dominic's Order in Italy
has a very remarkable charaćter.   The Friar-Preachers
always arrived in the great towns as ambaffadors of
peace, and enemies reconciled together gave them
churches and convents in token of their gratitude.

The thirteenth century was bloody on account of
the ftruggle between the Guelphs and Ghibelines.   In
a high point of view, this was a war between Chriftian
and pagan principles, and of the liberty of the Church
againft imperial defpotifm ; and Providence, for the
welfare of modern nations, brought out the profound
diftinćtion between the fpiritual and the temporal
power.   But when we come to the details of the war,
what a variety of epifodes, what confufion of interefts,
and what outburfts of private paffion ! Venice, Milan,
Sienna, Pifa, and Florence, efpecially, become arenas
where the parties wreft bloody vićtories in turns.
The names of Guelph and Ghibeline are only the rally-
ing cry of hoftile races.   Sometimes rival lords are
aiming at power, fometimes the people are defending
againft feudal ambition the immunities granted to them
by the Church.   Error, whofe only expedient againft
truth is always violence, takes advantage of this univerfal turmoil to enlift its foldiers.   The Manichean
herefy preaches the theories which appear in every
focial revolution ; and religion, rifing to confound

them, is once more honoured with the martyr's palm. S. Pietro of Verona writes his victorious *Credo* with his blood.

His death was not the only glory of the Friar-Preachers. S. Dominic fent his difciples to the devaftated towns of Tufcany, with words of peace and love. The little band arrived at the town towards evening, lodged in fome hofpital, and in the morning, after offering prayers to God and confolations to man, went down to the public fquare, to fulfil the object of the journey. Not by fkilful arbitration did the Dominicans triumph, but by fpeaking of the love of Jefus crucified, and of the peace He gives to men of good-will. The moft exafperated enemies liftened weeping, to things which hatred had made them forget; their weapons fell, and they took each other by the hand, to accompany the good religious, who led them into fome neighbouring church, to give fraternal thanks to Heaven.

Twelve Friar-Preachers thus arrived at Florence, about 1219, under the guidance of Beato Giovanni of Salerno. That fame year, S. Dominic, on his return from Sienna, found them in the hofpital of S. Maria Maddalena, where they remained till 1221. The small church of Santa Maria della Vigna was then given them as a recompenfe for their fervices; but it could not hold thofe whom their eloquence and virtues attracted. When S. Pietro of Verona was fent by Pope Innocent IV. to combat the Manichees, he had to preach in the open air in a neighbouring fquare; and as room was ftill wanting, the Republic of Florence ordered the demolition of as many houfes

as the crowd of hearers would require, as truth
appeared to be the principal neceffity of the people.[1]

The Dominican colony foon made rapid progrefs.
The ufefulnefs of a religious order always produces alms to fupport and devotion to multiply.
Thofe whom the Friar-Preachers had fnatched from
hatred gave themfelves up to love, and the grateful
city lavifhed its treafures and its youth on its paci-
ficators. The year 1279 witneffed a feftival deftined
to be one of the moft glorious dates in Chriftian art.
P. Latino Malabranca, Cardinal legate of the Holy
See, after he had appeafed the troubles of Bologna
and reconciled the Guelphs and Ghibelines of the
Romagna, went to Florence to conclude a folemn
peace between the parties. He convened the people
on the ancient fquare of Santa Maria Novella, the
whole of which was decorated with fuits of tapeftry
and with galleries wherein were ranged bifhops, pre-
lates, clergy, religious, authorities, the captain and coun-
cillors of Florence. The Cardinal made a difcourfe
worthy of the occafion and of his eloquence. Then
he gave the fignal for a general embrace between the
reprefentatives of the Guelphs and Ghibelines, who
numbered one hundred and fifty on each fide, and
peace was concluded amidft the joyous acclamations
of all the citizens.[2]

In teftimony of this great act, the firft ftone of
the new church of the Friar-Preachers was laid and
bleffed. Like the people of God on entering the

---

[1] The decree of the Republic, dated Dec. 12th, 1244, is found in P. G. Richa,
Notizie ftoriche delle Chiefe Fiorentine.

[2] Gio. Villani, *Cronica*, lib. vii, cap. 6.

Promifed Land, the Florentines wifhed to pile up ftones to perpetuate the memory of their deliverance, and thofe ftones became a mafterpiece.

Santa Maria Novella is the pureft ray of the artiftic glory of Florence. The magnificence of Santa Croce and Santa Maria dei Fiori, which were built fome years later, have not eclipfed it ;[1] and Michael Angelo, who could not weary in admiring it, gave it the fweet name of *Spofa*. This fair bride was prefented to the genius of Italy by Fra Sifto and Fra Riftoro, two poor Dominican religious. Some have wifhed to affociate thefe two architects with the great fchool of Pifa, but it is moft probable that they ftudied chiefly under James of Germany, who built the church and convent of Affifi, and executed great works for the Republic of Florence. This connection would explain the relations of their work with the wonders of French architecture : in it, we find the fame elegance and poetry ; it is the fame art and infpiration under a different fky and with other materials. The erection of that church offers a peculiarity not to be paffed over in filence. Not only were the two architects Dominicans, but the convent furnifhed mafons and carpenters as well. This temple, raifed by pure and confecrated hands, amidft recollection and prayer, was thus, more than any other, the fymbol of the fpiritual Church built by the faints on the plan of Chrift, and to be confecrated by the laft judgment to ever-lafting joy.

The two religious, whofe genius Rome and Florence

---

[1] Arnolfo laid the foundations of Santa Maria dei Fiori in 1294, and thofe of Santa Croce in 1298.

had admired, feem to have fallen afleep in the peace
of a holy obfcurity. In 1283, the afhes of Fra Riftoro
difappeared beneath an unknown flab in Santa Maria
Novella; and fix years later, the nuns of the folitary
convent of San Sifto at Rome were praying around
the lifelefs remains of Fra Sifto, who in his latter days
had become their humble fervant. Hiftory, however,
has not forgotten them in its pages.[1]   But their
higheft praife is in the pofterity of artifts they left to
complete their work. The names of Fra Mazzetto,
Fra Borghefe, Fra Mazzanti, Fra Giovanni da Campi,
and Fra Jacobo Talenti, are identified with the fineft
monuments, the pride of Italy. The Dominican fchool
of architecture, which built Santa Maria Novella at
Florence, SS. Giovanni e Paolo at Venice, San Niccolo
at Trevife, Santa Maria fopra Minerva at Rome, and
San Domenico at Naples, is diftinctively characterized
by a fimplicity full of noblenefs and grandeur, and
recalls the ftyle of the reign of S. Louis, the traditions of
which it might eafily have received through the convents of S. Jacques and of Touloufe.

The Order of Friar-Preachers alfo furnifhed its
fhare to the celebrated fchool of fculpture, which un-
queftionably caufed the progrefs of painting in Italy.
One of the beft pupils of Niccolo of Pifa was Fra
Guglielmo Agnelli, whom his mafter wifhed to affociate in all his moft beautiful works. He entrufted to
him the execution of part of the baf-reliefs on the
tomb of S. Dominic at Bologna; and the chronicle

---

[1] Vasari, *Vita di Gaddo Gaddi.* Baldinucci, *Vita di Arnolfo.* Cicognara,
Storia della fcultura. P. V. Marchese, *Memorie dei più infigni pittori, fcultori,
e architetti Domenicani,* lib. i, c. 2.

of the convent of S. Catterina tells us how this good
religious paid himfelf for the mafterpieces his filial
hand had wrought for the glory of the holy founder.
During the tranflation of the facred relics, he ftole a
rib, and hid it under the altar of his convent. All his
life, he enjoyed his treafure in fecret ; but at his death,
he owned his pious theft, and bewailed it as a great
fault. Fra Guglielmo executed important works in
his own country, and worked on the bas-reliefs of the
façade of the cathedral of Orvieto, falfely attributed
to his mafter. This magnificent church, where later
on we meet again with Beato Angelico, was begun
in 1290, when Niccolo of Pifa was repofing in the
tomb.

Our painter's moft direct predeceffors in the Order
of S. Dominic, were the miniaturifts, whofe naive compofitions embellifhed monaftic manufcripts, and prepared for Chriftian art its iconography and doctrine.
From the beginning, the Dominicans rivalled the Bene-
dictines and Camaldolefe, who have produced fo many
remarkable artifts. The chronicles of their convents,
in touching notices dedicated to the memory of their
departed brethren, make conftant mention of good
painters and writers of ability: Fra Pietro Macci (1301),
Fra Caro Belloci (1316), Fra Tommafo (1336), Fra
Matteo Marconaldi (1348). In 1348, alfo died of the
plague at Florence, Fra Guido, the fuppofed author
of the choir-books preferved in the noviciate of Santa
Maria Novella. There alfo, are admired two large
pfalters painted by Padre Michele Sertini della Cafa,
who died in 1416, and no doubt, knew Beato Angelico
in his youth. Our painter's vocation was probably

influenced by this friendſhip ; but it ſeems alſo that the
principal honour of it muſt accrue to Beato Giovanni
Dominici, founder of the convent of Fieſole.

This religious, of ſuch great energy and activity of
life, loved and cultivated painting. In the convents
he eſtabliſhed or reformed, he recommended the ſtudy
of it " as a powerful means of elevating the ſoul and
developing the holy thoughts of the heart." There
are a great number of his letters addreſſed to the
Dominicans of the convent of Corpus Domini at
Venice. He gives them advice on the method of
executing miniatures, and offers himſelf to finiſh what
they could not do.¹ From the moment he met him,
he muſt have underſtood and longed for the young
man, whoſe ſoul was ſo pure and talent ſo precocious.
Beato Angelico, on his part, became an eaſy conqueſt,
becauſe nothing has greater ſympathy for ſtrength
than meekneſs. God makes the meek maſters of the
earth, and puts honeycombs into the mouth of the lion.

The convent where Beato Angelico preſented himſelf, ſtands on the declivity of the mountain of Fieſole,
one of the moſt beautiful of thoſe ſurrounding Florence.
Boccacio, whoſe ſenſual pen was purified later on by
penance, has not found a more enchanting ſpot for
telling his profane ſtories.² He took pleaſure in
deſcribing its verdure, ſhades and limpid waters, its
peaceful valleys and rich horizons. But it was not
theſe that moſt charmed the ſoul in the convent of
Fieſole. All its beauty, like that of the ſpouſe in the

---

¹ *Commentario della vita del B. Giovanni Bacchini,* vol. in fol. MS. Arch. di
S. Marco, V. § xxx. P. V. MARCHESE, l. v, p. 181.
² *Decameron,* vi giourn, 10 nov.

Canticles, was from within; reform had there efta-
bliſhed its rule.

The reform of a religious order is a great miracle
of Divine grace. At every inſtant, God is drawing
from His power new germs of life; but how few He
brings back from death! He created the world by a
word, but what heroic means has He not choſen to
fave the world from the ruin of ſin! If the con-
verſion of one ſoul is an event that gladdens all the
angels, what a feſtival muſt there not be celebrated in
heaven, when a religious order which relaxation was
extinguiſhing returns to its firſt fervour!

When God would fave the people He had ſettled
in the Promiſed Land, He choſe a man to reſtore their
courage and their victory. The man of God of the
Dominicans, at the beginning of the fifteenth century,
was Beato Giovanni Dominici. Abuſes had been introduced into the Order in the train of the two great
ſcourges, by which Italy had been deſolated during
the preceding century. The plague had cut down the
holieſt and moſt devout;[1] and the ſchifm which the
Church was ſtill experiencing caſt the ſurvivors into uncertainty as to their courſe. Beato Giovanni Dominici
combated the evil with zeal. He choſe generous
aſſiſtants from the convents, and thus formed new
houſes, which brought back the primitive rule in
vigour. In 1400, he eſtabliſhed himſelf at Fieſole,
with fourteen religious taken for the moſt part from
the reformed convent of Cortona; and in the follow-

---

[1] In 1348, the convent of Santa Maria Novella loſt ſeventy-ſeven religious in
the ſpace of four months.

ing year, the two brothers of Mugello went to increaſe this little Dominican family.

When a man leaves the world to enter the cloiſter, he receives a new name which.ſymbolizes his new life. Religious profeſſion is regarded as a ſecond baptiſm. Our painter was called Fra Giovanni, and his brother Fra Benedetto. The name of John was more ſuitable than any other, ſince "S. John, the apoſtle, evangeliſt and prophet, was, of all the friends of Chriſt, the one who penetrated fartheſt into the myſteries of beauty and of Divine love, the eternal objeċts of the true artiſt's contemplation."[1] Poſterity, however, has forgotten that name for two others merited by his life and works. Fra Giovanni is now ſometimes called *Fra Angelico*, the *Angelic Brother*, and by his more devoted admirers *il Beato*, *the Bleſſed*, Angelico. This laſt name we give him in our hiſtory, becauſe it beſt expreſſes the purity of his talent, and the charaċter of his ſanċtity.[2]

The firſt days of religious life have a charm which the world cannot underſtand. God clothes the beginnings of everything with a particular beauty and ſweetneſs. In it, He is intimately preſent, in order to receive its firſt fruits, of which He declares Himſelf jealous. The noviciate of a cloiſter is the dawn, the ſpring-tide and infancy of a higher exiſtence ; and its peace, delights, joys and hopes, none can tell.

---

[1] R. P. LACORDAIRE, *Règlement de la confrérie de Saint-Jean-l'Evangéliſte*.

[2] Some authors call Beato Angelico *Fieſole;* but this is a wrong appellation. If we would deſignate our painter, in the Italian mode, by his native place, we ſhould have to ſay *Mugellano,* or *Fieſolano,* as we ſay *Perugiano,* or *Parmeſano;* but Fieſole is only the name of a place.

There God fhows Himfelf like a mother towards her
fon who has to undertake a long and painful journey:
fhe preffes him more tenderly than ever to her heart,
and lavifhes careffes on him, the remembrance of
which will fweeten his fatigues and confole him in his
abfence. When we ftudy the works of Beato Angelico,
it is natural to go back to the epoch which prepared
them, and was their fource. But we find that foun-
tain fealed and that garden fhut, the purity and
abundance of which only angels know. We may
judge the caufe, then, from the effect, and believe the
flower as beautiful as the fruit has been delicious.

Another means of appreciating Beato Angelico's
early years, is by knowing the religious who were his
friends at that time. Firft of all, was Beato Giovanni
Dominici, of whom we have already fpoken. God
made him to be born of poor parents, and let him
earn his bread by the fweat of his brow, till he was
eighteen years of age. When he afked for the habit
of S. Dominic, the religious of Santa Maria Novella
were on the point of refufing a young man, whofe
exterior and education gave fo flight hope ; but from
his noviciate, his progrefs in letters and virtue was
fuch, that his fuperiors took him for a model and a
mafter. During his protracted vigils, he made fo
good ufe of his rare intellect and prodigious memory,
that he rapidly overcame the difficulties of theology,
philofophy, mathematics and canon law. The fuccefs
of his preaching caufed him to be compared with
S. Vincent Ferrer, who was exercifing his miraculous
apoftolate at the fame time. Florence, Pifa, Lucca,
Venice and Rome were reformed at his word ; and

with religion and morality, peace for the people and
happinefs for families everywhere reappeared. His
biographer remarks that, notwithftanding the vigour
with which he purfued vice, his charity taught him
the fecret of never wounding the feelings of any one.
Thofe who wifhed to hinder him from preaching, on
account of the crowds he converted and withdrew from
the world, could not refift the pleafure of hearing and
applauding him. The work he had moft at heart,
was the reform of his Order, and fuccefs crowned his
efforts to fuch a degree, that the rule was foon flourifh-
ing again throughout all Italy. After he had founded
the convent of Fiefole, God called His fervant to
greater things, and made him His chief inftrument
in putting an end to the fchifm which had fo long
defolated the Church.

The other companions of Beato Angelico were
Beato Marco of Venice, his prior; Beato Lorenzo
of Ripafratta, his novice-mafter; Beato Pietro Capucci,
who, when fifteen years of age, forgot the nobility of
his family for that of Jefus Chrift, by begging in the
ftreets and ferving in the hofpitals; Beato Coftanzo
of Fabriana, whofe ardent charity obtained everything
from God and man, and Beato Antonio Neyrot, who
fo glorioufly redeemed his fall by voluntary martyrdom. Pirates had made him prifoner and carried
him to Tunis. After having at firft generoufly con-
feffed his faith amidft torments, he let himfelf be overcome by pain, and was weak as S. Peter had been at
the voice of a fervant maid. But a merciful look
from his Divine Mafter touched his heart alfo, and
he refolved to take a great revenge. He purified

himſelf by tears and prayer, and exerciſed himſelf for
the combat by bloody penances; and then, being
clothed again with the ſtrength of Chriſt and the
habit of his Order, he went before the judges, to
accuſe himſelf of his guilt and to preach the Goſpel.
Five days of threats, promiſes and torments, could
not break him, and he died, kneeling, with arms up-
raiſed to heaven, buried under a ſhower of ſtones.

Beato Angelico's moſt eſteemed friend was S. Antoninus, younger than him in years but older in the
cloiſter. At thirteen, he went to offer himſelf to
Beato Giovanni Dominici, who, ſeeing his diminutive
ſtature and delicate conſtitution, promiſed, with a
ſmile, to receive him when he thoroughly knew canon
law. The boy took the anſwer in earneſt, and returned, ſome time after, when he had learned by heart
the voluminous treatiſes of that difficult ſcience. This
aɛt of courage and memory opened the convent doors
to him. His learning and virtues ſoon raiſed him to
the greateſt charges, in which he was diſtinguiſhed as
much by his parts as by his deep humility. All their
lives, Beato Angelico and his brother Fra Benedetto
were united with S. Antoninus by the ties of a lively
friendſhip. Our painter pointed him out for the ſee
of Florence, when it was himſelf whom the Pope wiſhed
to raiſe to that high dignity. S. Antoninus made as
many efforts to avoid honours as people generally do
to obtain them; but he found no refuge from the
Divine will, and had to become the model of biſhops
as he had been of religious. He made no change, on
that account, in his mode of living, but retained his
habit, rule and laborious and mortified life; baniſhed

every luxury from his houfe, and corrected abufes with energy and mildnefs. He was eminently the apoftle of peace and father of the poor, and at the age of feventy years died in the joy of his Lord, pronouncing thefe beautiful words, "To ferve God is to reign."

To fpeak of thefe faints is no digreffion from our fubject. Virtue in a convent is like light in nature; it is reflected on everything, and from the rays croffed and blending together, refults a general harmony in which nothing is ifolated. The merit of each belongs to all, becaufe all really have but one heart and one foul in God.

Chapter III.

BEATO ANGELICO'S RESIDENCE AT FOLIGNO AND CORTONA.—HIS ARTISTIC STUDIES (1408-1418).

HE peace of the convent of Fiefole was of no long duration. God often takes the tempeft as the minifter of His will. Events are like the winds He commands to purify the air, fertilize plants, and carry their rich feeds to a diftance. In the confufion of the ftorm, we fee nothing but ruins and tears; but afterwards, when the fun of hiftory fhines, it is perceived that the ruins were thofe of error, and the tears a dew fertile for good and truth. The troubles which agitated Italy removed Beato Angelico from his fweet retreat; and we fhall fee that this was a bleffing for his talent and for Chriftian art.

The bark of Peter was then in peril, and Chrift flept the fleep that tries faith. The Church, wounded in the centre of life, feemed to be lofing unity; fhe deeply felt thofe ambitious ftruggles which deftroy empires. The refidence of the Popes in the county of Avignon had clearly proved the neceffity of their political independence, and S. Catherine of Sienna, the Joan d'Arc of catholicity, had received the miffion to bring Gregory IX. back to Rome, the predeftined city. The Sovereign Pontiff has the whole earth for his country, but the place whence he muft blefs it will ever be the tomb of the Apoftles.

The Cardinals who nominated Urban VI. maintained that the election had not been free, and made a new one under the preffure of their paffion and private interefts. Robert of Geneva took the name of Clement VII., and went to rule at Avignon under the patronage of France. Then began the fchifm of · the Weft which had fuch deplorable refults. The world was divided, and the ftruggle in the Church became more fatal to civilization than the moft bloody wars. Excommunications, or favours ftill more dangerous, were the weapons of the combat. The defire of creating partizans led to an indulgence which deftroyed difcipline, and to nominations which kept up anarchy even in the fmalleft localities. Cities had two bifhops, convents two fuperiors; and troubled confciences no longer perceived the vifible order eftablifhed by God on earth to convey even to the weakeft the infallibility of His doctrine and the ftrength of His facraments. In this difordered hierarchy, each chofe, not a guide for his foul but a protector for his affairs, or an accomplice for his covetoufnefs. This ftate of things would have been the deftruction of the Church, had fhe not poffeffed the eternal promifes.

When Pope Innocent VII., fucceffor of Urban VI.
and Boniface IX., died at Rome, the Republic of
Florence deputed Beato Giovanni Dominici to the cardinals of the conclave to engage them to fufpend the
election, in order that the extinction of the fchifm
might be rendered eafier; but when he arrived, Pope
Gregory XII. had been oppofed to Peter de Luna,
who kept his fee at Avignon, under the name of
Benedict XIII. The illuftrious Dominican exerted
the influence which his virtues and enlightenment
gave him over the Sovereign Pontiff, to determine
him on renouncing the tiara, in cafe his competitor,
on his fide, would renounce *his* pretenfions. The
negotiations undertaken in this matter led to the
Council of Pifa, which increafed inftead of refolving
the difficulties; for the two adverfaries found, in their
mutual conduct, reafons for not keeping their word;
and their colleges being again met together, after
depofing them, nominated Alexander V. in their ftead.
Inftead of two Popes there were now three.

. Beato Giovanni Dominici remained, as the ambaffador of peace, with Gregory XII., and the fequel
juftified his fympathies and conduct. The Council
of Conftance, which terminated the fchifm, was fuc-
cefsful through the obedient and voluntary abdica-
tion of Gregory XII.; whilft John XXIII., fucceffor
of Alexander V., yielded only to force, and Peter
de Luna died in his criminal obftinacy.

Meanwhile, the Republic of Florence had declared
itfelf for Alexander V. On the contrary, the religious
of Fiefole, being faithful to the direction of their
founder, remained firm to Gregory XII.; and as it

was fought to make them change fides by violence, they protected their liberty by flight. The town they chofe for their afylum was Foligno. God led them, for a particular end, to that ·part of Italy, as it was there He would prepare Beato Angelico for his fair deftinies.

The Florentine fchool from which He feparated him, was then in a new phafe of its development. It was abandoning by degrees its hieratic types, and feeking in its compofitions rather the perfection of form than the manifeftation of the religious thought. The mind, diverted from the true aim of art, reflected the beauties of earth, to the detriment of the beauties of heaven. Ghiberti ftudied antiquity, in order to fteal from it the nobility of its figures and the elegance of its proportions.

Paolo Ucello had a ftrong paffion for perfpective, and chofe fubjects which could beft exhibit its illufions. Exactnefs in anatomical details, the truth of likenefs, the difficulties of forefhortening, precifion of· movements, and harmonious combination of lines, were the fingle prepoffeffion of the artifts who already preferred the admiration of connoiffeurs to the pious fympathy of the crowd. Painting became more learned, but alfo lefs Chriftian.

Beato Angelico, already feparated from the world by the cloifter, was removed, too, from Florence, the neighbourhood of which might trouble the purity of his talent, and went to grow up under another fky, like thofe dear children who are fent far from the turmoil of the city, to be nurtured in a purer air and by a more tranquil breaft.

The influence of locality plays a great part in the life of man; efpecially it makes a difference between one people and another. God made the human race to flow into the world from a fingle fource, but He has prepared various channels for its waves. Nations are rivers which vary with their banks. Some precipitate their noify courfe through wild rocks, others roll their waters over the quiet fand. Country makes our exiftence : every day it gives its reports, its lights and imagery to feed our fenfes; from it come the forms of our thought and the reminifcences of our heart; there every joy finds its mark, each event its place. We imbibe it at every pore, of it make up our whole being, and when abfence feparates us from it, we underftand to what degree it is our element. This union of man with what furrounds him, is a law of the Creator. God has made us the fouls of the world and difperfed us over the whole earth, in order that every mountain, valley and fhore may have a voice, a prayer.

Italy is, perhaps, the moft varied country of the globe, and this will be one of the obftacles to the unity fhe dreams of, under the fhadow of her ancient glory. The mountains trace out feparations there, which it will be difficult to deftroy. The traveller is aftonifhed at changing his scenery fo frequently, and at meeting fo many different beauties within fo fmall a fpace. There are the rich plains of Piedmont, of which Germany is jealous; the bright coafts of Genoa, which make us forget thofe of France and Spain; the majeftic folitude of the Roman Campagna; the wild afpects of the Abruzzi; the intoxicating fky of Naples;

the volcanic lands of Sicily, with their ruins myfterious as thofe of Egypt; and the fhores of the Adriatic, once crowded with fhips from the Eaft in the great days of wealthy Venice.

In the centre of thefe countries is Umbria, which fums up the whole of them. More uneven than Lombardy and the Romagna, frefher than Tufcany, fweeter than the environs of Naples, it leaves the deareft memories in one who has gone over it. How can one forget the light fo pure, the atmofphere fo tranfparent, the lakes reflecting mornings fo frefh and evenings fo calm; the mountains topped with towns for diadems; the hills all wreathed with beautiful ravines, brought out, rare fhapes, againft the cloudlefs fky; the valleys, torrents, roads, where the vine-garlands lend to the elms their rich fruit and graceful foliage? No! never has artift vifited that country without experiencing its happy influence. There the fchool of Perugino copied its chafte landfcapes, and Milton found verfe to paint his Paradife.[1]

Spots fo beautiful could not fail to have a hiftory; antiquity and the middle ages have left traces of their paffage. There Rome and Carthage difputed the empire of the world; and when feudality had built its caftles on the ruins heaped up by the barbarians, Umbria became the lifts where chivalry unfurled its banners. Thofe were not the wars of now-a-days, begun in the darkneffes of diplomacy and ended in the calculations of ftrategy; but Homeric combats mingled with difcourfes and feftivals, tourneys held

---

[1] Milton vifited Italy, and fojourned a long time at the Abbey of Vallombrofa. He was particularly infpired in his defcription by the banks of the Arno.

on the plain, and gazed upon from the neighbouring heights by towns deftined for the conqueror.

God alfo chofe thofe places, as the theatre of one of his faireft victories. Thofe who had been to the Eaft to recover the fepulchre of Chrift had very quickly forgotten the aim of their holy enterprife. Mahometanifm, vanquifhed by arms, triumphed by its cuftoms; and the Crufaders, being compelled to ftrike their tents, brought vices back to Europe which endangered Chriftian civilization. In order to fave it, God inftituted that chivalry of poverty of which S. Francis was the grand mafter. None felt the folly of the Crofs more deeply than that young man of Affifi. He overcame the world by contempt for riches, and formed legions of apoftles who traverfed the earth, teaching by word and example the paffion for facrifice. The plains of Umbria faw the beauty of the tents of Jacob, and the Church exulted at the fight of its wondrous fruitfulnefs.[1] The life of S. Francis was like a great fhout of victory re-echoed in the neighbouring valleys and mountains. S. Clare of Affifi repeated it firft, then Rofe of Viterbo, Angela of Foligno, Agnes of Montepulciano, Catherine of Sienna, and Margaret of Cortona, all of whom celebrated the divine nuptials of love and poverty.

When the new Crucified had gone to reft upon the hill of Affifi, his tomb, like Chrift's, became glorious; for God made grace and pardon ftream from it. The church by which it was covered was the dawn of a new architecture, and fucceffive painters, from

---

[1] At the fecond General Chapter, held May 26th, 1219, more than five thoufand difciples of S. Francis encamped on the plains of Affifi, around the Portiuncula.

Cimabue to Perugino, decorated it with their fweeteft infpirations. Under what purer fky and into what holier place could Providence lead Beato Angelico for developing his talent?

Hiftory does not tell us who was Beato Angelico's firft mafter. Some authors mention Gherard Starnino (1354-1403), and give him Mafolino da Panicale (1378-1415) for his fellow-pupil; but this opinion has no other foundation than a certain fimilitude of ftyle. It is, befides, a matter of little importance to clear up. The mafter is a great deal to mediocrity, but very little to the genius taught directly by nature and the paft. It is evident that Beato Angelico formed himfelf outfide the artiftic movement of Florence. Miniature was his firft occupation and real fchool. He grew up alone, like one of thofe vigorous faplings rifing from the very root of the tree to renew it.

It is a miftake to feparate miniature from hiftorical painting; the image is like the thought it reprefents, independent of its dimenfions. God and man can manifeft the beautiful in little and in great things. The cedar and its vaft fhades are in the feed which is carried by the wind; but to fulfil the myfteries of its life, and prepare its magnificence, the feed requires a good and undifturbed foil: the art of miniature found this in the cloifter.

We have already quite corrected the ftrange judgment formerly paffed on convents, and it is now almoft a commonplace to fay that religious life has been the holy ark in which the Church has renewed human nature. In going back to the fource of all the progrefs our age boafts of, we always arrive at the cloifter and monks, who ferve us as links with antiquity; they are the unwearied workmen who have civilized barbarians, cleared forefts, taught fciences, created univerfities, developed induftry, and built the marvellous monuments which we are beginning to underftand. But whatever be the fhare affigned them in thofe mafterpieces of the middle ages, we fhall do them only juftice in recognizing what they have done in giving it a fcientific formula.

Science is truth known by the intelligence, and art is truth expreffed by love. As truth needs to be known before it is expreffed, between art and truth there is always fcience, and this fcience is the meafure of the art it infpires. The fcience of art does not confift, as feems now-a-days believed, in certain external laws and proceffes. Geometry and ftones are only the means for the architect. Science is a tongue which names things and arranges them together. To difcover fcience is the great work of man. Hollowing out a furrow and laying in it the grain which is to multiply and feed, is nothing; a little toil and fun are enough, and the crop comes. But to penetrate the nature of things ; to know their elements, properties and relations ; to arrive by analyfis at fynthefis ; to difcover, in fhort, unity, the plan of the Creator, is a work that wears out generations and ages. What refearches, what vigils, what chances, what miftakes, before reaching certainty ! A fingle affirmative acquired is fufficient to make a life illuftrious ; and after fo much time and efforts what have we ? Some materials ranged in a certain order, but the edifice has yet to be built.

Art receives its ſcience from a religion. Religions are developed in the world by three degrees. They are firſt impoſed by faith; men accept a revelation, a tradition, and recognize its authority. They are afterwards extended by ſcience, which explains the relation of the viſible and inviſible, of the cauſe and effeᶜt. Finally, they are communicated by ſigns and images always neceſſary for our nature, and only when they have tranſlated their doᶜtrines by outward forms, do they attain their full empire. To refuſe the language of art to a religion, is to dry up its ſource for the majority of mankind.

This aſſimilation of artiſtic forms to doᶜtrine is very remarkable in the religions of antiquity. Their theologies being baſed only on the confuſed traditions of a primitive revelation, created, in order to expreſs the relations of the Supreme Being with the univerſe, a vaſt ſyſtem of ſymbols calculated to render the explanations of them palpable to the people. But the ſages kept the key, and gave it up only in the ſecret of the initiations. Thus the people ſtopped at the form and fell into idolatry.

The religious form of the Greeks was the moſt favourable one to the development of art, becauſe to give the inviſible they took the moſt perfeᶜt viſible being. Inſtead of creating, like the Orientals, fantaſtical figures as ſymbols of their belief, they choſe man whom God Himſelf had made to His own image, and their genius ſtrove to expreſs in his perſon their ideas of the Firſt Cauſe. Not only did they invent types repreſenting the higher powers of nature, but they alſo compoſed hiſtories to recount their phenomena.

That vaft affemblage of allegories became a language, with which artifts could exprefs everything. The figures and fcenes on their monuments had a fenfe known to the people, and that focial language was the life of art and favoured its development. We are beginning to decipher heathen iconography, defpite the obfcurity the Romans brought into it by mixing together all the religions of the nations they conquered. When fhall we alfo revive Chriftian iconography, fo ufeful and fo admirable!

·The middle ages had an iconography, an artiftic fcience, as fuperior to heathen iconography as light is to fhade. Inftead of fictions, Chriftians have realities for images. God has really become incarnate, and Chrift, in putting on the human form, has become the type of beauty and virtue. All that is admirable in the univerfe is a reflection of His light; and all that is fublime in the heart of man is a ray of His grace. His thoughts make faints, His words make worlds. He is the centre of time and fpace, the meeting-point of the prefent and the future, the mafter of events, the argument of hiftory, the tie of the Old and New Teftaments, the fource of the Church, the purity of virgins, the ftrength of martyrs. This primal and fruitful beauty, religion prefents to Chriftian art. What fcience did it not require to comprehend and reproduce it! This fcience the Fathers of the Church prepared in their commentaries on the Holy Scriptures; but they who gave it fyftem and merit to be called the fathers of Chriftian art, are the patient and unknown monks who were turning the text of manufcripts into pious images, and creating a fign and fymbol for each bright thought and each affection of the heart. By them, the moft elevated truths and the moft ufeful leffons of religion were brought within the reach of all. Chriftian art became a book wherein the moft ignorant could read, an univerfal mirror wherein hiftory and nature were delineated in their moral forms—a mirror dimmed by our ignorance, but ftill ferviceable, if ftudy reftores to us its brightnefs and its images.

There artifts will find again the fcience, the language, which gives power over the multitude. What is art without iconography? Mere ifolated acts, individual reveries, a relation between the initiated few. But with iconography, with figns and fymbols comprehenfible to every one, art becomes a focial power, and a means of fubduing minds and hearts, of carrying them on to virtue and uniting them in love.

Let painters and fculptors ftudy miniature, who have the holy ambition to renew the wonders of Chriftian art. The figures ftocking our cathedrals are often unexplained; they will be found again in manufcripts befide the text. Manufcripts are a mine ftill unopened, we may fay, by archæology. What riches, what pious and genuine beauties! Every page has its joys and tears, as each day its light and dew; there are flowers and fruits for every feafon. And they were poor monks who have thus identified the life of art with the life of the Church, in praying to God by images, and having no other ambition but to excite a holy thought in the heart of their brethren! Sometimes the Father of the family gave them a higher place at His banquet; their tafk was increafed, and they painted their mafterpieces on the walls of churches and cloifters. Fame paid them a vifit, and forced them to appear on a wider ftage : princes and cities invited them to decorate their monuments, and to affociate them with the moft celebrated artifts.[1]

Such was the deftiny of Beato Angelico. Miniature was his firft fchool. He ftudied the holy truths of religion in thofe beautiful manufcripts, in which the text is tranflated and commentated by the pencil. But he was not fatisfied with that teaching, and, like the Chriftian orator, who becomes the difciple of the holy fathers like them to clothe doctrine with the charms of eloquence, profoundly ftudied the great mafters, and appropriated their works fo well, as to become the moft illuftrious reprefentative of the great fchool of Giotto. He did not go aftray in fearch of originality, as is done in our own days. Now the moft indifferent painter thinks to redeem his want of talent by novelty of compofition, whilft the greateft artifts of Greece and of the middle ages were not afraid to follow the track of their predeceffors, and to exercife themfelves on models already confecrated. Chriftian compofitions belong to every one ; they are like the prayers adopted by the Church, which each one repeats indifferently, according to his degree of faith and the rapture of his heart. Beato Angelico dedicated to the ftudy of the great mafters his years of exile paffed under the fair fky of Umbria. His pictures prove it better than hiftorical documents. The

---

[1] Dom Bartolomeo della Gatta, a Camaldolefe religious, arrived at great hiftorical painting through miniature. He was charged, with Luca Signorelli and Perugino, to paint the Siftine Chapel.

E

earlieſt eſpecially ſhow the influence of the ſchool of
Giotto, and in them are found types and figures borrowed from the paintings at Aſſiſi.

Aſſiſi was to Chriſtian art what the univerſities of
Paris and Bologna were to ſcience in the middle ages.
Great artiſts came ſucceſſively to depoſit their nobleſt
inſpirations at the tomb of S. Francis; and when the
walls of his ſanctuary were entirely adorned with theſe
ex-votos of genius, other churches were opened to
receive them, and all the ſacred edifices of the city
were beautified with paintings, which new generations
of artiſts ſought to make worthy of the maſterpieces
they came to admire. Deſpite the ravages of time
and men, Aſſiſi is ſtill the moſt intereſting and complete Chriſtian muſeum for the ſtudent of tradition.
Foligno and Perugia are only a few hours' diſtance
from it, and Beato Angelico, who long dwelt in thoſe
two towns, muſt have very often made a pilgrimage
ſo ſweet to the artiſt and the Chriſtian. He travelled
through that beautiful valley ſtudded with ſanctuaries;
viſited the church of Santa Maria dei Angeli, conſecrated by ſo many recollections, and the convent of
S. Damiano, ſo faithful to its virgin poverty; knelt at
the tombs of S. Clare and S. Francis, and received
in the Sagro Convento the fraternal hoſpitality never
refuſed, during ſo many ages, to the children of
S. Dominic. Thus he found again the maſters he
had loved at Florence. He ſtudied the magnificent
Crucifixion by Pietro Cavallini, ſtill ſo remarkable
notwithſtanding mutilations, for its beauty of colouring and energy of expreſſion; the Life of the Virgin,
by Taddeo Gaddi; the Chapel of the Bleſſed Sacra-

ment, by Giottino; the Hiftory of S. Mary Magdalen, by Buffalmaco; and the great poem in four
cantos, with which Giotto crowned the altar over the
body of S. Francis. But the painter who perhaps
moft engaged his fympathies was Simone Memmi, in
the admirable chapel where the Hiftory of S. Martin
is reprefented. Thefe paintings have recalled to our
mind more than any others the charaĉter and grace
of his talent.

To us, it is beyond doubt that Beato Angelico
ftudied the old paintings of Sienna: from them he
moftly borrowed the type of his Madonnas with looks
fo pure and fweet.[1] Sienna is not far from Florence:
Beato Angelico often paffed it on his journeys, and
probably went there to affift at the annual feftivals celebrated by his Order in honour of S. Catherine, before
her canonization.[2] He muft have known Andrea Vanni,
the difciple of that great faint, the portrait of whom
he has left us; as well as Taddeo di Bartolo, who,
in 1409, was painting the beautiful Annunciation preferved in the public gallery of the city.[3] If Beato
Angelico found mafters and friends at Sienna, there
too he had difciples and imitators; for later on we
fhall fee Giovanni di Paolo infpired by his compofitions, and borrowing whole figures from his Laft

---

[1] We will cite particularly the fine Madonna by Guido of Sienna, at the foot
of which the painter has written thefe verfes:—

> ME GHVIDO DE SENIS DIEBVS DEPINXIT AMENIS,
>
> QUEM Xps LENIS NVLLIS VELIT AGERE PENIS. ANNO D. MCCXXI.

The church of S. Domenico at Sienna.—ROSINI, *Storia della Pittura*, plate iv.

[2] *Vie de S. Catherine de Sienne*, part ii., chap. 11. See the procefs of Venice,
DOM MARTENE, *Veterum Scriptorum et Monumentorum ampliffima Collectio*,
tom. vi, p. 1238.

[3] *Catalogue*, third room, No. 1.

E 2

Judgments. No school has greater conformity with the talent of Beato Angelico than the school of Sienna.

To the study of the old masters, Beato Angelico added that of nature, and thereby surpassed preceding painters. He certainly did not use a model, as the artists of the Renaissance did. He had no ambition for the science of the nude ; and on the rare occasions when he painted the human body, it would be easy to mark down faults in anatomy. Was he thinking of avoiding them, when, on bended knees and with tearful eyes, he was painting his Christs? But if he neglected a talent more advantageous to the senses and to the artistic vanity than to piety and the glory of God, he did his utmost to give the beauties of nature truthfully. His movements are exact, his proportions happy, and he condenses on his figures a life and an expression which imagination alone could not have yielded. In place of mercenary models, whose indifference stifles inspiration, he found in the religious surrounding him friends, to whom he could communicate his thoughts and feelings. This explains the life-like expression of his saints, who seem to be painted from nature. It is evident, also, that Beato Angelico's poetic soul took pleasure in studying the riches with which the Creator has decked the earth. In his first pictures particularly we find flowers copied with all the joyousness and patience of love, and his compositions sometimes present landscapes, which for freshness and truth would do honour to the ablest Flemish painters.

Beato Angelico must have had cartoons well filled with studies. He carefully prepared his pictures, and preserved the drawings of them ; for we find the same figures in works executed at very remote places and periods. His drawings are numerous at Florence, but we have few of them in France. The Mufeum of Sketches at the Louvre has one, and M. de Reifet two in his valuable collection.' That in the Louvre is the oldeft, and might be a ftudy made during his years paffed in Umbria. It is executed on coloured paper, fet off in white. It reprefents a S. Francis in a glory: its bad prefervation is to be regretted. At the back of this drawing, is the face of a little ftag, charmingly graceful and natural. M. de Reifet's drawings are more important. The firft (No. 5 in the catalogue) prefents ftudies for a compofition of the Laft Judgment; they are done with the pen and in 'biftre, with great freedom. Chrift as Judge, and the three angels accompanying him, recall the picture in the Corfini gallery. At the top, is a hand drawn from life, and given with the precifion and livelinefs admired in the hands of Holbein's portraits. On the reverfe of the fheet, on a yellow ground, is a fine head of a religious feen in front, half in the light and half in fhade; and this portrait prefents a furprifing character of truth. The fmalleft details are reprefented in it with the fidelity of daguerreotype; a little fwelling over the left eye is given carefully. A painter of the Renaiffance could not have drawn it with greater breadth and fkill.

The fecond drawing of M. de Reifet (No. 6 in the catalogue) is alfo double. It contains two ftudies of

---

' We were not able to ftudy the drawings at Florence, as they were not exhibited in the Gallery of the Uffizi at the period of our laft journey. We here thank M. de Reifet for his kindnefs in allowing us to enjoy the treafures in his poffeffion, which he is fo well qualified to appreciate.

the evangelifts S. Mark and S. Matthew, painted on
the arch of the chapel in the Vatican. The former is
wafhed and fet off in white on a green ground; he
holds with both hands a book opened on his right
knee. The latter has a pen in his right hand, and a
clofed book in his left : it is with the pen, and wafhed
with biftre on white ground. Thefe two ftudies are
very beautiful and well finifhed, and make us underftand how our painter prepared and executed his
works.

Thus Beato Angelico neglected no means of cultivating and developing his talent. He ftudied tradition
and nature. Manufcripts taught him to clothe his
faith with images and fymbols all could underftand.
The old mafters taught him the great principles of
art, and he imitated their mafterpieces, as the defcendant of a noble race imitates the exploits of his
anceftors, by following their virtues without aping
their actions. Beato Angelico did the fame in regard
to his predeceffors, by appropriating their good qualities, without fervilely copying their pictures. He
fought progrefs, and found it in the ftudy of nature.
He ftudied her not through vanity and to furpafs
others, but through love for the Creator, and to
glorify them in the beauty of His works.

CHAPTER IV.

THE FIRST WORKS OF BEATO ANGELICO (1408-1418).

HE works of Beato Angelico are
very numerous, but our bleſſed
painter counted time and glory as
nothing, and never ſigned nor dated
them. Still we will endeavour to
claſſify them, by the aid of hiſtory,
and as the different phaſes of his
talent point out to us. His pictures do not preſent
the changes of ſtyle undergone by other artiſts through
external influences. The love of God, being his only
inſpiration, diffuſed over ·them unity and perfect harmony; but that very harmony has delicate tints, even
as the heart has different tones, according to its years,
whilſt repeating the ſelf-fame prayers and canticles.

The life of Beato Angelico is divided into a certain
number of epochs, in which it will be eaſy for us to
arrange all his pictures. The hills of the neighbourhood

of Florence had feen his artiftic and religious childhood. His youth expanded under the fair fky of Umbria, amidft the archaic works of Chriftian painting. The ten years between his departure from Fiefole and his return were not entirely fpent in ftudying the old mafters, and he confecrated, no doubt, a great part of the time to making pictures.

The religious, whofe voluntary exile he had fhared, remained four years in the convent of S. Domenico, at Foligno. But the plague, afflicting Umbria about 1413, caufed fome relaxation in it, and they quitted it, fearing more the fcourge menacing their fouls than one which might attack their bodies. They withdrew to the convent of Cortona, the cradle of Beato Giovanni Dominici's reform, and noviciate of moft of them. Beato Angelico went with them; but he ftaid, doubtlefs, at Perugia alfo, and perhaps then executed the picture in the convent of his Order. This painting and thofe at Cortona feem to us to belong neceffarily to this period. He probably made many others now loft or hidden in the obfcurity of cloifters, there to delight fome holy fouls. The paintings at Perugia and Cortona were done under the influence of the fchool of Giotto, and they fuperabound in the naturalnefs of heart and frefhnefs of imagination, which a youth nurtured by pious meditations can alone poffefs.

The picture executed for the chapel of San Niccolo dei Guidalotti is now in the chapel of S. Orfola, in the church of S. Domenico, at Perugia. It muft originally have been oblong, and divided, like triptichs, into three compartments terminated in angles, and with a gradino.[1] It reprefents, on a gold ground, the Holy Virgin and her Divine Son. On both fides of the throne, angels are carrying bafkets of flowers, whence the child Jefus feems to have taken the rofe he is holding in his hand. The expreffion of the Son and the fmile of the Mother feem to fay that this rofe is the emblem of the Myftical Rofe which God has chofen, amongft the faireft and pureft creatures, to defcend there and put on our humanity. In the two compartments ferving as fhutters for this picture, Beato Angelico has painted S. John the Baptift, S. Catherine, S. Dominic, and S. Nicholas.

The gradino is alfo divided into three pictures, reprefenting the legend of S. Nicholas. The firft two are at Rome, in the Mufeum of the Vatican. The third has remained at Perugia, and is in the facrifty of the convent of S. Domenico. The firft picture comprifes three fubjects.

1. The birth of S. Nicholas. His mother is put to bed, and a female wafhes the child, who is ftanding.[2] His little body is well drawn.

2. The young Nicholas hearing a fermon. His delight was to frequent churches; and he retained all he heard out of the facred fcriptures.[3] A bifhop is in the pulpit; and his audience are women feated upon a flowery turf.

3. After the death of his parents, S. Nicholas em-

---

[1] Padre Marchefe thinks with Padre Bottonio, that this picture was executed in 1437, but its form and ftyle make us believe it to be older.

[2] Hic prima die, dum balnearetur, erectus ftetit in pelvi *(Legenda aurea, de vita S. Nicolai).*

[3] Factus autem juvenis, aliorum devitans lafcivias, ecclefiarum potius terebat limina, et quidquid ibi de facra Scriptura intelligere poterat, memoriter retinebat.

ploys his riches in good works. The daughters of a gentleman are in danger of lofing their virtue, on account of their poverty. S. Nicholas faves them from difhonour, by throwing a confiderable fum through the window, in the night-time. The fubject is expreffed with great fimplicity of compofition. The interior of the young girls' bed-chamber is feen, and the father, in the foreground, is fitting to watch his benefactor.

In the fecond picture, S. Nicholas, become Bifhop of Myra, is having unladen from a veffel bound for Rome, a hundred meafures of corn, to feed the city defolated by famine. By a miraculous multiplication, the freight of the veffel is not diminifhed, and the hundred meafures fuffice the poor for two years. In the mid-diftance, behind the rocks, the faint appears to people who are invoking him, and calms the tempeft threatening their fhip.

The third picture, ftill at Perugia, contains two fubjects. The firft fhows S. Nicholas faving three Roman princes from the death by which an unjuft governor would have them perifh. The fecond reprefents the obfequies of the holy bifhop. He is extended on his bier, furrounded by religious, by women and the poor, whofe tears tell his virtues and charity. In the upper part, angels conduct his foul to heaven, and with their harmony celebrate his triumph.[1]

The Madonna of S. Domenico, at Perugia, had fome little pictures for a frame, now feparated and fhown in the facrifty. There are twelve figures painted with extraordinary delicacy. Two pictures reprefenting the

---

[1] Cœleftium melodia audita eft.

Annunciation formed, probably, part of the top of the compofition. By Mariotti, all thefe paintings at Perugia have been afcribed to Gentile à Fabriano; but the miftake is evident, for the ftyle of that mafter is too different from Beato Angelico's to let us confound them. Befides, the fame compofitions have been repeated by our painter; and we have,. on our fide, the authority of Rofini and of Padre Marchefe.[1]

The convent of Cortona, where Beato Angelico paffed the laft years of his exile, ftands on the Cyclopian walls of the town, and commands one of the moft magnificent landfcapes in Italy. Beyond the wild declivities of the foreground, the view is extended over a rich plain bordered by mountains, and over the beautiful lake of Perugia, which reflects like a mirror the clear light of Umbria. The poetical foul of

---

[1] V. MARCHESE, lib. ii, c. 4, p. 217.

["On a gold ground he (Beato Angelico) painted the Bleffed Virgin, feated on a throne, with the Divine Babe on her knees. Two Angels ftand at either fide, with bafkets of flowers, from which the infant feems to have taken a rofe that he holds in his right hand. At the foot of the throne are fome fhrubs, with white and red rofes; a beautiful idea, that the painter repeated afterwards in Cortona and elfewhere. The Virgin, rejoicing in her maternity, fmiles on her Son; and this portrait appears to us to be the nobleft and fweeteft of the many he has executed. Its grand characteriftics, like thofe of all his other paintings of the Madonna, are purity and grace, fo well befitting the Mother of the Son of God. I think, however, that the defign of the nude in the infant, as well as angels, is feeble. Retouchings, or, perhaps, the injuries of time, prevent us from recognizing the drapery of the Virgin's robe. In the two lateral compartments, now divided, there were four figures, two on the right, and two on the left; thefe were S. John Baptift, S. Catherine, Virgin and Martyr, S. Dominic and S. Nicholas, all in one line, according to the Giottefque; and, if we except the fecond of thefe figures, all the others are moft beautiful and excellently executed. But truly beautiful was the gradino of this picture, on which he painted three hiftories of the life of S. Nicholas, of which only one remains, the other two having been removed to the Vatican. This, that may ftill be feen in the church of S. Domenico (Perugia), over the great door of the facrifty, is divided into two compartments; in one of

our painter muſt lovingly have enjoyed that fine ſpec-
tacle, which recalled the grand ſcenery of Fieſole.
On the façade of the church of S. Domenico, at Cortona, he executed, probably his firſt painting in freſco.
He has repreſented, on the tympan of the door, a
Madonna, with the child Jeſus holding a globe.
S. Dominic and S. Peter Martyr are in adoration
before their throne. This painting is damaged in the
lower part. The four Evangeliſts adorning the arch
are better preſerved, and allow of our admiring now
the ſimplicity of execution, delicacy of touch, and
purity of colouring, which are natural qualities in
Beato Angelico.

In the interior of the church, the beautiful architecture of which has been unfortunately modified, are
ſeen, on the left of the high altar, the ſhrine of Beato

which he repreſents the holy biſhop, and two youths, who, with bandaged eyes,
are in the act of waiting the headman's ſtroke ; multitudes, aſſembled to witneſs
the execution, ſeem to ſhudder and groan ; and the ſudden appearance of the
Saint ſtays the axe of the executioner, and ſaves them. In the other he painted
the funeral of the Saint, whom he repreſents ſtretched on the bier, and ſurrounded
by the poor, by monks and women, who exhibit ſigns of the deepeſt grief. But
that which is ſtill more exquiſite is the action of the two youthful acolytes, one of
whom raiſes the hem of his ſurplice to wipe away the tears which he could not
reſtrain. In the upper part of the ſame compartment he painted the ſoul of the
Saint conducted to heaven by angels. Amongſt the works of the Angelico,
executed in the miniature ſtyle, this appears to me to be truly beautiful, the little
figures being exquiſitely deſigned and coloured. The cornice [frame] that
adorned this picture, (now divided into twelve pieces, each having a little figure,)
may be ſeen near the ſame door of the ſacriſty ; but, although they poſſeſs great
merit, no one that has ſeen his Depoſition from the Croſs in Florence, will
pronounce them to be his beſt performances. To complete the entire picture, we
want the points of the upper part ; and, probably, the two little pictures in the
ſame ſacriſty formed a part of them. Theſe repreſent the Annunciation and the
angel Gabriel, on a gold ground. They appear to me to have been executed by
the ſame painter, but I would not dare to affirm it."—Marchese, *by Mcehan,*
vol. i, p. 177.—Translator's note.]

Capucci, and on the right, a picture by our painter.
The remembrance of thefe two contemporaries over
the altars, before which they had prayed together,
ftruck us, and we confefs that the work of Beato
Angelico feemed to us a holy relic, like the bones of
his friend : for is it not a living remnant of himfelf,
a ray of his foul, a perfume from his heart ? This
picture ftrongly recalls the one at Perugia, by its
arrangement and principal fubject ; only the dimenfions are larger and the execution is fuperior. Its
form is ogival. In the centre, is feated the Virgin,
one of the moft beautiful by the painter. The child
Jefus, ftanding on her knees, is covered in the lower
part with a red drapery ; he holds a rofe in his hand,
and is looking at his mother with a delightful fmile. ·
Around the throne, four angels, whofe heads are ravifhing. On the two fhutters, on the right S. John
the Baptift and the well-beloved Apoftle, on the left
S. Mary Magdalen and S. Mark. The upper part of
the triptich reprefents, in the principal angle, Chrift
on the Crofs, and at his feet the Virgin and S. John
the Evangelift, the Mother and the adopted fon.
In the exterior angles, the two figures of the
Annunciation.

The gradino of this picture is now in the church
of the Gefu at Cortona, which ferves as a baptiftry
for the cathedral. It is a little poem in honour of
S. Dominic. His hiftory is reprefented in fix compartments. The firft prefents two fubjects, the Dream
of Pope Innocent III, who fees in his fleep S. Dominic
fupporting the tottering Church; and the inexpreffible
embrace of S. Dominic and S. Francis, which was

the fignal for the conqueft of the world by fcience and love.

The fecond compartment reprefents S. Dominic in exftacy before the altar. The Apoftles S. Peter and S. Paul appear to him, and give him the book of the Gofpels and the traveller's ftaff, fymbols of his divine miffion. A young religious paufing on the threfhold of the oratory, happily contemplates this fcene.

In the third picture, S. Dominic difputes with the Albigenfes, and propofes to them to try their oppofite doctrines by fire. The flames confume the writings of the heretics, and, on the contrary, refpect the book of S. Dominic.

In the fourth picture, the holy patriarch raifes the young Napoleon to life, and gives him back to his mother. This compofition recalls the bas-relief of Niccolo of Pifa on the tomb of S. Dominic, at Bologna. Our painter appears to have been feveral times infpired by the fculptures of that monument, which filial piety doubtlefs led him to vifit.

The next picture makes us prefent at the repaft where S. Dominic and his brethren receive miraculous bread from two angels. The laft painting prefents the bleffed death of the Holy Founder. The religious furround him, weeping, and kifs his hands, whilft angels carry his foul into the bofom of God. We do not ftop at thefe compofitions, becaufe we fhall have to examine them more attentively in another gradino. Four charming figures feparate thefe pictures into pairs. The firft is S. Peter Martyr, from whofe head and breaft efcapes the generous blood with which he wrote, expiring, the firft words of the creed; the

fecond, S. Michael the Archangel, remarkable for its
purity and dignity; the third, S. Vincent, deacon and
martyr, with the mill-ftone which was tied to his body
when he was thrown into the fea, that the faithful
might be deprived of his holy relics;[1] and the laft is
an admirable S. Thomas Aquinas.[2]

Beato Angelico painted for the church of his own
convent a fecond picture, now at the Gefù. It reprefents the Annunciation, a fubject he was fo fond of
repeating. It was his *Ave Maria*, that prayer every
Chriftian loves fo much, becaufe it recalls the words
whereby Mary was made mother of God and men.
" When fhe heard it, for the firft time, from the lips
of Gabriel, fhe immediately conceived within her

---

[1] S. Vincent is reprefented, with his mill-ftone and the raven which defended his body, on the fine fouth door of Chartres cathedral.

[2] [" In fix compartments he painted eight hiftories of the life of the Saint (Dominic) ; and, from time to time, by way of epifodes to that epic, he introduced fome graceful little figures of faints, which, far from violating the unity of the fubject, tend to heighten the beauty and perfection of the entire compofition. Firft, there is S. Peter, Martyr, the wound in whofe head and breaft tells how generoufly he laid down his life for the faith ; then comes the compartment in which he executed two hiftories—the firft is the vifion of Pope Honorius [*read* Innocent] III., who, after having refufed to fanction the new Order, dreamt that he faw the Lateran Bafilica falling, and S. Dominic fuftaining it ; the fecond is, S. Dominic meeting S. Francis of Affifi, who, recognizing each other by Divine revelation, kneel and embrace. The fecond compartment, like the firft, is divided into two parts, one of which reprefents the poor cell, and the other the oratory of the faint. The perfpective in both is admirable. In the oratory we fee S. Dominic before the altar, in exftacy receiving the gofpels and ftaff from Saints Peter and Paul, who fend him forth to evangelize peoples and nations. One of the moft charming figures in this compofition is that of a friar, who, fetting out on his miffion in obedience to the command of his fuperior, paufes on the threfhold of the cell to fteal a glance at this wonderful apparition. Next comes a beautiful little figure of S. Michael the Archangel, light, airy, and full of grace. In the third compartment there are alfo two hiftories ; in the firft, he reprefents S. Dominic difputing with the Albigeois; and in the fecond the ordeal of fire, in which he depicts the aftonifhment of the Saint's adverfaries, on feeing their book

moft pure womb the Word of God; and now every time the mouth of man repeats to her thofe words, the fignal of her maternity, her heart thrills with joy at the recollection of a moment which never had its like in heaven nor on earth, and all eternity is filled with her happinefs."[1]

The Annunciation at Cortona reminds us particularly of the old mafters. The Virgin is on a throne covered with rich drapery, and her arms are croffed upon her breaft. An angel[2] with golden hair advances towards her, and his hands fhow the text of S. Luke, " *Spiritus Sanctus fuperveniet in te, et virtus Altiffimi obumbrabit tibi :*" "The Holy Ghoft fhall come upon thee, and the power of the Moft High fhall over-

burn and his unfcathed. In the picture of the Saint refufcitating the young Napoleone at Rome, he faithfully carried out the idea of Niccola Pifano, and placed the afflicted mother near the dead body, imploring the Saint to call back her fon to life. Then follows the figure of a martyr, beautifully painted. I am ignorant, however, of the fubject. By the dalmatic we know that he is a holy deacon, and that the heavy weight fufpended from his neck defcribes the mode of his death. He produced only one hiftory in the compartment that follows; and here he reprefents the Holy Founder feated at table with his brethren, and the angels bringing them food. In the laft he painted the death of the holy patriarch; and this, in my judgment, excels all the others. The holy foul has been already borne into the bofom of the Eternal by angels; his bereaved children furround the lifelefs body; fome of them kifs his hands, others raife their arms to heaven; fome of them, almoft petrified by grief, fix their eyes on his beloved features; whilft others, unable to reftrain their tears, raife their garments to their eyes. This is a work calculated to awaken piety in every heart. The actual gradino has a moft graceful figure of S. Thomas of Aquino. All thefe hiftories are beautifully defigned and coloured, and are moft fimple in their compofitions."—MARCHESE, *by Meehan*, vol. i, p. 182.—TRANSLATOR'S note.]

[1] *Vie de Saint Dominique*, par le R. P. Lacordaire, p. 332.

[2] ["In the wings of this angel there is a profufion of gold and colouring unexampled in the other pictures of the fame; nor does the drapery of this figure deferve fo much praife as that which we find in the generality of Fra Giovanni's works. Here, indeed, it is too much elaborated and confufed."—MARCHESE, *by Meehan*, vol. i, p. 184.—TRANSLATOR'S note.]

fhadow thee." The Virgin anfwers, "*Ecce ancilla Domini :*" "Behold the handmaid of the Lord." This ufe of infcriptions on the field of a picture is regarded by many as a cuftom of barbarous times; it exifted, however, in the moft glorious epochs of Greek art, but will always fhock thofe who feek to addrefs the fenfes rather than the foul, and place all the perfection of painting in the knowing combinations of lines and colours.

The fcene takes place under a fmall portico with graceful little pillars. In a landfcape vifta, is feen an angel driving Adam and Eve out of the terreftrial paradife, who are clothed in the drefs God made for them. Bringing thefe two fubjects together was very frequent in the middle ages, becaufe it explained the caufe and manner of our redemption. Our mother by nature ruined us by gathering the forbidden fruit; our mother by grace has faved us by accepting the redeeming fruit. She it is who, according to the promife, crufhes the tempter-ferpent's head.

The gradino of this picture is alfo at the Gefù. It reprefents the hiftory of the Holy Virgin; and is divided into feven compartments, with thefe fubjects.

1. The Nativity of the Virgin. S. Anne herfelf configns the infant to a midwife. This picture is damaged.

2. The Marriage of the Virgin and S. Jofeph. The fcene takes place at a city-gate; the high prieft is uniting the efpoufed. This picture is very remarkable as a work of art. S. Jofeph, particularly, is in a beautiful ftyle. The women accompanying the Virgin

F

are draped and grouped perfectly. The men placed before S. Joseph express their joy by dance and song.

3. The Visitation. The Virgin and S. Elizabeth reverentially embrace each other. Two women only are present at the interview between the blessed mothers. One contemplates it from the threshold of the house, the other, kneeling in the road, raises her arms to heaven and gives thanks for this joyful mystery. The landscape is one of the most remarkable by our painter, who was inspired by the pure and peaceful spots of Umbria.

4. The Adoration of the Magi. This composition is one of rapturous simplicity. S. Joseph is speaking with the oldest of the three Magian kings, and affectionately presses hands.

5. The Purification. The aged Simeon clasps the Infant to his heart. The Virgin stretches out her hands to him. Behind her, S. Joseph is carrying two little doves; on the other side, the prophetess Anna is devoutly advancing.

6. The Burial of the Virgin, as the Golden Legend so poetically relates it.

7. The Virgin gives the habit of the Friar-Preachers to the Blessed Reginald.[1] The artist has thus bound up the history of the Virgin with that of his Order, of which she is the patroness. Marchese thinks this picture did not form part of the gradino; but it evidently does belong to it. It is narrower than those before it, and of the same size as the first, of which it formed the pendant. Three of these charming little

---

[1] *Vie de S. Dominique*, p. 443.

pictures, the fecond, fourth, and fixth are found alfo
in the gallery of the Uffizi, at Florence.

We feel how incomplete are the indications we are
giving of the earlieft works of Beato Angelico. To
defcribe a picture is always difficult, becaufe words
ill exprefs what the pencil reprefents. As for other
artifts, however, there is a means of making the refult
of their infpiration underftood, and criticifm may
analyze the peculiar qualities of their talent; but
Beato Angelico is not a painter only, he is alfo a faint.
How tell celeftial mufic, which earthly inftruments
could not yield? An engraving or even a copy leaves
much to wifh for. The pictures of our faint muft be
feen, and feeing them, we feel that we fhould underftand them better, were we ourfelves better. They
are like thofe pages of the Gofpel, which proportion
the intenfity of their light to the purity of the heart.

Our purpofe is to infpire artifts to love and ftudy
the works of Beato Angelico. Shall we gain it? Will
not our efforts be fruitlefs? Many pafs before thefe
pious pictures with indifference, and if they ftop for
an inftant, fafcinated by a myfterious attraction, they
foon fhake off the fecret call of virtue, and go away
faying, "It is myftic painting." Yes, but what is
myftic painting? And why cannot every one do it,
nor even underftand it?

There is a myftic painting, becaufe there is a myftic
life and a myftic fcience. Art only gives what the
fpirit fees, and the fpirit fees only what exifts. By
his foul and body, man has relation with two worlds,
the vifible world and the invifible world; and he can,
by his will, place the activity of his life in either

of them. If he choofes the vifible world, and feeks
in matter the gratification of his fenfes only, he may,
even by his intellect, defcend below the brute, and
fall into exceffes unknown to it. If, on the contrary, he choofes the invifible world, and feeks God,
his beginning and end, he may difengage himfelf from
earth, and let his foul breathe in higher regions.
Thefe two lives fo different lead to oppofite phenomena. The world perceives thofe produced by the
brutifhnefs of man, becaufe there are infamies and
crimes againft which it is obliged to defend itfelf; but
the fupernatural life of the foul efcapes it, becaufe it
is fulfilled in a fphere not its own. But what matters
ignorance? It is as powerlefs againft truth, as nothingnefs is againft Being. Myftic facts exift, and modern
fcience will be forced, one day, to ftudy them, in order
to underftand matter itfelf. Form, motion and life
are problems not to be folved without the interven-
tion of a fpiritual power.

Myfticifm is the interior life of the Church, its intimate union with Chrift, the unfpeakable love which
Solomon has made known to us in the Canticle of
Canticles. The difciple whom our Lord loved was its
Evangelift and Apoftle, and, fince his bleffed repofe
on the facred bofom of his Mafter, there have always
been fouls who have enjoyed thefe familiarities and
divine careffes. We doubt not Beato Angelico tafted
this happinefs, and it explains to us the myfterious
charm diffufed over all his works.

But you will fay, this fupernatural life, this higher
ftate of the foul, is it not a hindrance to the development of art? Is it not oppofed to the realization of

natural beauty? Strange error, to believe that thofe only who abufe nature love and know it! Thefe pretended lovers of the creation are only profaners of it, and their fcience is as falfe as their love. Outfide God, what can we know in its beginning and end? And when the beginning and end of a thing is not known, what is left except vain appearances? Myftics, by purifying their fenfes, become ftrangers to the forms of our coarfe paffions; they are like to God, who in His perfect liberty cannot do evil. But precifely on this account, they are capable of feeing and rendering true natural beauty. They leave to others the fields defolated by original fin; they enter again the terreftrial paradife of grace and tafte its delights. Seated under the fhade of the tree of life, they contemplate at its fountain-head the river which is carrying its fertilizing ftreams to the extremities of the earth. God accompanies them through all creation, like a friend who himfelf will put his friend in poffeffion of his domain; and becaufe the leaft object becomes valuable when a friend has given it, everything is tranffigured and appears divine to him who loves God.

And without here recalling the paffion of the faints for their fellow-men, the love which makes them find Jefus Chrift in the leaft and moft miferable, the ardour which fends the miffionary to martyrdom and the fifter of charity into the hofpitals, how much have not the faints loved and cherifhed nature! Look at the heart of S. Francis of Affifi dilating itfelf through the whole univerfe. Liften to him hailing his brother the fun, and fpeaking to his fifters the doves. He has knit again the true relations of man with creatures; they

underftand and love each other, becaufe they converfe
with God their Father.

Poor ignorant men! You believe that you have
the monopoly of artiftic enjoyments, and imagine that
in loving God we cannot love His works! You think
that you fee the light, becaufe you fee its reflection
on the duft around you. To contemplate it, we need
to be upon the mountain of a holy life. There we are
bathed in its fplendour, which we fee filling vaft horizons, rejoicing the eagle in the air, giving ftrength
to the cedars and fertility to the plains, and drawing
dew-drops from the ocean, to fhed them with its heat
upon the flower of the prairies. Artiftic enjoyments!
There are more of them in the heart of the monk, who
gathers that little flower to copy it on the margin of
his manufcript, than in all your refearches and learned
works. Of what good are all your refearches, your
analyfes, if in nature you do not love its Author? To
know without loving, is to poffefs without enjoying.
Blind flaves! Under the mill-ftone of ftudy, you are
grinding the good grain of fcience; the pure wheat
from it is referved for love. You believe that your
works are monuments which will protect the memory
of you; and they are fteps which will aid thofe who
love God to love Him more.

CHAPTER V.

HE exiles of Fiefole fighed after their dear retreat. But the foundation-deed purported that an abfence of two months fhould caufe them to lofe all right to the convent; and thus they found many difficulties in re-entering it. Beato Giovanni Dominici took fteps with the bifhop, who confented to their return by the way of a fet-off of a hundred ducats. This fet-off was paid out of the paternal inheritance which fell to S. Antoninus at this time. Providence did not ftop there with regard to the Friar-Preachers: a rich merchant of Florence bequeathed them a fum of fix thoufand florins, and they employed it, not in embellifhing, but in enlarging the convent.

The mountain of Fiefole is one of the moft beau-

tiful of thofe which fhelter the valley of the Arno
againft the north winds. A powerful town once occupied its fummit; but Florence, its rival, overcame it,
one day, and left nothing but ruins and recollections.
Rich and wooded hills ftorey the fides of the mountain, and their loweft declivities watered by the Mug-
none end at the gates of the Athens of the middle
ages. On every fide rife magnificent villas, to which
the Platonifts of the Renaiffance repaired, to forget
the divine teaching of the Gofpel, and renew, beneath
the beautiful fhades, the learned converfations of the
gardens of the Academy.

The convent of S. Domenico of Fiefole is built about
midway up the mountain. The church opens on the
high-road, and attracts the wayfarer by its pure and
fimple architecture, like the fountains which formerly
offered a feat and limpid water to the weary traveller.
The apfe is furrounded with buildings and cloifters, all
protected by a filent valley. Their quiet lines and
fimple difpofition recall the Francifcan convents, fo
full of peace and lowlinefs. Nothing is finer for the
foul than thofe palaces of poverty, the long corridors,
the walls without ornament, the little windows, and the
fweet light meeting with a holy image or a pious fentence. The ray of the fun penetrating the cells is like
Jacob's ladder; angels are paffing up and down, to
exchange grace and prayer between God and man.

In this convent, Beato Angelico paffed the beft years
of his life, and his mafterpieces executed there have
made it believed *that* folitude was his native place.
He might have figned himfelf Fra Giovanni da Fiefole,
as S. Louis ufed to fign Louis de Poiffy; for there he

was born to religious life, and had received the moſt precious favours of heaven. He lived eighteen years there under the ſhadow of the altar, amidſt his brethren, and in the joys of prayer and ecſtaſy.

How different is the life of the artiſt in the world! He who believes he has a vocation for the fine-arts has magnificent hopes at the beginning of his career. He aſpires to a higher ſphere, where he will contemplate ſupreme beauty and reflect it in his works. He hails from afar thoſe pure enjoyments, the glory of which is but a ſet-off. He ruſhes with ardour forward towards the brilliant future; obſtacles, privations, fatigue, nothing arreſts him, and with all the enthuſiaſm of youth, he overcomes the difficulty of the firſt ſtudies. But when he has put on the manly robe of talent, when he muſt needs enter into the public life which he had dreamed independent and glorious, he often finds himſelf in the preſence of a ſad reality. He meets with the world's injuſtices, perfidious envy, and the ſtupid encouragements of ignorance. Diſquietude comes to trouble his boundleſs hopes, and need intercepts, like a fog, the diſtant light of glory which had miſled him. When the artiſt is alone, he may ſtruggle yet, and prolong his dream; but if he has united a wife to his lot, if he has a family to maintain, his heart trembles, his eyes are troubled, and it is no longer the palm, but bread, his hand is aſking for. He will have to ſacrifice his taſtes, undergo the caprices of thoſe that pay, endure their contumely, and exchange for a lucrative handicraft the holy miſſion which he thought he had received from heaven.

In a convent, on the contrary, the artiſt finds the happieſt conditions for working out his noble deſtiny. He
enjoys a profound peace, and there is nothing perſonal
in his ambition. He ſeeks beauty in the love of Him
who is its beginning; and all around puts far from
him what might trouble the contemplation of it. His
vows protect him with a triple rampart : chaſtity
defends him againſt the paſſions which would ſully
the purity of his ſoul; poverty ſhelters him from diſquietude of life; and obedience arreſts diſcourage-
ment, and makes him ſtrong againſt himſelf. His
exiſtence flows away, peaceable and orderly as a brook
encloſed in a marble conduit that it may not lead
a-wandering over its flowery banks the valued waters
deſtined for the ornament of the city. For him, art
is a ſong, a prayer. He ſeeks not the praiſes and
honours of the world. Can he even think of them
when he enjoys the affection of his brethren, and
hopes for the rewards of heaven?

Such was the life of Beato Angelico, and his years
paſſed in the convent of Fieſole were, without doubt,
the ſweeteſt and the richeſt. From thirty to fifty
years in his age, the artiſt is in all the activity of his
mind and talent; afterwards the ſap is leſs vigorous,
and more ſlowly fruitful in new works. To this period,
doubtleſs, we muſt attribute the greater number of our
painter's pictures; for his laſt years were occupied
eſpecially in painting the freſcoes in San Marco and
the Vatican. Glory came early to viſit his retreat, and
every one would have pictures from his hand. He
refuſed no one; and Vaſari has preſerved this pleaſing

anfwer, " Obtain the Prior's confent, and I will always do what may pleafe you."[1] It is difficult for us to claffify thefe pictures, which are not dated. We will, neverthelefs, examine them in a certain order, aiding ourfelves by fome facts and documents. Firft of all, we will fpeak of the paintings he executed for the convent of Fiefole : he muft have done them before he dwelt at Florence, and they have a great refemblance to thofe of Cortona and Perugia.

Beato Angelico did two paintings in frefco ; one for the refectory, the other for the chapter-room, which afterwards became the hofpice for ftrangers. The frefco in the refectory reprefents our Lord crucified, and the Holy Virgin, S. John the Evangelift and S. Dominic, kneeling at the foot of the Crofs. The compofition is fimple and grave ; its execution muft have been remarkable, judging by the portions which have efcaped the reftoration made, in 1566, by one Francefco Mariani.[2] The heads and hands are ftill beautiful, but the feet and draperies have fuffered much. The room in which this painting is, ferves as a ftore for greens and garden-tools.[3]

---

[1] " Con amorevolezza a ogniuno che ricercava opre da lui, diceva, che ne faceffe effer contento il Priore, ed egli fempre farebbe cofa, che gli foffe in piacere.— (VASARI, edition of 1550.)

[2] *Chron. of S. Domenico of Fiefole*, fol. 164. Similiter pinxit aliquas figuras hic Fefulis in refectorio, in capitulo veteri quod modò eft hofpitium fecularium. *And fol.* 10. Reftaurata eft etiam pictura ipfius refectorii, in quâ Crucifixi imagines, et beatæ Virginis ac beati Joannis vifuntur. Hæc omnia quæ artis pictoriæ funt, faciebat peritiffimus juvenis, et qui magnam de fe fpem excitavit, Francifcus Mariani de Florentiâ. Expofuit autem in his omnibus prior ipfe ven. libras fexaginta ex R. P. F. Angeli Diaceti et aliorum amicorum elemofinas.—(P. MARCHESE, lib. ii, c. 5, p. 232.)

[" On the front wall of the refectory he painted a Crucifixion (life fize), with the Bleffed Virgin on one fide, and S. John the Evangelift on the other : at

The fecond frefco is now feen at the top of a ftair-cafe in a private dwelling. It reprefents the Virgin on her throne, holding on her knees her Son, whom a portion of her veil covers. On her right and left, are S. Dominic and S. Thomas Aquinas, with open books. The head of the Virgin, although it is very beautiful, feems to have been retouched by a painter of Perugino's time, perhaps by Lorenzo di Credi.'

the foot of the Crofs, kneeling, and feen from from behind, is S. Dominic ; but this laft figure feems to have have been introduced at a fubfequent period. We cannot now appreciate the colouring or defign of this painting, as the hand of fome very ignorant perfon, who undertook to reftore it, and the vandalifm of the parties who got poffeffion of it, have all but cancelled it. The continuator of the Chronicle of the convent of S. Domenico at Fiefole, tells how it was reftored by a young Florentine artift, named Francefco Mariani, in 1556 ; but, heavens, after what a fafhion ! enlarging the outlines, and heightening the colours, fo as to efface altogether thefe delicate mezzotints, thefe lines fo beautifully varied, and the fimplicity of the drapery, in order to introduce all the defeéts peculiar to an age when art was in its decadence. Finally, when the convent was taken from the religious, the refeétory was turned into a fruit ftore, to the great injury of this painting. Notwithftanding, the beauteous head of S. John is admirably pre-ferved, as is alfo the nude of the Redeemer."—MARCHESE, *ly Meehan*, vol. i, p. 193.—TRANSLATOR'S note.]

' [" But the hiftory that he painted in the chapter-room, though known to very few, is well preferved, and deferves to be claffed amongft the beft works of the Angelico. Here he painted the Bleffed Virgin feated, and, as in the Perugian piéture, holding the Divine Babe on her knees. The Infant is nude, but the white veil that covers our Lady's head and bofom falls gracefully over Him. On her right is S. Dominic, ftanding ; on the left, S. Thomas of Aquino ; both having an open book. The Founder of the Preaching Friars (a mode of reprefenting him unufual to this painter) has his chin covered with a flowing beard, and holds in his hand a lily, the emblem of his virginity—a fimple compofition, and well calculated to awaken devout feelings in the fpeétator. Few of the Angelico's works prefent more beauty in the expreffion of the countenances, or more negligence in the extremities and neceffary acceffories, than this does. The type of the Virgin is perhaps lefs ideal than ufual ; it reminds us of Raffaello and Pietro Perugino ; and it is impreffed with fuch beauty and majefty, that we are almoft forced to kneel down and worfhip in prefence of that image. Wonder-fully beautiful are the faces of S. Dominic and the Infant ; that of S. Thomas is the moft beautiful in its defign and colouring. But we no fooner fet about examining the extremities of thefe figures, and the folds of the drapery, than we are

Vafari informs us that Beato Angelico painted three pictures for the conventual church. "He alfo painted," fays he, "the picture on the high altar, at S. Domenico of Fiefole; but this, perhaps becaufe it appeared to have been injured, has been retouched by other mafters, and fpoiled. Still the predella and the tabernacle of the B. Sacrament are much better preferved; and the numerous little figures feen there, furrounded by a celeftial glory, are fo beautiful that they feem truly to belong to paradife, nor can he who approaches them be ever weary of regarding their beauty."[1] This picture, in fact, was reftored by Lorenzo di Credi, when the tribune of the church was repaired, in 1501, and the high altar reconftructed. Even the fhape of it was changed, and the gradino replaced by a copy. The original muft be now in the poffeffion of the heirs of Sig. Valentini of Rome. The tabernacle has been loft.[2]

This picture reprefents the Virgin on a throne with

---

obliged to afk ourfelves, whether the fame hand that outlined and coloured the countenances finifhed the reft of the work. So much fo, that in many places we do not recognize thefe exquifite foldings of the robes, fo peculiar to Fra Angelico; and the feet of S. Thomas and S. Dominic look like a large blot. This led me to fufpect that the fame artift who had attempted to reftore the frefco in the refectory, had likewife injured the drapery and the extremities of that in the chapter-room. A diftinguifhed painter, who examined it with me, is of opinion that it exhibits evident· figns of having been retouched at a later period."— MARCHESE, *by Meehan*, vol. i, p. 194.—TRANSLATOR'S note.]

[1] Dipinfe fimilmente a S. Domenico di Fiefole la tavola dell' altar maggiore: la qual perchè forfe pareva che fi guaftaffe, è ftata ritocca da altri maeftri, e peggiorata: ma la predella ed il ciborio del Sacramento fonofi meglio mantenuti.— By the words *predella, gradino*, are defignated the feries of little fubjects, which the old painters placed beneath their pictures.

[2] Circa anno Domini 1501 .... tabula altaris majoris renovata eft et reducta in quadrum, et additæ picturæ fupius (*fic*) et ornamenta tabulæ per fingularem pictorem Laurentium de Credis.—(*Chron. of S. Dom. of Fiefole*, fol. 5 à tergo.)

her Divine Son, having on one fide S. Peter the Apoſtle
and S. Thomas Aquinas, and on the other S. Dominic
and S. Peter Martyr : in the foreground, angels are in
adoration.   By its ſimplicity and dignity, this compoſition recalls the great ſchool of Giotto.   The
gradino juſtifies Vaſari's eulogy ; it is the *Alleluia* of
the reſurrection of our Saviour.   The ſubject is divided
into three compartments.   In the centre, Chriſt riſes
with his victorious ſtandard ; a multitude of angels
ſurround him, and appear to carry him on a buckler ;
they announce his glory to all the world, to the ſound
of trumpets and inſtruments.   On each ſide, a great
crowd of ſaints take part in the joy of the triumph.
It is difficult to conceive a more lyric compoſition.

The ſecond picture repreſented an Annunciation.
" In the chapel of the ſame church," ſays Vaſari, " is
a picture from the ſame hand, repreſenting our Lady
receiving the annunciation from the angel Gabriel,
with a countenance in profile ſo devout, ſo delicate,
and ſo well executed, that it appears truly not by man,
but to have been made in paradiſe.   In the landſcape
forming the background, are Adam and Eve, who were
the occaſion of the Redeemer's incarnation by the
Virgin.   In the predella are likewiſe ſome extremely
beautiful little hiſtories."[1]   This picture, which muſt
have very cloſely reſembled the one at Cortona, has
been loſt ; it was parted with, after two years' negotiations, to Mario Farneſe, for 1500 ducats, which ſerved

---

[1] In una cappella della medeſima chieſa è di ſua mano, in una tavola la noſtra
Donna annunziata dall' Angelo Gabbriello, con un profilo di viſo tanto devoto,
delicato, e ben fatto, che par veramente non da un uomo, ma fatto in paradiſo.
E nel campo del pacre è Adamo ed Eva, che furono cagione che della Virgine
incarnaſſe il Redentore.   Nella predella ancora ſono alcune ſtoriette belliſſime.

to rebuild the campanile, and to do the wainſcotings
of the choir. The religious, who has entered the
bargain on the regiſters of the convent, gives thanks
to God, and to the angelic painter who, after one
hundred and ſixty years, has again rendered ſo great
a ſervice to the convent.[1]

France has the good fortune to poſſeſs the third
picture executed for the church of Fieſole. Vaſari
thus expreſſes himſelf about this picture : " But above
all the works of Fra Giovanni, and one in which he
has ſurpaſſed himſelf, is a picture in the ſame church,
near the door on the left hand of the entrance. In
this he proves the high quality of his powers, as well
as his profound intelligence of the art he practiſed.
The ſubject is the Coronation of the Virgin by Jeſus
Chriſt: the principal figures are ſurrounded by a choir
of angels and a vaſt number of ſaints, male and female.
Theſe figures are ſo numerous, ſo well executed, in
attitudes ſo varied, and with expreſſions of countenance ſo diverſified, that one experiences incredible
pleaſure and delight in looking at them. Nay, it
ſeems as though theſe bleſſed ſpirits cannot be otherwiſe in heaven ; or, to ſpeak more correctly, could
not, if they had forms, appear otherwiſe. For all the
ſaints here, male and female, have not only life and
expreſſion moſt delicately and truly rendered, but the

---

[1] Qual tavola ſi conſegnò come ci era ordine al P. Carlo Strozzi, inſieme con
la ſua predella, dove erano dipinte cinque ſtoriette della B. Vergine, tutte opera del
detto pittore, etc. . . . Di tutto fia lode e onore al Signore, ſi ancora al noſtro
Angelico pittore, dal quale, dopo l'età di circa 160 anni ha ſentito il noſtro convento cotanto benefizio.—(P. MARCHESE, t. i, p. 400.)

[This painting was ſold in 1611, but a copy of it was left in the church of
S. Domenico. The original and the copy are now both loſt.—TRANSLATOR'S
note.]

whole colouring of this work feems to have been executed by the hand of a faint or of an angel like themfelves. Thus it was with fufficient reafon that this good religious has been always called Fra Giovanni Angelico. The hiftories of our Lady and S. Dominic adorning the predella are in the fame divine manner; and, for myfelf, I can in truth affirm that I never fee this work without its appearing to me fomething new, nor do I ever leave it fatiated."[1]

We do not, like Vafari, rank this painting above all the works of Beato Angelico, but we regard it as one of the moft remarkable. The detailed examination we are going to make of it, will juftify, we hope, to our readers the fincere enthufiafm of the celebrated critic of the Renaiffance.

What was the artift's thought? How has he expreffed it with his heart and pencil? The fubject of the picture is the Coronation of the Virgin, fo often reprefented by the painters of the old fchool. No fubject can be more pleafing to God and man : to God, becaufe it is the glorification of His moft perfect creature ; to men, becaufe they find in this triumph the moft fruitful caufe of their joys and hopes. Thus Beato Angelico has very often treated it ; but he has almoft always followed tradition, by reprefenting Mary feated at the right of her Son and receiving the crown from Him : it is the triumph of her maternity. Here the fubject is treated differently. The age and attitude of the Virgin, the manner of arranging the fcene, and the faints affifting at it, would make us

---

[1] E io per me poffo con verità affermare, che non veggio mai quefta opera che non mi paia cofa nuova, nè me ne parto mai fazio.

believe that the painter has chofen a particular title in the litanies fung by the church in praife of Mary, and that he has wifhed to crown her *Queen of Virgins.*

To give expreffion to his idea, his chafte pencil feems to have tranflated the verfes of the Canticle of Canticles explained and paraphrafed with fo much purity by S. Bernard and S. Thomas Aquinas; and he fet himfelf to the work, no doubt, after he had chanted with his brethren the fweet words commencing the office of the Affumption in the Order of S. Dominic:—" Thou art all fair, O my love, and there is not a fpot in thee: thy lips are as a dropping honeycomb; honey and milk are under thy tongue: the odour of thy garments is beyond all fpices. For the winter is now paffed, the rain is over and gone, the flowers have appeared, the vines in flower yield their fweet fmell, and the voice of the turtle is heard in our land. Arife, make hafte, my love, and come from Libanus; come, and thou fhalt be crowned."[1] The ceremony takes place before the porch of the heavenly Jerufalem. The throne upon which our Lord is to feat Mary is raifed upon nine fteps, figurative of the nine choirs of angels. " The things which have been faid unto thee are accomplifhed in thee; behold, thou art exalted above the choirs of angels."[2] Under a rich Gothic canopy ornamented with magnificent tapeftry,

---

[1] Tota pulchra es, amica mea, et macula non eft in te: favus diftillans labia tua, mel et lac fub lingua tua, odor veftimentorum tuorum fuper omnia aromata : jam enim hiems tranfiit, imber abiit et receffit, flores apparuerunt, vineæ florentes odorem fuum dederunt, et vox turturis audita eft in terra noftra : Surge, propera, amica mea, et veni de Libano; veni, coronaberis.

[2] Perfecta funt in te quæ dicta funt tibi : ecce exaltata es fuper choros angelorum.

"Chrift has prepared for his moft chafte Mother the place of her immortality : it is a feftival incomparably more excellent than all the feftivals of the faints,"[1] and in it the Bleffed Virgin is to triumph in prefence of all the heavenly court. Our Lord holds with both hands the crown he is going to place on his Mother's head. Mary is kneeling before him, bending a little, and with her arms croffed upon her breaft. Around the throne, four-and-twenty angels fing her praifes, and play on various inftruments. Near them, and upon the fteps of the throne, are arranged the faints of the Old and New Teftament: Mofes, David and the Apoftles S. Peter and S. Paul. In the foreground, are placed two groups of privileged faints who have glorified virginity the moft by their example and teaching. All are kneeling, and the pofition of their heads and the expreffion of their countenances indicate the fweeteft and pureft joy.

If we feek now to penetrate the idea of the artift and to analyze the perfection of his work, we fhall fee how he has followed tradition, and clothed the ancient types with his angelical individuality.

The Supreme Artift has created types by realizing, in time and fpace, His eternal ideas. Thefe types are perpetuated by immutable laws, and manifeft, according to their kind, the invifible things God has willed to make them fay.

Man alfo creates types. He expreffes his religious and focial ideas by works of art, which generations

---

[1] Afcendit Chriftus fuper cœlos, et præparavit suæ caftiffimæ Matri immortalitatis locum. Et hæc eft illa præclaia feftivitas, omnium fanctorum feftivitatibus incomparabilis.

underftand and tranfmit to each other. Genius, firft
realizing thefe types, does nothing but give the belief
of his age, and renders to it a form, which thofe who
come after may modify, but without changing its
effential charaćter, which remains invariable, as in the
fpecies of Divine creation.

Pagan art has created types for all religions, and
Greece efpecially had remarkable ones. Its poets,
painters and fculptors perfonified the Divine attributes which they faw reflećted in nature. They
deified the effećts of the Firft Caufe, and endeavoured
to exprefs His power, wifdom, intelligence and beauty,
by human forms. All their belief, ideas and paffions
were an image, a type. Error had narrowed the
field of truth for them, but their genius knew how to
fill up the limited horizon. Phidias was worthy of
Plato, and the artift rofe to the height of the philo-
fopher. There was balance between the interior and
the exterior form.

For Chriftians, this balance is, fo to fay, impoffible,
fo fublime are the ideas they have to give. Supreme
Truth, by defcending on the earth and rendering it
fertile, has opened an immenfe, an infinite horizon
to the fine-arts. Between Chriftian and Pagan types
there muft be the diftance of truth and error. Thefe
types the Church has fixed by her dočtrine and worfhip, and for many ages artifts have been feeking to
clothe them with their form. It is not the queftion to
know if thefe artifts have equalled the material perfection of the ancients ; we fay only that the models they
have to give are fuperior to thofe of the Greeks, and

that the Gofpel calls them to a progrefs without bounds.

The fupreme type of Chriftian art is Jefus Chrift, the perfect image of God, the fplendour of the Father ; beauty inexpreffible, a ray of which burft forth on the day of the transfiguration ; beauty fo fweet and ravifhing, notwithftanding the veil covering it in the Incarnation, that it was neceffary to take away its fenfible prefence from the Apoftles and difciples, becaufe the enjoyment would have rendered virtue too eafy, and the happinefs of it is referved for eternity.

After Chrift, comes Mary, the type of all graces and virtues : Mary, the pureft mirror of the divinity : Virgin, Spoufe, and above all Mother, carrying thefe titles as a triple and indivifible crown to the higheft heavens.

Angels alfo have put on bodies, and artifts may effay to give under human forms the fublime functions of their different hierarchies. Then come the multitude of faints, male and female, of the Old and New Teftament, lighting up with their prefence the fucceffion of ages, and being united to us by the Church in the bofom of their eternity : the patriarchs, prophets, martyrs, confeffors, virgins, all thofe living beauties that the artift can contemplate and invoke by the light of faith : inexhauftible ocean of infpirations for thofe who do not fatisfy themfelves with the grofs individualities which are infults to truth.

Types fo perfect cannot be realized by one fingle artift : ages work flowly at them, and the firft duty of him who wifhes to give them is to confult tradition.

Beato Angelico has faithfully done this. He has collected the light of thofe who had gone before him, whilft increafing and endowing it with his own colouring. By examining his works, it is eafy to fee that he has confulted the two great fchools, Greek and Latin. His types of Chrift fhow remarkable differences. His heart feems never to have been fatisfied. Sometimes he follows the type of Giotto, and gives our Saviour a powerful manlinefs. Sometimes, on the contrary, his types are extremely youthful, and it is the tender Lamb who redeemed the world. In the picture now occupying us, the painter has given Chrift a middle age. The Faireft of the children of men is arrayed with magnificence; a rich crown glitters on his brow, luxuriant hair falls down on his neck, and the mantle thrown over his fhoulders envelopes the lower part of his body. Everything in his perfon is calm and pure; truly it is he, whofe blood buds forth virgins.[1]

For his types of the Bleffed Virgin, Beato Angelico, we have already faid, feems to have ftudied much the Madonnas of the fchool of Sienna, fo fweet, fo melancholy, and fo full of the love of God and the thought of the Paffion. He ufually reprefents Mary in the glory of her maternity, but here fhe is the virgin rather than the mother. He has given her the age when fhe sought to hide her virginity under the marriage-veil : the age of fourteen years, which death reftored to her when fhe left the earth to go and reign with her Son. This figure of the Bleffed Virgin makes us

---

[1] Quid enim bonum ejus eft, et quid pulchrum ejus, nifi frumentum electorum et vinum germinans virgines ?—(ZACHARIAS, ix, 17.)

underſtand what S. Thomas ſaid of her beauty, the ſight
of which purified the ſenſes inſtead of diſturbing them.
It is, indeed, the dove of the Canticle of Canticles, that
goeth up by the deſert as a light cloud of ſmoke of
myrrh, frankincenſe and the ſweeteſt perfumes.'   Rich
garments hide the ſhape of her body, and allow her
face and hands alone to appear, the only parts of her
moſt pure being which man's eye had ſeen.   She is
kneeling, bowed ſweetly towards her Son, her eyes caſt
down, and her arms croſſed upon her breaſt.   Her hair is
platted and arranged as a crown with charming grace;
her head is covered with a tranſparent veil falling
down upon her neck; and a richly-fringed mantle falls
from her ſhoulders and covers her feet.   A more chaſte
and heavenly figure cannot be imagined.

But the genius of our painter ſhines moſtly in his
types of the angels.   It is very difficult to clothe the
bleſſed ſpirits with a body;   and there are, perhaps, no
Chriſtian ſubjects more unworthily profaned by the
Renaiſſance.   The old ſchools had repreſented angels
ſuch as they appear to us in the Bible.   At one time,
they are the cherubim of the prophets, with their bodies
of flame and their wings to veil themſelves before the
Eternal; at another time, the angels of Abraham, of
Jacob and Tobias, clad in the ſhape of youth, to viſit
men and bring them meſſages from on high.   This type
prevailed in the ſchool of Giotto, who always knew how,
deſpite the elegance of their ſhape and the length of
their robe, to preſerve his angels from a feminine
character.   Beato Angelico has imitated the angels of

' Quæ eſt iſta, quæ aſcendit per deſertum, ſicut virgula fumi ex aromatibus
myrrhæ et thuris, et univerſi pulveris pigmentarii ?—(*Cant.* iii, 6.)

Giotto, but he has made them younger, in order to give them a more virginal beauty. They are not infants like thofe of the fchool of Perugino : that age does not fufficiently exprefs the zeal and intelligence of thofe minifters of God. They are youths, at that time of life when the expanding heart is all light and fincerity, unruffled by the breath of the paffions. The angels affifting at the coronation of the Queen of Virgins are the pages of the heavenly court ; their whole being expreffes intelligence and love. If nature has been confulted in painting them, the artift has altogether fpiritualized it ; but it is more probable, as Vafari thinks, that he copied his graceful models by the light of his ecftacies.

Thefe angels are twenty-four in number. They recall thofe that are celebrating the Triumph of S. Francis on the arch of the lower church at Affifi. They are clothed in embroidered tunics which veil their feet; a little flame fhines above their heads. The moft diftant are founding the trumpet, and announce on every fide the coronation of their Queen : the neareft are finging and accompanying themfelves on various inftruments. So fweet is their expreffion and fo graceful their attitude, that they exprefs to the eye the charm of their heavenly harmony.

The choice of the faints affifting at this feftival muft be remarked. Beato Angelico has written their names and glorious titles in the aureolas of fome of them. The Old Testament is reprefented by Mofes and David, the law and the prophets. Mofes, the chofen fervant of God, *fanctus Moïfes Dei famulus et electus*, contemplates the ftar come forth from Jacob, the woman who crufhed the ferpent's head by efcaping original fin. David hails the honour of his pofterity, the Queen who is going to fit at the right hand of the Saviour, in the gold of her veftments and the variety of her attire.[1]

After Mofes and David, comes S. John Baptist, the precurfor of Chrift, *Johannes Baptifta, precurfor Domini*, the link between the old and new law, the man vifited by the Bleffed Virgin before his birth who died at the court of Herod in defending chaftity. Afterwards come the Apoftles, having at their head S. Peter, doorkeeper of the kingdom of heaven, *fanctus Petrus claviger regni cœlorum conftitutus ;* and S. Paul, doctor of the Gen-tiles, *fanctus Paulus, doctor Gentilium vocitatus.* Both have their traditional emblems and places. S. Andrew ; S. Bartholomew ; S. James ; S. Simon ; S. Matthias ; S. Philip ; S. Thaddeus ; S. Matthew ; S. James the Greater ; and neareft to the throne and to the angels, S. John the Evangelift, the well-beloved difciple of God, *fanctus Johannes evangelifta, dilectus Deo,* the virgin-apoftle, the adopted fon of Mary, the gentle old man, who faw in Patmos *her* who is clothed with the fun, with the moon under her feet, and a crown of twelve ftars upon her head.[2]

On the right of the throne, below S. John the Evangelift, the artift has placed S. Dominic, the founder of the Order cherifhed by the Bleffed Virgin, holding the fpotlefs lily of virginity, *confervans fine macula virginitatis lilium.* Beato Angelico has painted

---

[1] Aftitit regina à dextris tuis in veftitu deaurato, circumdata varietate.— (*Ps.* xliv, 9.)

[2] Mulier amicta fole, et luna fub pedibus ejus, et in capite ejus corona ftellarum duodecim.—(*Apoc.*, xii, 1.)

the glorious patriarch with filial love. He has written upon his open book, as a promife to be faithful to them, the three recommendations left by him for an heritage to his difciples : " Have charity, keep humility, poffefs voluntary poverty ;" then he has added the prayer recited every day in his Order: " O wondrous hope, which thou gaveft to thofe that wept for thee at the hour of death, when thou didft promife after death to do thy brethren good. Father, fulfil what thou haft faid, and help us by thy prayers : thou who haft fhone by fo many figns wrought on the bodies of the fick, bring us the help of Chrift to heal our fickly ways."[1] Near S. Dominic is S. Auguftin, whofe rule the Friar-Preachers follow. He holds in his hand the pen with which he celebrated fo well the wonders of divine grace.

At the foot of the fteps, and on the fame fide, are kneeling other founders of Orders: S. Benedict, S. Anthony, S. Francis, and perhaps S. Bernard, whofe figure is not feen. In the foreground, S. Louis, with his crown of fleurs-de-lis.[2] The presence of S. Louis is eafily explained by his tender devotion to the Holy Virgin, and by his connection with the Friar-Preachers,

---

[1] Charitatem habete, humilitatem fervate, paupertatem voluntariam poffe-dete.—O fpem miram quam dedifti, mortis horâ te flentibus, dum poft mortem promififti te profuturum fratribus. Imple, Pater, quod dixifti, nos tuis juvans, precibus ; qui tot fignis claruifti in ægrorum corporibus, nobis opem ferens Chrifti ægris medere moribus.

[2] Schlegel wifhed to fee in this perfonage a S. Charlemagne, and has explained even to the three little crowns ferving for ornament to his mantle, by his threefold title as Emperor, King of the Franks and King of the Lombards. The cultus of Charlemagne has never been accepted in Italy. The Golden Legend only repre-fents the great emperor delivered from the hands of the devil, in confideration of his pious foundations ; and the monk Vetin, in his vifion, fhows him to us in the flames of purgatory, being purified from the pleafures of the flefh which he loved too well.

his confeffors and friends. He was of the Third Order
of S. Dominic,[1] and very intimate with S. Thomas
Aquinas, whom he often invited to his table. Beato
Angelico has reprefented him converfing with the
angelic Doctor, who feems to be explaining to the holy
king the fcene he contemplates. In the open book
S. Thomas carries, are written the firft verfes of the
Te Deum.

Near this group, is S. Nicholas, the protector of
purity. At his knees, the painter has placed three
gold balls, to recall the three purfes he threw into the
houfe of the poor nobleman to preferve his daughters
from feduction. The coftly chafuble of the bifhop is
ornamented with a large figured band, on which are
reprefented fome features of our Lord's life. Thefe
fketches are painted with an aftonifhing freedom of
pencil. They feem done after the pictures by Giotto,
preferved in the Academy of Florence.

On the oppofite fide, is a group of female faints,
whose expreffions and figures are as poetical and pure
as their legends. They are feparated from the Apostles
on the left of the throne by feveral young faints,
patrons and defenders of virginity. S. Peter Martyr,
his head bathed with the blood with which he writes
the words, *Credo in Deum*, at the moment he gave up
his laft breath. S. George, the Chriftian knight, who
faves a virgin from the fangs of the infernal monfter.
S. Stephen and S. Lawrence, the two young deacons
of the Eaftern and Weftern Churches, who bear the
double aureola of charity and purity. Death united

[1 This is an error of the author; S. Louis was a *Francifcan* Tertiary, not a
Dominican Tertiary.—TRANSLATOR's note.]

them in a fweet brotherhood. Thofe who were carrying the body of S. Stephen to Rome were miraculoufly forced to go and lay it in the tomb of S. Lawrence, whofe bones drew back of themfelves to make room for the holy relics, and to fhare with them the homage of the faithful.[1]

The group of holy women affifting at the Corona-. tion of the Virgin is one of rapturous beauty. It is perhaps the moft admirable part of this work of Beato Angelico.

Below S. George is S. Urfula, holding the arrow which unites her by death to her divine fpoufe. Nothing is more pure and graceful than the movement of her head. Kneeling in front of her, with the wheel and palm of her martyrdom, is S. Catherine of Alexandria, the learned virgin, who converted fifty philofophers to the faith. She forms a pendant to S. Thomas Aquinas, and converfes with S. Agnes, who carries in her arms the lamb fymbolical of meeknefs. Near S. Catherine of Alexandria, between two female faints not made known by any fymbol, is S. Catherine of Sienna in the joys of ecftacy.[2]

Nearer towards the centre, S. Cecilia, with the crown of flowers, which never lofe their frefhnefs and perfume and chafte hearts alone can fee.[3] Laftly, S. Mary Mag-

---

[1] Laurentius adventui fratris fui quafi congratulans et arridens, in alteram partem fepulchri feceffit, et medietatem illius vacuam fratri reliquit.—(*Leg. aurea*, c. cxii, de Inventione S. Steph. Protom.)

[2] In the "Life of S. Catherine of Sienna," I have given the reafons which make me fee in this figure the very faithful portrait of that great faint. Schlegel has taken the figure for a S. Clare, but without giving any proof of it.

[3] Angelus autem duas coronas ex rofis et liliis in manu habebat, et unam Cæciliæ, et alteram Valeriano tradidit, dicens : Iftas coronas immaculato corde et mundo corpore cuftodite, quia de paradifo Dei eas ad vos attuli, nec unquam

dalen, with her long hair that wiped our Saviour's feet,
and the little vafe of fpices defigned to honour his burial.
S. Auguftine and S. Mary Magdalen are the patron
faints of the Order of S. Dominic; but it may alfo be
believed that the artift, by placing them in this picture,
wifhed to honour purity recovered by the tears of
.repentance.

No defcription can give the holinefs of all thefe
figures; and to underftand them well, it would be neceffary to read and meditate the texts which have infpired the artift, the beautiful prayers he addreffed to
the faints in the office of the Order, and the pages of
the Golden Legend, that inexhauftible fource of
poetry.

The talent of the artift has been worthy of his
infpiration, and the execution of this picture is very
remarkable. The compofition of it is happy, and
it is impoffible to arrange fo great a number of figures
more fkilfully in fo fmall a fpace. They form a
circle around the throne, the elevation of which on
fteps has allowed their being difpofed one over another
without confufion or monotony. The centre is free
and leaves to the two principal perfonages the whole of
their importance. The variety of the groups and the
movement of the heads concur to unity inftead of
obfcuring it. Notwithftanding the difficulty of the
point of fight taken from the laft ftep, the perfpective
is unblameable. The canopy crowning the throne
prefents a charming defign of Gothic architecture, and

marcefcent, nec odorem amittent, nec ab aliis, nifi quibus caftitas placuerit,
videri poterunt.—(*Leg. aurca*, de Sanctâ Cæcilia, c. clxix.)

the long trumpets fetting off the top of the compofition enlarge the fpace in an ingenious manner.
The drawing leaves nothing to be wifhed for; although the long draperies hide the fhape of the bodies
and the feet of all the perfonages, the attitudes are very
well given, and the movements of the heads efpecially
are admirably fine. The figures are drawn with inimitable purity, and the model has a perfection which
can only be underftood by trying to copy it. The
hands alone are a little neglected. The draperies are
quiet and graceful. The artift has difplayed in them
an unheard-of luxury of ornament. All the ftuffs
are enriched with magnificent defigns and delicate
embroidery. The aureolas are loaded with gold and
jewels. All thefe details are varied with an incredible
fertility of imagination, and executed with a care which
might be called devotion.

This picture is painted with egg, upon wood, on a
gold ground. The colouring is agreeable to the eye;
and notwithftanding the multiplicity of the details, the
injuries of time and fome clumfy reftorations, the
look of it is fweet and harmonious. The more we
view this painting, the more do we underftand
Vafari, when he fays, " I never fee this work without
its seeming fomething new to me, nor do I ever
leave it fatiated."

The great Chriftian fchool painted beneath their
pictures a feries of little compofitions reprefenting the
legend of a faint. The artift difplayed in them with
more liberty the treafures of his imagination and the
originality of his talent. This little poem in honour
of a faint was called in Italy a *predella*, a *gradino*, a

ftep, becaufe it raifed the principal picture, and ferved
as a ftep to the altar-piece.' Cannot there alfo be feen
a fymbolical fignification in thefe words very natural
to the language of the middle ages? The Chriftian
artift reprefented the faints in the repofe of glory, as
the Greek artift reprefented heroes in the immobility
of triumph. The lower pictures were confecrated to
the life on earth, which is the ftep to the life to come.
The gradino fhowed that we reach heaven by trial and
combat : it taught the fundamental truth of religion,
that by imitating the Paffion of our Lord, we arrive
at his glory.

This explanation is proved by the gradino of the
Coronation of the Virgin, fince the central fubject is
what Italians call a *Pietà*, a compaffion. In it, our
Lord appears coming out of the tomb and furrounded
by the inftruments of his punifhment, to show us
his wounds and invite us to fhare in his fufferings.
In front of him, are feated, in contemplation and
prayer, the Holy Virgin and S. John the Evangelift,
the two great reprefentatives of humanity on Calvary :
Mary who has brought us forth in pain, and the well-
beloved difciple who inherited the rights of Jefus
Chrift in his Mother's heart.

The fix fubjects into which this compofition is
divided, are taken from the life of S. Dominic. The
choice was natural enough in a convent of Friar-
Preachers. The life of the glorious Patriarch is as
rich in infpirations as that of S. Francis of Affifi. It

[' The gradino was adopted, in order to raife the picture quite above the foot of
the candlefticks on the altar; and it was ornamented with pious fubjects calculated
to excite the devotion of the prieft.—Translator's note.]

prefents the fame virtues, and thofe virtues were developed on a fcene more vaft and mingled with greater events. Spain, France and Italy were witneffes of the apoftlefhip of S. Dominic, and the moft cele- brated and learned cities of Europe admired his miracles and learning.

The firft compofition reprefents the vifion of Innocent III. When he hefitated to give his approval to a new order in the Church, he faw during fleep S. Dominic fupporting the bafilica of S. John Lateran, as it was about to fall. The figure of the faint is admirable for movement and impulfe. With the ftrength of faith and love, he fupports the gaping walls of the building which proudly bears the title of " Head and mother of all the churches of the world." In the background of the picture, the Sovereign Pontiff repofes on an ´eftrade, above which is drawn the caftle of San Angelo. He is lying on his bed in full coftume, with the tiara on his head and his whole body enveloped in a magnificent cope. This luxury and thefe veftments during fleep may fhock fuch as fee hiftorical truth only in coarfe reality, and Schlegel himfelf begs pardon for the painter, by excufing this fimplicity of the times, and by praifing the gracefulnefs and eafe of the calmly-fleeping figure. He would, no doubt, have preferred that the Sovereign Pontiff were reprefented in common *déshabille*, with fome device and details indicating his name and dignity; and the dream would have been feen in the diftance or on a cloud. Beato Angelico has conceived his fubject more happily. S. Dominic is in the foreground, and his fymbolical action is given perfectly. We underftand

that this fcene is a vifion. At the end of the little deferted and flowery court, the bed, whereon the Sovereign
Pontiff repofes, is raifed like a throne: his attitude
is chafte and refpectful, and if his veftments are not
thofe of a sleeping man, they are thofe of a pope
receiving a divine communication. There. is intelligence and truth, then, in what appears only fimple.
The aim of art is to exprefs ideas, and to this all its
means should concur. The details are at the fervice
of thought, as the body is at the fervice of the foul.
Thus have the ancients underftood art, and thus will
true artifts always underftand it.

The fecond picture reprefents the miffion of S.
Dominic. "The two Apoftles, S. Peter and S. Paul, appeared to him, S. Peter prefenting him with a ftaff,
S. Paul with a book, and he heard a voice faying to him,
'Go and preach, for unto it thou art chofen:' and at
the fame time he faw his difciples, two and two, fpread-
ing over the whole world to evangelize it. From that day
forward, he conftantly carried with him the epiftles of
S. Paul and the gofpel of S. Matthew, and whether
travelling or dwelling in a town, he never walked
without a ftaff in his hand."[1] The figures of S. Peter
and S. Paul hover majeftically in the air; the perfpective of the nave of the church hides the lower part
of their bodies, and gives the idea of an apparition.
The eagernefs of S. Dominic to receive the fymbols
of his miffion, happily exprefs his zeal to fulfil it.
The beautiful church in which the fcene paffes, is not,
as Schlegel fuppofed, a faithful reprefentation of the
ancient bafilica of S. Pietro. Beato Angelico had not

[1] *Vie de S. Dominique,* p. 392.

yet been at Rome when he painted this picture; but
in default of an archæological exactitude, we may
admire the graceful architectural defign, a creation,
doubtlefs, of his own talent, like the one adorning the
next picture.

It reprefents the raifing to life of the young Napoleone. This miracle is celebrated in the life of
S. Dominic. It marks one of the great epochs of his
Order, the taking poffeffion of the convent of Santa
Sabina and the furrender of the convent of San Sifto
to the nuns of Santa Maria in Traftevere, whom
S. Dominic reformed, by fending for five French
nuns from his dear convent of Our Lady of Prouille.
All thofe who were to take part in that double event
were affembled, Feb. 18th, 1218, at San Sifto, when
some one came to announce that the nephew of cardinal Stefano da Foffanuova had juft been killed by
a fall from his horfe. S. Dominic celebrated the holy
facrifice of the mafs, and went with all the affiftants
to the room where the body had been laid; and after
having prayed and made the fign of the crofs over the
dead body, he commanded him, in the name of Jefus
Chrift, to rife. The young man arofe, and the faint
reftored him joyful and without hurt to his uncle, the
cardinal, who was prefent.[1]

[1] The room in which this miracle occurred ftill exifts. The Dominican pope
Benedict XIII, a defcendant of the young man reftored to life, went every year,
in fpring or autumn, to pafs fome days of retreat in the chambers above this room.
The Rev. P. Beffon has juft decorated it with large mural pictures, which prove
that, in the Dominican Order, talent ftill continues to be the ornament of virtue.
[P. Beffon was an artift of great fkill, and his early death is much deplored.
He executed, too, fome frefcoes of the life of S. Dominic on the wall of the re-
fectory of San Clemente in Rome. They were done at the requeft of the Rev.
F. Jofeph Mullooly, prior of that convent, who is himfelf now rendering the

H

The fcene is given with rare merit in the compofition. In a corner of the picture, is feen the horfe
trampling the young Napoleone beneath his feet.
Under a little building, open, and fupported by elegant pillars, the various fpectators are fkilfully grouped.
The young man, ftretched on the foreground, holds
up his arms to S. Dominic, who, ftanding, commands
him calmly and fweetly. All the affiftants are in
aftonifhment and in the act of giving thanks. The
cardinal, Stefano da Foffanuòva, is near the faint.
Kneeling in front of him with clafped hands, is a young
woman, fifter or fpoufe of the refufcitated man.
Behind him, an older woman, no doubt his mother,
is leaning forward, to affure herfelf of his perfect
cure. The figure of S. Dominic is in a fine ftyle,
and the profile of the woman on her knees, of enchanting purity. It is evident that the fame ftudy
has ferved for this figure and for the Virgin in the
Coronation. It is the fame kind of nature, the fame
face, the fame head-drefs and the fame coftume; but
we may admire how well the artift, to paint the
Bleffed Virgin, has known how to fpiritualize a type
already fo perfect.

The fourth fubject reprefents the ordeal of doctrines which took place at Montreal, in the diocefe
of Carcaffone. After many difcuffions with the Albigenfes, S. Dominic propofed to them to caft into
the fire the books containing the expofition of their

greateft fervices to art and to Chriftian archæology, by his difcovery of the ancient
fubterranean bafilica of S. Clemente. The frefcoes which he is ftill exploring and
reftoring poffefs a value and an intereft unfurpaffed by any fimilar ancient
Chriftian monuments in the firft city of the world.—TRANSLATOR'S note.]

doctrine. The book of the heretics was inftantly confumed, whilft that of the faint was thrice fpared by the flames.[1]

This compofition has many points of refemblance with the gradino at Cortona; but it fhows the artift's progrefs fince his return to Fiefole. In the firft pic-ture, the figures recall the fchool of Giotto, by the fimplicity of the drawing and the naturalnefs of the movements. In the fecond, whilft preferving the dignity of the ftyle and the truth of the expreffions, Beato Angelico has given more freedom to his groups, more pliancy to his draperies, and more feeling to his figures. The pupil of tradition has been developed by the ftudy of nature. The double fcene of the delivery of the book and the ordeal by fire is arranged perfectly. S. Dominic's gefture explains his propofal very well. The young brother who is following him is a model of religious modefty. The different feel-ings agitating the heretical witneffes of the miracle are alfo very fkilfully expreffed.

The next picture is a literal rendering of the charm-ing recital in the account Sifter Cecilia has given of the life of S. Dominic. " When the brethren were ftill living at the church of San Sifto, and were a hundred in number, on a certain day, Bleffed Dominic commanded Fra Giovanni of Calabria and Fra Al-berto the Roman to go about the town and queft for alms. But they employed themfelves to no pui pofe from morning to the third hour of the day.

---

[1] A like miracle took place alfo at Fanjeaux; and in the church of that town are ftill feen the hearthftone on which the fire was kindled, and a beam bearing the traces of the fire.

They were then returning home, and had already reached the church of Santa Anaſtaſia, when a woman who had a great devotion to the Order met them, and seeing that they carried nothing back with them, gave them a loaf, ſaying, " I will not have you return quite empty." A little farther on, they were accoſted by a man, who earneſtly begged charity of them. They excuſed themſelves from giving, becauſe they had nothing for themſelves; but when the man continued all the more importunate, they ſaid to one another, " What ſhall we do with one loaf? Let us give it to him for the love of God." Then they gave him the bread, and immediately loſt ſight of him. Now, as they were entering the convent, the pious Father, to whom the Holy Ghoſt had already revealed all that had paſſed, came to meet them, and ſaid with a cheerful air, " Children, have you nothing?" " No, Father," they replied; and they related to him what had happened, and how they had given the loaf to a poor man. He ſaid to them, " It was an angel of the Lord. The Lord will know well how to feed His own. Let us go and pray." Thereupon he went into the church, and coming out at the end of a ſhort time, he told the brethren to call the community into the refectory. They anſwered, " But, holy Father, how can you wiſh us to call them, as there is nothing to ſerve them with?" And they purpoſely delayed to do what he ordered them. Thereupon the Bleſſed Father ſent for Fra Roggero the cellarer, and commanded him to aſſemble the brethren for dinner, becauſe the Lord would provide for their wants. Then the cloths were laid, and the cups ſet out, and at a given

fignal the whole convent entered the refectory. The
Bleffed Father pronounced the bleffing, and all being
feated, Fra Enrico the Roman began the reading.
Meanwhile the Bleffed Dominic was praying, with his
hands clafped upon the table: and, lo! all at once, juft
as he had promifed by the infpiration of the Holy Ghoft,
two beautiful young men, minifters of Divine Providence, appeared in the midft of the refectory, carrying loaves in two white napkins, which hung from their
fhoulders before and behind. They began the diftribution by the lower rows, one on the right, the other
on the left, and fet an entire loaf of admirable beauty
before each brother. Then when they were come to
Blefled Dominic, and had likewife placed before him
a whole loaf, they bowed their heads and difappeared,
without any one knowing to this day whither they
went or whence they came. Bleffed Dominic faid to the
brethren, " My brethren, eat the bread which the Lord
hath fent you." Then he told the ferving brothers
to pour out the wine. But they replied, "Holy Father,
there is none." Then the Bleffed Father, full of the
fpirit of prophecy, faid to them, " Go to the cafk and
pour out for the brethren the wine which the Lord
hath fent them." They went, in fact, and found the
cafk filled to the brim with excellent wine, which they
haftened to bring. And Bleffed Dominic faid, "Drink,
my brethren, of the wine which the Lord hath fent
you." Then they eat and drank as much as they
would, that day, the next and the day after. But after
the repaft of the third day, he had all given to
the poor that remained of the bread and wine, and

would not have any of it kept any longer in the houfe." [1]

The painter has been worthy of the writer : his pencil has given the original faithfully. The religious are feated in the refectory, in the order and recollection which gives fomething fo grave and poetical to monaftic repafts. S. Dominic is in the centre, his hands joined together, waiting for the good turn of Piovidence. Fra Enrico the Roman is reading, and Fra Roggero the cellarer is bringing, in a large wicker bottle, the wine which the Lord hath fent. The two angels, who have begun with the laft, as is ftill the cuftom, are come before S. Dominic, and are going to lay upon the table the loaf defigned for him. The whole of this fcene is as calm and fimple as the confidence of thofe who hope in the Lord.

The laft picture reprefents the Death of S. Dominic. The holy Founder, fitting on his bed, is giving his bleffing and laft inftructions to his religious. Before him, we read thefe words of his will, " Have charity, keep humility, poffefs voluntary poverty." The painter, who had written them on the book S. Dominic is carrying in the upper picture, took delight in repeating them, becaufe they were dear to the reformed convent of Fiefole. The children of the dying faint liften to him with love and veneration. Grief is depicted in different fhades on the countenances of all. Two religious in particular cannot reprefs their fobs. In the upper part, is drawn the dream of Fra Gualo, prior of the convent of Brefcia, who, at the moment when the

---

[1] *Vie de S. Dominique*, p. 415.—Narrative of Sifter Cecilia, No. 3.

faint was giving his laſt ſigh, ſaw two ladders reaching
from earth to heaven : one was held by our Lord, the
other by the moſt Holy Virgin, and angels were going
up and down, playing glad inſtruments and bearing
a beautiful crown. In the midſt, two angels carried
the luminous throne deſtined for the holy Patriarch.
This viſion does not injure the unity of the compoſition : it is ſweetly blended with the azure ſky.[1]

The type of S. Dominic in theſe pictures comes up
to the portrait Siſter Cecilia has left us of him. " His
ſtature," ſhe ſays in her narrative, " was of middle ſize,
his ſhape ſlender, his face fine and rather ſanguine in
its hue, his hair and beard fair and bright, and his
eyes beautiful. There came out from his forehead
and from between the eyelaſhes a certain radiant light,
which attracted reſpect and love. He was always
cheerful and agreeable, except when moved to compaſſion by ſome affliction of his neighbour. He had
long and beautiful hands, and a powerful, noble and
ſonorous voice. He was never bald, and had his religious tonſure perfect, ſprinkled with a few white
hairs."[2]

We muſt not ſuppose, however, that Beato Angelico
has adopted only one type. On the contrary, we
have been ſtruck with the diverſity of face he has
given to S. Dominic ; and we conclude from it that,
in his time, no traditional likeneſs of him exiſted.
He choſe amongſt the religious around him thoſe who

---

[1] This compoſition may be compared with the Death of S. Bruno, one of the
fineſt ſcenes in the celebrated Gallery of Leſueur. Notwithſtanding the merit of
that picture, which diſplays an admirable effect of light, Beato Angelico's compoſition is more religious, more true and more learned.

[2] *Vie de Saint Dominique,* p. 432.

by their fanctity and dignity beft reprefented the holy
Founder to him, and gave them his name by placing
above their head the ftar which characterizes him.
Beato Angelico is one of thofe painters who have
ftudied nature moft. In his pictures, are found faces
with fuch marked individuality, that it is evident they
are portraits. But they were not common mercenary
models which the artift chofe ; they were religious
who underftood the actions of the faints, and made their
virtues live again. Beato Angelico put them in the
fcene, and did not make them groups of diftracted
fpectators, as the painters of Renaiffance did.

Chapter VI.

BEATO ANGELICO AS A THEOLOGIAN.— LIFE OF OUR LORD.

F all the works executed by Beato Angelico during his abode at the convent of Fiefole, the moft important is affuredly the Life of our Lord, in thirty-five pictures. Vafari tells us that it was painted for the chapel of the Nunciata at Florence, which Cofimo de Medici had built with fuch magnificence by his architect Michelozzi.[1] The paintings once formed the panels of a prefs intended for the treafures of the chapel; they are now in the Academy of Fine Arts.

Never has that great epopee of Chriftianity been reprefented with more learning and piety. Not only

[1] Nella cappella fimilmente della Nunciata di Firenze, che fece fare Piero di Cofimo de' Medici, dipinfe gli fportelli dell' armario dove ftanno l'argenterie, di figure piccole condotte con molta diligenza.

has Beato Angelico followed the traditions of the great fchool of Giotto, but he has himfelf drawn from the fources of Holy Scripture and of theology. This merit in our painter has not been fufficiently remarked by hiftorians ; feveral have even fuppofed that he held a fecondary rank in the Order of S. Dominic, and that he had put on only the humble habit of a lay-brother, in order to cultivate his art more readily. But the ftudy of his life and works proves to us that he was a prieft, and a prieft, too, as remarkable for learning as for holinefs. At firft fight, the text is pofitive. The chronicle of the convent of Fiefole fays, "In the year 1407, Fra Giovanni received the clerical habit in this convent, and made his profeffion in the following year."[1] He was amongft the choir-religious then, and muft have made his theological ftudies along with his companions in the noviciate. His brother, who was an artift like himfelf, was certainly a prieft, fince he was nominated fub-prior of San Marco and prior of San Dominico of Fiefole, and fulfilled the duties of thofe offices, whilft executing the choral books which he enriched with fuch beautiful miniatures. Beato Angelico was a prieft, fince Pope Eugenius IV. wifhed to nominate him Arch-bifhop of Florence. In the fifteenth century, they did not raife at once to the fulnefs of the priefthood one who was not already in orders ; and if the Sovereign Pontiff wifhed to place Beato Angelico in the fee of

[1] Fr. Joannes Petri de Mugello, juxta Vichium, optimus pictor, qui multas tabulas et parietes in divefis locis pinxit, accepit habitum clericorum in hoc conventu . . . . et fequenti anno fecit profeffionem. Beato Angelico is reprefented on his tomb in the choir-habit. Paul Delaroche has depicted him in a lay-brother's habit, in the hemicycle of the fchool of fine-arts.

Florence, before he feated S. Antoninus there on his recommendation, it was that he might receive the high dignity his humility made him refufe. The title of artift, which is given even to God, does not ill become a prieft. In Chriftian antiquity, many religious and bifhops have borne it with glory, and Greek tradition has put the pencil into the hand of S. Luke, who wrote the gofpel.[1]

Beato Angelico has alfo written the Life of Our Lord. The facerdotal unction had prepared his hands, as the coal from the altar purified the lips of Ifaias; and it is not furprifing that the fingers which daily held the Body of the Holy Victim fhould have produced fuch pure mafterpieces. Painting formed a part of his miniftry. Charged to diftribute the light of grace and truth to the faithful, he did it by prefenting to them pictures, which converted and fanctified their hearts. Thefe preachings of art have not loft their eloquence. At Florence, we have been told of Proteftants who have come back to a religion capable of infpiring fuch paintings.

Our Beato ftrengthened his talent by theological ftudies. His pictures evince fruitful meditation and profound intelligence of the Holy Scriptures. He borrows numerous texts from them to complete his thought and exprefs his fentiments better. We be-

---

[1] In the middle ages, the Latin Church did not believe that S. Luke was a painter. S. Thomas Aquinas, in his *Catena Aurea*, and Bleffed James de Voragine, in his *Legenda Aurea*, give to this Evangelift the title of phyfician, after the Epiftle of S. Paul: *Salutat vos Lucas, medicus cariffimus* (Colofs. iv. 14). The numerous Greek Madonnas attributed, in Italy, to S. Luke are by different painters, and of various epochs. The one in Santa Maria Maggiore, which we were able to examine very clofe, appeared to us the moft ancient. We believe it to be contemporary with the paintings of Santa Sophia at Conftantinople.

lieve we can recognize traces of his ftudies in the two
little panels preferved in the Academy of Fine Arts
at Florence. In them, he has painted the two great
glories of the Dominican Order, Bleffed Albert the
Great and the Angelic Doctor S. Thomas Aquinas.
The panels, in a femi-circle terminated by fcrolls, were
doubtlefs placed over the doors or pulpits of the halls
ufed for teaching philofophy and theology. The firft
reprefents Albert the Great furrounded by his numerous
difciples, religious and laymen; and at his feet is read
this infcription :—Bleffed Albert the Great, BEATV.
ALBERTVS MANGNVS [sic].[1] In the fcrolls, is feen, on
the left, a figure holding a fphere, *aftrology*, ASTRO-
LOGIA; on the right, a figure holding two ferpents
attempting to bite each other, *logic*, LOICHA. This
perfonification of logic is found on feveral of our
monuments.

In the fecond panel, S. Thomas Aquinas is teaching
theology; at his feet, three perfonages are overthrown,
pointed out by their names, VILIELMVS. AVERROIS.
SABELLIVS, William de Saint-Amour, Averroës and
Sabellius, reprefenting the three great herefies victo-
rioufly combatted by S. Thomas. In the fcrolls, on
the left, a figure holding an eagle, and on a banderole, THEOLOGIA SPECVLATIVA; on the right, a
figure holding a globe, THEOLOGIA PRATICA.

Thefe two pictures fhow us the whole of the fciences
of the middle ages, and the happy agreement between
reafon and faith. Aftrology, in its ancient fignification, indicates the knowledge of natural caufes; and

---

[1] This mis-fpelling appears in other pictures, and indicates, perhaps, a pro-
nunciation at that period.

logic, the knowledge of the intellectual powers, the ufe of which it directs. Albert the Great unveils the fecrets of the vifible and invifible world; but his more illuftrious pupil, S. Thomas Aquinas, whofe reafon is enlightened by fuperior light, rifes into the regions of faith, and contemplates by fpeculative theology the fplendours of the infinite, afterwards to follow its rays, which come down upon things and acts of life by means of practical theology.

Theological fcience, in which, by a fublime prodigy, the mind of man is united to the mind of God, is the focus where all the rays of light converge, coming either directly or indirectly from the Firft Caufe. Diftinct from the other fciences, of which it is the judge and queen, it exceeds them in its beginning, object, certainty, and its aim, which is the perfection of man and his eternal happiness.[1] It embraces the paft, prefent and future, and lights up the triple face of time, by fhowing us under the literal fenfe of the revealed word, the allegorical, moral and anagogical fenfes; that is, the teachings of faith, the rules of virtue, and the promife of its rewards.

Theology is alfo the queen of the arts; for, with the knowledge of the truth, it gives the love for it: the light of faith gives birth to the ardour of charity. By theology, the heart goes higher than the underftanding. When the mind is fixed in the obfcurity of a myftery, the heart leaps forward ftill, attaches itfelf to the unknown, and dilates in the infinite. It is imagined that theology is a ftern fcience, and that its only part is to fill the pulpits of the

---

[1] Summa Theol., 1, q. 2, 3, 4.

fchools and the columns of folios with fyllogifms. But theology is the infpirer and moft faithful friend of Chriftian art. It has given to art its fymbolifm ; it has traced the plan of the cathedrals ; it has guided the hand of fculptors and of painters, and has revealed to them, by the commentaries of the holy fathers, the poetry of the Bible and the fublimity of the Gofpel.

In proving that Beato Angelico was a theologian, and more of a theologian than any of the artifts who have preceded or followed him, we make known one of the fources of his genius, one of the caufes of his glory. Not only did he receive the infpirations of theology by artiftic tradition, of which he was the faithful difciple, but he appropriated its lights by fpecial and profound ftudies. He has given proofs of it in painting the Life of our Lord, and has underftood all its hiftorical and dogmatic grandeur. The life of our Lord is the key of hiftory, the centre of time and eternity, the higheft and moft complete manifeftation of truth.

Beato Angelico has known how to fhow us the Word, the Son of God playing in the creation,[1] announcing Himfelf by the prophets, becoming incarnate to fave us, dying on the Crofs, leaving us His life and teachings, and coming at the end of ages to reward and punifh according to each one's works; and he has painted thefe fubjects with his eyes fixed on the two Teftaments, of which Chrift is the infpirer and the hero. Each fubject has a double text giving the meaning of it.

As a prologue to his poem, Beato Angelico has

---

[1] *Prov.* viii, 30.—[TRANSLATOR's note]

painted the vifion which begins the prophecies of Ezechiel, and he explains it by the magnificent commentaries of S. Gregory the Great. On the banks of
the river Chobar, Ezechiel contemplates the fymbolical wheel. Oppofite him, the Pope, S. Gregory,
meditates on it and writes the explanation. In the
corners above their heads, great parchments are un-
rolled, whereon fome paffages of their texts are read.

Above Ezechiel :—" And I faw, and behold a whirlwind came out of the north; and a great cloud, and
a fire enfolding it. . . . . And now as I beheld the
living creatures, there appeared upon the earth by the
living creatures one wheel with four faces. And their
appearance and their work was, as it were, a wheel in
the midft of a wheel."[1]

Above S. Gregory :—" What is it that, when one
wheel is fpoken of, it is added fhortly after, ' as it were
a wheel in the midft of a wheel,' except that, in the
letter of the Old Teftament, the New Teftament lay
hid in allegory? Whence, alfo, the fame wheel that
appeared near the living creatures is defcribed as
having four faces, becaufe facred Scripture, by both
Teftaments, is divided into four parts, the Old Teftament into the law and prophets, the New into the
Gofpel and into the acts and fayings of the Apoftles."[2]

[1] Et vidi, et ecce ventus turbinis veniebat ab aquilone, et nubes magna et ingnis
(*fic*) involvens . . . Cumque afpicerem animalia, apparuit rota una fuper terram,
juxta animalia, habens quatuor facies. . . . Et afpectus eorum et opera, quafi fi
fit rota in medio rotæ. (EZECHIEL, ch. i., v. 4, 15, 16.)

[2] Quid eft hoc, quod cum una rota diceretur, paulo poft adjungitur : Quafi fi
fit rota in medio rotæ, nifi quod in Teftamenti Veteris littera, Teftamentum
Novum latuit per allegoriam ? Unde et rota eadem, quæ juxta animalia apparuit,
quatuor facies habere defcribitur, quia Scriptura facra per utraque Teftamenta in
quatuor partibus eft diftincta. Vetus etenim Teftamentum in lege et prophetis,
Novum vero in Evangelii atque apoftolorum actibus et dictis.

This paffage is taken from the beautiful homilies of S. Gregory the Great, explaining the vifion of Ezechiel by the coming of our Saviour and by the fpread of the holy Gofpel, which he relates by employing the figures of the prophet. At the time of the Incarnation, he fays, the whirlwind came from the north ; the breath of the evil fpirit was ravaging the world ; the great cloud of idolatry blinded men ; and the fire of perfecution encompaffed truth. Light then fpread ; in the midft, was, as it were, a metal compofed of gold and filver, of juftice and mercy: the gold of the Divine nature was united with the filver of the human nature in the perfon of our Saviour. In the midft, alfo, was the image of the four living creatures refembling the Son of Man ; for the Evangelifts have imitated our Lord in all things. They have four faces and four wings, for they all fay the fame thing, and their flight tends to the fame perfection. Their way is ftraight forwards, and their feet are like thofe of the ox, the fymbol of ftrength and difcretion, and fparks of truth go out of them like glowing brafs. The hand of the Man-God makes itfelf felt by the ardour of their zeal in the four quarters of the world, and they carry to them the fame teftimony of words and virtues. They do not recoil before any obftacle, and always advance towards things eternal. They refemble man by reafon, the ox by facrifice, the lion by courage, and the eagle by the flight of contemplation. They triumph on the right and on the left, in profperity as well as in adverfity, becaufe they know how to foar above the things of earth. The two wings of their foul are love and hope ; and the two wings of their body, fear and penance. They

go whither the breath of the Holy Ghoſt carries
them. They are like burning coals of fire, like burning lamps; and they ſhed everywhere the flames of
love and the light of truth. They go and come like
the thunder-clap, and ſcatter Holy Scripture everywhere. Holy Scripture is like a wheel with four ſides:
the ˌlaw, the prophets, the Goſpel and the words of
the Apoſtles; and this wheel is double, for the New
Teſtament is the centre to which the Old converges.
Holy Scripture is like the ſea by its extent and depth,
and by it we may arrive, upheld by the ſacred Tree of
the Croſs, at the heavenly country.[1]

This beautiful commentary developed in the firſt
homilies of S. Gregory on Ezechiel, muſt naturally
have been familiar to a religious of the Order charged
to continue the miſſion of the Apoſtles. Beato Angelico was very capable of underſtanding and loving the
genius of that great ſaint, the moſt perfect repreſen-
tative of the papacy in its ſocial action. In the perſon
of S. Gregory the Great, Providence inaugurated the
temporal power of the ſovereign pontiffs, which was to
be the centre of progreſs and civilization during all the
middle ages. Sprung from ancient patrician families, he
was inveſted with the firſt magiſtracy of Rome by the
Emperor Juſtinus. And when the acclamations of the
whole people had ſeated him, in ſpite of himſelf, upon
the pontifical throne, he became the light of the Church
and the ſaviour of Italy, which he defended againſt the
corruption of Byzantium and the violence of the
Lombards. No pope was more zealous in ſending mis-

---

[1] SANCTI GREGORII PAPÆ Opera omnia, è Congr. S. Mauri, 1705; tom. i,
lib. i, Hom. 2, 3 et ſeq.

I

fiɔnaries to the barbarians, in creating fchools, in founding hofpitals, and in maintaining ecclefiaftical difcipline, the code of which he digefted in his *Paſtoral.* He was alfo the legiflator of Chriftian art, by regulating the liturgy, its moft divine and living part. An artift himfelf, he compofed hymns, and gave to the faithful the Gregorian chant, that precious fragment of the ancient melodies. His works excel in poetry, and his *Dialogues* have been the moft fruitful fource of our marvellous legends. He protected particularly painting, and the artifts of his time took pleafure in multiplying his portrait. They reprefented him as receiving the infpirations of the Holy Ghoft in the form of a dove.

Let us fee how Beato Angelico has tranflated the commentary of S. Gregory with his pencil. Around two concentric wheels reprefenting the Old and New Teftament, are written the beginning of Genefis and of the Gofpel of S. John.

The creation is the firft manifeftation of the Son of God. "In the beginning God. created heaven and earth. And the earth was void and empty, and darknefs was upon the face of the deep; and the Spirit of God moved over the waters. And God faid: Be light made. And light was made. And God faw the light that it was good: and He divided the light from the darknefs. And He called the light Day."[1]

The Incarnation is the fecond manifeftation of the

---

[1] In giving the infcriptions on the pictures by Beato Angelico, we fhall adhere to the orthography. We will occafionally correct the texts in italics.

In principio creavit Deus cœlum et terram. Terra aut. erat innanis *et vacua* et tenebræ erant fuper faciem abiffi et Spiritus Dni ferebatur fuper aquas dixitq. Deus fiat lux *et* facta eft lux et vidit Deus lucem q. effet bona et divifit ucem ac tenebras (*à tenebris*) appellavitq. lucem diem.

Word. The Evangelift relates His eternal generation. " In the beginning was the Word, and the Word was with God, and the Word was God. The same was in the beginning with God. All things were made by Him, and without Him was made nothing that was made."[1]

On this account, all the fpokes of the two wheels, like all the events of the Old and New Teftament, end in one only centre, the Man-God, whofe double nature is reprefented by the union of gold and filver in a fingle metal. The outer wheel reprefenting the Old Teftament is divided into twelve compartments. In the higheft, is feated Mofes, his brow armed with the reflexions of the Divine light, holding the two tables of Sinai in his hands. On his right and left, are fitting David and Solomon, and next them Ifaac, Ezechiel, Daniel, Jeremias, Efdras, Micheas, Malachias, Jonas and Joel. These perfonages are not only the hiftorians of our Lord, but alfo types of Him : their very names have a prophetic fignification not unknown to art in the middle ages.[2]

DAVID REX. David (dilectus) the well-beloved fits on the right hand of Mofes, as the well-beloved Son of God is fitting on the right hand of His Father. He reprefents the prophets. His eyes are fixed on heaven, in which he is faluting his Lord, the inheritor of his race: and his hands accompany his fongs on the pfaltery.

On the other fide, SOLOMON (*pacificus*), the peaceful

---

[1] In principio erat verbum et verbum erat apud Deum et Deus erat verbum. Hoc erat in principio apud Deum omnia per ipfum facta funt et fine ipfum factu. eft nichil.

[2] See the explanation of the names of the forefathers of Chrift, in the *Catena a urea*, chap. i of S. Matthew.

king, who holds the fword and the book of the law.
Forefather of Him who is to make all nations at peace
by the fword of the word and by the fweetnefs of the
Gofpel, Solomon celebrates the nuptials of Chrift and
the Church.

ISAAC (*rifus*), the laughter of Abraham, who is ready
to facrifice him upon the mountain. His attitude expreffes ecftacy. He rejoices becaufe all nations are to
be bleffed in his pofterity.

The other prophets hold phylacteries in their hands,
to indicate the texts relating to the Saviour.

EZECHIEL (*fortitudo Dei*), the ftrength of God. He
announces Him who is to reign over the nations, and
the only Paftor who is to lead them.

DANIEL (*judicium Dei*), the judgment of God. He
delivers truth from the hands of falfehood, and indicates
the day and hour when juftice and peace will embrace
upon Calvary.

JEREMIAS (*celfitudo Domini*), the highnefs of the
Lord. He laments over the fufferings of the Paffion,
and fhows Him who will draw all things to Himfelf,
when He fhall be lifted up on the Tree of the Crofs.

ESDRAS (*adjutor*), the helper. He is the fupport and
light of the captivity, and teaches the faithful the law
and divine worfhip.

MICHEAS (*quis ficut Deus*), who as God. Micheas
fees in the Child of Bethlehem, the Ruler of Ifrael, the
God gone forth from the days of eternity.

MALACHIAS (*nuncius meus*), my meffenger. Malachias,
the prophet of the forerunners of Chrift, announces
S. John Baptift before the Incarnation, and the prophet Elias before the laft judgment.

JONAS (*columba*), the dove of the deluge, the fymbol of the refurrection. He holds in his hand the fifh by which he became the fign of the Saviour.

JOEL (*volens, incipiens*), willing, beginning. He celebrates the power of the Name of Jefus invoked over the whole earth, and the triumph of His law in the valley of Jofaphat.

All thefe prophets, who have written and reprefented the life of our Saviour, are feated on the ground and furrounded by flowers and trees, becaufe they lived amidft fleeting images and the fhadows of the Old Teftament, whilft the hiftorians of the New Teftament are ftanding and in the pure light of truth.

The wheel of the New Teftament is divided into eight compartments. The four Evangelifts form a crofs, the intervening fpaces of which are filled with the Apoftles who wrote the epiftles. S. John, like Mofes, is at the top, S. Matthew on his right, S. Mark on his left, and S. Luke at his feet. They hold the book of their Gofpel open, and are reprefented with the fymbolical heads of the vifion of Ezechiel. This perfonification of the Evangelifts is found on a great number of monuments: and the explanation of it given by S. Gregory the Great has been adopted by all the theologians and artifts of the middle ages. We will quote it in full, in order to underftand what light the Church has elicited from the letter of Sacred Scripture.[1]

" Thefe four-winged living creatures," fays S. Gregory, " defignate the four holy Evangelifts, as the very beginnings of the evangelical books evidence. For as

---

[1] See the learned differtation of Mde. Félicie d'Ayza on this fubject. *Annales Archéologiques*, 1847-1848.

Matthew began from Chrift's human generation, he is rightly reprefented by the man; as Mark has begun by the voice crying in the defert, he is well reprefented by the lion; as Luke proceeds from facrifice, he is well reprefented by the calf; and as John began from the divinity of the Word, the eagle worthily fymbolizes him, who fays, 'In the beginning was the Word, and the Word was with God, and the Word was God.' Whilft he contemplated the very fubftance of the Divinity, he fixed his eyes, as the black eagle's, on the fun."

Thefe four fymbols alfo reprefent the Saviour. "For the only-begotten Son of God Himfelf was truly made man. In the facrifices of our redemption, He deigned to die like the calf; by virtue of His ftrength, He rofe again like the lion. The lion is alfo accounted to fleep with open eyes: for in that death, in which by His humanity our Redeemer could be fleeping, by His divinity He was watching by remaining immortal. Also after His refurrection, afcending to heaven, He was raifed above, like the eagle. To us, therefore, He has become, at once, the man by being born, the calf by dying, the lion by rifing again, and the eagle by going up to heaven."

But Chrift is the chief of the elect, and all the elect muft be like their Head. "Therefore, every elect and perfect in the way of God is at once the man, the calf, the lion and the eagle. For man is a rational living creature; the calf is ufually offered in facrifice; the lion is a ftrong beaft, as it is written, 'A lion, the ftrongeft of beafts, hath no fear of anything he meeteth.' The eagle flies up into the air and turns to the fun-beams with unquailing eyes. Every one, therefore, who is perfect in reason, is the man. And as he mortifies himself in worldly pleasure, he is the calf. When by his own voluntary mortification he has the strength of security against all adversity, as it is written, 'The just man, bold as a lion, shall be without dread,' he is the lion. As he sublimely contemplates heavenly and earthly things, he is the eagle. Therefore, as the just man is by his reason man, by the sacrifice of his mortification the calf, by the strength of security the lion, and by contemplation becomes the eagle, so by these sacred living creatures every one perfect may be rightly typified."[1]

Such are the principal ideas Beato Angelico has recalled, by giving the commentary of S. Gregory in this first picture of the Life of our Lord. The twenty-two figures which it contains are in noble style; the prophets especially, representing the Old Testament, may be compared, for style and draperies, with the finest statues adorning our cathedrals.

The pictures following represent the Life of our Lord. Each subject is accompanied by a verse from the Old and New Testament, which explains the idea of the artist.

The Incarnation. "Behold a Virgin shall conceive, and bear a Son, and His name shall be called Emmanuel." "Behold thou shalt conceive in thy womb, and shalt bring forth a Son, and thou shalt call His name Jesus."[2]

---

[1] S. Gregorii Opera, lib. ii, Hom. 3, p. 1200.

[2] Ecce virgo concipiet et pariet filium, et vocabitur nomen ejus Emmanuel. —*Isaias*, vii, 14.

Ecce concipies in utero et paries filium, et· vocabis nomen ejus ihesum.—*S Luke*, i, 31.

The angel and the Bleſſed Virgin are kneeling, to treat together of the great affair of our ſalvation. Mary has come down from a little ſtool before her, as if to lower herſelf ſtill more, and bows down whilſt ſtyling herſelf the handmaid of the Lord. The Holy Ghoſt hovers over the compoſition. The ſcene takes place in the middle of a rich porch, at the back of which is opened the avenue of a beautiful garden. The architecture already no longer preſents the ſimple and graceful notions of the firſt pictures by Beato Angelico: it recalls the claſſic taſte and magnificence of the Medici.

The Nativity. "A Child is born to us, and a Son is given to us, and the government is upon His ſhoulder." "Her days were accompliſhed that ſhe ſhould be delivered, and ſhe brought forth her firſt-born Son."[1]

He, in whoſe Name every knee muſt bow, is laid upon the ground, in front of a ruſtic and ruinous ſtable; and has nothing to cover him. He extends his arms, to offer himſelf already in ſacrifice. Mary and Joſeph adore him in ſilence. Behind him, the aſs and ox are kneeling, according to the legend, and warm him with their breath. Over the thatched roof of the ſtable, ſix angels chant the *Gloria in excelſis*. On the left, are ſeen the ſhepherds, haſtening on with devotion. The ſchool of Perugino ſeems to have been often inſpired by this compoſition.

The Circumciſion. "Be circumciſed to the Lord, and take away the foreſkins of your hearts, ye men of

---

[1] Parvulus *enim* natus eſt nobis . . . . et factus eſt principat*us* ſup. humeru. ej. —*Iſaias*, ix, 6.

Impleti ſunt dies ut pareret, et peperit filium ſuum primogenitum.—*S. Luke*, ii. 6.

Juda." "And after eight days were accomplifhed that the Child fhould be circumcifed, His name was called Jefus."[1]

A little table covered with a worked cloth, and a gold difh reprefent the altar, upon which the Saviour is to offer the firft fruits of his blood. The prieft advances to fhed it. The Child Jefus has his eyes and hands raifed to heaven. Mary and Jofeph are affociated with his facrifice by holding him; but the Virgin mother turns her head away. Behind the prieft, are three perfons, who feem to be waiting upon him. The building in which the fcene paffes is like a church; the lancet windows and the vaults of pointed arches fupported by fluted pilafters indicate the tranfition that fhowed itfelf at Florence in the beginning of the fifteenth century.

The Adoration of the Magi. "The kings of Tharfis and the iflands fhall offer prefents: the kings of the Arabians and of Saba fhall bring gifts." "And opening their treafures, they offered Him gifts; gold, frankincenfe and myrrh."[2]

This compofition is very fine. The Holy Virgin is feated in the centre; her figure ftands out from the hut of Bethlehem as it were from the drapery of a throne, and is admirable for dignity and purity. The Child Jefus fitting on his mother's knees bleffes the king

---

[1] Circumcidimini Domino, viri Juda, et auferte præputia cordium veftrum —Jeremias, iv. 4.

Poftquam confummati funt dies octo ut circumcideretur puer, vocatum eft nomen ejus ıнefum.—*S. Luke,* ii, 21.

[2] Reges Tharfis et infulæ munera offerent; reges Arabum et Sabba dona adducent.—*Ps.* lxxi, 10.

Et appertis thefauris obtulerunt ei *munera* thus et mirram.—*S. Matt.,* ii, 11.

proftrated to embrace his feet. The young king bearing the gold vafe is very elegant. On the right of the
Bleffed Virgin, is feen the retinue of Orientals. The
neareft refpectfully contemplate the scene; the more
diftant are looking at, and pointing out, the ftar which
has guided them. On the left, S. Jofeph is difcourfing
with one of the kings.

The Purification. "Prefently the Lord whom you
feek, and the Angel of the Teftament whom you defire
fhall come to His temple." "They carried Jefus to
Jerufalem, to offer a facrifice for Him."[1]

The Ruler of the nations is ftraitly confined in his
fwaddling clothes. The Holy Virgin is giving him
into the hands of the aged Simeon, who lovingly contemplates and adores the Salvation and Glory of Ifrael.
Behind the Bleffed Virgin, S. Jofeph comes up carrying two little doves in a bafket. On the oppofite
fide, the prophetefs Anna is advancing, with clafped
hands. This figure is admirable, and is worthy of
Raphael.

The Flight into Egypt. "I have gone far off flying
away, and I abode in the wildernefs." "Arife, and take
the Child and His Mother, and fly into Egypt."[2]

The Virgin is going away, fitting on an afs; fhe
tenderly preffes the Child Jefus in her arms. S. Jofeph
follows on foot, with his poor provifion for the journey;
he holds, in his left hand, a ftone bottle, with a ftaff and

---

[1] Statim veniet ad templum sanctum fuum *dominator* (dominus) *quem vos
quæritis* et angelus (eft) teftamenti quem vos vultis.—*Malachi,* iii, 1.
Tulerunt ineſum in Jerufalem ut darent oftiam pro eo. (An inexact quotation;
ee S. Luke, ii, 22-24).

[2] Elongavi fugiens: et manfi in folitudine.—*Ps.,* liv, 8
Surge, *et* accipe puerum et matrem ejus, et fuge in Egiptum.—*S. Matt.,* ii, 13.

his cloak on the end of it; and in his right, a fmall round bafket. This compofition reminds us of Taddeo Gaddi's, in Santa Croce, at Florence.

The Maffacre of the Innocents. "They have done unjuftly againft the children of Juda, and have fhed innocent blood in their land." "And Herod was exceeding angry, and fending killed all the men-children that were in Bethlehem."[1]

This is a very remarkable compofition. Herod orders the maffacre from the top of a terrace of his palace. A troop of foldiers purfues the weeping mothers. The tears and cries of the inconfolable Rachel are given with an infpiration and intenfity of expreffion feemingly incompatible with Beato Angelico's fweet and contemplative foul. It is true, the executioners do not appear to be furious; but the defpair of the mothers is fhown by the trueft and moft varied movements. Two women, in the foreground, are fenfelefs with grief. Their children are dead, and they take no more notice of the fcene of flaughter around them; one is lying on the body of her fon; and the other contemplates her child extended on her knees; whilft another tears the face of a foldier with her nails. The moft diftant fly, whilft preffing the objects of their tendernefs to their bofoms. One of them feems to hope to fave him; her profile recalls the one we have admired in the Coronation of the Virgin and in the raifing of the young Napoleone to life. All thefe female heads are drawn and modelled with rare perfection.

---

[1] Ineque egerunt in filios Juda, et effuderunt fanguinem innocentem in terra fua.—*Joel*, iii, 19.

Iratus *eft valde* (Herodes) *et mittens* occidit omnes pueros qui erant in Bethlehem.—*S. Matt.*, ii, 16.

Jefus in the midft of the Doctors. "The wife men are confounded, they are difmayed and taken. There is no wifdom in them." "They found Him in the temple fitting in the midft of the doctors, hearing them and afking them queftions."[1]

This compofition is full of quiet and fweetnefs. He who confounds human wifdom is fitting in the centre. His heavenly look appears to contemplate truth in the bofom of his Father. The doctor on his right has fought to anfwer him: his book is open on his knees but his gefture expreffes furprife and embarraffment. The one on his left has humbly clofed his book, and liftens with compunction and veneration. The countenances of the others exprefs various feelings. The Holy Virgin and S. Jofeph are refpectfully advancing.

The Baptifm. "He went down, and wafhed in the Jordan feven times." "Jefus came and was baptized by John in the Jordan."[2]

The Marriage in Cana. "You shall take of the river-water, and it fhall be turned into blood." "The voice of the Lord hath thundered upon the waters."[3]

The Transfiguration. "And the houfe was filled with the glory of the Lord." "And He was transfigured before them."[4]

---

[1] Confufi funt fapientes, perterriti et capti funt . . . . Sapientia nulla eft in eis.—*Jeremias,* viii, 9.

Invenerunt eum in templo fedentem in medio doctorum, audientem illos et interrogantes *eos.—S. Luke,* ii, 46.

[2] Defcendit et lavit fepties in Jordane.—*4 Kings,* v, 14.

Venit Jefus et baptifatus eft à Johane in Jordane.—*S. Mark,* i, 9.

[3] Haurietis aquam . . . et vertetur in fanguinem.—*Exod.,* iv, 9.

Vox Domini intonuit fuper aquas.—*Ps.,* xxviii, 3.

[4] Et repleta erat gloria domus Domini.—*Ezech.,* xliii, 5.

Tras fighuratus eft ante eos.—*S. Matt.,* xvii, 2.

Thefe three pictures are not by Beato Angelico, and we do not know how to explain their prefence amongft the others. Perhaps the originals had been accidentally deftroyed, and fome artift of very inferior talent wanted to replace them; but he has ill fucceeded, for his figures do not approach our painter's, neither in ftyle nor in execution. Thefe three pictures on the fame panel are befides almoft effaced.

The Raifing of Lazarus to Life. "I will bring you out of your fepulchres, O my people." "Jefus cried with a loud voice, Lazarus, come forth. And prefently he that had been dead came forth."[1]

This compofition recalls the frefco of Buffalmaco in San Francefco, at Affifi. Lazarus is ftanding, with his hands ftill bandaged. Thofe who have taken away the ftone recoil on perceiving the corruption of the tomb. Martha and Mary are kneeling at the Saviour's feet. Their countenances exprefs at once both grief and hope. Chrift, at the head of his apoftles, looks kindly on his friend Lazarus.

The Entry into Jerufalem. "Behold thy King cometh to thee meek, fitting upon an afs and a colt, the foal of her that is ufed to the yoke." "Hofanna to the Son of David: bleffed is He that cometh in the name of the Lord."[2]

That King, full of meeknefs, comes to take poffef-

---

[1] Educam vos de fepulcris populus meus.—*Ezech.*, xxxvii, 12.

Clamavit Jhs voce magna : Lazare, veni foras. Et ftatim prodiit qui erat mortuus.—*S. John*, xi, 43.

[2] Ecce rex tuus venit tibi . . . . manfuetus fedens fuper afinam et filium fubjugalem.—Inexact ; fee *Zach.*, ix, 9. [It is exact from *S. Matt.*, xxi, 5.—TRANSLATOR'S note.]

Hofanna filio David, benedictus qui venit in nomine Domini.—*S. Matt.* xxi, 9.

fion of his empire on the heights of Calvary. He is croffing the Mount of Olives, which is to be the witnefs of his agony, and he bleffes the faithful band accompanying him. As yet we fee neither Jerufalem nor the enthufiaftic and fickle crowd. Only a few difciples and the college of the Apoftles, holding branches, follow him. This march in folitude has fomething fad and folemn in it.

The Betrayal by Judas. "And they weighed for my wages thirty pieces of filver." "What will you give me and I. will deliver Him unto you? But they appointed him thirty pieces of filver."[1]

The hiftory of our Saviour's Paffion begins with the treafon of Judas. The bargain has juft been concluded, and Judas, before going away, ftretches out his hand, into which the price of his crime is being counted. This compofition is diftinguifhed amongft all the others, by the grandeur and fimplicity of the lines. The phyfiognomy and geftures of the perfonages are very expreffive, and the type of Judas is quite that of the avaricious and treacherous man. The building that ferves as a background for the picture feems copied from the baptiftry at Florence.

The Laft Supper. "A lamb of the fame year without blemifh he fhall offer." "And they made ready the pafch. And when the hour was come, Jefus fat down and the twelve difciples with Him."[2]

---

[1] Appenderunt mercedem meam triginta argenteos.—*Zach.*, xi., 12.

Quid vultis *dare* mihi et ego *vobis* tradam illum. At illi conftituerunt ei **xxx** argenteos.—*S. Matt.*, xxvi, 15.

[2] Agnum ejusdem *anni* immaculatum faciet facrificium (*holocauftum*).—*Ezech.*, xlvi, 13.

Paraverunt pafca. Et cum *facta* effet hora difcubuit (Jhs) et duodecim difcipuli (*apoftoli*).—*S. Luke*, xxii, 13.

The moment chofen by the painter is when our Lord announces to the Apoftles that one of them will betray Him. This picture is inferior to the others. Judas, who betrays himfelf by putting out his hand to the difh, has not the type which we have juft noticed.

The Wafhing of the Feet. "Wafh yourfelves, be clean, take away the evil of your devices." "He putteth water into a bafin, and began to wafh the feet of His difciples, and to wipe them with the towel."[1]

The fcene takes place under a gallery furrounding a little court planted with trees and turf. The Apoftles are attentive and recollected. Our Lord is kneeling before S. Peter, who withdraws his feet, whilft he looks on his Mafter with refpectful adoration. The group is a mafterpiece. Never, perhaps, has the text of the Gofpel been more admirably given.

The Inftitution of the Holy Euchariff. "I will flay for you a great victim upon the mountains of Ifrael, to eat flefh and drink blood." "He that eateth my flefh and drinketh my blood, hath everlafting life."[2]

Our Lord is giving communion, as a prieft, to the Apoftles on their knees. This is one of the occafions in which myftic truth may put on hiftorical truth. The provifion for the repaft muft difappear amidft fo great a myftery; and Nicolas Pouffin had a more Chriftian infpiration, when he reprefented the

---

[1] Levamini, mundi eftote, auferte malum cogitationum veftrarum.—*Ifaias*, i, 16.
Mifit aquam in pelvim et cepit levare pedes difcipulorum et extergere linteo.— *S. John*, xiii, 5.

[2] Ego imolabo vobis victimam *grandem* fuper montem *Ifrael* ut comedatis carnes et bibatis fanguinem.—*Ezech.*, xxxix, 17.
Qui manducat meam carnem et bibit meum fanguinem habet vitam eternam. —*S. John*, vi, 55.

inftitution of the Holy Euchariſt after Beato Angelico,
than when, in his Seven Sacraments, he ſought to
ſhow his talent by the luxury of an ancient ſupper.

Jeſus in the Garden of Olives. " Fear not, for I am
with thee: I am Thy God. I have ſtrengthened thee."
" And there appeared to Him an angel from heaven,
ſtrengthening Him."[1]

The apparition of the angel preſenting the chalice
to our Lord at prayer is a deſign from the ſchool of
Giotto. But the poſture of the three Apoſtles aſleep
on the foreground is remarkable for its originality. It
is ſeen that they wanted to watch, but that ſleep has
overcome them. S. Peter is ſitting in front, with his
forehead ſupported and hidden by his hand.

The Kiſs of Judas. " He who ate my bread hath
greatly ſupplanted me." " And Judas forthwith coming
to Jeſus, said, Hail, Rabbi. And he kiſſed Him."[2]

The principal group is very beautiful. The hypo-
criſy of Judas contraſts with the calmneſs and ſorrow
of Jeſus, who weeps for him whom he would even ſtill
call his friend. The ſoldiers and the Jews overturned
on his left ſomewhat injure the unity of the ſubject.

Jeſus is Bound. " Behold, they ſhall put bands
upon thee, and they ſhall bind thee with them." " But
they holding Jeſus led Him bound to Caiaphas the
high prieſt."[3]

---

[1] Ne timeas quia *ego* tecum ſum . . . . Ego Deus *tuus* confortavi te.—*Iſaias*
xli, 10.

Apparuit autem ei angelus de cœlo, confortans eum.—*S. Luke,* xxii, 43.

[2] Qui edebat panes meos, magnificavit ſuper me ſupplantationes.—*Ps.,* xl, 10.

Et confeſtim accedens (Judas) ad xpm dixit ave rabbi et oſculatus eſt eum —
S. Matt., xxvi, 49.

[3] Ecce data ſunt ſuper te vincula, et ligabunt te in eis.—*Ezech.,* iii, 25.

Beato Angelico does not excel in reprefenting fcenes of violence. The figure of our Lord always remains calm and dignified. The foldiers furrounding him are well drawn, but execute without emotion the miffion they are charged with. In the foreground, S. Peter, armed with a not very dreadful fword, cuts off the ear of the overturned Malchus.

Jefus is treated ignominioufly. "I have not turned away My face from them that rebuked Me and fpat upon Me." "And they mocked Him and ftruck Him. And they blindfolded Him."[1]

This compofition, imitated from Giotto's, is very beautiful. The fervants of the high prieft infult our Lord, pull his hair and fpit in his face. Jefus, motionlefs on his throne of derifion, holds in one hand a reed for a fceptre, and in the other the globe of the world. The bandage covering his eyes is tranfparent, and allows his look to be feen full of meeknefs and patience. Does not this admirable figure well reprefent Him, who is the truth, fitting in the midft of ages, receiving the infults of error and the grofs outrages of vice; feeing all, fuffering all, becaufe He awaits the tears of penitence or the juftice of eternity? In a corner of the picture, is painted the Denial of S. Peter.

Jefus before the High Prieft. "They fhall ftrike the cheek of the Judge of Ifrael." "One of the officers

---

At illi tenentes Jhm duxerunt eum ligatum ad Chaipham principem Judeorum. *S. Matt.*, xxvi, 57.

[1] Faciem meam non averti ab increpantibus et confpuentibus in me.—*Ifaias*, l. 6. Illudebant ei cædentes. Et velaverunt faciem ejus.—*S. Luke*, xxii, 63.

K

ftanding by gave Jefus a blow, faying, Anfwereft thou the high prieft fo ?"[1]

Our Lord is ftanding before the tribunal of the high prieft. Around his neck is a noofe, and a foldier holds the end of the cord. Behind him is the fervant, who is going to ftrike him. The judge and the falfe witneffes furrounding him are well drawn and well draped.

The Scourging. "I am ready for fcourges, and My forrow is continually before Me." "Then therefore Pilate took Jefus and fcourged Him."[2]

This fcene is painted with piety and compaffion. Beato Angelico feems to have heard from the mouth of our Lord the Pfalm of David, and to have applied it to himfelf. He muft have fhed many tears in thus reprefenting Him who had fuffered for him, and his grief was very truly before his eyes, as it was in his heart. Nothing is more fimple and affecting than this compofition. Jefus is bound to the pillar. Two executioners hold the cord binding him, with one hand, and with the other ftrike him with rods. Our Lord cafts upon the one on his left a fweet deep look, which ought to convert him.

Jefus carries His Crofs. "He was led as a fheep to the flaughter." "And bearing His own crofs, He went forth to that place, which is called Calvary."[3]

---

[1] Percutient maxillam judicis Ifrael.—*Micheas,* v, 1.
Unus affiftens miniftrorum dedit alapam Jhu dicens: Sic refpondes pontifici ?—*S. John,* xviii, 22.

[2] Ego in flagella paratus fum, et dolor meus in confpectu (tuo) *meo* femper.—*Ps.* xxxvii, 18.
Tunc *ergo* apprehendit Pilatus Jhm et flagellavit eum.—*S. John,* xix, 1.

[3] Tanquam ovis ad occifionem ductus eft.—*Ifaias,* liii, 7.

There is much movement and grandeur in this scene. Thofe who go firft are entering upon the mountain-roads, whilft thofe who clofe the train are ftill at the gates of the city. Jefus follows the two enchained thieves. He turns his head to look at his mother, whofe grief weighs on him more than his Crofs. A foldier menacingly repulfes Mary, who, weeping, follows the footprints of her Son. The lines and drapery of this figure are as beautiful as the expreffion. The holy women who accompany him are alfo very remarkable. One of them is turning as if to afk a favour from the Roman officer.

Jefus is ftripped of His garments. "They parted My garments amongft them; and upon My vefture they caft lots." "The foldiers divided His garments, cafting lots."[1]

This fubject is reprefented in an unufual manner: nothing in it indicates Calvary and the neighbourhood of Jerufalem. On the contrary, the fcene is commanded by high mountains furnifhed with towns and fortified caftles. The holy women who accompanied our Saviour are abfent, the Crofs and the two thieves have difappeared. Chrift is furrounded only by the foldiers, who are ftripping him, and two of them are playing at dice for his feamlefs coat. Has not Beato Angelico had fome particular intention, and may we not fee in this picture a memorial of the events he had witneffed and been the victim of, when he was

---

Bajulans xps fibi crucem exivit in eum, qui dicitur Calvariæ locum.—*S. John,* xix, 17.

[1] Diviferunt fibi veftimenta mea, et fuper veftem meam miferunt fortem.— *Ps.* xxi, 19.

Diviferunt (milites) veftimenta ejus, fortem mittentes.—S. *Matt.,* xxvi, 35.

obliged to abandon the convent of Fiefole? Does not Chrift naked reprefent the Church ftript by fchifm and herefy? And the two foldiers difputing for the coat without feam, are they not the two competitors of Gregory XII, who want to inveft themfelves with the papacy?

The Crucifixion. "He was wounded for our iniquities, He was bruifed for our fins." "And when they were come to the place which is called Calvary, they crucified Him there."[1]

This picture is a prayer at the foot of the Crofs. The facrifice is confummated: the open fide of our Lord has even poured out water and blood, to prove to us his inexhauftible love. The new Adam feems to awake and contemplate the fpoufe taken from his breaft during his fleep. His eyes are opened upon the Church, which is before him. His executioners are converted; the centurion confeffes his divinity; he who had given him gall and vinegar to drink raifes towards him eyes full of repentance and love. The foldiers are on their knees, and Longinus, ftill holding the lance with which he ftruck him, gathers up the precious blood that reftored his fight. On the right, S. John and the holy women fupport the Mother of Grief, who fwoons away. This group is as beautiful as the chant of the *Stabat.*

The Burial. "Him the Gentiles fhall befeech, and His fepulchre fhall be glorious." "Jofeph wrapped the

---

[1] Ipfe *autem* vulneratus eft propter iniquitates noftras, et attritus eft propter fcelera noftra.—*Ifaias,* liii, 5.

Poftquam venerunt in locum qui dicitur Calvarie, *ibi* crucifixerunt eum.—*S. Luke,* xxiii, 33

body of Jefus in fine linen, and laid Him in a fepulchre."[1]

The perfons who are burying the Saviour pay him their laft homage. We fhall find the fame compofition again in one of Beato Angelico's mafterpieces, in the Academy at Florence.

The Defcent into Hell. "He brought them out of darknefs and the fhadow of death, and broke their bonds afunder." "Thou haft redeemed us to God in Thy blood, out of every tribe and tongue and people."[2]

Jefus enters triumphant into limbo. The gate of hell has fallen upon the demon, who kept the key of it. The patriarchs haften towards their Redeemer; Adam and Eve ftretch out their hands to him. Behind them, are advancing the innocent Abel, Noe with the model of the ark in his hands, Abraham holding the knife of facrifice like a palm, David and the prophets. In the corner of the picture, are feen two fcenes of hell: demons fighting with a club and a trident, and a hideous monfter fqueezing a woman in his arms, as a punifhment, no doubt, for her voluptuoufnefs. This picture leaves much to be defired in the drawing; for the figures are heavy and ill-proportioned.

The Holy Women at the Sepulchre. "I rofe up and

---

[1] Ipfum gentes deprecabuntur, et erit fepulchrum ejus gloriofum.—*Ifaias*, xi, 10.

Jofeph depofitum corpus JHU, involvit in findone, et pofuit *eum* in monumento.
—*S. Luke*, xxiii, 53.

[2] Eduxit eos de tenebris et umbra mortis, et vincula eorum difrupit.—*Ps.* CVI, 14.

Redemifti nos Deus (*Deo*) in fanguine tuo, ex omni tribu linguarum et populorum.—*Apocal.*, v, 9.

am ftill with thee." "You feek Jefus of Nazareth ; He is rifen, He is not here."[1]

The angel who fpeaks to the holy women is fitting upon the ftone where the Saviour's body lay. Two young women ftoop down to look into the interior of the grotto. The three Marys are retiring : their attire, by its noblenefs, reminds us of that of the Saints admired in the Paradife of Orcagna, at Santa Maria Novella.

The Afcenfion. "He afcended above the heavens, and He flew upon the wings of the wind." "And the Lord Jefus, after He had fpoken to them, was taken up into heaven."[2]

In the upper part of the painting, is feen nothing but the bottom of our Lord's garment, and the luminous circle furrounding him. The Apoftles and difciples, with the Holy Vigin at their head, are kneeling in a circle, and follow him with their eyes who is withdrawing his fenfible prefence from them. Two angels ftanding near them announce to them his return at the end of the ages.

Pentecoft. "I will pour out My fpirit upon all flefh, and your fons fhall prophecy." "They were all filled with the Holy Ghoft, and they began to fpeak with divers tongues."[3]

---

[1] Refurexi (*exfurrexi*) et adhuc tecum fum.—*Ps.* cxxxviii, 18.
Jhefum queritis Nazzarenum *crucifixum ;* furrexit, non eft hic.—*S. Mark,* xvi, 6.
[2] Afcendit fuper celos [*cherubim*] . . . et volavit fuper pennas ventorum.— *Ps.* xvii, 11.
Deus Jhus poftquam locutus eft *eis,* affumptus eft in celum.—*S. Mark,* xvi, 19.
[3] Effundam Spiritum meum fuper omnem᾽ carnem, et prophetabunt filii veftri. —*Joel,* ii, 28.
Repleti funt omnes Spiritu fancto et ceperunt loqui variis linguis.—*Act. Apoft.,* ii, 4.

The upper part of the fupper-room is open, like a church-tribune. The Apoftles and difciples, with their heads illuminated with the divine fire, furround the Holy Virgin. Before the clofed door, five per-fonages, whofe head-dreffes mark them to be of foreign nations, are liftening, and teftify their aftonifhment at underftanding one fame word in different languages.

The Coronation of the Virgin. " I faw the Lord fitting upon a throne high and elevated . . . and all the houfe was full of His majefty." "Behold the taber-nacle of God with men, and He hath dwelt with them; and they fhall be His people, and God Himfelf with them fhall be their God."[1]

This picture feems to us to reprefent the commu-nion of faints. The luminous centre whence the rays iffue which light up the faces of all the faints, is the fymbol of Jefus Chrift uniting all the faithful by the power of the Sacraments and by the outpouring of charity. Our Lord was not fatisfied with fending us the Holy Ghoft ; He crowned His work by making His mother and ours, Queen of Heaven, of grace and mercy. In her, alfo, is truly the Tabernacle where God communicates with men, fince in Mary He has united together all His treafures, in order to diftribute them to us through her.

A proof that Beato Angelico has wifhed to repre-fent the Communion of Saints by the Coronation of the Virgin, is, that he has given no individuality to

---

[1] Vidi Dominum sedentem fuper folium excelfum et elevatum. Et plena domus majeftate ejus.—*Ifaias*, vi, 1, 3. (Inexact.)

Ecce tabernaculum Dei cum hominibus et habitavit cum eis, et ipfi populus ejus erunt et ipfe Deus *cum eis erit* eorum *Deus.—Apoc.*, xxi, 3.

any of the perfonages affifting at her triumph. He has
made them only reprefentatives of thofe who form the
Church in heaven and on earth. Some have the
aureola, others have none, and many are accompanied
by angel-guardians, who look upon them with folici-
tude and affection. The hierarchy of the Church is
indicated by a pope and a bifhop with the tiara and
mitre, without the aureola. Befide them, are religious of
various orders, and below them the laity of both fexes
and of different profeffions. All thofe kneeling on
the ground cannot as yet contemplate the glory of
Jefus and Mary, but await that happinefs in the joy
of hope.

We do not pretend to explain each of the fifty-
eight ravifhing figures of this picture. It would
require the painter himfelf to reveal to us the beauty
of his thoughts. What is the meaning of the young
girl and knight crowned with flowers; the king holding a rofe, and the angel who feems to wifh to open a
little precious vafe for him? The two muficians playing
on their inftruments, do they not reprefent Chriftian
art in its fweeteft and moft fpiritual expreffion? Beato
Angelico might then have been placed near them with
his brufh. He muft have been in communion with
the faints, when he made this picture fo pure and perfect. Our Lord and the Holy Virgin are admirable:
they are clothed in garments of the fame colour, as
their fouls were clothed with the fame flefh. The
effect of this compofition is truly heavenly.

The pictures of the Life of our Lord prefent great
differences in merit and execution. Heavy and badly-
drawn figures contraft fometimes with others of ex-

traordinary exactnefs in movement and elegance of
drapery. Sometimes, alfo, the work is hard and unfinifhed, whilft it is almoft always remarkable for
freedom and finifh. Muft this difference be explained
by the inequalities of genius and the negligences of
improvifation? If we muft believe Vafari, our painter
never reconfidered his firft thought. We do not think
fo. Genius certainly does not always maintain itfelf
at the fame elevation, and the humility of Beato
Angelico might make him renounce perfections which
would have merited for him more glory before men.
But the painter, like the orator, when lefs infpired,
does not change his ftyle; and we do not find Beato
Angelico's ftyle in the defects we have pointed out.
We will explain them then by the joint-labour of his
brother Fra Benedetto. The latter cultivated painting:
Vafari tells us that he was very well practifed in it,
and that he affifted his brother in his works. We
have ftudied the large miniatures in the choir-books
of the convent of San Marco, and that ftudy has
enabled us to diftinguifh the hand of the two brothers
fometimes in the fame picture.[1]

We fhall, therefore, diftinguifh the works of Fra
Benedetto from Beato Angelico's, not by the greater
or lefs quantity of gold they have put into their
pictures, as Chevalier Roffini propofes,[2] but by the
character of the drawing and the proceffes of execution. Fra Benedetto's perfonages are generally
dumpy and ill-fet; their heads are too broad, and the

---

[1] Ben è vero che a far quefti fu aiutato da un fuo maggior fratello che era fimilmente miniatore ed affai efercitato nella pittura.

[2] *Storia della Pittura Italiana*, vol. ii, ch. xvii, p. 257.

extremities badly joined: the feet efpecially are often difagreeable. His figures are fketched with a heavy brown touch, whilft thofe of Beato Angelico are prepared with very great lightnefs, and the touch, hardly perceived, is of a brilliant red. The two brothers worked without rivalry and with the fame infpiration; but Beato Angelico had a happier and better cultivated talent for rendering his own.

Chapter VII.

THE LAW OF LOVE.—THE LAST JUDGMENT.

HE Life of our Lord is cloſed by two compoſitions, the ſummary and concluſion of it. They. repreſent the *Law of Love* which the Goſpel has given to the world, and the Laſt Judgment, which is the ſanction of it.

Doubtleſs, it was difficult to expreſs within a narrow compaſs the fundamental truths of religion : the unity of the two Teſtaments, the fulfilment of the prophecies, the revealed and accompliſhed myſteries, the eſtabliſhment of the Church, the dogmas of the faith, the reign of charity, the hopes of a perfect happineſs and the means of arriving at it. See how Beato Angelico has overcome the difficulty.

In the middle of the picture, on a ground covered with verdure and flowers, is raiſed the triumphant

Crofs. It is the Tree of Life planted in the midft of the new earthly paradife. It has produced the divine Fruit which has faved us; its fhadow can alone protect us, and its fap render us fertile. A crofs-bearing ftandard waves there; it is the fign to point out the way and animate us to the combat. Around the ftaff is rolled a banderol, on which the twelve articles of the Creed are indicated: DEUS PATER. JHS. XPS. NATIVITAS. PASSIO. RESUREXIO. ASCENSIO. ADVENTUS IN MUNDO. SPIRITUS SANCTUS. ECCLESIA CUM SCIS. VENIA CRIMINUM. SUSCITATIO HOMINUM. VITA ETERNA.

On both fides, the perfonages of the Old and New Teftament repeat the Creed with fublime accord. The Prophets and Apoftles prefent their banderols, whereon correfponding texts are read. They have all had the fame God, the fame faith, the fame Redeemer; and what the Prophets hailed in the rifing glimmer of dawn, the Apoftles have contemplated in the broad light of day.

Jeremias has faid: Thefe fhall call me Father, and fhall not ceafe to walk after Me.—*S. Peter* replies: I believe in God, the Father Almighty.

David. The Lord hath faid unto Me: Thou art My Son.—*S. John.* And in Jefus Chrift His only Son, our Lord.

Ifaias. Behold a virgin fhall conceive, and bear a Son.—*S. James (son of Zebedee).* He was conceived of the Holy Ghoft, born of the Virgin Mary.

Zacharias. All fhall look upon Me, becaufe they have crucified Me.—*S. Andrew.* He fuffered under Pontius Pilate, was crucified, dead and buried.

Osee. O death, I will be thy death; O hell, I will

be thy bite.—*S. Philip.* He defcended into hell.—
S. Thomas. The third day, He rofe again from the
dead.

Amos. He hath built His afcenfion in heaven.—
S. Bartholomew. He afcended into heaven, fitteth at
the right hand of the Father Almighty.

Malachias. And I will come to you in judgment,
and will be a fpeedy witnefs.—*S. Matthew.* From
thence He fhall come to judge the living and the dead.

Joel. I will pour out My fpirit on all the land.—
S. James (fon of Alpheus). I believe in the Holy
Ghoft.

Solomon the King. She will communicate to me
of her good things.—*S. Simon.* The holy Catholic
Church, the communion of Saints.

Micheas. The Lord will put away our iniquities.—
S. Jude. The remiffion of fins.

Daniel. I will bring you forth from your fepulchres,
O my people.—*Ezechiel.* Some fhall awake unto life
everlafting, and others unto reproach.—*S. Matthias.*
The refurrection of the body, life everlafting.[1]

---

[1] Tradition attributes to each of the Apoftles one article of the Creed, which
they may have repeated by infpiration before they feparated to evangelize the world.
But the affignation of the articles to each Apoftle is not uniform : there are even
two modes of dividing the Creed into twelve articles, according as we difjoin or
unite the defcent into hell and the refurrection of our Lord, or the refurrection of
the body and life everlafting. It is to be remarked that our painter has followed
both thefe methods. The Apoftles' Creed proffers the divifion adopted by
S. Thomas Aquinas, and the Symbol of the Prophets that of Durandus. (*See*
Bibliothèque Dominicaine, *la Foi, les Œuvres et la Priere,* d'après S. Thomas
d'Aquin, p. 46; and the *Rationale* of Durandus, lib. iv. § 25.)

We have given the names of the Apoftles according to S. Thomas : the following are the texts of the Prophets' Symbol :—

1. Patrem vocabis me, et poft me ingredi non ceffabis.—*Jeremias,* iii, 19.

2. Dominus dixit ad me : Filius meus es tu.—DAVID. *Ps.,* ii, 7.

3. Ecce virgo concipiet et pariet filium.—*Ifaias,* vii, 14.

The foot of the Cross is formed of a candlestick with seven branches, representing the seven Sacraments. The Blood of Jesus Christ is the oil which feeds the light of grace in the Church. Banderols passed in the branches of the candlestick point out the Sacraments in the following order, and the texts of the Old and New Testament which refer to them.

Baptism. "All in Moses were baptized, in the cloud and in the sea." "Go and teach all nations, baptizing them."

Confirmation. "Seek the Lord, and be strengthened." "And thou being once converted, confirm thy brethren."

Orders. "The priests stood in their order." "Thou art a priest according to the order of Melchisedech."

Eucharist. "Melchisedech brought forth bread and wine." "This is My body: do this for a commemoration of Me."

Penance. "If a soul hath sinned, let it do penance for its sin." "Except you do penance, you shall all perish."

Marriage. "What God hath joined, let no man put asunder." "This is a great Sacrament, but I speak in Christ and in the Church."

4 Aspicient omnes ad me quoniam confixerunt.—*Zacharias,* xii, 10.

5. O mors, ero mors tua ; ero morsus tuus, O inferne !—*Oseas,* xiii, 14.

6. Qui edificat in cœlo ascensionem suam.—*Amos,* ix, 6.

7. Et accedam ad vos in judicio et ero testis velox.—Sophon. *Malach.,* iii, 5.

8. Effundam de spiritu meo super omnem terram.—*Joel,* ii, 28.

9. Comunicabit mecum de bonis.—Solomon rex. *Sapient.* viii, 9.

10. Deponet Dominus omnes iniquitates nostras.—Malach. *Micheas,* vii, 19.

11. Educam vos de sepulchris vestris populus meus.—Daniel. *Ezechiel,* xxxvii, 12.

12. Evigilabunt (omnes) alii ad vitam *eternam* et alii *in opprobrium.*—Ezechiel. *Daniel,* xii, 2.

The painter is often mistaken in pointing out his texts : no doubt he wrote them from memory.

Extreme Unction. "He fhall make up ointments of health." "Is any one fick among you. Let him bring in the priefts, and let them pray over him, anointing him with oil: and the prayer of faith fhall fave the fick man, and if he be in fin, it fhall be forgiven him."[1]

On the right of the Crofs, a nimbed female figure perfonifies the Law of Love. She does not hold a fword and a clofed book, like Solomon, who reprefents the Old Law in the vifion of Ezechiel. Her book is open, becaufe the truth is now without figure and fhadow. Her only arms is a fhield infcribed with thefe words, LEX AMORIS (the Law of Love). Therein is the whole Gofpel, the new commandment our Lord has come to teach by His life and words, To love God and men, as God Himfelf has loved us: this law

---

[1] Thefe are the texts of the picture :—

BACTISMUS. Omnes in Moyfe baptizati (eftis) *funt* in nube et in mari.—S. PAUL. 1 *Cor.*, x, 2.

Ite, docete omnes gentes baptizantes eos.—*S. Matt.*, xxviii, 19.

CONFIRMATIO. Quærite Dominum, et confirmamini.—*Ps.*, civ, 4.

Tu aliquando converfus confirma fratres tuos. —*S. Luke*, xxii, 32.

ORDO. Sacerdotes fteterunt in ordine fuo.—2 *Paralip*, xxx, 16.

Tu es facerdos fecundum ordinem Melchifedec.—*Ps.*, cix ; *Heb.* v, 6.

EUCHARISTIA. Melchifedec proferens panem et vinum.—*Genefis*, xiv, 18.

Hoc eft enim corpus meum. Hoc facite in meam commemorationem.—*S. Luke*, xxii, 19.

PENITENTIA. Si peccaverit anima, agat pœnitentiam pro peccato fuo.—*Levit.*, v.

Nifi pœnitentiam (egerris) *habueritis*, omnes fimul (*fimiliter*) peribitis.—*S. Luke*, xiii, 3.

MATRIMONIUM. Quod Deus *ergo* conjunxit, homo non feparet.—*S. Mark*, x, 9.

Sacramentum hoc magnum est, ego autem dico in XPo et in Ecclefia.—S. PAUL. *Eph.*, v, 32.

EXTREMA UNCTIO. Unctiones conficiet fanitatis.—*Ecclus.*, xxxviii, 7.

Infirmatur quis in vobis ? Inducat prefbyteros (*Ecclefiæ*), et orent fuper eum, ungentes eum oleo (*in nomine Domini*), et oratio fidei falvabit infirmum, et alle-viabit eum Dominus, et fi in peccato fit, remittetur ei.—*S. James*, v, 14.

includes all others; and the Church is eftablifhed
to realize and fpread it. The Church is the law
of the living and eternal love. The fpoufe of
Chrift is artless and weak like this young female
holding the book and fhield; fhe has no other
attire but her poverty, no other fword but her
doctrine, no other power but her law of love,
lex amoris. She makes the martyrs triumph, pro-
tects the feeble and lays the mighty at their feet:
fhe eftablifhes the family and fociety. Love one
another, and all human laws will become ufelefs;
the fword of juftice will no longer find the guilty,
and peace will reign throughout all the earth.

The law of love which Chrift has come to give the
world, is alfo the new law of art. S. Jerome, commenting on the verfe of S. Matthew, "the things which
proceed out of the mouth, come forth from the heart,"
fays, "the principle of the foul is not, as Plato fays, in
the brain, but, according to Chrift, in the heart."[1] This,
it feems to us, is an admirable diftinction between
Pagan and Chriftian art. Art is a language, of which
the mouth is the moft fublime organ. Antiquity
places the principle of art in the intellect; Chriftianity,
in the will: our Lord has re-eftablifhed the foul in its
true centre. Memory and intellect are the means and
minifters of the will. The will is free and fupreme,
and our heart is its throne and empire; it may uphold
it againft God Himfelf, and it is to fubdue this one
thing, which may truly be ours to do, that the Word

---

[1] Quæ autem procedunt de ore, de corde exeunt.—*S. Matt.,* xv, 18.
Principale igitur animæ non, fecundum Platonem, in cerebro eft, fed juxta
Chriftum in corde. (*Catena aurea.*)

has wrought all the marvels of creation and redemption. He has taken a heart in order to captivate ours; by our heart only can we honour God and pleafe Him.

Greece made Minerva iffue from the brain of . Jupiter; the Church has drawn Chriftian poetry from the Heart of Jefus Chrift. Pagan Art has never loved its gods; it has expreffed the beauties of nature, the intoxication of the fenfes, or the terrors of man. Perfonal intereft has been its fole aim; the palms of Olympus or the bounties of the Emperors: whilft the life of Chriftian art is, to love and make Him loved who is the firft caufe and the end of it. There its miffion lies, like that of the Apoftle and martyrs, and outfide this law of love it fees only falfehood and vanity.

This law of love, fo beautiful and fweet, but fo difarmed and forgotten, muft have a fanction. The work of our Lord has not ended on earth: all He has faid and done, is, fo to fpeak, only the preparation for the folemn act which will terminate the ages, and open to us the boundlefs fcenes of eternity: Chrift will come in all His majefty, to judge the living and the dead.

The laft day of the human race is the vafteft and moft fublime fubject art can reprefent. The Chriftian religion alone was able to give its match. Heathen antiquity had imagined in the fhadows of death a myfterious place, whither each foul went to receive its fentence feparately; but painters and fculptors employed themfelves little in expreffing the joys of the Elyfian fields and the torments of the infernal regions recounted by the poets. The theology of the Eaft offered beyond the prefent, only fucceffive changes of the metempfycofis, which granted delays to crime, and

L

allowed it to brave divine juftice indefinitely. All in its doctrines was indecifive, obfcure and individual. The Gofpel-light alone has made to fhine on the confines of time and on the threfhold of an immutable eternity, that laft fcene, in which heaven, earth and . hell, all ages, peoples and conditions will be called together: that decifive moment when the Saviour will come and demand of each an account of his life, when all actions will be judged, truth made plain, hiftory explained and Providence glorified; that defirable · moment, when thofe who have thirfted after juftice fhall be fully fatisfied.

This fublime fubject was the great poem of the mediæval artifts. Sculptors placed it at the doors of cathedrals, as at the entrance of heaven. In this prophetic vifion of the Laft Judgment, Chrift is feated on his throne furrounded by angels and faints, and near him is the Crofs, as the text of the law. The Virgin without fpot bends towards her Son, to ferve as advocate for us. S. John the Evangelift or S. John Baptift intercedes in the name of love and peni-tence. Angels found the trumpet, and the dead raife up their tombftones: the bleffed are led into Abraham's bofom, whilft the reprobate are caft down into the yawning jaws of hell. On the lower courfes, the vices and virtues are reprefented, which, higher up, receive their chaftifements or rewards. Such is the theme which fculptors in the middle ages have rendered with incredible variety.

Reprefentations of this kind offered their indelible inftruction in the public fquares; and there all found fears or hopes. If tyranny did not ceafe its violence, fervitude at leaft was confoled, when it perceived, beyond the pangs of life, the glory of virtue and the delights of eternity.

The great fchool of Giotto was worthy to paint fo vaft a fubjeft, which the genius of Dante had explained to it. Orcagna efpecially gave it an admirable manner, in the church of Santa Maria Novella, and under the galleries of the *Campo Santo.* But Beato Angelico, in the reprefentation of the Laft Judgment, has furpaffed all who have preceded and followed him, by compre-henfion of the fubjeft, beauty of compofition and grandeur of charaéter.

The oldeft Laft Judgment by Beato Angelico is the one clofing the Life of our Lord. It is inferior to to the others, but ftill prefents beauties of the firft order. This compofition, double the fize of the other piétures, is framed, like them, with texts of Holy Scripture. " Let the nations come up into the valley of Jofaphat ; for there will I fit to judge all nations." " He fhall fit upon the feat of His majefty, and judge the good and the bad." " Come ye bleffed of My Father, poffefs the kingdom prepared for you." " Go, ye curfed, into everlafting fire."[1]

Chrift is fitting in the midft of a circular glory ; and near him, the Bleffed Virgin, S. John Baptift, the Apoftles, and the founders of Orders are ranged on the clouds of heaven. In the lower part, the refur-

---

[1] Afcendant gentes in vallem Jofaphat ; quia ibi fedebo, ut judicem omnes gentes.—*Joel*, iii, 12.

Sedebit fuper fedem majeftatis fuæ (et judicabit bonos et malos).—*S. Matt.*, xxv., 31.

Venite, benediéti Patris mei ; poffidete paratum vobis regnum.—*S. Matt.*, xxv, 34.

(*Difced*) ite *à me*, malediéti, in ignem eternum.—*S. Matt.*, xxv, 41.

rection of the dead is fhown in two perfonages iffuing
from their tomb, whofe expreffion and geftures make
known their different lots.   On the right, on a flowery
turf, the bleffed of every ftate contemplate the heaven
awaiting them, and receive the fraternal kifs of their
guardian-angels; whilft on the left, the reprobate are
dragged pell-mell by devils into hell.

The upper part of this compofition is admirable.
Chrift is calm and terrible: his uplifted right hand
is full of power. His half-opened garment lets the
wound of his fide be feen.   The adjuftment of his
mantle has a fulnefs and noblenefs which recalls the
fineft Greek types.   The two groups of faints com-
pofing his tribunal may be compared with thofe feen
in the Difpute of the Holy Sacrament. If Raphael
has a purer defign, a more learned pencil and more
varied lines, Beato Angelico has graver attitudes, more
truthful expreffions and a more religious character;
and in relative talent, it muft aftonifh us that there
was the interval of nearly a century between the two
painters.   The elect ftill on the earth breathe peace,
the certainty of happinefs, and all that fenfe of love
and adoration which Beato Angelico knew fo well how
to give.   The reprobate are painted with extraordinary
force and freedom of pencil.   They prefent fore-
fhortenings and movements, which remind us of the
hell and thunder-ftricken of Luca Signorelli in the
frefcoes of the cathedral at Orvieto. The two fides
of this compofition are united together by a remarkable group: an angel who is feparating the good from
the bad, drags along one damned, whofe gefture and
figure exprefs all the anguifh of defpair.

The other Laſt Judgment, which the Academy of Fine Arts at Florence poſſeſſes, is grander and more complete. It was executed for the church of the Camaldoleſe, and ſerved to ornament the ſeat of the celebrant at high maſs.[1] We may perhaps be allowed to borrow the beautiful deſcription of it given by Comte de Montalembert, who is ſo capable of appreciating and praiſing the merit of Beato Angelico.

"Imagine a board of ſome feet ſquare. In the middle of the upper part, our Lord is ſeated in his glory. His arms are ſtretched out ; his right hand, imprinted with the radiant wound of the crucifixion, is open on the ſide of the elect, whom he ſeems inviting to enter into his kingdom: his left hand is equally extended on the ſide of the damned, but it is cloſed, and they can only ſee the back of it. This geſture alone ſays everything ; it has a ſublime ſimplicity. Our Lord is in the midſt of a cloud of ſeraphim, diſpoſed in the form of an almond (a form conſecrated to the Trinity, of which that fruit is the ſymbol) : theſe ſeraphim are red, to expreſs the ardour of the love conſuming them. Around them, is ranged, in concentric ellipſes, the whole heavenly hierarchy in adoration, each order with its ſymbol, the Archangels with the *pallium*, the Powers with helmets and lances, &c.: each little figure is a charming miniature in

[1] Fece . . . nella chieſa de' monachi degli Angeli un Paradiſo ed un Inferno di figure piccole, nel quale con bella oſſervanza fece i beati belliſſimi e pieni di giubbilo e di celeſte letizia, ed i dannati apparecchiati alle pene dell' inferno in varie guiſe meſtiſſimi, e portanti nel volto impreſſo il peccato e demerito loro. I beati ſi veggiono entrare celeſtemente ballando per la porta del paradiſo, ed i dannati dai demoni all' inferno nell' eterne pene ſtraſcinati. Queſta opera è in detta chieſa andando verſo l'altar maggiore a man ritta, dove ſta il ſacerdote, quando ſi cantano le meſſe, a ſedere.

itfelf.   At the feet of Chrift, an angel raifes a
triumphant Crofs, and two others are ftill founding
long trumpets, which have wakened the human race.
On his right, Mary, clothed with a long white
robe ftudded with ftars and lined with green (the
emblematic colour of hope), with her .hands timidly
croffed on her breaft, raifes towards her Son a tender
look of love and prayer for poor mortals.   On his
left, S. John Baptift prefents the fymbolical lamb
to the Supreme Judge, as if to appeafe him.   Behind
the Queen of Angels, are the greateft of the faints :
Jofeph, at the fide of Mary, and as if protected by
her; Peter, with the gold key of paradife and the
filver key of purgatory; Paul, with his fword ; Mofes;
David, with his harp; Francis of Affifi, with his bright
ftigmas; Stephen, his figure all impreffed with
the joy of martyrdom ; and many others.   Light white
clouds enfhroud their feet ; and long rays of fire glitter
on every fide around them, for they are already in the
bofom of celeftial glory.   Nothing can equal the expreffion of all the heads, that ineffable mingling of
calm and ferene beatitude and of holy reverence, with
which the burft of divine juftice ftrikes them.   The
moft exacting imagination remains fatisfied and even
furpaffed ; it feems, as Vafari himfelf writes, that the
fouls of the bleffed cannot be otherwife in heaven.
The lower part of the picture perfectly correfponds
with the upper half : the centre is occupied with a long
avenue of open and empty graves, and the perfpective
of them is terminated with the great tomb of Chrift,
which alone is clofe, *becaufe it has nothing to give up.*
The judgment is being pronounced ; and every one

knows his lot. On the left, the damned of every clafs, amongft whom our Beato (although born in an age of fanaticifm and oppreffion) has not feared to place kings, cardinals and a great many monks, are dragged by a throng of devils towards hell at the extremity of the picture, where the feven capital fins are feen punifhed in feven different circles; and at the bottom, . the great Lucifer of Dante, devouring a finner in each of his three chaps. On the right, are the elect ; and here may be feen to what degree Chriftian genius gets the better of difficulties, and how an inconceivable variety may be reconciled with the moft complete unity: all have the head raifed towards heaven, and look on their Saviour, whilft thanking and adoring him, and not one is like his neighbour. In the firft rank, is a pope, whofe calm and lofty coun- tenance feems to exprefs efpecially the joy of repofe after his hard labours ; behind him, an emperor, type of Chriftian chivalry ; then a king, and befide the king a poor pilgrim, who has journeyed even to heaven ; a young princefs all radiant with purity and faith ; very many religious, bifhops, lay- men and monks of ravifhing beauty, but in whom it is well feen that the phyfical beauty is only the outward beaming of moral beauty. But fee the guardian-angels who go feeking the elect, over whom they have watched during the time of trial. Each angel is kneeling at the fide of his elect, impreffes a fraternal kifs upon his lips, and then conducts him to heaven acrofs a flower-enamelled meadow, where angels and faved men dance together, *Cantantes cho- rofque ducentes in occurfum regis.* Both are crowned

with white and red rofes; and in the fingle expreffion
of their hands holding each other, there is a treafure
of poetry. The round being finifhed, two and two they
wing away towards the heavenly Jerufalem. Its glit-
tering walls are feen in the diftance; the half-opened
portal allows a torrent of golden rays to efcape, in the
midft of which two of the bleffed are being loft, it
may be an angel and an elect, or two fouls who have
loved each other and been faved together.

" ' Sufo alle pofte rivolando iguali.—*Purg.*, c. viii.

"Add to this fketch the preftige of a frefh and
pure colouring, a correct defign without anatomical
exaggeration, draperies of perfect grace, and expreffions of countenance truly divine, and we fhall have
a feeble idea of this *Laft Judgment*. When we have
feen and underftood it, we remain quite cold before
that of Michael Angelo."[1]

[1] *Du Vandalifme et du Catholicifme dans l'Art*, p. 99.
["It is about feven palms long, and its fummit is in the form of three arches,
the central one being largeft, and the two fide ones fmaller. The Final Judgment
occupies the central one; in that on the right, he painted Paradife; and in that on
the left, Hell. The figures are of the dimenfions of thofe which he painted on
the gradini of his pictures." . . . . "But more charming than even this, are
the kiffes and embracings which the Elect interchange with the Angels who protected and guided them on the path of peril. Kneeling, they clafp each other in
heavenly affection. The idea of the painter, probably, was to exhibit the angels,
venerating in thefe bodies, humanity glorified. The greetings between the angels
and the elect terminated, we fee them linking hands and gracefully dancing on a
fweet meadow, enamelled with moft beauteous flowers. Their garments gliften
with innumerable little golden ftars; the head of each is wreathed with a garland
of white and red rofes, whilft a brilliant little flame burns on the forehead of each
angel. Then light, aery, graceful, and even during the dance abforbed in ecftatic
contemplation, carolling and finging they advance towards the celeftial Jerufalem;
and the nearer they approach to it, the more etherial and luminous do their bodies
become; till at laft, arrived at the gates of the holy city, they appear to be trans-

After this fine defcription, it remains for us only to prefent fome obfervations on the execution of the picture. The upper part is admirable for light, colouring and purity. The lower part is far from offering the fame qualities. The compofition of it is fine, and the groups well difpofed; but the figures are fhort and ill-defigned.[1] How explain this contraft? We do not hefitate to perceive in this picture the joint workmanfhip of the two brothers, Beato Angelico and Fra Benedetto. The attentive ftudy of the painting will juftify, we hope, what we have faid of the ftyle and execution of the two artifts. There was a great inequality between their talents; but Beato Angelico was too modeft to retouch his brother's paintings and harmonize them with his own. He has begun the painting, and Fra Benedetto finifhed it, by copying doubtlefs the lower part of fome other Laft Judgment, of which this one appears to be a repetition.[2]

This Laft Judgment is the one which forms part of the gallery of Cardinal Fefch.[3] A great number

muted into moft fubtile and refplendent fpirits; and then, two by two, holding each other's hand, they are introduced into eternal beatitude. Where did the painter find this fweet conception? How was he able to develop fuch varied beauties? We confefs our inability to give or imagine a reply."—Marchese, *by Meehan*, vol. i, pp. 235, 238. Translator's note.]

[1] P. Marchefe has remarked this difference. " E quefta parte del dipinto, fe nella compofizione non è del tutto infelice, cede di gran lunga al rimanente, cofi nel difegno come nella efecuzione " (p. 281).

[2] On the gold of the framing thefe words, traced with a point, are read beneath the hell, " *In inferno nulla eft redemptio.*"

[3] I have not been able to ftudy this picture at leifure. Cardinal Fefch died in 1839, juft when I was to have had the honour of being prefented to him, and I only ran over his gallery on the day of his interment. I have been affured that this Laft Judgment is now in England, in the gallery of Lord Ward.

of artifts look on it as the mafterpiece of Beato Angelico. The compofition is the fame as the one of
which Count de Montalembert has given a defcription,
that cannot be repeated. All its fuperiority lies in the
execution, in the purity of drawing, fweetnefs of
pencil and elegance of the figures. We have been
able to compare together fome outline drawings of
the angels flying towards heaven with the elecft, with
the celebrated female dancers found at Pompeii and
preferved in the Bourbon Mufeum at Naples.[1] Thefe
picftures, executed on a black ground, are perhaps the
moft •perfecft relics of ancient painting we poffefs.
They have many points of refemblance with the
work of Beato Angelico; in the matter of art,
there is the fame talent, the fame grace, the fame
lightnefs, but employed with a different infpiration
and with quite a different aim. The half-clothed
females in tranfparent draperies difturb the fenfes, by
their wanton poftures and voluptuous forms. The
artift has placed them on a black ground, like evil
defires in the fhades of our heart, and has decorated
the walls of a banquet-hall with them, in order to
aroufe thoughts of debauchery amidft the pleafures
of the table. Our painter, on the contrary, has confecrated the delicacy of his pencil to reprefent the joys
of ecftacy and the triumph of virtue : in the full light
of truth, he has painted heavenly dances, which infpire
peace and hope. The chafte figures flying away two
and two attracft and purify our foul, by detaching it
from the feducftion of the fenfes. God has created

---

[1] See *Antiquités d'Herculanum*, par David, graveur, 1 vol., p. 64 et feq.

ártifts as the angels ; according as they are faithful or unfaithful to Him, they remove us from, or bring us nearer, the Creator.

Another mafterpiece of Beato Angelico is the fmall Laft Judgment in the Corfini Gallery, at Rome.[1] None of his pieces have been painted with greater care and love. The compofition is not fo extenfive as the others : it feems to have been executed for a religious order. Chrift is feated in his glory : with one hand he curfes the damned ; and in the other he holds an open book, wherein are the fymbolical Alpha and Omega. In front of him, on his right, is S. Peter with the keys ; on the left, S. Paul with the fword upon his knees. They hold open books, and might be hearing the fulfilment of the text more unchangeable than earth and heaven. Behind thefe two great faints of the Church, are two Apoftles ; a pope (S. Gregory ?) ; a bifhop (S. Auguftin ?) ; a deacon (S. Lawrence ?); and the founders of orders, S. Benedict, S. Dominic and S. Francis of Affifi. In the upper part and as the back-ground, is a multitude of angels varioufly difpofed and of charming expreffion. At the bottom of the tribunal, and in the azure fky, an angel with golden wings raifes the Crofs which judges the world ; on his right, an angel makes the trumpet of the refurrection heard ; whilft on his left, another angel fhows, with one hand, the crown of recompenfe, and with the other, the rod of chaftifement.

---

[1] This picture and two others which accompany it and reprefent the Pentecoft and the Afcenfion, came out of a church in the environs of Florence, of which the Corfini family had the patronage. The figure of Chrift in the *Afcenfion* is very beautiful ; the picture of the *Pentecoft* has been unfortunately retouched.

In the lower part, a line of empty tombs divides the bleſſed from the reprobate, repreſented on both ſides by religious of various orders. Again the angels come to embrace, with overflowing joy, thoſe who were entruſted to them on earth. This idea was like a devotion in Beato Angelico; but it muſt be remarked that he never repreſents angels embracing females, fearing, no doubt, to arouſe ſome profane thoughts by that heavenly kiſs.

Hell is expreſſed with an extraordinary energy and vivacity of pencil. This picture, deſtined for the inſtruction of a cloiſter, reminds us that Beato Angelico belonged to the part of the reform of which the great S. Catherine of Sienna had been the Apoſtle. The vices of religious are particularly attacked in it. The hideous embraces of devils contraſt with thoſe of the angels. One devil drags to himſelf a monk, whoſe purſe, hung at his neck, points out his crime; another lifts from the head of a Franciſcan the cardinal's hat, the dream of his ambition and the cauſe of his perdition. All theſe figures expreſs remorſe and deſpair. In the midſt of the damned, a terrified nun raiſes her veil with a dramatic geſture, which proves how greatly our painter poſſeſſed all the reſources of his art. This picture, which has the dimenſions of a miniature, has all the grandeur and ſtyle of a monumental painting.

A fifth Laſt Judgment attributed to Beato Angelico is in the Muſeum at Berlin. M. H. Fortoul has eulogized it in his work on Germany.[1] Yet this is only a repetition, or perhaps a copy, of the picture

---

[1] *L'Art en Allemagne*, vol. ii, p. 248.

at Florence, and an awkward reftoration has a great deal leffened its value. In the gallery of the Uffizi, is alfo preferved the original defign of another Laft Judgment, but we are not acquainted with the picture.

Thus our painter has, many times, and always admirably, reprefented this grand fubject, which, in our days, we dare no longer undertake. We feem to have loft the comprehenfion of it, fince the gigantic talent of Michael Angelo has profaned it in the Siftine chapel, to the pitch of fcandalizing Aretino himfelf.[1] Painters have feen in it nothing more than an occafion of fhowing their talent by picturefque pofitions and fine laying-

---

[1] Cæfar Cantu, in his *Hiftorie Univerfelle*, vol. xiv, p. 255, gives this letter of Aretino, dated Venice :—"November, 1565. Is it poffible," fays he, " that the great Michael Angelo has wifhed to fhow as much religious impiety as artiftic perfection? Is it poffible that you, fo fuperior to men that you difdain their fociety,—*you* have done this in the greateft temple of God, over the firft altar of Jefus, in the moft renowned chapel of the world, in a place where the great cardinals of the Church, where venerable priefts and the Vicar of Chrift confefs, contemplate and adore His body, blood and flefh ? Your work would have been better fuited for a faloon of voluptuous baths than for fo auguft an affembly. But our fouls have more need of devotion than of vigour of defign. May God then infpire the fanctity of S. Paul, as He infpired the bleffednefs of Gregory, who preferred to ftrip Rome of the fuperb ancient ftatues rather than, on account of the perfection, to deprive the humble images of the faints of the reverence of their faithful."

Salvator Rofa, in his Satyres, alfo reproaches Michael Angelo for the nudities of the Siftine chapel, which to him looks like a ftove :—

" Dovevi pur diftinguere e penfare
Che dipingevi in chiefa : in quanto a me
Sembra una ftufa quefto voftro altare . . .
   Dunque là dove al ciel porgendo offerte
Il fovrano paftore i voti fcioglie,
S'hanno a veder le ofcenità fcoperte ?"

out of fcene. Therein is not the true aim of art. The love of glory is an egotiftical feeling, which leads genius aftray as it difturbs fociety. The love of God can alone realize the True, the Beautiful, and the Good, and preferve them in an admirable unity.

Chapter VIII.

PICTURES BY BEATO ANGELICO IN THE MUSEUMS AND CHURCHES OF FLORENCE.

HE painter of Fiefole has enriched particular churches, convents and chapels of Florence with his pictures. Thefe mafterpieces were made to be placed near the tabernacle, amidft the incenfe and lights, in order to ftir up the piety of the faithful. Revolutions have torn them from their fanctuaries, to expofe them in mufeums, where they contraft with all around them. Thofe Virgins, thofe Chrifts, thofe angels fo beautiful and pure, are now found mixed with ordinary portraits and the profane nudities of the Renaiffance: they are the facred veffels of the temple in the midft of Belthafar's feaft. Mufeums offer to 'the mind an idea of pillage and a proof of decay. Art is become enflaved and mercenary, when it no longer works for public monuments. It went and offered its works to the caprices of princes; and then palaces were filled with pictures infpired by intereft and vanity, but have afterwards received better guefts. They have collected religious paintings made for other places and other times. Mufeums are medleys like the world; each one can there choofe friends after his heart. Let us go there and feek Beato Angelico; and if we fome-times find him in bad company, the prefence of vice will make his virtue fhine more bright.

The gallery of the Academy of Fine Arts at Flo-rence is the richeft in Beato Angelico's pictures. Befides thofe we have fpoken of, it poffeffes other mafterpieces, which we are about to examine.

Without contradiction, the moft remarkable is the Defcent from the Crofs, in the room of the great pictures, No. 14. Vafari informs us that it was in the church of Santa Trinita. "In Santa Trinita," he fays, "a picture in the facrifty, reprefenting a Defcent from the Crofs, is executed with fo much care, that it may be reckoned amongft the beft works he ever did."[1] This picture is nearly one metre and feventy centimetres in height, and eighty centimetres in width: the upper part is divided into three ogives correfpond-ing with the three principal groups. The fummit of Calvary has been abandoned to the faithful difciples; the Crofs is placed in the centre of the compofition, two ladders are applied to it, the difciples refpectfully take down the body of our Lord laid in the fleep of death, and S. John is going to receive it tenderly into

---

[1] "In S. Trinità una tavola della fagreftia dove è un depofto di croce, nel quale mife tanta diligenza, che fi può fra megliori cofe che mai faceffe annoverare."

his arms. . This group is admirable for lines and expreffions. The Chrift is a very remarkable defign :
his fair body bears the marks of the fcourging; his
head is of a divine purity; on his cruciform aureola
are read the words, " CORONA GLORIE," the crown of
glory; for He had need to fuffer thus, to enter into
glory. On the right of the Saviour, is the group
of holy women bringing the linen for the burial;
S. Mary Magdalen is ftill kiffing his feet; and the
Holy Virgin contemplates him in the trance of grief.
The pious hand of the artift has written on her aureola
the praife he was daily reciting in her office : " O Virgin
Mary, there is none like unto thee," " VIRGO MARIA
N. E. T. SIMILIS." The other females furrounding her
are admirable for their attitude and expreffion. On
the oppofite fide, the difciples contemplate the fcene,
and difcourfe on the Paffion; the one neareft the Crofs
fhows with one hand the crown of thorns, and with
the other the three nails. It is impoffible to render
compaffion and gratitude in a more ftriking manner.
In the foreground of the picture, between this group
and the central one, a young man on his knees prays
to the Saviour, and, ftriking his breaft, adores him.
The painter has lent him all his own feelings. On
the frame beneath the Chrift, is read, " I am counted
among them that go down to the pit;" beneath the
holy women, " They fhall mourn Him as an only fon,
for He was innocent;" beneath the difciples, " Behold
how the Juft One dies, and no one thinketh of it in
his heart."[1]

---

[1] Eftimatus fum cum defcendentibus in lacum.
  Plangent eum *planctu* quafi *fuper* unigenitum, quia innocens.
  Ecce quomodo moritur Juftus, et nemo percipit corde.

M

Yet this fcene of anguifh has fomething of a
heavenly peace. It is the Paffion meditated with love
in folitude, and the tears it caufes to flow are fweeter
than all the joys of earth. A divine light feems to
illumine all the perfonages; and the painter has fpread
a beautiful carpet of flowers and verdure beneath their
feet. The landfcape is executed with incredible charms;
it is as fine and lightfome as the moft graceful per-
fpectives of Flemifh pictures. On one fide, is feen
the city of Jerufalem, and on the other, the mountains
of Judea. Angels appear in the fky, to unite in the
adoration of men. There is no picture which makes
the foul of Beato Angelico better underftood.[1] Here
are the holy thoughts with which he infpired a young
perfon, whofe impreffions the Count de Montalembert
has greatly wifhed us to impart. She wrote: "Oh,
what excefs of love of God, of immenfe and burning
contrition, muft that dear Beato Angelico have had
on the day he painted it! How he muft have meditated and wept, that day, in the depth of his little
cell, over the fufferings of our Divine Mafter! Every
ftroke of the pencil, every tint which came from it,
feem to be fo many acts of forrow and love iffuing from
the bottom of his foul. What a moving fermon is
the fight of fuch a picture! . . . O delicious mafterpiece! Oh, what a happinefs, what true grace, to be
able to contemplate, in this marvellous reprefentation
of our Lord's Paffion, the heart fo ardent and contrite
of the faint, which thus breathes the fentiments of

---

[1] There is a Defcent from the Crofs, by Starnina, which has fome refemblance
with Beato Angelico's. There are found in it, again, the difciple who carries the
crown and nails, and the one who is kneeling in the foreground. But what
inferiority! (See ROSINI, *Storia della Pittura*, t. xxxi.)

forrow and love inundating his foul, during his long hours paffed in the calm of folitude and in the prefence of God. Grant me, O Lord, fome part in this exceeding contrition, that whilft contemplating thefe works, my heart may be fo profoundly initiated, by this feraphic religious, into the way of Thy forrows, that I may inceffantly think of fharing in them, and urged by love, of entering into this road of the Crofs, every time it pleafeth Thee to fend me troubles. Perhaps I ought to limit my requeft to fubmiffion ; but it is too little. Oh ! yes, the force of love, that is what I figh for, that is what I entreat Thee to grant me, after having feen all the works of Thy painter. Others look at them fimply as works of art. I myfelf have drawn from them—I feel it—unfpeakable confolation and deep inftruction."[1] It is impoffible to make a more fplendid eulogy on this picture. Has ever work of art infpired fuch feelings ?

This compofition is framed with little pictures, as a diamond is furrounded with precious pearls. Thefe pictures, twenty in number, are real mafterpieces. We will particularly point out, on the left, S. Lawrence, of an admirably purity ; S. Francis of Affifi ; S. Michael, whofe head is fet off by his golden wings : on the right, S. Jerome, holding an iron difcipline and a ftone, with which he has made his breaft bleed ; S. Stephen, of charming youth ; S. Dominic, with the capuce on his head ; S. Peter Martyr ; and S. Peter the Apoftle, holding the keys and book. All thefe figures are admirable in execution and of great character. The upper part of the picture is crowned with three fub-

[1] *Du Vandalifme et du Catholicifme dans l'Art*, p. 97.

jeéts, not by our painter, but attributed to Lorenzo
degl' Angeli, a Camaldolefe monk. The fubjeéts of
them are, the Refurreétion, the holy women at the
fepulchre, and the *Noli me tangere.*[1]

[1] ["The painting of the Depofition from the Crofs is about feven palms high
by eight wide; its upper part is pointed, or, to fpeak more intelligibly, is in
the form of three triangles, which are divided from the principal painting by a
gilded cornice. The points and cornice are beautifully chifelled and painted, the
former being ornamented with many little hiftories, and the latter with fome
minute figures of Saints, fomewhat larger in their dimenfions, and certainly far
more perfeét than thofe which he executed in the Perugian painting. Contrary to his ufual idea, he here reprefents Mount Calvary clothed with flowers and
verdure, as though he meant to fignify that the foot-prints and blood of the
Redeemer caufed the moft beautiful vegetation to flourifh on that accurfed hill.
That fuch was the painter's idea may be colleéted from the faét of the diftant
mountains in the back ground (the perfpeétive of which is admirable,) being tree-
lefs and herblefs, if we except here and there fome ifolated palm. On the oppofite fide is a good perfpeétive of Jerufalem, defigned and finifhed with incredible
diligence. The figures are difpofed in three groups; in the centre are two
difciples, who, ftanding on the fteps of the ladder that leans againft the Crofs,
lower the Redeemer's body; at the ladder's foot two difciples fupport the fanctified remains, and the youngeft of the two who betrays fuch wonderful emotion
is the Evangelift John; a fifth, proftrate on the earth, adores the body, and raifing
his hand to his breaft feems to fay, '*I fhould have died this ignominious death!*'
The group on the left prefents fix figures, one of which holds the thorny crown
in his right hand, and in his left the bloody nails wherewith the Redeemer's
hands and feet were pierced; whilft he exhibits them to an old man who contemplates them in profound dolor. . . . Two of the difciples gaze intently on
the dead body of Chrift, and in their midft is one who, unable to reftrain his tears,
buries his face in his hands and fobs almoft audibly. . . . The group on the
right is compofed of pious women. Whofoever would find the tender and loving
Magdalene let him feek her at the feet of Jefus. The Angelico reprefents her
fupporting them and imprinting her laft kifs on them. Behind her is the Mother.
Oh! what a woe-begone Mother! Grief and agony have fo wrung her heart,
that the eye knows not on which of the two objeéts it fhould reft—the lifelefs
body of the Lord, or on her, the moft afflicted of women! Who can behold this
work and not feel love and forrow ftirring in his heart? Two women hold the
winding-fheet, and two others contemplate the poignant anguifh of Mary; but
the laft figure at the fide is the moft beautiful of all; it is that of a woman whofe
whole perfon is robed in a violet mantle, which fhe gracefully gathers over her
bofom, thus revealing only the exquifite beauty of her face. The figure of the
Redeemer is perfeétion itfelf, and nothing can exceed the foftnefs of the lines or

The Academy of Fine Arts poffeffes a picture which feems to be the continuation of this Defcent from the Crofs, and to have been executed at the fame time. It is the Burial, found in the room of little paintings, and made for the confraternity of Santa Croce del Tempio.[1]

This compofition is full of touching melancholy. It is no longer the heavenly brightnefs which fhone juft now on the height of Calvary, but the fweet evening twilight when the day is only a recollection. The fcene takes place near the walls of Jerufalem, in a lonely garden. All are paying their laft homage to the Sacred Body of the Saviour. The inftruments of his Paffion, his crown, and the nails which lefs than his love faftened him to the Crofs, are placed near him as the infignia of his royalty. Amongft the holy women and difciples, Beato Angelico has painted S. Dominic and Beata Villana, a tertiary, whofe relics repofe at Santa Maria Novella. In front of her we read thefe words : xpo ihv, lamor mio crvcifisso : Chrift Jefus, my crucified love. It is the cry of all thefe perfonages, as well as of our painter.

In the fame room, are alfo many pictures by Beato Angelico. No. 43, a picture in two parts : below, the Adoration of the Magi ; above, a Pietà. The head of Chrift is very beautiful. Unfortunately this painting is damaged. Nos. 51 and 54, fragments of the Legend

the delicate tranfparency of the mezzotints. The nude which exhibits the ftripes of the fcourge and the marks of the nails is moft correct. The anatomy is well defined ; nor is there a fingle trace of that harfhnefs that offends us in the productions of the Giotto fchool.—Marchese, by *Meehan,* vol. i, p. 231. Translator's note.]

[1] Per la compagnia del Tempio di Firenze fece in una tavola un Crifto morto.

of S S. Cofmas and Damian. Thefe two pictures are badly preferved and much inferior to thofe we fhall find in the chapel of the Painters at the Nunciata. No. 39, a Madonna holding the Child Jefus. The ftyle recalls the painting at Perugia and Cortona. The head of the Virgin is of great purity. This picture is furmounted with a reprefentation of the Holy Trinity.

The exhibition-room of the Academy of Fine Arts offers us three other very remarkable Madonnas.

No. 13. The Bleffed Virgin, clothed in a blue mantle, holds the Child Jefus on her knees; two angels in bright red robes are behind her throne; on the right, S. Peter Martyr, S. Cofmas and S. Damian; on the left, S. Francis, S. Antony and S. Auguftin. The architectural background recalls the defigns of Brunel-lefchi. This picture is remarkable for drawing and colouring. The gradino is not fo well preferved: in the centre, a Pietà; on one fide, S. Dominic, S. Bernardine and S. Peter the Apoftle; and on the other, S. Peter Martyr, S. Mark and S. Auguftin.

No. 16 is probably the altar-piece executed by Beato Angelico for the high altar of San Marco.[1] Accord-ing to the teftimony of Vafari, it was one of the moft beautiful works of the artift, but its ftate of preferva-tion now leaves much to be defired. The Holy Virgin is

---

[1] Ma particolarmente è bella a maraviglia la tavola dell' altar maggiore di quella chiefa, perchè oltre che la Madonna muove a divozione chi la guarda per la femplicità fua, e che i fanti che le fono intorno fono fimili a lei, la predella nella quale fono ftorie del martirio di S. Cofimo e Damiano, e degli altri, è tanto ben fatta, che non è poffibile immaginarfi di poter veder mai cofa fatta con più dili-genza, nè le più delicate o meglio intefe figurine di quelle.—This gradino is in the chapel of the Painters, in the cloifter of the Nunciata.

feated upon a throne, furrounded with angels. On her right, are S. Dominic, S. Francis and S. Peter Martyr; and on her left, S. Lawrence, S. Paul and S. Mark. S S. Cofmas and Damian, patrons of the Medici, are kneeling before her. All thefe perfonages are grouped with great fkill: there is no longer the fymmetry of the fchool of Giotto. The back-ground is decorated with architecture and garlands of flowers. A magnificent carpet is fpread before the throne, whereon a Crucifixion is painted, which the prieft faw from the altar.

No. 17. This picture is well preferved. The Madonna is upon her throne, and the Child Jefus holds an opened pomegranate, fymbol of the charity which would lead him to Calvary. His mother contemplates him with a kind of fear. Around the throne are S S. Cofmas and Damian, S. Peter Martyr, S. John the Evangelift, S. Francis and S. Lawrence. This picture is feebler in drawing than the preceding ones.

On entering the gallery of the Uffizi, at Florence, one of the firft pictures we met with, on the left, is the magnificent altar-piece executed by Beato Angelico for the Guild of flax-workers,' about 1433. The Guilds of workmen played a great part in the hiftory of the Italian Republics. At Florence, it was neceffary to belong to them, in order to take part in the government; and on that condition only was Dante, in 1300, nominated prior of the city. We have not to examine what thefe Guilds did, in the middle ages, for liberty and for

---

' Vafari and Marchefe both ftate that the painting was executed for the Guild of *Joiners*. TRANSLATOR's note.

developing induftry; we will only remark that they were intelligent and powerful protections to the arts. As their conftitution was eminently religious, they raifed monuments, chapels which the moft fkilful artifts decorated; and a noble rivalry exifted amongft them, and led them to make the greateft facrifices. They carried on their work with perfeverance, and paid with royal munificence. Tafte for the Beautiful was thus developed in the multitude, and art remained religious and popular. The flax-workers defired to have a fine altar-piece with doors, for their place of affembling. They had afked a defign from Lorenzo Ghiberti, which did not pleafe them; fo they applied to Beato Angelico, and our painter knew better than that celebrated artift how to fatisfy their defire and devotion. The panel was prepared October 29th, 1432;[1] and, July 11th, 1433, the Guild fettled the conditions following:—"They have agreed with Fra Guido, called Fra Giovanni, of the Order of S. Dominic, of Fiefole, to paint a tabernacle of our Lady, to be painted infide and outfide, with colours, and diverfified with gold and filver the beft and fineft to be found, with all his fkill and induftry: and for all and for his pains and labour, to have one hundred and ninety florins in gold, or what lefs he can in confcience, and with the figures in his drawing."[2]

[1] BALDINUCCI, *Notizie di profeffori del difegno*, decenn. 2, part i, § iv.

[2] Allogorono a frate Guido, vocato frate Giovanni dell' ordine di S. Domenico di Fiefole, a dipingere un tabernacolo di noftra Donna, nella detta arte, dipinto di dentro e fuori, con colori, oro e argento variato, de' megliori e più fini che fi trovino, con ogni fua arte e induftria, per tutto et per fua fatica e manifattura, per fiorini cento novanta d'oro, o quello meno che parrà alla fua cofienza, e con quelle figure che fono nel difegno.—P. MARCHESE, t. i, p. 235.

Beato Angelico was faithful to thefe conditions. He was lavifh of his gold and fkill: and it is one of his richeft and moft remarkable pictures. The Bleffed Virgin is entirely covered with a blue mantle all embroidered with gold. She holds, ftanding upon her knees, the Child Jefus, who carries the world in his left hand, and bleffes with his right. The Holy Ghoft is hovering in the upper part. The background of the picture is fpread with a magnificent curtain of cloth of gold. In the breadth of the frame, are painted twelve angels adoring and playing on various inftruments. Thefe angels are mafterpieces of gracefulnefs and purity. We will efpecially point out the one clothed in a red robe and founding a kind of crooked trumpet. On the little doors of this altar-piece, are reprefented, infide, S. John Baptift and S. Mark, and outfide, S. Mark and S. Peter. S. Mark is on both fides, being patron of the flax-workers.

This picture is executed on a ground of gold, which muft have produced a very happy effect in the place, doubtlefs a little obfcure, where it was fixed. It is now too much lighted, and the painting appears too tranfparent. The gradino of this altar-piece is at the fide, and reprefents three fubjects.

1. The Preaching of S. Peter. S. Mark feems to be writing his fermon, to fhow that he wrote his gofpel under the dictation of the chief of the Apoftles.

2. A beautiful Adoration of the Magi.

3. The Martyrdom of S. Mark.

The Coronation of the Virgin, in the gallery of the Uffizi, is later than the one in the Mufeum of the Louvre, and recalls many parts of it; but the composition is more airy and more heavenly. The scene takes place in the splendour of glory. From the centre, as from the bosom of God, golden rays issue and serve for the background of all the picture. Christ and his Mother are seated on light clouds. The Blessed Virgin is clothed in a blue mantle studded with small stars, her hands are crossed on her breast, and she bends down, with love and respect, towards her Son. The Saviour, vested in a blue mantle and bright red robe, is not crowning Mary, but stretches out his hand to add a magnificent diamond to her crown. What thought has inspired the artist? What privilege, what divine grace has he wished to represent by this diamond? We do not know. But could we not thus figure the honour which the Church is rendering to Mary, in proclaiming the dogma of the Immaculate Conception? Is not this the fairest jewel in the crown which God destined for her in His eternal designs? A troop of angels surround the Queen of Heaven, and celebrate her triumph with dances and concerts. To paint angels so beautiful, Beato Angelico must have seen them. He has heard their songs, and shared their joy, and he has reflected them in all these charming figures.

In the lower part of the picture, are disposed on clouds two groups of saints, male and female, reminding us of those in the Coronation at the Louvre. The chief ones are, S. Nicholas of Bari, S. Giles, S. Dominic, S. Jerome, S. Benedict, S. Peter and S. Paul. S. Dominic again holds a book and a lily, but the head is not the same, as it is a three-quarter face and bearded.

Amongſt the female ſaints, are remarked, S. Mary Magdalen, S. Catherine of Alexandria, S. Catherine of Sienna, and one who carries a lighted lamp like the wiſe virgins. Near this group, is alſo found S. Stephen, protećtor of the weak, and S. Peter Martyr, patron of virginity. This maſterpiece was executed for the Chartreuſe at Florence.[1] We cannot forbear regretting that it is now in a muſeum, and that this pićture, made for praying and meditating on heaven, is placed beſide one of the ſaddeſt nudities of the Renaiſſance.

The ſame room poſſeſſes three other ſmall pićtures by Beato Angelico.

1. Zacharias writing the name of S. John Baptiſt. The woman holding the ink-horn is charmingly natural.[2]

2. The Marriage of the Bleſſed Virgin. This ſubjećt, which we have already ſeen at Cortona, recalls the freſco of Taddeo Gaddi, eſpecially in the three principal perſonages. In the two compoſitions, a dove is placed on the bloſſomed branch of S. Joſeph, to mark his purity.

3. The Death of the Virgin. The painter has followed the traditional compoſition. Our Lord holds the ſoul of the Holy Virgin, and bleſſes her body, which muſt ſoon be glorified in heaven. Angels are holding torches and cenſers; and the Apoſtles are ranged all

---

[1] Una delle prime opere che faceſſe queſto buon padre di pittura, fu nella Certoſa di Florenza una tavola che fu poſta nella maggior capella del cardinale degli Acciainoli. . . . Nella crociera di detta cappella ſono due altre tavole di mano di medeſimo; in una è la Incoronazione di noſtra Donna.

[2] Lanzi loved this little pićture very much: "La R. Galleria ne ha diverſi, e il più gajo e finito è quello della Naſcita del Batiſta."

around, with their names written in their aureolas.
This auguſt ceremony cannot be repreſented in a
nobler and more ſolemn manner.

The gallery of the Pitti palace poſſeſſes only one
picture by Beato Angelico. It is found in the Hall
of Juſtice, No. 399, and calls to mind the firſt Madonnas of our painter, by its ſtyle and ogival ſhape.
The Bleſſed Virgin is holding a gold vaſe, whence her
Divine Son takes a piece of gold. By this pure
metal, the painter has perhaps wiſhed to expreſs the
moſt pure fleſh, which the Word has taken in Mary's
moſt pure womb. On the right, S. Dominic and
S. John Baptiſt; on the left, S. Peter and S. Thomas
Aquinas. In the three angles of the upper part, are
repreſented, in the middle, the Crucifixion; and on
each ſide, the Annunciation. In the arch which frames
the ogives, are ſeen the Preaching and the Martyrdom
of S. Peter, who is writing with his blood the firſt
words of the Credo.

If the religious of Santa Maria Novella had loſt the
fervour and ſanctity of their founders, they had
preſerved at leaſt the artiſtic traditions. They ſtill called
for the moſt celebrated painters to decorate the walls
raiſed by Fra Siſto and Fra Riſtoro. Simone Memmi,
Orcagna and Taddeo Gaddi had enriched their church
and cloiſters with maſterpieces, and they invited Beato
Angelico to execute ſome pictures near thoſe of theſe
great men, whom he worthily ſucceeded. He worked
there, doubtleſs, at the ſame time as Maſſacio, who was
ſo well qualified to underſtand and love his talent.
Vaſari tells us that he painted in freſco, in the
tranſept of the church, in front of the choir-door,

S. Dominic, S. Catherine of Sienna and S. Peter Martyr, and fome little pictures in the chapel of the Rofary. He alfo painted on canvas an Annunciation for the little doors of the old organ.[1] Thefe paintings no longer exift; but there are ftill three pictures which adorned the reliquaries made by Giovanni Mafi, a religious of the convent, who died in 1430.[2] The picture on another reliquary and the decoration of a pafchal candle, fpoken of by Vafari, have been loft.[3]

The firft reliquary at Santa Maria Novella reprefents a Madonna ftanding, with a ftar over her head. The Child Jefus leans on her neck, and feems to be fpeaking to her, and lavifhing his divine careffes: the Bleffed Virgin is liftening with a tender melancholy. In the upper part and almoft outfide the ogive framing it, the Saviour, furrounded by angels' heads, regards her and lets a crown fall upon her head. In the border, are painted angels offering their homage and incenfe to her. The two angels feated at her feet are fingering a little organ, and are feparated by a beautiful vafe of flowers. In the part ferving as the bafe of the picture, are reprefented

---

[1] Dipinfe dopo nel trameffo di S. Maria Novella in frefco, accanto alla pofta dirimpetto al coro S. Domenico, S. Caterina da Siena, e S. Pietro Martire, ed alcune ftoriette piccole nella capella dell' Incoronazione di noftra Donna, nel detto trameffo. In tela fece nei portelli che chiudevana l'organo vecchio una Nunciata, che è oggi in convento dirimpetto alla porta del dormentorio da baffo fra l'un chioftro e l'altro.

[2] Habemus et multas plurimorum fanctorum reliquias, quas quidam Fr. Joannes Mafius Florentinus, multæ devotionis et taciturnitatis vir, in quatuor inclufit tabulas, quas Fr. Joannes Fefulanus pictor, cognomento Angelicus, pulcherrimis beatiffimæ Mariæ Virginis et fanctorum Angelorum ornavit figuris. Obiit Fr. Joannes Mafius anno M CCCC XXX.—BILIOTTI *Chronica*, MS., c. xix, p. 24.

[3] In S. Maria Novella, oltre alle chofe dette, dipinfe di ftorie piccole il cereo pafquale, ed alcuni reliquieri che nelle maggiori folennità fi pongono in full' altara.

S. Dominic; S. Peter Martyr; and S. Thomas Aquinas bearing a little church whence a light iffues, to call to mind the eulogy of the fovereign pontiffs, who have proclaimed him *the Light of the Church.*

The fecond reliquary is divided into two parts, reprefenting the Annunciation and the Adoration of the Magi, the homage of heaven and earth.

The Annunciation. The Holy Virgin is feated, with her arms croffed on her breaft. She is receiving the falutation of the angel who inclines before her. Between the heavenly ambaffador and Mary, who was to be mother of the Saviour, is placed a vafe full of rofes, out of which three beautiful lilies efcape, in honour of her who was thrice virgin,—before, in, and after her delivery. In the upper part, is feen the youthful figure of our Saviour carrying the world, and advancing, preceded by the Holy Ghoft.

The Adoration of the Magi. The Bleffed Virgin, clothed in a magnificent mantle, prefents the Child Jefus to the old Magian king, proftrate at his feet. S. Jofeph is holding the prefent he is come to make. The two other kings wait for their turn. The perfonages of their fuite are looking at the ftar, which appears above the roof of the ruftic ftable. All the background is ornamented with rich tapeftry. This picture is executed with an admirable grace and purity.

In the part ferving to fupport the picture, are fketched ten ravifhing figures of female faints, and one of them, the Virgin embraced by her Son, occupies the centre.

The firft is S. Catherine of Sienna, with the infcription, B. CATHERINA DI SEIS. She is reprefented hold-

ing a book in her right hand, and in her left a heart
with a golden centre. Her mantle is black and veil
white, like thofe of tertiaries. Her profile recalls the
type we have remarked at the Louvre and in the
gallery of the Uffizi. The picture is anterior to the
canonization of this great faint, which took place in
1460; but the procefs of Venice made in 1411 for
the Dominicans who celebrated her feftival, had, fo
to fay, authorized her cultus.

After S. Catherine, come S. Appollonia with the
pincers, S. Margaret, S. Agatha carrying eyes in a
vafe, S. Mary Magdalen, S. Agnes, S. Cecilia,
S. Dorothy with her mantle full of flowers, and
S. Urfula with her arrow.

The third reliquary reprefents the Coronation of
the Virgin, and recalls by its difpofition the picture at
the Louvre. The Holy Virgin, kneeling before her Son,
is furrounded with angels; a great number of faints
are grouped below the fteps of the throne. To us, it
is evident that this picture is not by Beato Angelico,
but by Fra Benedetto. It fuffices to compare it with
the works of our painter, to comprehend the difference
of talent in the two brothers. Here are feen a religious thought and a wifh to follow his model; but
the whole compofition is wanting in order and fpace.
The figures are heavy, the attitudes awkward, the proportions fhort, the outlines clumfy and the painting
painful. On the pedeftal, the fame hand has reprefented the Child Jefus adored by the Holy Virgin and
S. Jofeph, in the midft of angels who are dancing
and playing the tabour.

The Chapel of Painters dedicated to S. Luke, in

the cloifter of the Nunciata, poffeffes fix charming
little pictures by Beato Angelico framed in the gradino
of the altar. They were formerly placed at the bottom
of the altar-piece made for the new church of the
convent of San Marco, and reprefent the legend of
S S. Cofmas and Damian.

1. Palladia, being cured by the two phyficians, prefents a purfe full of gold to S. Damian, who will not
receive it.

2. S S. Cofmas and Damian and their three brothers appear before the proconful Lilias.

3. The two faints are caft into the fea, and are
brought out by an angel.

4. They are condemned to the fire; the flames rufh
on the by-ftanders.

5. They are crucified, and the arrows intended to
pierce them recoil on the executioners.

6. The five brothers are beheaded.

Vafari cites thefe pictures amongft the mafterpieces
of Beato Angelico, and fays it is impoffible to imagine
anything executed with greater care, or figures more
delicate or more judicioufly conceived.[1] In fact, the
poetry of the legends of the middle ages cannot be
given in a happier manner.   Beato Angelico preferved
at Fiefole the frefhnefs and gracefulnefs of his imagination, for all he was developing his talent by the
ftudy of the material progrefs which art was then
making at Florence.

[1] See the text of Vafari, p. 166.

CHAPTER IX

*BEATO ANGELICO AT FLORENCE.—HIS RELATIONS
WITH BRUNELLESCHI, GHIBERTI AND MASSACIO.*

LORY had vifited the cell of the humble religious; churches and princes contended for his mafter-pieces, and Cofimo de Medici, who particularly loved our painter, wifhed to have him near him, in the convent of San Marco, where he had eftablifhed the reformed Dominicans of Fiefole. Beato Angelico was obliged to quit his dear folitude, and go to mingle in the artiftic movement at Florence. He had certainly obferved it already from the heights of his mountain, and had profited by it, but he now found himfelf more in connection with the celebrated artifts of that time; and it is very important to examine what he did amidft their new tendencies.

The firft half of the fifteenth century is perhaps the moft interefting epoch of art. Then really began the

N

Renaiffance, which has been the object of fuch contradictory appreciations: and at Florence muft be ftudied the various elements that compofe it. Beato Angelico knew how to diftinguifh and choofe them out; and his example muft be followed by all who defire a better future for Chriftian art.

Three contemporaries of Beato Angelico may be regarded as the fathers of the Renaiffance, and they are Brunellefchi, Ghiberti and Maffaccio. To them, architecture, fculpture and painting owe a new direction. We proceed to examine in what it was favourable or prejudicial, and will feek the truth amidft extreme opinions, at the rifk, perhaps, of not conciliating any one. Architecture, fculpture and painting are three means of art which muft not be feparated from each other, any more than the thought of the orator from his word and gefture. They have always been clofely united during the great epochs of art, and their tendency to feparation has been one of the chief defects of the Renaiffance. Still architecture has always preferved a certain paramount influence: the fculptor and painter are fet off by the architect. The architect is the leader of the orcheftra, who conducts the concert.

To comprehend the influence of Brunellefchi at Florence, it is neceffary to know what was the ftate of architecture before him.

Every nation has its architecture, becaufe every nation has its character, fcenery and different materials, which explain the diverfities of forms invefting the fame doctrines. Thefe diverfities are very ftriking in the Italian Republics of the middle ages, although they were fo near together. Florence, Sienna, Perugia, Pifa and Bologna have not the fame monuments, and their monuments always harmonize with the type of their population. Man, as God does, leaves his ftamp and image on his works. Every national architecture, in its regular developement, creates three ftyles correfponding to the three periods we have marked out in art: the hieratic, the learned and the naturaliftic periods.[1] Form is fucceffively developed, juft as human thought expreffes itfelf, firft by affirmation, then by precifion, and at length by the embellifhment of imagery. Thence three ftyles of architecture, the chief qualities of which are fimplicity, elegance, or richnefs. Thefe three ftyles have received in Greece the name of the people whofe genius they beft reprefented, and have been called the Doric, Ionic and Corinthian orders. Thefe orders are diftinguifhed by the embellifhments, and efpecially by the proportions. Vitruvius has given the ftandard of thefe proportions; but this ftandard has nothing abfolute, for genius cannot be imprifoned within invariable limits. The proportions of the Parthenon, the mafterpiece of ancient art, do not agree with the ciphers of Roman architecture. The columns themfelves are not equal between them. The artift acts on matter with the liberty of the Creator, who, in nature, is pleafed to vary the geometrical forms of flowers.

Roman art has gone through the three phafes we are about to point out. Under Greek influence, it

See page 5.

has paſſed from the Tuſcan to the Compoſite ſtyle. In regard to the nations of the middle ages, united by the Church in relations not to be ſlighted when we wiſh to ſtudy the hiſtory of art, architecture has followed the ſame rules with greater or leſs rapidity, according to circumſtances and countries. An original architecture is raiſed on the ruins of the ancient monuments; its firſt form becomes developed from Charlemagne until the Cruſades, and is the Romaneſque ſtyle. It then appears elegant and noble in the reigns of Philippe Auguſte and S. Louis. It has at laſt diſplayed its richneſs down to the years of the decadence preceding the Renaiſſance. Theſe three epochs correſpond with the three Greek ſtyles.

We regret that we are unable to examine at greater lengths the connections between ancient and mediæval architecture. We will only ſay that if Greek architecture attained perfection within a narrow ſphere, Chriſtian architecture developed a vaſter doctrine and greater liberty with more powerful reſults. Its ſtyles are not defined by columns and capitals, but by more general characteriſtics and more varied ornaments. Its moſt perfect ſtyle, uniting in an admirable elegance the ſimplicity of the firſt epoch with the richneſs of the third, has laſted throughout all the Cruſades, and has employed two different forms, the rounded arch and the ogive.[1] Theſe two ſtyles, dialects of the ſame language, are intereſting for the ſtudy of our ſubject. Some have wiſhed to eſtabliſh a rivalry or antagoniſm between them: and the ogive has had, in theſe latter

---

[1] The Ogive is deſignated by Engliſh writers, the *Pointed Style*. [TRANSLATOR's note.]

times, as paffionate admirers as it formerly had unjuft detractors. Some enthufiafts have wifhed to fee in it the exclufive and abfolute fet-form of Chriftian archi-tecture, and the greateft reproach they make againft the Renaiffance is for having abandoned it. Brunel-lefchi is the firft culprit, and we fhall fee if Beato Angelico has not been his accomplice.

What is the origin of the ogive? A great deal has been faid on this queftion, which has long been a butt for the reveries of poets and for the erudition of the learned.[1] The former feek its origin in foreft fhades, the latter have given the honour of it to the genius of the Eaft, whilft archæologifts have been willing to affign it a place, name and date glorious to their own country. For our part, ogival architecture is no more an imitation of forefts than it is a foreign importation, nor is it the patented invention of any individual. It is the natural developement of the rounded arch, not belonging to any one in particular, but fettled and perfected by artifts in general. What is a monument, a work of architecture? It is an affemblage of lines, ftraight or curved, perpendicular or horizontal, com-bined fo as to produce an impreffion on man. For a church particularly, it is a means, an optical effect created by the artift. The ogive and the rounded arch produce different effects; but we fay that the effect of the ogive or pointed arch has been fuggefted by the very effect of the femicircular arch. Ogival

---

[1] M. l'Abbé Bouraffé, in his *Archeologie chretienne*, chap. x, has thoroughly fummed up and determined the opinions of the learned on the origin of the ogive. This excellent manual has very much contributed in France to fpread the ftudy of our old monuments. A good elementary work is one of the greateft fervices which could be rendered to the fcience.

architecture is the legitimate offspring of Romanesque architecture. With us its name is the certificate of its birth.

Whilst erecting churches in the rounded style, architects employed stone arches to support the ridges of the vaulted roofs. These supports were called *ogives*, and the curves of these ogives, by meeting at right angles, gave in geometry and perspective all the variations of the equilateral arch. If a person is placed under the vaults of a church in the rounded style of the twelfth century, he will experience the same optical effect as in an ogival church. The only line interrupting the upward tendency of the lines is the principal arch which separates the bays. This arch, in the rounded style, becomes pointed by degrees, first in the arch of the sanctuary, then in the arches of the nave, either as a means of construction for diminishing the pressure of the roof, or for unity and harmony, because the pointed arch agrees better with the tracery of the ogival windows. The pointed arch is also placed upon the rounded arch, which separates the nave from the aisles, just as in the same monument the Ionic order has been placed upon the Doric, because what supports must be simpler and stronger than what is supported. These two different styles do not destroy unity, but only give to the eye the impression of greater height, like the lessening dimensions of a column.

The pointed arch or ogive has thus been naturally and progressively systematized in architecture, and to explain it we have no need of recourse to a foreign importation, or to a local and individual invention.

The adoption of the ogival ftyle was not effected in Italy as in France and Germany. Architecture was lefs rapidly and freely developed there, becaufe it was more tied to imitating ancient edifices better preferved than in other countries.

The rounded arch was an Italian creation, and the employment of it forms the difference between the architectures of Rome and Athens. It was precifely the Etrufcans, forefathers of the Florentines, who introduced it into Rome, whilft building the earlieft monuments there. The North had ftill an influence on the architecture of Italy in the middle ages. In our opinion, the fineft church of the ancient Republic of Florence is San Miniato, evidently built by German artifts during the omnipotence of the empire.

In Italy, the ogive is an importation due to the triumph of the architects of the North, in the competition opened to the whole of Europe for the church to crown the tomb of S. Francis of Affifi. It is an exotic plant which languifhes in a foreign land. James of Germany, after he had raifed his mafter-piece, went to Florence, where he worked for the Republic, and died in 1360. He founded a fchool, and the beft pupils of it were the Dominicans, Fra Sifto and Fra Riftoro, who built Santa Maria Novella, the *Bride* of Michael Angelo.

Arnolfo di Lapo, who was the fon of James of Germany, as many learned think,[1] did not manage the ogive with the fame liberty as the architects of the North did. He was pre-occupied with the great maffes

---

[1] Lapo might be the Tufcan diminutive of Jacopo.

of the ancient bafilicas, and his chief works (Santa
Croce and Santa Maria dei Fiori) cannot be compared
with the other ogival churches of Tufcany. They
have neither the gracefulnefs of the cathedral of Sienna,
nor the richnefs of San Martino at Lucca, nor the
character fo impofing of Santa Petrona at Bologna.
Their façade has not been finifhed: it feems that the
national impulfe had failed. Santa Croce, in the huge
ogives of which are encafed the pagan tombs raifed by
the Florentines to their great men, with its bare beams
refembles an unfinifhed church. Its beauty is altogether in the fine line of chapels at the farther end,
which dazzles the eyes by the glare of the large
glafs windows. Santa Maria dei Fiori is gigantic; but
the effect of the interior, which is the moft important
in Chriftian architecture, is not happy: the light does
not lighten up the barenefs of the walls. It is true
Arnolfo did not finifh it, but left the central part to
be crowned by Brunellefchi. The exterior is decorated
rather by a painter than by an architect. The ancients
fet off the details of their architecture with colour;
but this was only a fecondary means, and they gave
deep fhadows to their maffes and profile. The exterior
of Santa Maria dei Fiori is an inlaid work of marble,
and the merit of it difappears at a diftance. The
influence of the artift is felt, to whom is attributed
the Campanile, much inferior to the Tower of Pifa, the
work of a German architect. The Campanile at Florence has beautiful details and great elevation, but it
feems to us to be as wanting in bafement as in crowning. The mafterpiece of the fchool of Giotti is the

Loggia, by Orcagna, which has the rounded arch, and takes on the national ftyle again.

Brunellefchi came at a moment when all artifts were paffionately ftudying ancient monuments, and he had to choofe between the ogive and the rounded arch. His ftudies and genius made him prefer the rounded arch. He was fettered in the completion of Santa Maria dei Fiori; he went back to ftudy the monuments of Rome, and wifhed to place the cupola of the Pantheon over the ogives of Arnolfo. He wrought perhaps a greater architectural miracle than that of Michael Angelo in the dome of S. Peter's, but the interior effect in his work is to be lamented; for the clear light of Florence never penetrates there, and the great offices have to be celebrated by candle-light.[1] Brunellefchi was not in his element, and returned to the rounded arch. His mafterpiece is the church of San Spirito. He refumed the ancient Latin bafilica, and wifhed to give it all the elegance and lightnefs of ogival churches, whilft wholly preferving the ancient forms and natural traditions. We believe that he was right, and that this Renaiffance in architecture has been legitimate. It has been a progrefs on the anarchy and decline caufed by the introduction of a foreign architecture, like as the Italian Renaiffance was, in our opinion, a progrefs for French architecture led away by Flemifh influence and the fhameleffnefs of the fifteenth century. Moreover, architecture, by its contact with pagan art, has to fear corruption lefs than fculpture and painting have, becaufe it is not fo eafily given over to

---

[1] We have feen the choir-books lighted at the High Mafs on Afcenfion-day.

individual caprice and paffions. We believe that the
era of Brunellefchi has been the great epoch in the
architecture of Florence.

Has Ghiberti rendered the fame fervice to fculpture? He had the fame tafte for the ftudy of the
antique; but his paffion for form made him forget
the great traditions of Chriftian art. The march of
his talent is feen in his gates of the Baptiftry at
Florence. Thofe made by him, in addition to the
ones by Andrea Pifano, harmonize with the lines of the
architecture, but they have not the noble and fimple
ftyle of his rival, whofe compofitions remind us of the
fkill and purity of the Greek bas-reliefs. His figures
project too much: ftill his vivacity is kept within
bounds, and he gives every liberty to his genius in
the central gate. We cannot, indeed, grow weary in
admiring the unheard of luxury in ornamenting there
difplayed, that vigorous modelling, thofe little ancient
ftatues, that marvellous chafing which time feems defirous to refpect. The compofitions on the panels
are very remarkable, the groups are excellent, the proportions elegant and the draperies graceful. Raphael
muft have ftudied them a great deal. But we cannot
equally praife the landfcape grounds. Inftead of fome
fimple lines ferving to frame-in the figures, the fculptor has modelled trees, deepenings and mountains,
and has led his art away into the domain of painting.
To fum up, we cannot fay, with Michael Angelo, that
thefe are worthy of being the gates of Paradife,[1] for
the artift made them for his own and not for God's

---

[1] Elle fon tanto belle, ch' elle ftarebbon bene alle porte del paradifo.—VASARI, *Vita di Lorenzo Ghiberti.*

glory, and has fought to give rather beautiful forms
than holy thoughts; but we look on them as the
principal work of the Renaiffance, and the richeft
ornament of the temple which the fixteenth century
would raife to natural beauty. Donatello followed in
the fame way as Ghiberti. The Chriftian fentiment
difappeared in his finging and dancing children, and
he replaces it by fimplicity of expreffion and the gracefulnefs of youth. It is a nature that fuffers itfelf to
be carried away by earthly paffions, but ftill preferves
the charm of bafhfulnefs. Lucca della Robbia better
refifted being dragged along by his epoch, and remained religious and popular in his works.

Maffaccio reprefents the progrefs of the Renaiffance
in painting: it is he that profited moft by the example of Ghiberti. Two principal works fhow how far
he went: his paintings in the church of San Clemente
at Rome, and in the chapel of the Carmine at Florence. Maffaccio, too, went to vifit the Eternal City;
and, as with Brunellefchi and the other artifts of his
epoch, it was no longer to pray at the tomb of S. Peter
and of the martyrs, but to admire the ruins and divini-
ties of the heathen world. When he arrived, he was
ftill the man of Chriftian traditions; all the poetry of
them is found again in his Hiftory of S. Catherine
of Alexandria. He is worthy to be compared with
Beato Angelico for the purity of his talent. But when
he returns to Florence, his mind is changed, and he
carries off the idea of a material perfection, which he
purfues and attains in the chapel of the Carmine.

This chapel is a celebrated date in hiftory, becaufe
for painting it marked out the advent of the Renaif-

fance.   The oldeft part was done by Maffolino da
Panicale, and the fubjeċts he reprefented are, Adam
and Eve driven out of the earthly paradife; S. Peter
healing the cripple at the Temple and raifing S. Pe-
tronilla from the dead ; S. Peter vifited in prifon by
S. Paul. In them, a noble and auftere ftyle is admired,
as a memorial of the great fchool of Giotto ; but there
is found, too, a real progrefs in defign, colouring, and
chiarofcuro, and a vifible prepoffeffion to ftruggle againft
the ancients in painting the nude. The figure of S. Paul
is worthy of Raphael.

Maffacio continued the work of his fellow-pupil
Maffolino, and painted, on both fides of the altar, the
preaching of S. Peter, the fhadow of S. Peter curing
the fick, and S. Peter giving alms and adminiftering
baptifm.   Vafari is in ecftacy at the nude man who is
being baptifed, and points him out for the admiration
of all.[1]

But the mafterpiece of Maffacio is the Payment
of the Tribute, which is in the upper part. In the
centre, Chrift fends Peter to catch the fifh to furnifh the tribute; and on the right, S. Peter delivers
the money to the young man who demands it. This
compofition can be compared with the beautiful cartoons of Raphael.   The ftyle is noble, the figures
well drawn and the draperies full and natural.
The play of expreffions is alfo very remarkable ; but
a religious fentiment muft not be fought there.   The

---

[1] Nell' iftoria dove S. Piero battezza fi ftima grandemente un ignudo, che
triema tra gli altri battezati, affiderando di freddo, condotto con belliffimo relievo
e dolce maniera, il quale dagli artefici e vecchi e moderni è ftato fempre tenuto
in riverenza ed ammirazione.

artift gets the ftart of the Chriftian. At the lower part of the fcene, Maffacio has reprefented the refurrection of a young man at the interceffion of S. Peter. He had not time to finifh this painting, and all the fpectators placed near the gate of the town are by Filippino, fon of Fra Lippi, whofe fall fymbolizes that of Chriftian art. The talent of Filippino is already a decline; S. Peter delivered out of Prifon, and S. Peter and S. Paul before the Proconful, tell of the exclufive ftudy of the antique, and the defire of making portraits to procure friends and patrons. The whole of this chapel gives a glimpfe of the anarchy which the new tendency of art muft caufe. It is no longer a poem conceived with unity, but an open competition, wherein each one feeks the means of making his talent valued. The aim of the artift is no longer to infpire the crowd with noble and pious fentiments, but all his ambition is to flatter the tafte and obtain the fuffrage of connoiffeurs. And this ambition is a caufe of ruin, becaufe, for art as well as for fociety, true progrefs lies only in moral perfection.

The three artifts we have named as the fathers of the Renaiffance were contemporary with Beato Angelico. They muft have loved him as a genius who could not give them umbrage, and often vifited his cell, when our painter went to fettle at Florence. Brunellefchi was then erecting his cupola at Santa Maria dei Fiori; Ghiberti had finifhed his gates of the Baptiftry, and was working on other mafterpieces; Maffolino was dead, and Maffacio was painting his chapel of the Carmine.

Beato Angelico, their match, regarded them, without

doubt, as his mafters, and profited by their progrefs, whilft he ftill preferved the great principles of Chriftian art. This is feen in the works of which we have already fpoken or which remain for us to ftudy. He under-ftood the happy revolution brought about in architec-ture by Brunellefchi, and did not think the ogive more Chriftian than the rounded arch; for we fee him abandoning the mediæval defigns with which he had decorated his early pictures, to adopt the lines and ornamenting of the new monuments of Florence. His figures continued to be no lefs holy: they only took on lefs lengthened proportions, whilft wholly retain-ing their noblenefs, becaufe the ftyle of architecture always affects the figures.

He was certainly capable of underftanding all the beauties of the gates of the Baptiftry of Florence, and he knew how to rival Ghiberti in grace and elegance; but for all that he did not neglect the expreffion of religious feelings; and that made him preferred before his rival for the altarpiece ordered by the Guild of flax-workers [joiners].

Without doubt, many place Maffaccio above Beato Angelico for perfection of form, becaufe they confider the fcience rather than the Chriftian infpiration; but even in that regard we do not find Beato Angelico inferior to his contemporary.

The chapel of San Clemente is not to be compared with the paintings we have already ftudied, and we believe it, above all, to be lefs beautiful than the chapel of Nicholas V, in the Vatican. As to the compofition in the chapel of the Carmine, we think that it cannot be preferred to moft of the works of Beato Angelico, whofe Laft Judgments efpecially offer firft-rate beauties. Maffaccio refembles Raphael more in the freedom and elegance of his figures; but Beato Angelico has a grandeur and ftyle he had from tradition, which often bring him nearer to the Greeks than Raphael himfelf.

Thus Beato Angelico, model of all artifts for the holinefs of his infpirations, is alfo their model for the form with which he knew how to clothe thofe infpirations. He affifted at the firft appearance of the Renaiffance. He difentangled what it had of progrefs towards natural beauty, but remained faithful to moral beauty. He not allowed himfelf to go aftray through defire of perfonal glory, and faw in the beauties of earth only the reflection of the beauties of heaven: he loved God, and defired to make Him loved. This was his higheft aim, and becaufe he was faithful to it, his talent has been preferved from all decay.

Chapter X.

*FOUNDATION OF THE CONVENT OF SAN MARCO
BY COSIMO DE MEDICI. — CHOIR-BOOKS BY FRA
BENEDETTO.*

HE convent of San Marco was
founded and protected by the
Medici, who grew great with the
Renaiffance, of which they were to
become the corruptors. It is interefting for the hiftory of art to examine
how thefe bankers purchafed Florence
by degrees, and ended by becoming its mafters.
Never was ufurpation more mild and in appearance
more happy.

Pope Innocent III, who has done fo much for the
liberty of Italy, had aided Florence to fhake off the
tyranny of the emperors. This city formed itfelf into
a republic, and the fourteenth century was a turbulent period for it, but full of glory and profperity.
The form of government often changed, through the

ftormy fedition of the democracy and the ftrifes of a
turbulent ariftocracy; but the popular element always
predominated. Weary, at times, of the rending of
anarchy, Florence fought fome repofe, by entrufting
power to foreign princes, a means which never re-
united it.

In 1267, it gave itfelf, for ten years, to Charles I, King
of Sicily, but foon renounced this protectorate. In
1301, Pope Boniface VIII. fent to it, as governor,
Charles de Valois, brother of the King of France, who,
inftead of re-eftablifhing peace, organized pillage and
enkindled the fire of civil war. In 1342, the Florentines nominated Gauthier de Brienne, Duke of Athens,
as captain and protector of the people, and afterwards
lord of Florence for life; but his odious tyranny caufed
him to be driven out in the following year. Then
the ftruggles of the people began afrefh againft the
nobility, who fought in power means only to fatisfy
private hatreds. The citizens triumphed, and the
nobles were excluded from every charge; and a government was eftablifhed, the peculiar combinations of
which gave great developement to private energy and
public wealth. The fyftem of guilds of art was exceedingly favourable to commerce and induftry. Florence
became the emporium of Europe, and its manufactures
fupplied every country; for woollen ftuffs, it reckoned
two hundred manufacturers, who employed thirty
thoufand perfons. Its revenues were confiderable, and
its unpaid magiftrates amaffed treafures which enabled
them to pay off the troops, purchafe towns, found public
eftablifhments, and organize feftivals, to which ftrangers
reforted in crowds. The fine arts alfo flourifhed: this

was the epoch of the fchool of Giotto and of the great monuments. An unheard-of luxury bred a corruption of manners, which the plague of 1348 chaftifed, when a hundred thoufand perfons died in Florence.

Amidft this feverifh agitation of induftry, the influence of the bankers grew very confiderable. They treated on an equality with crowned heads. The King of England borrowed 900,000 florins of gold from the Bradi and 600,000 of the Perruzzi. The auguft debtor did not pay, and ruined his bankers. The Medici were more prudent and more clever. They chofe lefs exalted and furer clients, and made partifans for themfelves amongft the people and citizens. Sylveftro de Medici is the firft illuftrious member of his family; he was created cavaliere by the revolted workmen, and was nominated gonfaloniere by them in 1378.

Whilft the nobles were returning to power by their alliances with the rich citizens, and Florence was increafing in profperity under Gino Capponi and Mafo Albrizzi, the Medici were extending their bufinefs without mixing up in the ambitious contentions of parties. Giovanni de Medici, in particular, made enormous profits during the Council of Conftance. He was banker to the Pope, and profited by the circumftance to acquire immenfe credit throughout all the world. He was the true founder of his dynafty. His courtefy towards the rich and generofity towards artifans commenced his power, and he attracted general efteem and knew how to keep himfelf adroitly in neutrality. In 1421, he was nominated to the office of gonfaloniere, which he honourably fulfilled; and he died in 1428, leaving to his children, his credit, his fortune, and the recommendation of never having offended anybody, and of always refpecting the laws and will of his fellow-citizens.

Cofimo de Medici profited moft by his leffons. To the ability of his father, he joined greater ambition, and he fought every means to advance his influence, by increafing his riches and enterprifes. Active, geneous and infinuating, he grew to be the friend and creditor of all the world. He attached to himfelf the families of the exiled by means of bills of exchange, received the money of the condottieri and made advances to them, protected letters and the arts, and furrounded himfelf with all who could have an influence on the public fpirit. He took the artifans into his pay, by furnifhing funds to induftry, and his bounty relieved the poor and decorated churches, whilft he remained himfelf in a comparative fimplicity, which is always feductive under a republic.

The nobles, who faw his powei increafing and confolidating, confpired to overturn it. Renaud, fon of Mazo Albizzi, prepared an infurrection inftead of an affaffination. Cofimo was arrefted and condemned, but in his prifon he bought the judges over who were fold to his enemies, and inftead of being fent to death, he departed only into exile. There was his triumph. He retired to Padua, and there received deputations from thofe who acknowledged his power. The city of Venice fent ambaffadors to him, and afked his counfels. All the vaffals commerce had given him came to pay him homage, whilft Florence fuffered all through by his abfence. He demanded his capitals back; it was neceffary to repay them, and they could not borrow

any more : induſtry flagged, artiſts had no longer a protector nor artiſans a patron. The city was compelled
to capitulate. Then the reign of the Medici began.

Coſimo was a ſovereign without taking the titles and
coſtly equipage of one. He was proclaimed the benefactor of the people and the father of the country : he
commanded, he revenged, he governed. His banking-
houſe was his palace, his caſh-box his throne ; and he
eſtabliſhed the royalty of money, the tyranny of riches
—a tyranny more terrible than any other, becauſe it
is more corruptive. It was a ſyſtem well organized
by him ; and when they complained of the injury he
inflicted on the city by the loſs of good citizens whom
his baniſhments and revenges drove away, he boaſted
that he could make good men with two ells of ſuper-
fine cloth.

He knew how to profit by the talent and warlike
qualities of Neri Capponi, whoſe independence he re-
ſpected in order to gain an influence by his means over
the ſoldiery. He allowed the ſoldiers to tyrannize over
the people, that his own apparent moderation might
be more valued, and he hurried on induſtry towards
luxury, a material progreſs which is a danger when it
is not guided by Chriſtianity. He gathered alſo a brilliant circle of learned men and artiſts, heaped preſents
on churches, founded numerous convents and neglected
no means to conciliate the maſſes.

The country-house of Coſimo de Medici was near
the convent of Fieſole, and he became the benefactor of
the religious inhabiting it. He had ordered many pictures by Beato Angelico, and he cauſed him to remove
to the new convent of San Marco. God thus always

mingles good and evil, to let us choofe between thefe two eternal enemies, and to perpetuate, amidft the ruins of corruption, the germs of life and the hopes of re-fufcitation. Providence placed not far from the palace of the Medici the holy dwelling, where the inexhauft-ible charity of S. Antoninus was to confole the victims of the vengeance of Cofimo the elder, and to folace the mifery bred by the excefs of luxury. From the con-vent of San Marco was alfo to iffue forth Savonarola, that tribune of the Church, who defired to direct towards God the progrefs of the Renaiffance, which was becom-ing more and more corrupted in the fervice of the paf-fions under the fatal influence of Lorenzo il Magnifico.

The religious of Fiefole had already fent a colony to Florence. On June 19th, 1435, they had obtained of Pope Eugenius IV, and the magiftracy of the city, the fmall church of San Giorgio beyond the Arno. The Sovereign Pontiff was then profecuting the reform of the religious orders, in which the fchifm and the plague had caufed relaxation. The religious who gave moft fcandal were thofe who inhabited the old convent of San Marco.[1] A petition from the magiftrates of Florence was prefented to the Pope by Cofimo de Medici, afking for a change. It fet forth that the convent of San Marco, fituated in the centre of the city, had need of zealous and numerous minifters; and that thofe who were occupying it could not do any good and were allowing the buildings to fall into ruins. The reformed Dominican religious were to take the place of them, and give in exchange the convent of San Giorgio, which was being granted them. Eugenius IV

[1] [Monks of the Order of S. Sylvefter.—TRANSLATOR's note.]

received this requeſt favourably; and a bull dated
January 21ſt, 1436, ordained the change.   The monks
of San Marco reſiſted, and appealed to the pſeudo-
ſynod of Baſle, one of the precurſive lightning flaſhes
of the Reformation.   But this means did not ſucceed
with them; they were obliged to give up, and the Pope
ordered that poſſeſſion ſhould be taken with unuſual
ſoleinnity. The Dominican religious went through all
the city, accompanied by the clergy, three biſhops, the
mazzieri and an immenſe concourſe of people.   Padre
Cipriano took poſſeſſion of San Marco in the name of
his congregation.

Beato Angelico aſſiſted, without any doubt, at the
ceremony, and ſettled in the convent, which was in a
deplorable ſtate. In the preceding year, a fire had
deſtroyed a part, and the roof of the church had been
burned.   The Dominican religious were obliged to
make wooden cells all open to the wind and damp.
ButCoſimo de Medici ordered his architect, Michelozzi,
to build them a more ſuitable abode.   The architect
pulled down the old convent, and left only the church
and the refectory.   He made two cloiſters, one on the
ſouth ſide of the church, and the other at the apſe.
Theſe buildings, commenced in 1437, were finiſhed in
1443, and the expenſe amounted to 36,000 ducats.
The reſtorations of the church were finiſhed in 1441,and
the conſecration took place on the Feaſt of theEpiphany
in the following year, in the preſence of Pope Eugenius
IV. and of the college of Cardinals. Coſimo de Medici
wiſhed to preſent all the choir-books, and charged Fra
Benedetto, elder brother of Beato Angelico, with the
execution of them.

We have feen that the two brothers, until this time, had the fame exiftence, and we have proved the joint labour of Fra Benedetto in the works of our painter. The teftimony of Vafari on this point is pofitive.[1] Fra Benedetto was particularly beloved by S. Antoninus, who chofe him as fub-prior every time he himfelf was nominated prior of San Marco. He lived in that convent with his brother, and quitted it only when he was elected prior by the religious of Fiefole; but the third year of his charge was not yet completed, when he died of the plague, in 1448. The two chronicles of San Marco and of Fiefole eulogife his talent and fanctity.

"Fra Benedetto," fays the one of San Marco, "fon of Pietro of Mugello, native fon and then prior of the convent of Fiefole, brother of Fra Giovanni, that admirable painter from whofe fkill almoft all the pictures of this convent proceed. Bleffed *(Benedictus)* in reality and name, he was moft upright in life and manners, and he converfed in the Order without a murmur. He was alfo the beft writer and miniaturift, not only of his own but of moft times. By whofe hand are the texts, muficnotes and miniatures of nearly all the choir-books of this church of San Marco, including the antiphonaries, graduals and pfalters, except only the laft gradual for feftivals. Being feized with the plague, and having cheerfully looked on death, after duly receiving the facraments, he fell afleep in the Lord that year, 1448, and was buried in the common fepulture of the brethren. May he reft in peace!"[2]

---

[1] Ben è vero che a far quefti fu aiutata da un fuo maggior fratello che era fimilmente miniatore ed effai efercitato nella pittura.

[2] Fra Benedictus Petri de Mugello, filius nativus et tunc prior exiftens Fefulani cenventus, germanus fratris Joannis, illius tam mirandi pictoris cujus arte picturæ

We have already compared the talent of Fra Benedetto with his brother's ; the ſtudy of the choir-books
at San Marco will make us better appreciate the difference.　Fra Benedetto did not give himſelf up ex-
cluſively to the practice of the art ; but was very much
occupied in the miniſtry and in the direction of ſouls,
as is proved by the duties to which he was called.　Still
the regularity of religious life left him much leiſure,
ſeeing that he aſſiſted his brother, and almoſt entirely
executed in a few years, from 1443 to 1448, the choir-
books, which ſerve the church of San Marco, and coſt
Coſimo de Medici 1500 ducats.

Theſe magnificent books are one of the moſt valuable texts of ancient religious muſic.　The annals of
the convent ſay that fourteen volumes of graduals
and antiphonaries were written by the hand of Fra
Benedetto, prior of the convent of Fieſole, except the
laſt volumes of the graduals for the ferias, which remained uncompleted on account of his death, and were
finiſhed by a religious of the order of Friar-minors.
At the requeſt of Coſimo, he alſo wrote two choir
pſalters and a book of invitatories.[1]

The books now ſerving the religious are twenty in
number, either becauſe they have been divided, or

---

fere omnes hujus conventus exſtant.　Hic re et nomine Benedictus moribus et
vitâ integerrimus fuit et ſine querelâ in ordine converſatus.　Exſtitit autem ex-
cellentiſſimus, non modo ſuorum, ſed et plurimorum temporum ſcriptor et
miniator.　Cujus manu, litteris, cantus nota, et minio ſt. (*ſic*) omnes fere libri
chori hujus eccleſiæ S. Marci : Antiphonaria videlicet, Gradualia, et Pſalteria,
dempto ultimo duntaxat feſtivo graduali.　Hic ex eâ peſte invaſus alacer mortem
intuitus, ſacramentis omnibus rite perceptis, in Domino requievit, ipſo anno 1448,
ſepultus in communibus fratrum ſepulturis.　Requieſcat in pace.—*Annalia conv.
S. Marci,* A, fol. 211.

[1] *Annal. conv. S. Marci,* fol. 8, a tergo.

others have been added to them. Thefe books have been repaired in the fixteenth century: the miniatures in them are generally well preferved. They bear the arms of the Medici; and numerous infcriptions give proof of the munificence of Cofimo the old. The writing is beautiful; the initials are a little heavy in defign, but encircled with flowers and fome grotefque figures. The miniatures are painted within the letters. The volumes moft ornamented are the firft marked A and B.[1] The following are the moft remarkable fubjects.

The Calling of S. Peter and S. Andrew.

The Martyrdom of S. Stephen. The background prefents a charming landfcape.

S. John the Evangelift. A beautiful figure, but unfortunately injured.

The Maffacre of the Innocents.

S. Agnes, virgin and martyr. She is carrying amidft the flames her palm and fymbolical lamb.

The Converfion of S. Paul. The Prefentation. The Annunciation.

Then follows the common of the Apoftles and Martyrs. Jefus bleffes them, to fhow that he is their ftrength and reward.

At the common of a virgin, virgins of every age are finging before an open book laid upon the palms. In it are read thefe words: GAUDEAMUS OMNES.

For the office of the Crofs is a very beautiful Crucifixion, feemingly done by Beato Angelico. Another miniature reprefents the Bleffed Virgin covering with her mantle the religious of the Order of S. Dominic.

---

[1] At the beginning is read :—*Hos libros fuis pecuniis, illuftriffimus civis* . . . . *multa et magna beneficia, et hoc templum extruxit Cofmas Medic.*

In the second volume, marked B, may be especially
pointed out, an Annunciation, in beautiful ftyle: S.
Peter of Verona receiving the three crowns of doctor,
virgin and martyr.   S. Mary Magdalen carried to
heaven by angels.   S. Dominic receiving his miffion
from S. Peter and S. Paul.   A magnificent Affumption.   A very remarkable S. Michael.   All the Saints,
who are celebrating their feftival whilft finging CAN-
TATE DOMINUM.

In another compofition, Chrift places his hand on
the head of a martyr, and with the other fhows him the
heavenly rewards, which he is contemplating with the
eyes of faith.

The other books are not rich in miniatures.   The
greater part have one only at the firft page.   The An-
tiphonary marked I, prefents a beautiful compofition.
Our Lord is fhowing to his apoftles a young man with
his eyes bandaged and his hands tied behind his back:
fuch is the lot awaiting them, and alfo the fureft means
to conquer the world, whilft rendering teftimony to
the truth.   The Book P prefents a very fine Adoration
of the Magi, the figures of which recall Beato Angelico's
mafterpiece in the cell of Cofimo de Medici.

All thefe miniatures exhibit defects and qualities
already pointed out in the pictures we have attributed
to Fra Benedetto.   There are found in them a profound religious feeling, a pious imagination, new fubjects and ingenious manner of giving them; but if
the artift has the fame faith and the fame piety as his
brother, he has not the fame talent; he has received
lefs and improved lefs.   He is not, as Beato Angelico,
the inheritor of the great mafters, nor has he, like him

ftudied nature. His figures are dumpy and ordinarily
badly placed, the movements untrue, and the heads
without vivacity and pattern. But above all, he has
not the noble elegance and admirable fimplicity of his
brother: evident proof that the Chriftian idea alone
does not make the artift; to give it well, a natural gift
developed by ftudy is needed.

We infift very ftrongly on this diftinction between
the works of Fra Benedetto and Beato Angelico. The
joint labour of Fra Benedetto has been prejudicial to
the glory of Beato Angelico. But by ftudying attentively the works, which, without any doubt, belong to
them, we come to recognize an evident inequality of
ftyle. They are two handwritings which it is impoffible to confound.

Did Beato Angelico work at his brother's miniatures?
We believe fo, and have remarked figures worthy of
him. Beato Angelico certainly made miniatures. Vafari
attributes to him two large books at Santa Maria dei
Fiori.[1] Padre Marchefe could not fee them; but
Profeffor Rofini feems to have been more fortunate.
The library of San Marco poffeffes other miniatures
afcribed to him; but we think it is neceffary to be
careful in thefe affignments. Beato Angelico is
pre-eminently the religious painter. Speculation or
unfkilled admiration gives to him a multitude of manufcripts of the fifteenth century, French or German.
Let us refpect the truth, and the glory of our painter.

[1] Sono di mano di Fra Giovanni in Santa-Maria-del-Fiore 'due grandiffimi libri
miniati divinamente, i quali fono tenuti con molta venerazione e riccamente
adornati, nè fi veggiono fe non ne' giorni folenniffimi.

CHAPTER XI

CONVENT OF SAN MARCO.—PAINTINGS IN THE CLOISTER AND IN THE CELLS.

HE convent of San Marco is noble and fimple in architecture. S. Antoninus moderated the liberality of Cofimo de Medici, and prevented grandeurs too much oppofed to the fpirit of the reformed Dominicans. The fkill of Machelozzi is fhown only in the two cloifters and in the library which is divided into three by two rows of fine Doric pillars. Beato Angelico worked only in the firft cloifter and in the cells connected with it. The reft of the convent was not finifhed before his departure or Rome.[1]

[1] This firft cloifter is called the cloifter of S. Antoninus, on account of the pictures reprefenting the life of the faintly Archbifhop of Florence, which were executed at the end of the fixteenth century.

[A great many, and certainly the moft perfect of thefe frefcoes, defigned and coloured by M. Laborde, have been publifhed in Paris, "Frefque du Couvent de Saint Marc, à Florence; par Beato Angelico da Fiefole, deffinées fur les Origineaux par M. H. de Laborde, et reproduites en Chromo-Lithographie, par les Procèdes de M M. Englemann et Graff, par MM. Moulin, Blanke, Colette, et

At the end of the fide of the cloifter running along the church and facing the entrance door, is a beautiful Chrift on the Crofs. According to his cuftom, Beato Angelico has reprefented him with eyes open on all men, and fhedding on the ground his divine blood flowing from its inexhauftible fource. S. Dominic on his knees embraces the Crofs and looks on our Lord with love and compaffion. This figure is impreffed with a moft marked individuality. It muft be the portrait of some religious, which was afterwards made into a S. Dominic, by the addition of the aureola and ftar of the holy Founder. Whofe portrait is it? Is it one of S. Antoninus, Fra Benedetto, or Beato Angelico? We have no authentic portrait of our painter. But cannot we allow a fuppofition, and believe that he defired to reprefent himfelf at the foot of the Crofs, as he placed himfelf fo often there? His brother might have drawn the profile, and this act of ardent adoration would be the fignature of all his works on the walls of the convent of San Marco. If thefe are not his features, they are at leaft his feelings, and he has written them at the bottom of this picture. In place of his name is read this touching infcription: " Hail! Salvation of the world: hail! dear Jefus, my Salvation; I would truly fix me to Thy Crofs. Thou knoweft wherefore; grant me power." [1]

Near this painting, and above the door leading to the facrifty, Beato Angelico has painted in an ogive a

---

Sanfon, fous la Direction de M. Paul Delaroche; précedés d'une Notice Hifto-rique fur Beato Angelico, par Ludovic Vitel."—MARCHESE, by *Meehan*, vol. i, p. 210 (note.)—TRANSLATOR's note.]

[1] Salve, mundi falutare; falve, falus Jefu chare; Cruci tuæ me aptare vellem verè: tu fcis quare; prefta mihi copiam.

S. Peter Martyr. In the left hand he holds a book and palm ; and the forefinger of his right hand placed on his mouth enjoins the filence which fhould reign in the cloifter and the recollection neceffary for approaching the fanctuary.[1]

Above the door of the chapter-room, a S. Dominic holds a difcipline and the book of the conftitutions. Can any one better point out the room where the religious meet to accufe themfelves publicly of their faults againft the rule and to receive the penance for it?

Near the door leading to the refectory, is painted a Pietà. The Saviour above his tomb fhows his hands pierced for men. This is one of the moft beautiful figures of Chrift by Beato Angelico. The head is of a divine purity, the body of very noble and very remarkable drawing. Over the door of the hofpice where ftrangers were entertained, Beato Angelico has reprefented two Dominican religious receiving our Lord Jefus Chrift clothed as a pilgrim. This compofition is admirable, and perfectly expreffes the kindly hofpitality, the tradition of which, as we ourfelves know, is not loft in the Order of S. Dominic. The two religious receive their gueft with joy and love : their heads, well drawn and well modelled, are full of life and charity.[2] To exprefs the fame idea, Fra Bartolomeo has painted the Difciples at

[1] [" Over the door that leads to the facrifty he executed a half-figure of S. Peter Martyr, indicating filence. He has the forefinger raifed to his mouth ; but far more impreffive, and far more calculated to invite us to filence and recollection, is the fevere, I would almoft fay threatening, afpect of the Saint."—Marchese, by *Meehan*, vol. i, p. 211.—Translator's note.]

[2] [" The three figures are fo beautiful, fo devout, and fo well coloured and defigned, that I do not hefitate to clafs them amongft the moft perfect works he executed for S. Mark's."—Marchese, by *Meehan*, vol. i, p. 211.—Translator's note.]

Emmaus above the door of the refectory ; but his work is very inferior to that of Beato Angelico, both as to religious expreffion and fkill.

A beautiful figure¹ of S. Thomas Aquinas, unfortunately very much injured, completes the decoration of the cloifter, where our painter has thus prefented to the thoughts of his brethren the example of recollection, of fcience and of all the religious virtues, along with the Paffion of our Lord.

The great compofition filling all the farther end of the chapter-room is ufually cited as the mafterpiece of Beato Angelico. This painting is the largeft and moft important, and reprefents the fcene of Calvary, the eternal object of the contemplation and love of the faints. Chrift on a very high Crofs rules the whole of the world ; he is placed between the repentant and impenitent, the good and the bad, thieves. At his feet, a death's-head marks the confequences of fin, of which he is the victim and vanquifher. Around him, are the faithful friends of his Paffion : the Bleffed Virgin, finking under the weight of her grief, is fupported by a holy female ; Mary Magdalen, kneeling at the foot of the Crofs, turns without rifing to receive the Mother of the Saviour into her arms. This group is one of the greateft beauty. On one fide, S. John Baptift ; S. Mark, hiftorian of the Paffion and protector of the convent ; S. Lawrence ; SS. Cofmas and Damian, patrons of the Medici. On the oppofite fide, are reprefented other witneffes of the Paffion of our Lord. At their head, S. Dominic, in an ecftafy of grief ; S. Zanobius, bishop of Florence, who feems to be addreffing

¹ [" A half-figure."—Marchese, *loc. cit.*—Translator's note.]

S. Jerome proftrate with his hands joined; behind him and above, S. Auguftin in the attitude of meditation; S. Francis of Affifi, with his little crofs and ftigmata, who, with his head leaning on his hand, cafts a feraphic look on his Divine Model; S. Benedict holding the rod of penance; S. Bernard preffing the gofpel to his heart and tenderly contemplating his mafter: a fublime figure of faith, ardour and purity; S. Romuald, bending under the weight of years; S. Gualbert breaking out into fobs; S. Peter Martyr and S. Thomas Aquinas. All thefe faints fuperabound in love, and the feelings they experience are rendered with a variety and intenfity of expreffion, of which it is impoffible to give an idea.

The whole compofition is framed in a broad and rich border divided by medallions, in which the prophets affift at the great event they had announced. They hold banderols, whereon are texts which form, as it were, a canticle in honour of the truth. At the right of Chrift, the first perfonage, whofe name is effaced, fays: "The God of nature is fuffering."[1] Then comes Daniel: "In feven weeks and fixty-two weeks, Chrift fhall be flain."

Zacharias. "See what I have fuffered."

The Patriarch Jacob. "To the prey, my fon, thou art gone up: refting thou haft crouched as a lion."

David. "In my thirft they gave Me vinegar to drink."

At the top of the compofition, is a pelican giving life

---

[1] [Perhaps S. Dionyfius the Areopagite. When he faw the miraculous darknefs at the crucifixion of Chrift, he exclaimed, "Either the God of nature is fuffering, or the fabric of the world is diffolved."—TRANSLATOR'S note.]

to its young ones with its blood. Below is read : "I am become like to a pelican of the wildernefs."

Ifaias. "Surely He hath carried our forrows."

Jeremias. "O all ye that pafs by the way, attend, and fee if there be any forrow like to my forrow."

Ezechiel. "I have exalted the low tree."

Job. "Who will give us of his flefh that we may be filled ?"

The Sibyll of Erythræa. "Dying he fhall die, and fleeping three days, then fhall he be the firft returned from hell to fee the light."[1]

In the lower border, Beato Angelico has reprefented the glories of the Order of S. Dominic. The holy Founder placed in the middle holds a genealogical tree, and the fcrolls on it form medallions, on which are the faints, popes, cardinals, bifhops and celebrated religious whom the Dominican family has given to the Church. On one fide, Innocent V., Cardinal Hugues de S. Cher ; the Patriarch of Gradi, Paolo Pilaftri ; S. Antoninus, archbifhop of Florence ; Bleffed Jordan of Saxony, Beato Niccola della Paglia, Beato Buoninfegna, martyr.

On the oppofite fide, Benedict XI, Beato Giovanni Dominici, Beato Pietro da Palude, Bleffed Albert the Great, S. Raymund of Pennafort, Beato Chiaro da

---

[1] Deus nature patitur.—Poft ebdomades viii et lxii occidetur xps.—*Dan.*, ix, 26. Ad predam defcendifti (*afcendifti*), fili mi dormiens (requiefcens). Accubuifti ut leo.—*Gen.* xlix, 9. In fiti mea potaverunt me aceto.—*Ps.* lxviii, 22.—Similis factus fum pellicano folitudinis.—*Ps.* ci, 7. Vere languores meos (*nostros*) ipfe tulit.—*Ifaias* liii, 4. O vos omnes qui tranfite (*fic*) per viam, attendite et videte fi eft dolor ficut dolor meus.—*Jeremias*; *Lam.* i, 12. Exaltavi lignum humile.— *Ezechiel*, xvii, 24. Quis det de carnibus ejus ut faturemur ?—*Job* xxxi, 31. Morte morietur tribus diebus fomno fubfcepto, et tunc ab infernis regreffus ad ucem veniet primus.

Sefto, S. Vincent Ferrer, and Beato Bernardo, one of the martyrs of Avignonet.[1] The figures in this vaft compofition are all admirable in ftyle, drawing and expreffion; one only makes a difparity, and it is S. Mark placed on the right of the Crofs, between S. John Baptift and S. Lawrence. It is badly placed and ill proportioned; and the head is evidently too large. We believe this figure to be Fra Benedetto's; his brother may have let him paint the patron of the convent, of which he was fub-prior.

This frefco has all the qualities of a great monumental picture. The execution of it is fimple and free, and the colouring foft and full of light. The perfonages are very well preferved, but the back-ground on which they are fet off is unfortunately in a deplorable ftate. It is covered with a heavy tint of dirty red, which has been fhaded off into a grey, whilft often carried over the outlines. It is impoffible to explain this act of vandalifm, of which we do not know the date and author.[2]

[1] Many of thefe names were not put by Beato Angelico; this is evident as to the faints beatified after his death. There is ftill feen beneath the name of S. Antonius, the one it has replaced.

[2] " In this work," fays Vafari, " are figures of all thofe faints who have been heads and founders of religious bodies, mourning and bewailing at the foot of the Crofs on one fide, and on the other S. Mark the Evangelift, befide the mother of the Son of God, who has fainted at the fight of the crucified Saviour. Around the Virgin are the Maries, who are forrowing with and fupporting her; they are accompanied by the faints Cofimo and Damiano. It is faid that in the figure of San Cofimo, Fra Giovanni depicted his friend Nanni d'Antonio di Banco, the fculptor, from the life. Beneath this work, in a frieze over the back of the feats, the mafter executed a figure of San Domenico ftanding at the foot of a tree, on the branches of which are medallions, in which are all the popes, cardinals, bifhops, faints and mafters in theology who had belonged to Fra Giovanni's Order of Preaching Friars, down to his own day. In this work the brethren of his

The chronicle of San Marco mentions another painting by Beato Angelico in the refectory of the

Order affifted him by procuring portraits of thefe various perfonages from different places, by which means he was enabled to execute many likeneffes from nature. Thefe are—San Domenico in the centre, who is grafping the branches of the tree ; Pope Innocent V ; a Frenchman. The Beato Ugone, firft cardinal of that order ; the Beato Paolo, the patriarch, a Florentine ; Bifhop (*sic*) Giordano, a German, and the fecond general of the order ; the Beato Niccolo ; the Beato Remigio, a Florentine ; and the martyr Boninfegno, a Florentine ; all thefe are on the right hand. On the left, are Benedict XI., of Trevifo ; Giandominico, a Florentine cardinal ; Pietro da Palude, patriarch of Jerufalem ; the German Alberto Magno, the Beato Raimondo, of Catalonia, third general of the order ; the Beato Chiaro ; a Florentine, and provincial of Rome ; San Vincenzio di Valenza ; and the Beato Bernardo, a Florentine ; all thefe heads are truly graceful and very beautiful." —VASARI, by *Fofter*, vol. ii, p. 25.

The garments of the Holy Virgin have unhappily fuffered from *reftorers.*

" In the chapter-room, of which we fpeak, he painted the Redeemer on the Crofs, and on either fide of Him the two thieves. At the foot of the Crofs, and on both fides of it, he introduced a great multitude of Saints. The figure of the Redeemer is one of rare beauty and noble form : the nude is flightly Giottefque ; neverthelefs, it is, in my judgment, far fuperior to the carnofe forms of the Cinque-centifts, not excepting even thofe of Fra Bartolommeo della Porta. The nude of the two thieves is inferior ; but on the countenance of one of them, you read the affurance of pardon, whilft that of the other bears the ftamp of blafphemy and the defpairfulnefs that feems a foretafte of hell. At the Crofs's foot, on the right, he painted the Virgin, who has fwooned, and is fupported by S. John and one of the pious women. Magdalene throws herfelf forward to help her, and clafps her in her arms. This is a group fo beauteous and fo touching, that it does not yield to Razzi's Swoon of S. Catherine da Siena—a compofition that fills every eye with tears. Then follows a beautiful figure of the Baptift, well defigned and well coloured, pointing with the index to that Saviour whom he had preached to the multitude in the wildernefs. S. Mark kneeling, points to the book of the Gofpels, in which he has defcribed the life and death of the Redeemer. The laft figures are SS. Laurence, Cofmas, and Damian. On the left a new fcene, not lefs tender and devout, prefents itfelf. Here are eleven faints, for the moft part Founders of the Religious Orders, who feem to meditate the Paffion of Chrift, and it may be that the Angelico introduced them to fhow that they had partaken copioufly of the fruits of the Redemption ; and as the chapter-room was meant to be the place for admonifhing, correcting, and infpiring the religious with fervour for the obfervance of conventual difcipline, perhaps, he defired to prefent them thefe faints as grand models for their imitation. And firft we fee S. Dominic proftrate at the foot of the Crofs, wrapt in profound contemplation ; a figure excellently defigned and coloured. Then follows S. Zanobi, bifhop of Florence, convent. It reprefented Chrift on the Crofs, affifted by the Holy Virgin and by S. John. It was deftroyed in 1534.[1]

The cells painted by Beato Angelico were conftruĉted under the infpiration of the moft fevere religious fim-plicity. They are ranged in two lines under an open wood-work roof, and are narrow, low, and lighted by little arched windows. The fpace is rigoroufly meted

who meditates the vaticinations of the prophets, realized in the Redeemer, to whom he points with his finger. That bald old man, with white beard, wafted and emaciated by years and faftings, is the great Jerom, in whofe breaft the love of the Crofs blunted the keeneft paffions, and who feems to beg aid in his moft direful need. Then comes S. Auguftin, who meditates and writes. The Patriarch of the Francifcans, the poor one of Chrift, is proftrate on the ground, in the moft overwhelming dolor : a wonderful figure, in which there is indefcribable affeĉtion. S. Benediĉt is in deep meditation; but I know not whether the Paffion of the Lord or the revival of monaftic difcipline in the Weft has moft of his thoughts. S. Bernard lovingly gazes at the Crucified, and, with both hands, clafps a volume to his bofom—that dear volume into which he has poured the tender effufions of his heart. S. Romuald, bending beneath the weight of years, fupports his feeble body on a ftaff, and feems buried in fome profoundly fad thought. A folitary, that I take to be S. John Gualberto, fobs and weeps. The laft are two Domi-nican faints, S. Thomas of Aquino, who contemplates the fublime myftery which faved the human race, and of which he wrote fo wifely; and S. Peter Martyr whofe gaping wound tells how he gave to Chrift *blood for blood*. . . . . The figures in this compofition are remarkable for flowing drapery, as alfo for the expreffion of the heads, not to fpeak of the relief and great power of the defign. I muft obferve, however, that I am not fatisfied with the extremities, in which there is a negligence not unufual to him; neverthelefs, whenever he wifhed, he removed fuch blemifhes. . . . .

"In order to develope ftill more effeĉtively this devout meditation, the painter executed, on the ten hexagons that furround the arch of the ceiling, ten half-figures of Prophets and Sybils, holding certain fcrolls with words relative to the Paffion of our Lord ; and they are as beautiful and graceful as it is poffible to imagine. On the frieze that runs under the frefco the entire length of the façade, he executed, in ten fmall circles, the portraits of S. Dominic and the illuftrious men of his inftitute. . . . ."—MARCHESE, *by Meehan*, vol. i, p. 212.—TRANSLATOR's note.]

[1 Probably it was a repetition of the one at Fiefole, deftroyed to make room for the great frefco by Antonio Sogliani, which reprefents S. Dominic and his brethren ferved at table by the angels.—MARCHESE, *by Meehan*, vol. i, p. 217.—TRANSLATOR's note.]

out for a table, chair, and a poor bed on which the
religious took reſt for ſome inſtants from his ſtudies
and prayer.   On theſe walls deſtitute of all ornament,
our painter has executed his maſterpieces.   Is there
not here truly a proof of touching humliity?   No idea
of human glory could have come into his mind in
decorating theſe obſcure cells.   The ſtrict encloſure of
the convent would withdraw them from the gaze of the
crowd; and yet he has put all his ſkill into them: like
other ſaints, who for the glory of God and the conſola-
tion of ſouls pour out in ſecret direction all the
treaſures of their heart and eloquence.

Beato Angelico has wiſhed to recount the Life of our
Lord again, and has left a page for each of his brethren to meditate.   He has often added to the ſcene
ſome ſaint who witneſſed it, male or female, to ſatisfy
doubtleſs the devotion of the religious who had to
dwell in the cell.   The figures are middle-ſized, and
the colouring admirably ſweet.[1]   Fra Benedetto has
helped his brother in the work: and we have even
remarked that their compoſitions were almoſt always
alternate.   Thus they worked ſide by ſide.   We will
follow the hiſtorical order in the examination of theſe
paintings.

On the outer wall of the range of cells is an Annunciation, which, whilſt it altogether recalls the one at
Cortona by its grace and purity, ſhows the artiſt's
progreſs.   The Bleſſed Virgin is ſeated on a little ſtool,
and bends forward before the angel kneeling in front
of her.   The ſanctuary where this heavenly ſcene paſſes

[¹ Vaſari declares that this hiſtory from the New Teſtament "is beautiful
beyond the power of words to deſcribe."—VASARI, by Foſter, vol. ii, p. 27.—
TRANSLATOR's note.]

is an open portico, on which the little cell of the Virgin
opens.   The architecture is the fame as in the cloifters
of San Marco.   It is furrounded by an enclofed garden,
all covered with beautiful flowers, which the foot of
man has never trodden.   The filial hand of the painter
has written at the bottom of this compofition, "Hail,
Mother of love, Mary, noble feat of the whole Trinity :"
and below, "When thou comest before this figure of
the fpotlefs Virgin, take heed in paffing it that the Ave
be not unfaid."[1]

Another Annunciation is painted in a cell, and has
perhaps fomething more heavenly.   The Holy Virgin
kneels on a ftool;   the angel is ftanding before her,
and feems to be waiting for her anfwer.   Behind him

---

[1] Salve, Mater pietatis, et totius Trinitatis nobile triclinium, Maria.   Virginis
intacte cum veneris ante figuram, pretereundo cave ne fileatur ave.—This infcription reminds us of the one adorning the ftatue of the Bleffed Virgin at the
beautiful portal of the Dalbade, at Touloufe :—

> "Chreftien, fi mon amour eft en ton cœur gravé,
>   Ne diffère, en paffant, de me dire un *Ave.*

["The firft that prefents itfelf is an Annunciation of the Bleffed Virgin, in the
upper dormitory, the figures of which are fomewhat lefs than life-fize. On a fuper-
ficies, ten palms in length, he painted the habitation of our Lady, furrounded by
a veftibule, which refts on Corinthian columns, much in the ftyle of that which
he executed at Cortona; and though the perfpective is not perfect, it is better
than that of the former.   On the outfide is the little Garden of Mary, enclofed
by a thick hedge and railing; a figure employed by the Church to denote her
unblemifhed virginity. The Holy Maiden of Nazareth is feated on an unadorned
chair; the colour of her tunic is a pale red, her azure mantle falls in folds over
her knees, her arms are croffed on her bofom, and her countenance, if not
remarkable for great beauty, is refplendent with the calm ferenity of Paradife.
Her fair hair falls gracefully on her fhoulders, and fo humble and devotional is
her whole attitude, that in the prefence of this dear image, we almoft feel the
Angelical Salutation, 'Hail, full of Grace,' trembling on our lips. . . . The figure
of the Archangel is truly beautiful.   A fweet fmile plays on his celeftial features,
and bending one knee, and croffing his arms on his breaft, he feems to await
anxioufly the announcement of Mary's confent : it is thus that Dante has defcribed him."—MARCHESE, *by Meehan*, vol. i, p. 218.—TRANSLATOR'S note.]

and outfide the portico, is feen S. Peter Martyr, fo
famous for his purity. This compofition is ravifhingly
beautiful.

The Nativity recalls the one on the panels in the
Academy of Fine Arts. S. Peter Martyr and S.
Catherine of Alexandria are kneeling, with Mary and
Jofeph, to adore the Divine Child lying on a little
ftraw, and ftretching out his little arms to his Mother.

The Prefentation in the Temple has great relation with
the compofition of Giotto. in the Academy of Fine Arts.
The figure of the Blessed Virgin is particularly remarkable for its fimplenefs. The ftraight lines of her mantle
and garment veil the form and movements of her body.
The aged Simeon lovingly preffes the Child Jefus to
his heart. S. Peter Martyr, and the prophetefs Anna
or Beata Villana are witneffes of the fame.[1]

The Adoration of the Magi is a mafterpiece, which may
be advantageoufly compared with all art then produced moft perfeft. It is executed in a cell larger than
the others; Cofimo de Medici had it made, to go
there and converfe with S. Antoninus and our two
painters, whom he particularly loved. Pope Eugenius
IV. alfo inhabited it, when he went to prefide at the
confecration of the church of San Marco, in 1442.
This ceremony took place on the feftival of the
Epiphany, and was the grand feftival of the period.
The Council of Florence had feen the Eaft adore

[1 "Nothing can be truer than his manner of pourtraying the affeftion of the
Mother, or the jubilee of the aged Simeon, clafping the Promifed One in his
arms. Although this pifture has fuftained injury at the hands of fome one who
removed the primitive ground, it is ftill very beautiful, particularly in the heads of
Simeon and the Mother."—MARCHESE, *by Meehan*, vol. i, p. 220.—TRANSLATOR'S
note.]

Chrift in the bofom of the Roman Church. The emperor and the patriarch of Conftantinople, the ambaffadors
of Ethiopia and Syria, were come to prefent their fubmiffion and homage to it in the perfon of the fucceffor
of S. Peter; and the fplendid feftivals which our
painter faw celebrated on that occafion, under the
vaults of Santa Maria dei Fiori, muft neceffarily have
influenced his imagination. The Adoration of the Magi
is a fubject often chofen by the painters of the Renaiffance, becaufe they could difplay in it great luxury of
coftumes and drapery. Beato Angelico painted it in the
cell of Cofimo de Medici as an inftruction to the rich
and powerful, who fhould lay down their fceptres and
their treafures at the feet of Chrift.

The fcene is admirably difpofed : the back-ground
reprefents the mountains of Judea the Magian kings
have croffed. The grotto of Bethlehem is indicated
by a flat furface of wall. The Holy Virgin's throne is the
faddle of an afs, and fhe holds the Child Jefus on her
knees, who bleffes the old Magian king, proftrate and
fcarce daring to put out his head and hand to
embrace the feet of the Defired of Nations. He has
offered his prefent, which S. Jofeph holds ftanding
near the Holy Virgin. Behind this perfonage are the
other two kings and their fuite, compofed of warriors
and fages in oriental coftumes. One of them holds a
fphere, to indicate the fcience which has led them to
the feet of the Saviour. Two men on horfeback look
up into the fky at the ftar which has ftood ftill over the
ftable. All thefe figures are full of life and drawn perfectly; no doubt they prefent portraits of celebrities of
the period, whom it is impoffible for us now to recognife.

Inftead of imitating the painters, who were then begin-
ing to fill their pictures with the liftlefs heads ftanding
before the fpectator, Beato Angelico has brought them
perfectly upon the ftage and imparted to them all the
fentiments of faith and adoration. By its beauty and
execution, this painting recalls the Defcent from the
Crofs in the Academy of Fine Arts, and it is very
much fuperior to the Adoration of the Magi, by Gentile
de Fabriano, in the fame Gallery.[1]

The Baptifm of our Lord takes place in a folitude
furrounded with rocks. The Holy Ghoft appears under
the form of a dove in the fky, and lights up all the fcene
with his rays. Our Lord is baptized by S. John.
Two angels are holding his garments, on the right;
and on the left, a female faint and a male faint, Domi-
nicians, are at prayer. The ftyle and the faults in proportion make us attribute this compofition to Fra
Benedetto.

Two cells have been fuppreffed, to open a commu-

---

[1] ["The back ground prefents a diftant view of the mountains of Judea; and
in order that nothing might feduce the eye or the foul from the contemplation of
the principal fubjects, he divefted them of verdure and foliage. Hollowed in the
living rock is feen the miferable grotto which firft fheltered the Saviour. The
poor Virgin is feated, and has her Divine Son on her knees. On her left is her
fpoufe, who contemplates an offering made by one of the Kings. Before them,
proftrate on the ground, in moft profound adoration, is a hoary-headed king, the
firft of the Magi, who, having laid down his diadem, approaches his lips to the
Divine Infant, who, with childifh grace, bleffes him. Behind him is the fecond,
who kneels, and evinces anxiety to perform the fame act of devotion. The third, the
youngeft of the three, is ftanding. Then follows a long train of footmen and
fervitors, admirably arranged and grouped; fome of whom difcourfe animatedly;
and in order to fhow that thefe princes were fkilled in aftronomy, he placed in
the hand of one of them an armillary fphere, as though he would thus feek to
account for that wonderful ftar which had lighted their way to Bethlehem. This
idea is beautifully expreffed. The others are engaged with the horfes; but
nothing can be more graceful than the laft figure on the left, which reprefents a

nication with the library. The fubjects reprefented
were, our Lord Jefus in the Defert, and his triumphant
entry into Jerufalem. There remains only of the firft
fubject a beautiful figure of the Saviour, fitting with
his hands clafped and his eyes raifed to heaven. His
garments are admirably draped.

The Sermon on the Mount. Chrift is fpeaking to the
Apoftles fitting in a circle at his feet. He has his
right hand raifed, and holds a paper rolled up in the
other. The fingular difpofition of the perfonages, and
their badly-drawn poftures and heads, make us recognize Fra Benedetto's hand again.

The Transfiguration. This compofition is full of
greatnefs and majefty. Chrift standing on a rock,
with his arms extended in a crofs, fhows himfelf in
his glory. This type is admirable for calmnefs and
grandeur. The Chrift of the Transfiguration by
Raphael may be more elegant and bold, but the one

man endeavouring to gaze at the ftar, beaming over the grotto, whilft he ufes his
hand to protect his eyes againft its blinding rays. Speaking of the artiftic merits
of this work, we may fay that the Bleffed Virgin and Infant are fupernaturally
beautiful. Nothing could have been better defigned and coloured than the firft
of the Magi, nor can anything better exprefs his burning defire to kifs the holy
feet of the Redeemer. The two other figures of the kings poffefs equal merit for
the nobility and grace that beam from their countenances ; but no words of ours
could defcribe the perfection of that group of courtiers and pages, who, gathered
together, converfe about the wondrous event. In fact one knows not which
fhould be moft praifed, the beauty of the attitudes, or the arrangement of the
draperies, that are in every refpect worthy of the moft celebrated painter. No
one will refufe to recognife in the whole compofition a happy imitation of that
life and grace fo peculiar to Mafolino; and thefe characteriftics are chiefly notice-
able in the relief which the Angelico has given to all the figures. The extremities
are well defigned ; nor does the entire lack a fingle beauty calculated to gladden
the heart or the eye. We grieve to think that time has done much injury to this
work ; nor do I know if it be in man's power to preferve it from approaching
ruin."—MARCHESE, by *Meehan*, vol. i, p. 221.—TRANSLATOR's note.]

by Beato Angelico is truer and more divine. The
heads of Mofes and Elias appear only in the clouds,
and leave to the principal figure all its importance.
The poftures of the Apoftles very well exprefs the daz-
zling of the light and the trouble of the exftacy.

The Inftitution of the Euchariſt. Our Lord gives
Holy Communion to the Apoftles fitting or kneeling.
Faith and love fhine on all their countenances. But
the falfe movements and heads too big give notice of
Fra Benedetto's hand.[1]

The Prayer in the Garden of Olives. Our Lord kneeling receives the chalice of the Paſſion from the angel.
The three Apoftles, whom fleep has overpowered, are in
the foreground. Near them, and as a contraft, Martha
and Mary are feen in a cell, who usually perfonify
the active and contemplative lives; but here Mary is
reading in a book, and Martha has her hands clafped.
Has not Beato Angelico wifhed to tell that it is neceffary to watch with the Saviour by meditation and
prayer ? All thefe figures are full of nature and noblenefs.

The Betrayal by Judas. The group of our Lord
and the faithlefs Apoftle is very fine. Chrift cafts a
look of compaſſion on him whom he ftill calls his
friend.

Chriſt in the Prætorium. The Saviour is feated in all
the majefty of his voluntary ignominies. He is crowned
with thorns, and has a tranfparent bandage over his
eyes. The reed he holds anfwers him for governing

[1 "The inftitution of the Sacrament, in which, following the method of the
Giottefque, he painted the Apoftles feated at the myftic Supper, and Jefus with the
chalice in his left hand whilft he prefents to them the confecrated hoft with his
right."—MARCHESE, by *Meehan*, vol. i, p. 222.—TRANSLATOR'S note.]

the world.   The executioners are abſent; but on the
hangings of the throne is ſeen, as ſet-off's the head of
the ſervant who ſpits in his face, and the hands that
ſtrike and outrage him.   On the ſteps of the throne, the
Holy Virgin and S. Dominic meditate the Paſſion.   This
compoſition is ſimple and ſublime.[1]

Chriſt goes up to Mount Calvary.   This is not an
hiſtorical ſcene, but a pious inſtruction.   The Saviour
carries his Croſs meekly, and his looks invite men to
follow him.   A holy woman, who repreſents the Chriſtian ſoul or the Church, walks in his footſteps in the
dolorous way.   A Dominican religious kneels on this
paſſage.

Chriſt faſtened to the Croſs.   This compoſition, particularly beautiful, is remarkable for the novel manner
in which the ſubject is rendered.   The Croſs is ſet up
like an altar for ſacrifice ; a little ladder ſerves as ſteps for
the victim.   Our Lord has voluntarily gone up, and
ſtretches out his arms to the executioners, who are
piercing his hands.   He bows his head and raiſes his

[1   " As the profound devotion of the Angelico would not allow him to repreſent
the ſacred humanity of the Redeemer expoſed to fiendiſh outrage and deriſion, he
ſtudied to make His divinity appear under the lowly garb of His mortality.   He
therefore painted Jeſus ſeated in great majeſty on a throne, but, though blindfolded, the tranſparency of the veil allows us to ſee His eyes, which are ſtern and
threatening.   His right hand holds the globe, and the left, inſtead of a ſceptre, a
bunch of rods.   Of the ſcoffers we can only ſee the hands and faces.   The white
garment that covers Him is beautifully draped.   Seated at the foot of the throne
are the Dolourated Virgin and S. Dominic, on the right and left; the latter,
whoſe attitude is graceful, holds an open volume on his knees and profoundly
meditates the humiliations of the Divine Word.   Motived by the ſame tender
devotion, inſtead of exhibiting the Redeemer writhing under the ſcourger's laſh,
he repreſents Him bound to the pillar; and places before Him S. Dominic, who
inflicts the diſcipline on his own naked ſhoulders.—MARCHESE, by *Meehan*, vol. i,
p. 223.—TRANSLATOR'S note.]

eyes to heaven, saying, "Father, forgive them, for they know not what they do!"[1] On his right, two holy women join in his grief; on his left, three persons feem to be prefiding at his execution: a doctor dis-cuffing, another looking infolently at the holy women, and a foldier clapping his hand on the hilt of his fword; that is, the injuftice, hatred and violence called up againft the Saviour. We do not know a more religious picture. The figure of Chrift efpecially is very beautiful; but ftill it caufes more compaffion than admiration.[2]

Padre Marchefe brings to this compofition the frag-ment of a legend of the thirteenth century, which feems to have infpired it. "And when they turned again, they perceived the Lord Jefus, who was going up the ladder with His feet and hand, and on feeing this fpectacle their lamentations were fo great and fo rending, that heaven and earth feemed to groan too. The other per-fons wept with compaffion over the Son, the Mother, and S. Magdalen who fpoke fo piteoufly that all who heard her feemed to have their hearts broken. It muft be believed that the Lord Jefus voluntarily mounted the ladder of the Crofs with His feet and hand. The cen-turion, who was afterwards faved, remarked Him, and as he was wife, faid within himfelf, 'O! what a wonder,

---

[1] Pater, dimitte illis, quia nefciunt *quid faciunt.*

[2] ["He painted the Crucifixion in many of the cells; and in that inhabited by the writer of thefe memoirs, he reprefented Chrift afcending the gibbet, to fhow the fpontaneity of His death, and Mary fainting and falling into the arms of Magdalene, at the foot of the Holy Rood. In the contiguous cell he painted the Dolourated Virgin and S. John weeping bitterly; then follow portraits of S. Dominic and Thomas of Aquino, abforbed in the contemplation of this ineffable myftery of love."—MARCHESE, by *Meehan*, vol. i. p. 223.—TRANS-LATOR'S note.]

the Prophet appears to go up voluntarily to be placed
on the Crofs ; He does not make any complaint nor
refiftance.' And whilft he was wondering at Him, the
Lord Jefus went up as high as was neceffary, then He
turned on the ladder, extended His arms in a princely
manner, and offered His hands to thofe who were
charged to pierce them."' How many infpirations
would art again find in thefe pious and poetic legends !

The Crucifixion. Chrift, amidft the agonies of death,
promifes the joys of paradife to the good thief.' At
.the foot of the Crofs, the Holy Virgin and S. John, who
are weeping. S. Dominic extends his arms, to imitate
the Saviour. Another Dominican kneeling holds an
open book. This compofition is beautiful ; but the
faults in drawing and proportions make us attribute it
to Fra Benedetto.

The Death of Our Lord is again reprefented in two
cells. Beato Angelico has chofen the moment when the
foldier Longinus pierces the Saviour's fide, and makes
gufh out under the head of his fpear the divine blood
which is to heal the eyes of his body, and to purify
thofe of his foul. A Dominican faint kneels at the
foot of the Crofs. The Virgin Mary turns away and
hides her face in her hands : Martha advances to fupport her. This fcene is full of devotion and recollection. The figure of Longinus is very fine. The
draperies are drawn very remarkably. In another cell,
Chrift has for witneffes of his death the Holy Virgin and
S. John on one fide, S. Dominic and S. Jerome on the
other. The ftyle of all thefe figures is very beautiful.

' S. Marco illuftrato e incifo.—V. MARCHESE, p. 40.

' Hodie mecum eris in paradifo.

S. Jerome prefents the fame type as in the frame of the Descent from the Crofs, in the Academy of Fine Arts, and in the great frefco in the chapter-room. His emaciation, his fhort and poor garment, his book and difcipline recall his life of ftudy and of penance in the defert.

The Burial. The holy women and S. John the Evangelift bury our Lord, in the prefence of S. Dominic. We believe this compofition to be by Fra Benedetto, who may have been infpired, efpecially for the head of Chrift, by the Burial we have admired in the Academy of Fine Arts.

We will alfo attribute to the fame artift the *Descent into Limbo*, in the cell where S. Antoninus dwelt. The compofition is the fame as the one he made in the Life of our Lord, in the Academy of Fine Arts. Chrift enters as conqueror, and ftretches out his hand to Abraham, the father of the faithful, who leads the juft, at the head of whom walk Adam and Eve. Satan is crufhed by the fall of the gate of hell, and the devils flee into the clefts of the rock. The figure of the Saviour has fome movement and noblenefs; but in the other perfonages there are grofs faults, which Beato Angelico could not have committed; the feet particularly are horribly drawn.

The Holy Women at the Tomb. The angel is fitting on the edge of the empty tomb, and announces the refurreftion by his gefture. Chrift appears in the upper part, with the palm and the ftandard of victory. The holy women do not fee him, and look into the tomb with fadnefs. This group is admirable and would do honour to the greateft mafters. Behind the angel is a kneeling figure of S. Dominic; it is faid to be a portrait. Beato Angelico has, perhaps, painted a religious, which may have been afterwards decorated with an aureola and a ftar. All this compofition is executed with wonderful fweetnefs of tone and foftnefs of light.

Noli me tangere. In a lonely and choice garden Jefus appears to Mary Magdalen, as the gardener who cultivates the flowers of virtue in the foul; but he paffes on, charging her, who is adoring him, not to be too much attached to the fweetnefs of his prefence. Mary Magdalen on her knees ftretches out her hands towards him; fhe is ardent but fubmiffive. It is impoffible to give this leffon in myftic life better.

The Coronation of the Virgin. Beato Angelico has treated his much-loved fubject with his ordinary perfection. Chrift and the Holy Virgin, in glory, are seated on light clouds. The Son puts the heavenly crown upon the head of his Mother, who humbly bows and feems again to fay, " Behold the handmaid of the Lord.'" It is the tranflation of the verfe of Petrarch,

> " E ftava tutta humile in tanta gloria."

Both are clothed with the fame white fhining garment, as with the fame flefh and fame purity. Some faints in exftacy affift at this triumph of the Bleffed Virgin ; S. Paul, S. Benedict, S. Dominic, S. Francis, S. Peter Martyr. Our painter may be said to have shared in their exftacy, to render it so well.'

[' "The laft of the frefcos, and the moft beautiful of them all, in which he difplays fuch maftery in depicting the ineffable joys of heaven, is the Coronation of the Bleffed Virgin. This, indeed, is far more celeftial than his picture on the fame fubject in the gallery of the Uffizj. We, however, will endeavour to de-

Beato Angelico has painted for another religious one of his moſt beautiful Madonnas. The Child Jeſus ſtanding on his Mother's knees, ſeems to be teaching the two greateſt theologians of the Church, S. Auguſtine and S. Thomas Aquinas.

Laſtly, on the wall of the upper dormitory, Beato Angelico has offered to the piety of his brethren another Madonna ſurrounded with the patron ſaints of the convent and Order, S. Mark, S. Coſmas, S. Damian, and S. Dominic, on the right ; and on the left, S. Paul, S. Lawrence, S. Thomas, and S. Peter Martyr. S. Dominic holds a book and points in it to the bequeſt he left his children : " Have charity, keep humility, poſſeſs voluntary poverty. I call down the

ſcribe how the artiſt developed his devout conception ; for, indeed, we confeſs our inability to expreſs the ſenſations which this glorious work has awakened in our heart. He painted the Virgin ſeated on a white cloud, which is overarched by a charming rainbow. She is robed in white, her arms are folded on her boſom, a gentle ſmile is on her lips, and ſhe leans gracefully forward towards her Divine Son. 'Mid all the glory, ſhe is the humbleſt of all. The Word is ſeated by her ſide, and ſeems to crown her. He does not, however, hold the golden diadem in His hands ; on the contrary, He barely touches it with the extremity of His fingers, as though He had ordered it to go and encircle His Mother's temples—a ſublime idea, that reminds us of the creative *Fiat.* He alſo wears a white robe, which is ſhaded with a light tint of chiaroſcuro, and appears to be as ſubtile as the air. In the drapery of theſe figures the Angelico has excelled himſelf. At their feet he painted three Saints on the right and three on the left ; they alſo ſtand on a white cloud, and are wrapt in ecſtaſy, contemplating this glory. Here he has more cloſely followed Dante ; for he diſpoſed theſe ſix figures on a ſemicircular line, as though they conſtituted one of thoſe garlands of Bleſſed ſpirits who inceſſantly ſing and dance round the throne of the Eternal. They are SS. Paul, Thomas, Francis, Benedict, Dominic, Peter Martyr ; and they all have their eyes and hands raiſed to heaven. From their countenances beam joy and beatitude. Whoſoever ſtands in preſence of it may almoſt fancy himſelf tranſlated to the ſociety of the Bleſſed. The tinting of this hiſtory is ſo delicate and tranſparent, and the pencilling ſo fine, that it looks more like a celeſtial viſion than a painting ; and, perhaps, it appeared as ſuch to the devout artiſt in the act of colouring it."—MARCHESE, *by Meehan,* vol. i., p. 225.—TRANSLATOR's note.]

curse of God and mine on him who fhall bring
poffeffions into my Order."[1]   This compofition is one
of the moft perfect in the convent of San Marco. The
execution is free, the figures well drawn and in an excellent ftyle.   All the perfonages are full of nobleness and
life : they well reprefent to us the religious who came
to plant the ftandard of the reform in the city of
Florence, which corruption was invading on every fide.
They were diftinguifhed as much for their fanctity as
for their fcience and genius. The great movement produced in the Church by S. Catherine of Sienna, made
itfelf particularly felt within her Order.   It was the
epoch of S. Vincent Ferrer and S. Antoninus ; and befide Beato Angelico fhone Padre Giovanni of Monte-
negro, the light of the Council of Florence, who was
admired by the moft diftinguifhed minds of the Eaft,
fent to conclude the reconciliation which unfortunately was of fo fhort duration.

O, fweet afylum ! fair convent ! little cells ! lonely
cloifters ! May you fee your ancient days again ! How
can I forget the time I paffed beneath your fhadow ! It
was eafy for me, whilft ftudying your mafterpieces, to
call up the recollection of the holy generation which
lived with Beato Angelico.   I faw its beautiful images
in thofe pictures, and once more found its virtues in
thofe who gave me fo benevolent a hofpitality.

---

[1] Caritatem habete, humilitatem fervate, paupertatem voluntariam poffidete.
Maledictionem Dei et meam imprecor poffeffiones inducenti in meo Ordine.

CHAPTER XII.

BEATO ANGELICO AT ROME.—CHAPEL OF THE
VATICAN.—(1445-1455.)

EATO ANGELICO had to paſs his
laſtyears at Rome. That city, the
centre of the world and of hiſtory,
ſeemed ſprung to life again after the
return of the popes. Its monuments were admired, its ruins interrogated, its maſterpieces dug up.
All artiſts made a pilgrimage to it; and we have ſeen
how architects, ſculptors and painters brought new
ideas back, and the germ of the Renaiſſance. Beato
Angelico was as capable as his fellow-citizens of admiring
theſe wonders; but it was not pagan Rome he wiſhed
to ſee, it was Rome the holy, the catacombs, the tomb
of the Apoſtles, that battle-field of Chriſtianity and
heatheniſm, thoſe temples conquered by the martyrs,
and the Croſs of Chriſt upon the Capitol. And if he

admired the ſtatues of the vanquiſhed gods and the wealth of their ſpoil, his heart was thereby made only more faithful to the Truth, which had triumphed over them.

Beato Angelico had to quit Florence for Rome about the year 1445. Pope Eugenius IV., who had particularly known him at the convent of San Marco, called him to decorate the Vatican. This was, without doubt, at the time of the deceaſe of Archbiſhop Zabarella, in 1445, and at that period muſt be fixed the faᶜt inexaᶜtly related by Vaſari.

This hiſtorian tells us that Beato Angelico was called to Rome by Nicholas V., who wiſhed to nominate him to the archbiſhopric of Florence. " And as Fra Giovanni appeared to the pope to be, as he really was, a perſon of moſt holy life, gentle and modeſt, he judged him, on the archbiſhopric of Florence becoming vacant, worthy of that dignity. But the Friar, when he heard it, beſought his Holineſs to provide ſome other perſon, as he did not feel himſelf capable of governing the people; and ſaid that there was in his religion a Friar, a lover of the poor, very learned, able to govern, and one who feared God, on whom it would be much better to confer the dignity than on himſelf. The pope hearing this, and remembering that what he ſaid was true, freely granted him the favour, and thus was Fra Antonino, of the Order of Preachers, made archbiſhop of Florence, a man truly renowned for holineſs and learning, ſuch an one in ſhort as to merit being canonized by Adrian VI. in our own time." [1]

---

[1] E perchè al papa parve fra Giovanni, ſiccome era veramente, perſona di ſantiſſima vita, quieta e modeſta, vacando l'arciveſcovado in quel tempo di Firenze

Vafari is evidently miftaken in attributing the nomi-
nation of S. Antoninus to Nicholas V., fince it took place
under the pontificate of Eugenius IV., in 1445. With
regard to the offer made to Beato Angelico, many, defpite fo pofitive teftimony of tradition, find it fcarcely
probable that the Sovereign Pontiff who had called
him to the Vatican would defire to take him away from
the pencil and caft him amidft the difficulties of the
adminiftration of a diocefe. He might be worthy of
the epifcopate for his virtues, but nothing had qualified him to difcharge its functions. Would it not be
more natural to fuppofe that the Sovereign Pontiff
only confulted Beato Angelico amidft the intrigues of
which the fee of Florence was the object, and that our
painter fixed his choice on S. Antoninus? A letter of
one of the holy archbifhop's friends, addreffed to the
Dominicans of Bologna, tells us that the pope hefitated for nine months, and that the counfels of fome
religious decided him to nominate S. Antoninus, whom
he already knew.[1] Eugenius IV. had appreciated S.
Antoninus during his ftay at the convent of San Marco,
and made him affift in the council of Florence. He

l'aveva guidicato degno di quel grado, quando intendendo ciò il detto frate, fup-
plicò à Sua Santità che provvedeffe d'un altro, perciocchè non fi fentiva atto a
governar popoli; ma che avendo la fua religione un frate amorevole de' poveri,
dottiffimo, di governo, e timorato di Dio, farebbe in lui molto meglio quella dig-
nità collocata che in fe. Il papa fentendo ciò e ricordandofi che quello che diceva
era vero, gli fece la grazia liberamente, e così fu fatto archivefcovo di Fiorenza frate
Antonino dell' ordine de' Predicatori, uomo veramente per fantità e dottrina chia-
riffimo, ed infomma tale, che meritò che Adriano VI. lo canonizaffe a' tempi
noftri.

[1] Ita novem menfibus ambiguus, fufpenfufque animo Romanus Pontifex per-
feverat. cui tandem fubjicientibus viris religiofis perfonam Antonini, cùm jam
antea virtutem hominis cognoviffet, ftatim eorum confiliis acquievit —BOLLAND,
Acta Sanctorum.

maintained the choice againſt the reſiſtance of his
humility, and wrote to him from Rome, ordering him
to return to the convent of Fieſole, where he would be
ſought in great pomp to take poſſeſſion of his ſee.

Beato Angelico enjoyed the friendſhip of two great
popes. Eugenius IV. and Nicholas V. were the beſt
gifts God made to His Church in the fifteenth century.
The miſſion of Eugenius IV. was to reform diſcipline
and heal the wounds inflicted by the ſchiſm on religion, and he had all the virtues and talents neceſſary
to carry it out. Noble and rich by birth, he might
have aſpired to every honour; but he ſtrove to fly
them by diſtibuting his fortune amongſt the poor,
and ſhutting himſelf up in a convent at Venice.
Thither his uncle Gregory XII. went, to take and place
him as the light upon the candleſtick. Endowed with
a ſuperior intelligence and a generous heart, he was the
devoted friend of the poor, and an apoſtle full of zeal
for the reform of the Church, the ſpread of the faith,
and the beauties of worſhip. When he mounted the
Chair of Peter, the ſynod of Baſle threatened the
Weſt with a new ſchiſm. We cannot admire too much
the mildneſs, patience and firmneſs he diſplayed to lay
the danger. But the great glory of his pontificate was
the Council of Florence : the good ſhepherd neglected
no means to bring back the ſeparated ſheep to the
fold. He ſpared neither pains, nor ſteps, nor expence ;
and at his coſt the emperor of Conſtantinople, the
patriarchs of the Eaſt, and the Greeks were conducted
over and received in Italy. This event was a brilliant
victory for the nations of the Weſt. The Greeks themſelves owned the ſuperiority of the Latins in the arts as

well as in the fciences. The truth united the conquerors
and the conquered again in one fame triumph, and the
ceremony which clofed the council, under the dome
of Santa Maria dei Fiori, was a fight worthy of the admiration of heaven and earth. The refult would have
been greater than that of the Crufades, if the bad faith
of the Greeks had not rendered it fo tranfitory. The
whole world was at peace; France and Germany were
reconciled with the holy fee, ambafladors haftened
from the moft diftant countries, and the faith fhone in all
the fplendour of its unity. It was perhaps this folemn
moment which rapt S. Catherine of Sienna in ecftacy,
when God willed to confole her for the horrors of the
fchifm fhe faw arife under Urban VI.[1] Eugenius IV. alfo
felt great joy, and might have fung the canticle of the
aged Simeon, when, juft before his death, he received
the laft ambafladors of the peace. Nothing is more
affecting than the account of his end. After he had celebrated holy mafs on Chriftmas-day, he fell ill all at once
and announced his approaching death. He called S.
Antoninus to affift him, who then faw Beato Angelico
again. Before receiving the facraments, Eugenius IV.
delivered an admirable difcourfe, in the prefence of
the affembled cardinals. In it he gives, with humility,
an account of his glorious pontificate; he rejoices to
fee all people united, and leaves them the heritage of
the peace and example of Jefus Chrift; he gives the
cardinals counfels for the future, and afks of them only
prayers and a fimple burial. The next day, the feaft of
S. Peter's Chair, S. Antoninus fpoke long to him on the
joys of heaven which he was going to enter, and he took

[1] *Vie de S. Catherine de Sienne*, ii. parte, chap. 10.

poffeffion of it at the very moment when the Church was faying to him "Depart, Chriftian soul."[1]

The conclave which named his fucceffor met in the Dominican church of Santa Maria fopra Minerva, and Beato Angelico was confequently one of the firft to pay homage to the Cardinal Archbifhop of Bologna, who took the name of Nicholas V. Tommafo de Sarzane had particularly known our painter during the Council of Florence, when he was charged by Cofimo de Medici to form the library of the Convent of San Marco; fo Beato Angelico found in the new Sovereign Pontiff an affectionate and worthy protector.

Nicholas V. is, perhaps, the moft glorious name to oppofe to those who pufh ignorance and falfehood fo far as even boldly to accufe the Popes of having been an obftacle to the progrefs of fcience and art. No one was more capable of inaugurating the new era which opened for the Church after the Council of Florence, and of guiding the intellectual movement at the moment of the Renaiffance in the direct and true path. Nicholas V. would have given his name to his age, if this movement, legitimate in its principle, had not allowed itfelf to be led aftray by idolatry of heathen antiquity. Leo X. gave his own only to an epoch of corruption and decay. Nicholas V. has certainly done more for the fciences and arts than all the Medici, and none afforded them a more intelligent and effectual protection.

Born in an humble ftation, and obliged to ftruggle againft poverty to inftruct himfelf, ftill at the age

[1] Hiftoire Univerfelle de l'Eglife Catholique, par Rohrbacher, tom. xxi., l. lxxxii., p. 587.

of twenty-two years, he won the firft honours of the
learned univerfity of Bologna. He merited, too, the
friendfhip of Beato Niccolo Albergati, and in remembrance of his benefactor, he chofe the name for his
pontificate. Being employed in difficult negociations
by Pope Eugenius IV., he turned his long journeys to
profit, by ftudying languages and manufcripts, and his
reputation led to his being entrufted with the organization of all the public libraries, on which the learned men
of the Renaiffance were bufied. Being unanimoufly
nominated pope by the college of cardinals, he accepted
the heritage of Eugenius IV., and effaced the laft traces of
the fchifm by pardoning Felix V. When the Greeks had
preferred the turban to the tiara, and drawn down upon
themfelves the chaftifements which are ftill lafting, he
acted againft Iflamifm with the zeal of S. Bernard.
The civilization with which he combatted the enemies
without, he protected and developed within. The great
jubilee of 1450 brought around him the reprefentatives
of all nations of the earth, a religious concourfe far
more impofing and far more civilizing than thofe
organifed in our days.

Nicholas V. fought, above all, to favour the progrefs
of fcience. To collect its facred and profane treafures
he fent all over the earth, and procured manufcripts
for their weight in gold; he dreamt of the library of
Alexandria for Rome. Men of learning were lodged
in the Vatican and magnificently entertained. He
caufed the poets, the Greek hiftorians, and the fathers
of the Church to be copied and tranflated, and placed at
the head of this movement the celebrated and pious
Manetto, fo well qualified to direct it. The fine arts

alfo owed much to him. He defired to reftore Rome,
as Auguftus had done. He made the ftreets larger,
raifed magnificent buildings, and laid the foundations
of the Bafilica of San Pietro. Truth was his paffion,
and he wifhed it in all and for all; he defired it efpecially for himfelf, and regretted the honours of his
pontificate as obftacles calculated to deprive him of it.
He called about him holy religious, with whom he
lived in the ftricteft intimacy. Beato Angelico was one
of his privileged friends. Vafari gives us a proof of
this intimacy. " Fra Giovanni," fays he, " was a man
of fimplicity, and moft holy in his habits ; and he gave
this evidence of his goodnefs, that when Pope Nicholas
V. wifhed one morning to give him dinner, he fcrupled
to eat flefh without his prior's licence, not reflecting on
the higher authority of the pontiff."[1] This affection
lafted until death. Nicholas V. would make the
epitaph himfelf, which was engraved on his tomb.
Under the charm of thefe glorious friendfhips, Beato
Angelico paffed the laft ten years of his life near the
pontifical throne. We have now to ftudy the influence Rome exercifed on his talent. This influence
was what it ought to have been. The artifts of Florence
were enamoured of ancient art, even to idolatry. Beato
Angelico was quite as capable as any of them of appreciating its mafterpieces ; but his admiration did not keep
him from remaining Chriftian. He did not employ the
precious veffels of Egypt to raife up the golden calf,

---

[1] Fu fra Giovanni femplice uomo e fantiffimo ne' fuoi coftumi, e quefto faccia
fegno della bontà fua, che volendo una mattina, papa Niccola V. dargli definare, fi
fece cofcienza di mangiar della carne fenza licenza del fuo Priore, non penfando all
autorità del Pontefice.

but melted them down to fet off the ark of the cove-
nant with the pureft ornaments, and to embroider the
magnificent draperies of the fanctuary. His infpiration
always remained the fame. His genius was not led
aftray into imitation of the ancients. His materials
only were richer, his ftyle assumed more grandeur, yet
without lofing any of the qualities we have already admired in him.

Beato Angelico painted two chapels in the Vatican,
the chapel of the Holy Sacrament which was deftroyed
under Paul III. to form the ftaircafe leading to the
Siftine chapel, and the chapel in which the hiftories of
S. Stephen and S. Lawrence are reprefented, called the
chapel of Nicholas V. This is how Vafari fpeaks of
the firft. " For the fame pope, he did the chapel of
the Sacrament in the palace, which was afterwards deftroyed by Paul III., to erect a ftaircafe there. In this
work, which was an excellent one, he executed in frefco,
in his own manner, fome hiftories from the life of
Chrift, and introduced portraits of many perfons eminent in his time. Thefe portraits would probably have
been all loft if Paolo Giovio had not had the following
taken off for his mufeum : Nicholas V.; the Emperor
Frederic, who, at that time, came into Italy ; Fra Antonino, who was then archbifhop of Florence; Biondo da
Forli, and Ferdinand of Arragon."[1] We do not know
what has become of thefe portraits. The deftruction

[1] Fece anco per il detto papa la cappella del Sagramento in Palazzo, che fu poi
rovinata da Paolo III. per dirizzarvi le fcale, nella quale opera, che era eccellente in
quella maniera fua aveva lavorato in frefco alcune ftorie della vita di Gefù Crifto,
e fattovi molti ritratti dinaturale di perfone segnalate di que' tempti, i quali per
avventura farebbono oggi perduti, fi il Giovio non aveffe fattone ricavar quefti per
il fuo mufeo : papa Nicola V., Federigo imperatore, che in quel tempo venne in

of this chapel is much to be regretted: we fhould have been able to compare the fame fubjects executed by the fame artift at the three principal epochs of his life, at Fiefole, at San Marco and at Rome.

Fortunately, the other chapel has been preferved. It is fmall,[1] and lighted by an arched window, below which is now placed the altar once oppofite to it. On the other three fides, Beato Angelico has painted two fets of compofitions over each other. In the arches of the upper part, he reprefented the hiftory of S. Stephen in fix compartments.

1. *S. Peter confers Deaconfhip on S. Stephen* in the prefence of the college of the apoftles. The head of the Church prefents the chalice and paten to the deacon, who touches them with reverence, whilft looking at him through whom all power comes down. The altar has an elegant ciborium upon it, and the bottom is orna-mented with a rich architectural defign. For this fubject, as well as for the others, we remark a change of ftyle; the lines become more fimple and the dra-peries more noble. The artift has ftudied the Roman toga on the ancient ftatues and bas-reliefs, and in order to difplay its magnificence, he covers the facerdotal veft-ment of S. Peter and the dalmatic of S. Stephen with it.

2. *Diftribution of the Alms.* S. Stephen gives the alms of the faithful to the poor. All is done orderly

---

Italia, frate Antonino, che fu poi arcivefcovo di Firenze, il Biondo da Forli, e Ferrante d'Aragona.

[1] It is 6 metres 75 centimetres long, by 4 metres 20 centimetres broad. The pavement is white marble beautifully inlaid. The fun is reprefented furrounded with the twelve months of the year, indicated by their Latin initials and the figns of the zodiac. On the fcrolls accompanying the extremities of the lozenges of the border is read—NICOLAVS PP. QUINTUS. We believe this pavement was executed under Benedict XIII., in 1725.

and quietly; a cleric calls out from a lift those who are to receive, fome are coming up, others going away. S. Stephen is giving a filver piece to a widow: his countenance breathes purity, he looks only at the hand extended to him. The three women in the foreground are in a fine ftyle, and have the dignity of the matron and the modefty of the Chriftian female. In this compofition is feen the ennobling of alms by charity, which unites before God him who gives and him who receives. A man coming up has an admirable truthfulnefs of drawing: the movement could not be given with more meafure and more happily.

3. *The preaching of S. Stephen.* After material alms follow fpiritual alms. The faint diftributes the bread of the word to an auditory feated at his feet. The women liftening to him are remarkable for pofture and draperies: their varied heads all exprefs attention and refpeét. Behind them, fome men hear the preaching with various feelings. This compofition might be compared with the legend of S. Nicholas, in which the youthful faint is liftening to a fermon;[1] the gracefulnefs and fimplicity are replaced by fuperior qualities. There is no longer the fmall lonely auditory on a flowery turf, but the populacy of a great city, in the midft of fplendid buildings, and on the irregular pavement of the Roman roads. The genius of the artift has reached its full maturity.

4. *S. Stephen before the great Council.* The faint delivers the fublime difcourfe, in which he unfolds all the hiftory of the truth.[2] His pofture is quiet; his intelligent gefture contrafts with the exafperation of

[1] Page 57.   [2] *Aéts of the Apoftles,* ch. vii.

the priefts, who can oppofe him only with falfehood and hatred. This fcene is a model of monumental painting; in the architecture is remarked a decoration of the defigns in mofaic which ornament a great number of the churches in Rome.

5. *S. Stephen led to Martyrdom.* This fcene of violence is rendered perfectly. A Jew drags the faint outfide the city, whilft others pufh him, and ftone in hand purfue him. We do not know how to praife too much the energy of expreffions, the juftnefs of the movements and the richnefs of the draperies. The walls forming the back-ground of the picture remind us of the admirable lines of the circuit-wall of Rome between the Porta di San Giovanni Laterno and the Church of Santa Croce in Gerufalemme.

6. *The Death of S. Stephen.* The faint receives the crown of martyrdom kneeling, with his hands and eyes raifed to heaven. His face is all bathed in blood. Behind the executioners, Saul, their accomplice, carries a cloak ; yet the faint is not ftripped of his clothes, for the toga ftill covers the dalmatic. All thefe compofitions indicate the ftudy of the ancient monuments; but the beauty of the lines and noblenefs of the draperies do not make any of the religious character and Chriftian thought be loft .

The hiftory of S. Lawrence approaches the mediæval ftyle in the coftumes; but ftill here may be feen the trace of the archæological ftudies then in vogue. It muft alfo be remarked that the painter knew how to vary his compofitions in fubjects pretty nearly alike.

1. *S. Lawrence receives the Deaconfhip.* The fuc-

ceffor of S. Peter is feated upon his throne, and makes S. Lawrence touch the chalice and paten. Three perfons vefted in magnificent copes affift at the ceremony, as alfo deacons and clerics who hold the book and the cenfer. All thefe figures are full of life and purity; and, without doubt, are portraits. Beato Angelico well knew how to choofe his models. The background of the picture is a Chriftian bafilica, in the apfe of which our Lord is feen reprefented, giving S. Peter the power to feed his fheep and his lambs.

2. *The Farewell of S. Sixtus and S. Lawrence.* The pope delivers the treafures of the Church to his deacon. A cleric placed behind him turns at the noife made at the door by the foldiers, who are coming to lead him to martyrdom.

3. *S. Lawrence diftributes his alms.* The faint who is clothed by Chrift, bears thefe words embroidered on the pectoral of his dalmatic, IHESVS ✠ CRISTVS. He is furrounded by the poor, the lame and the blind, whom he called the treafures of the Church. Beato Angelico could poetife fuffering and deformity by the truth of the movements and livelinefs of the expreffions. The blind man advancing on the right, whilft groping along with his ftick, is a mafterpiece. Raphael feems to have been infpired by it in his admirable cartoon of the magician ftruck blind by S. Paul, in the prefence of the pro-conful Sergius.[1] It is impoffible to give life and movement better.

4. *The Condemnation of S. Lawrence.* The emperor is feated on his tribunal, and fhows the faint the inftruments of torture in ftore for him, if he does not

---

[1] *Acts of the Apoftles*, xiii. 2.

sacrifice to the gods. This composition presents a singular medley of costume. It may be said to be a memorial of the coronation of Frederic III., which Beato Angelico witnessed, March 15th, 1451.

The medley of ancient armour of dubious archæological exactness, with the costumes of the middle ages, is very much in conformity with the idea of reviving the empire of the West. The emperor Decius has the cuirass and the draped mantle of the imperial busts of the Renaissance. His sceptre is tipped with a little ancient divinity. The personages around him have the large hanging sleeves and the close cut of the fifteenth century. In all ages, fashion often outrages good taste. The architecture is decorated with ancient ornaments. On the entablature of the tribunal, is seen the Roman eagle, with wings displayed, in a crown of laurel. Above the head of the emperor, is read, DECIUS IN-PERATOR, and on the step, A.D. CCLIII., about the date of S. Lawrence's martyrdom, or MCCCCLIII., which would be the year of the execution of the picture.

5. The study of the antique appears still more in the composition following, which represents *The Martyrdom of S. Lawrence*. The emperor, surrounded by his court, assists from the top of a terrace at the punishment of the saint. Between the pillars supporting the terrace, are placed five ancient statues well drawn. Thus may artists, whilst treating subjects of the earliest ages of Christianity, represent the monuments of a religion triumphed over by the Cross; truth even demands it, as it also requires Christian expression and moral beauty to prevail over all these magnificences. It is necessary to look on and express these

fcenes with the faith of the firft Chriftians, and not with the incredulity of the heathen, who faw in their victims only dangerous fanatics.

On the left of the fpectator, a window of the prifon lets S. Lawrence be feen converting a man on his knees, doubtlefs S. Hippolytus. In the foreground, S. Lawrence extended on his gridiron raifes his hand, and feems to be fpeaking to the emperor, to tell him he was fufficiently burnt on one fide, and he might have him turned on the other. The figure is well drawn, and decent defpite its nudity. The executioners are varied in pofture and expreffion; one of them is carrying wood; the other turns the faint with a long fork; another makes up the fire, and fhows the intenfity of the heat by his geftures.

The execution of thefe pictures is very remarkable. Beato Angelico has not loft any of his qualities and has acquired new ones. To the purity of his drawing and the tranfparency of his colouring, he has joined more fcience in the lines, more vigour in the tones, and more power in the modelling.

Thefe compofitions are framed with the figures of the greateft doctors of the Church. In the choice of them may be feen a memorial of the Council of Florence. The popes S. Leo and S. Gregory the Great are the fovereign pontiffs who reprefent beft for the Eaft, the primacy of the Bifhop of Rome. S. John Chryfoftom and S. Athanafius are the two fathers whofe works ferved moft to convince the Greeks on the fubject of the proceffion of the Holy Ghoft. S. Leo is fhowing a text open. S. Gregory holds a book and a pen, and is liftening to the infpiration of the Holy

R

Ghoft under the form of a dove. St. John Chryfoftom holds a book, in which this infcription is read: ATTENDE TIBI IPSI, NE FORTE FIAT IN CORDE TUO OCCULTA, IMPIAVE COGITATIO; "Watch over thyfelf, left perhaps a hidden or unholy thought be in thy heart."

From his crofier hangs the *fudarium*, which expreffes well the sweat of his laborious epifcopate. On the embroidery of his cope are decyphered words which ferve as ornaments, and are, as it were, confufed traces of the artift's thoughts and prayers. *Jefus of Naz-areth, King of the Jews ... Jefus. Mary ... of finners ... our advocate:* CHRISTUS NAZARENUS REX JUDE-ORUM. A. MAL. JHESUS-MARIA ... DE PECATORIBUS. ET SE. NOSTRA AVOCATA ... S. Athanafius is in ori-ental coftume : he feems to be commenting on a paffage of the Holy Scriptures.

Above thefe figures are placed thofe of S. Auguftine, S. Ambrofe, S. Bonaventure, and S. Thomas Aquinas holding a book in which is read: VERITATEM MEDIT-ABITUR GUTTUR MEUM, ET LABIA MEA DETESTA-BUNTUR INPIUM (*fic*): "My mouth fhall meditate truth, and my lips fhall hate wickednefs." His breaft is decorated with an eye beaming like the fun, to exprefs the light of his intellect which enlightened the Church. All thefe beautiful figures are placed under fmall gothic canopies, to be compared for elegance with thofe which crown the ftatues of the faints at the porches of our cathedrals. It is feen that Beato Angelico, amidft his ftudies of ancient Rome, did not repudiate the architecture of the middle ages. The four evangelifts are painted in the compartments of the vaulted ceiling, on an azure ground ftudded with gold ftars. The ridges of the roof are ornamented with defigns. In the lower part of the walls a rich drapery is painted. The whole decoration of this chapel is conceived perfectly, and proves how well the artift underftood monumental painting for the compofition as well as for the execution. The figures are of a fuitable fize; the general lines and the tones do not difturb the architecture; and the whole is harmonious and full of poetry.[1]

[1] ["In the fecond chapel (now called "of Pope Nicholas V."), he painted fome hiftories of the protomartyr S. Stephen, and S. Laurence, in the manner which we will now defcribe. He coloured the whole ceiling in ultramarine blue, and ftudded it with many golden ftars, according to the Giottefque, and he introduced the four Evangelifts, and eight Doctors of the holy Church. On the right, are S. John Chryfoftom and S. Bonaventure. Above thefe are S. Gregory and S. Auguftin. On the left, in the under part, are S. Athanafius, and S. Thomas of Aquino, and over them S. Ambrofe and S. Leo, the laft of which figures is almoft wholly effaced. All thefe Doctors are reprefented as ftanding erect under a little Gothic temple. The hiftories of the Martyrs he executed in fix compartments, wherein he painted the principal facts of the lives of two of them, in order to fhow the great refemblance that the hiftory of the one bears to that of the other. They are as follows:—S. Peter at an altar giving the chalice to the firft confecrated Deacon, S. Stephen, who receives it kneeling.—The holy Martyr giving alms to the poor. In the under part, he introduced Pope S. Sixtus. In the upper part is the Sermon of S. Stephen, and the fame Saint before the Jewifh high prieft. . . In the under part he introduced Pope S. Sixtus blefling S. Laurence, and giving him the treafures of his church to difpenfe them to the poor, at the very moment that two armed men are ftriking the door in order to gain admittance. Then comes the holy Deacon, giving alms to a great multitude of poor and infirm. On the left wall he painted the Stoning of S. Stephen, and in the under part S. Laurence before the tyrant, who, pointing to the various inftruments of torture, ftrives to fhake his conftancy. In another compartment, he executed a little window, through which we can fee the Saint in his dungeon, baptizing his fellow-captives. Finally, comes the martyrdom of S. Laurence. Under thefe little hiftories he painted a rich ornamentation of fruits and flowers, varioufly intertwined and alternated with the heads of angels and the triple crown: rofes and ftars exquifitely arranged complete the adornment of this work. I doubt not that Benozzo Gozzoli, who was celebrated for fuch decorations, was the author of thefe. Of the merits of the hiftories, we will now hear two of the moft celebrated writers on

This chapel, fo important for the hiftory of Chriftian art, was long forgotten.　Its exiftence was fcarcely known, and the learned Bottari, in order to vifit it, had to get through the window, as the key of the door was loft.　The profeffors of painting at Rome forbad the ftudy of it to their pupils as dangerous for their tafte :

art.　M. Seroux D'Agincourt fpeaks of them thus:—"The ability with which thefe frefcoes are finifhed is truly prodigious, and nothing can be more delicious to the eye than their colouring.　The fhadings are not ftrong, but the chiarofcuro is harmonious.　On near infpe&ion, thefe frefcos have all the graces of miniature. At a diftance, the vigour of their tints produces the effe& of a bold and free pen-cilling," etc.　He then lauds the artift for the beauty of the expreffion, in which he recognized a happy imitation of Mafaccio.　He likewife praifes the perfpe&ive of the buildings.　The criticifm of M. Rio is as follows :—" The work which excels that of which I fpeak (the reliqu*a*ries of S. Maria Novella)—I will not fay in beauty, as that is impoffible, but in dimenfions, and perhaps, too, in hiftorical importance, is the great frefco in the Vatican, in which Fra Angelico, who was invited to Rome by Eugene IV., painted, in fix compartments, the principal fa&s of the life of S. Stephen and S. Laurence, thus uniting thefe two Chriftian heroes in the fame poetic commemoration, as it is the cuftom of the faithful to invoke them conjointly, fince one and the fame fepulchre enfhrines the afhes of both in the ancient bafilica of San Lorenzo, outfide the walls of Rome.

"The Confecration of S. Stephen, the Diftribution of the alms, and far better ftill the Preaching, are three paintings as perfe& in their ftyle as any of the grandeft produ&ions of the moft diftinguifhed mafters ; it would be difficult to fancy a group that could excel the life and attitudes of thefe figures, and particu-larly of the women who are feated and liftening to the holy preacher.　If the beftial fury of the murderers who ftone the Saint be not adequately expreffed, we fhould attribute it to a glorious impotency of that Angelic imagination which teemed with ecftacies of love, and was never accuftomed to thefe dramatic fcenes in which it is neceffary to depi& violent paffions.

"The figures are difpofed with equal grace and nobility, and this merit that is always to be admired in all the works of the Angelico, is here, if poffible, ftill more admirable, fince he has paid marked attention to the coftume and other adjun&s belonging to the period, which he copied from the monuments of the Primitive Church.　Not fo, however, can we fpeak of the inferior compartments in which the painter has given the hiftories of S. Laurence."　We will finally obferve with Profeffor Rofini that, in this work, more than in any other, he feems to have enlarged his ftyle, and to have carried it to fuch perfe&ion as to difpute the palm with the nobleft geniufes of that age.　For the altar of the fame chapel he alfo painted a Depofition from the Crofs, which, I believe, is now loft."—MARCHESE, by *Meehan*, vol. i., p. 243.—TRANSLATOR'S note.]

a fad proof of the debafement of artiftic and religious feeling. The fovereign pontiffs have preferved thefe mafterpieces for us. Gregory XIII. (1572-1585) ordered the firft reftoration of them, as the infcription under the Diftribution of the Alms by S. Stephen informs us.[1] The infcriptions which fet off the altar make us acquainted with other reftorations. In 1712, Clement XI. repaired the chapel, ruined by the injuries of time, and reftored it for worfhip. Benedi&t XIII., of the Order of Friar-Preachers, confecrated the altar, April 7th, 1725.[2] Laftly, the fovereign pontiff, Pius VII., in 1815, had this pi&ture by Beato Angelico di Fiefole repaired and cleaned, *to preferve for the defire and ftudy of all* the only mafterpiece of this great painter which Rome poffeffes.[3]

Beato Angelico inaugurated art at the Vatican, and the painters who fucceeded him could find beautiful infpirations and great inftru&tions in his works. If the Siftine chapel is compared with the chapel of Nicholas V., it will be feen that art loft more than it gained amidft its material progreffes. The artifts who were fucceffively called to work at the Siftine chapel,

---

[1] Gregorius XIII. Pont. Max.—Egregiam. hanc pi&turam a F. IOANNE Angelico—Fefulano. Ord, Præ. Nicolai. papæ. V Ivssv—elaboratam ac. vetuftate. pæne. confvmpt.—inftaurari mandavit.

[2] Sacellvm—A Nicolao V—Pont. Max.—Conftru&tum—a Fr. IOANNE—Fefulano. celebri. Illius—evi pi&tore—Sacris—imaginibus—decoratum—† CLEMENS XI—Pont. Max.—Temporis. Inivriis—Deformatum—Ac obfoletum—priftinam—in fpeciem—ufumque. Reftituit. Anno Salutis—M D CC XII. † BENEDICTVS XIII. Ord. prædicator. altare. hoc. erexit. et confecravit. Die XI. Aprilis. M D CC XXV.

[3] Anno M DCCC XV—PIVS VII. Pont. Max.—Pi&tvram. IOANNIS Angelici Fæfvlani—viri beati—Hiftoriae præconio nobilitatem—negligentia temporum obfoletam—uti quod unicum pi&toris elegantiffimi—In Urbe exftat artis exemplum—omnium ftudio et defiderio ne deeffet—Squalore deterfo et lumine addito —reftituendam curavit.

did not underftand the laws of monumental decoration as the great fchool of Giotto had done: the
figures are too fmall for the fpace. Michael Angelo,
who ended their work, fell into the contrary error; he
piled up colossuses, as the Titans did mountains.
None will difpute his prodigious talent; but if they can
fet themfelves free from the admiration excited by the
powerful figures of the fibylls and prophets on the
vaulted roof, which are ftill more aftounding than thofe
of the Last Judgment, they will, indeed, be obliged to
acknowledge that there is a violation of the laws of
beauty and of monumental painting. A jury compofed of the great artifts of Rome and Athens would
have condemned fuch a mafterpiece. Michael Angelo
is an unique and a folitary genius, who has ruined all
that have wifhed to imitate him. He has violated
tafte by making it believed that beauty is in ftrength
and great dimenfions. He it is who has procured
us all thofe ridiculous giants with which the fchools
of the decline have encumbered the churches and
palaces of Italy: he it is who invented the theatrical
contrivances of our cupolas and the rout of figures
which fpoil the architecture under pretext of decorating the ceilings. The ancients, if they returned,
would treat us as barbarians.

In the Vatican, as elfewhere, art deferted the fanctuary
for the apartments of princes. The holy patronage of
Eugenius IV. and of Nicholas V. was replaced by that
of the Medici and the Borgia. The treafures art owed
to Chriftianity were fquandered on the caprices of
the paffions: the impure images of the gods profaned
the Vatican as they formerly did the fanctity of

Calvary, and facrilegious hands dared to trace upon its walls fubjeéts which might have made the debauchees of heathen Rome blufh.   The fovereign pontiffs have wifhed to have thefe obfcene paintings effaced ; but men are always found to elude their orders and defend thefe infamies as models of art and the Palladium of civil-ization.[1]   For all that, hiftory fpeaks loud enough in ancient and in modern times.   Moral beauty is infepar-able from natural beauty ; God has made them for each other, like the foul for the body ; and when man feparates them for the benefit of his fenfes, art is no more than a tree which has loft its fap, a corpfe given up to the corruption of death.

[1] Gregory XVI. ordered the paintings to be effaced which are fhown to ftrangers like the fecret mufeum at Naples.   They have been only covered with a cloth.   Pius IX. has in vain given orders to veil the nude caryatides at the arch of the hall of Conftantine ; the painter of the Renaiffance had a way for compreffing the indecency by making them hermaphrodites.

Chapter XIII.

PAINTINGS IN ORVIETO CATHEDRAL, AND PICTURES AT NAPLES:

UR humble religious enjoyed the ſweeteſt glory which can crown man on this earth. Admiration was even exceeded by the affection he inſpired: popes and princes ſought his friendſhip as much as his works.

Whilſt he was painting the chapels of the Vatican, the city of Orvieto was going on with its cathedral commenced at the end of the thirteenth century, and called for the moſt renowned artiſts of the world to embelliſh it. Beato Angelico was applied to, and his aſſiſtance was obtained. The unfiniſhed work of our painter marks, in our opinion, the apogee of his talent, and may bear compariſon with what art has produced moſt perfect.

On this work of Beato Angelico we poſſeſs the moſt

documents ; and they not only concern our painter, but alfo give us valuable information on the organization of mediæval art. It is impoffible to underftand the hiftory of art without taking into account the influence which the popular element has exercifed over its developement. The popular element is the caufe of the greatnefs of art; it is the foil which bears it, the light which makes it fruitful. The maffes are as neceffary for artifts as the crowd is for orators. The people are the only protectors rich enough in power and means to encourage art, which requires the thought of all to render, treafures to lay out, the multitude to comprehend it, and a long pofterity to admire it. What is art patronized by one man, even were he mafter of the world ? Genius itfelf, if it is not defeated by intrigue, muft be infpired with a caprice, to obtain a protection which paffes away like him who grants it. Its work, often haggled over, goes to difappear in the room of a palace which will be vifited by a revolution, and it will fall as an heritage or a conqueft into ignorant and mercenary hands ; whilft the work of art patronized by the people and confecrated in their monuments, fhines for the eyes of all, and may hope for ages of immortality.

But if the people do much for art, art alfo recompenfes the people ; it inftructs them, elevates them, and withdraws them from their material and dependent life by giving them pure enjoyments, the contemplation of the beautiful, the greateft good man can claim. . Art makes him know and love his country, and infpires him with the virtue of devotion ; it tells him of the paft and points out to him the future. Monuments are forefathers that look down on him, and give teftimony of him to his defcendants.

Religion alone is able to unite the people and art : it is equally neceffary to both, and it is in the temple that it confecrates their alliance. The rocks of the Parthenon and the flopes of the Capitol have feen the people and art mount up to the altars of the gods, and celebrate together feftivals fo magnificent that they feemed to juftify the triumph of error ; but a Chriftian people has nothing to envy the people of Rome and Athens for, as their alliance with art is far more intimate and far more admirable. The cathedral is the work in which art appears in all the majefty of its unity. A divine doctrine lays the foundations of it upon an immoveable rock, and traces the fymbolical plan ; architecture raifes the walls, pillars, arches and noble fpires : it entrufts the embellifhment to fculpture and painting, which it keeps in a perfect hierarchy ; then, when its work is over, and the rich light of the windows fhines peacefully on all the wonders of the chifel and the pencil, the Church difplays the pomp of her liturgy, and, amidft the chant of pfalms and the memorials of the faints, adores God Himfelf, who crowns all by His prefence. It is impoffible for art and the people to find better conditions for uniting.

The cathedral is not like the heathen temple which concealed a ftatue in its walls, and fent its prieft to make a little incenfe fmoke on the fteps of the portico. The Church is a mother who opens her bofom to receive her children, and to diftribute truth and goodnefs to each one. The cathedral is altogether for the people :

it is their life, faith, hope, baptifm, family, glory, hiftory and eternity. Before ignorance and falfehood had eftranged the people from the cathedral, and had difabled them for underftanding it, they found in it joy, courage and wealth: they received there a fimple and powerful doctrine, and knew what the moft learned are now ignorant of, the problem of their deftinies, their origin and their end. The ftatues and glafs-windows were their library, and they read in an open book all the hiftory, the poetic legends, and the aftonifhing fymbolifm, of which we fcarcely find out the meaning.

Can we be furprifed at the beauty of the Chriftian monuments of the middle ages? Whilft feudalifm was tearing itfelf to pieces in its bloody ftruggles, and building caftles to opprefs others or to defend itfelf, the people were building cathedrals; there was the centre of the commonalty, the donjon of their powers; and they neglected nothing in order to make the edifice worthy of God and of His adorers. This noble ambition explains the wondrous developements of art in the Italian republics of the thirteenth and fourteenth centuries; and it alfo makes it underftood why artifts remained Chriftian: the people kept them nobly employed on their cathedrals, whilft literature had already become corrupted by felling its verfes to princes and their paffions. Between the towns and commonalties there was a rivalry who fhould have the largeft and moft magnificent church. The people were once confulted by Phidias whether he fhould employ marble or ivory in making the ftatue of Minerva? There was a vaft difference in the price of the materials;

but the people replied to Phidias, "Do what will be moſt worthy of the city."

The people of Florence ſaid the ſame to their archi-tect Arnolfo, when he ſet about erecting Santa Maria dei Fiori :—"Foraſmuch as the ſovereign prudence of a great people wills that they proceed in affairs of ſuch ſort that their external works prove that they are as enlightened as generous, we ordain to Arnolfo, architect of our commonalty, to make the model or deſign for the rebuilding of Santa Reparata ſo great and magnificent, that it be impoſſible for art and human power to imagine anything more beautiful and more vaſt. This is what has been ſaid and counſelled by the wiſeſt of the city in public and private aſſem-blies. For the affairs of the commonalty ought not to be undertaken if it is not intended to render them worthy of an immenſe ſpirit, as it is compoſed of the ſoul of all the citizens united in the ſame will."[1]

All the Italian Republics gave the ſame programme, and they were faithful to it. They have done well; their churches are the only things remaining to them of ancient days. Who would now turn out of his way to climb the rock upon which the city of Orvieto uprears itſelf, were it not to admire the marvels of its cathedral, in which, for three centuries, a religious people entruſted the expreſſion of their faith to the moſt celebrated artiſts of the world?

A prieſt had doubted the real preſence of our Lord upon the altars; and the Holy Victim had been pleaſed to raiſe the veil which hides Him from our ſenſes, and to allow the Divine Blood ſhed on Calvary to

---

[1] *Cantu, Hiſtoire univerſelle,* tom. xi., p. 578.

flow anew. The corporal was foaked with it. The people were witneffes of this miracle which attefts the myftery the moft confoling to human nature : and to preferve this fenfible proof which divine goodnefs had vouchfafed to give them, they raifed a monument to receive the linen fteeped in the Precious Blood, but did not find it magnificent enough. Yes, that vaft bafilica, with its courfes of white and black marble, the façade fo rich in fculpture and mofaics, the columns, ftatues, lancet arches, paintings, gold, ftained glafs ; the reliquary with its enamels and precious ftones, all is an act of faith in the Real Prefence! The people believed that God was pleafed to dwell with them; and, if they had been able, they would have raifed to Him a dwelling ftill more magnificent.

This church, the firft ftone of which was laid November 13th, 1290, was a national work, carried on with enthufiafm and perfeverance throughout the revolutions and turmoils of the fourteenth century. The hiftory of this building is like that of other cele-brated mediæval monuments in France and Italy. It makes us acquainted with the means then adopted to enfure the completion and perfection of it.

So foon as the inhabitants of Orvieto had decreed the work, " they eftablifhed a magiftracy compofed of feveral intelligent and upright perfons, who were named fuperintendents of the fabric; they were to call in the beft artifts, and to pay the works agreed on with the chamberlain. Thefe magiftrates were obliged to give an account of the receipts and expenditure to the reprefentatives of the people, who were the captain, confuls, judge and fyndics. They were diftinguifhed from the other functionaries of the city by the title *della fabbrica.* Their efcutcheon is ftill feen, as in many other places, particularly in Tufcany."[1]

There was alfo a lodge of artifts " near the cathedral-church, a houfe where the architects, painters, and fculptors affembled to prefent their defigns and models to the mafter of mafters, and to carry them out when they had been approved by him, by the chamberlain, and by the fuperintendents. Each art had its chief, and over all was placed the mafter of mafters, who was ofteneft an architect, painter, or fculptor."[2] This unity of direction is a happy condition of fuccefs.

The firft mafter of mafters was Lorenzo Maitani, an artift of Sienna, who directed the works for forty-three years. He inceffantly traverfed the whole of Italy to choofe men and materials. Rome furnifhed him with its ancient marbles, Sienna with its black marble, Carrara with white marbles, Saint-Anthime with alabafter; and he had legions of artifts under his orders. Thofe who quitted Rome during the great heats worked for Orvieto at Albano and Caftelgandolfo.[3]

When Maitani died, his two fons fucceeded him; only one other artift, Meo d'Orvieto, was added to them. At this time, merit alone feems to have decided the

[1] *Storia del Duomo di Orvieto, fcritta dal padre maeftro Guglielmo della Valle,* Minor Conventuale, one volume in quarto, with an atlas : Rome, M DCC XCI, page 97.

[2] Era quefta una cafa vicina al Duomo, in cui architetti, e pittori e fcultori, fi radunavano per prefentare al maeftro de' maeftri il loro difegni e modelli per efeguirli, dopo che da effo, dal camerlingo, e dai fopraftanti, erano ftati approvati . . . Ogni arte aveva il fuo capo, e a tutti prefideva il maeftro de' maeftri che per lo più era architetto, pittore o fcultore.—*Storia del Duomo,* p. 101.

[3] *Storia del Duomo,* p. 103.

choice of the artifts; the interefts of the monument
prevailed over private interefts and local intrigues.
The greateft part of the directors of the work were
from Sienna or Pifa, but none were excluded, and a
Frenchman was preferred before an artift of Orvieto
in 1446, the period at which Beato Angelico was
fent for.[1]

The moft celebrated artifts of Europe gave their
concurrence; the Dominican Fra Guglielmo of Pifa
fculptured the bas-reliefs of the façade; Donatello
made the ftatue of S. John Baptift, in 1423; and in
the fame year, Gentile da Fabriano painted a Madonna.
After Beato Angelico, Luca Signorelli, Perugino and
Pinturricchio alfo executed paintings at Orvieto. For
decorating the baptifmal fonts, an artift of Friburg
was chofen, who paffed for the moft fkilful fculptor
of his time; but as foon as he was at the work his
ftyle was not liked, and he was replaced by Jacopo
Guido, from Florence.[2]

A matter worthy of remark is the contingent of
artifts furnifhed by the religious orders. Befides
Beato Angelico and Fra Guglielmo, the Order of
S. Dominic fupplied two glafs-painters, Fra Mariotto,
and Fra Mariano who was afterwards rejected kindly
becaufe he did not know how to draw well enough.
The *fabbrica* ordered a fubftitute for him to be fought
at Sienna and Florence, if it were neceffary. A Cifter-
tian, Fra Francefco d'Antonio, executed the ftained

---

[1] *Storia del Duomo*, docum. lxx, p. 304.

[2] In the lift of foreign artifts we alfo find, in the fixteenth century, two French
Mofaifts, Ferdinand Sermois and Francois-Etienne; a Flemifh painter, Henri
(1563), and Nicolas Cordier, a Lorrainefe, who was living at Rome, and called
himfelf Il Franciofetto.—*Storio del Duomo*, p. 170.

glaſs placed behind the high altar, repreſenting the life and miracles of the Bleſſed Virgin.

Fra Franceſco, of the Order of Minors, worked at the glaſs in 1446, at the ſame time as the Benedictine Dom F. Baroni of Perugia. It was this religious who ſent for Beato Angelico to Orvieto.

The deliberation which concerns our painter is dated May 11th, 1447.

"Conſidering that the chapel facing the one of the Corporal is blank . . . it would be fitting to have it painted by ſome good and famous maſter-painter. At this moment there is in Orvieto a religious of the obſervance of S. Dominic, who has painted, and is painting, the chapel of our moſt holy Father in the palace of the Vatican, who might perhaps be perſuaded to come and paint the chapel; *he is the moſt famous of all the painters of Italy,* and would paint in the church only three months in the year, that is, in June, July, and Auguſt, becauſe during the other months he is obliged to ſerve the Holy Father; but in theſe three months he will not remain in Rome. He aſks a ſalary for himſelf at the rate of 200 ducats of gold a-year, with the expenſes of food, and colours, ſcaffolding, etc. And this maſter-painter is named Fra Giovanni." [1] The council met again June 2nd in the

[1] Congregatis in unum in reſid. camerarii . . . pro laboreriis d. E. ordinandis ad honorem d. E., conſiderato quod cappella nova . . . in conſpectu cappelle corporalis eſt ſciabbida . . . et pro honore d. E. eſt dipingenda per aliquem bonum et famoſum mag. pictorem, et ad preſens in Urbe veteri ſit quidam, etc., obſervantie S. Dominici qui pinſit et pingit cappellam SS. D. N. in palatio ap. S. Petri de Urbe qui forſan veniret ad pingendum d. E. et EST FAMOSUS ULTRA ALIOS PICTORES YTALICOS, et ſtaret ad pingendum in d. E. tantum tribus in anno menſibus, ſcilicet Junio, Julio, Auguſto; et quia aliis menſibus . . . . non vult ſtare Rome, et petit ſalarium pro ſe ad rat. cc ducat. auri in anno, cum expenſis

fame year, and the chamberlain announced that " Fra Giovanni di Pietro has accepted the invitation given him, to come and paint the new chapel; and as he is to be in Orvieto a little before the feaft of *Corpus Domini*, it is neceffary for the council to decide on what he fhall paint. After much fpeaking, it is decided that they fhall wait for the painter, and determine when they have his advice." Beato Angelico, in fact, arrived ; and, June 14th, the deed was paffed. " After feveral converfations with the painter, it is unanimoufly agreed on every point. The chamberlain has led the religious, Fra Giovanni di Pietro, mafter-painter, of the Order of Preachers of the Obfervance of S. Dominic, to the new chapel to be painted, and there given over to him all the work on the following conditions :—

" Fra Giovanni fhall himfelf work on the pictures, together with Benozzo Cefi of Florence, Giovanni Antonio of Florence, and Jacopo de Poli, well and diligently, and with befitting fkill and care.

" Alfo he fhall labour and take care that the figures of the pictures be beautiful and commendable. Alfo the undertaking fhall commence to-morrow, June 15th inftant. Alfo every year he fhall paint, with the above-named perfons, in June, July, Auguft and September, until the entire chapel is painted. Alfo he fhall do all without fraud and deceit, at the commendation of any good mafter-painter.

" And for the aforefaid, the chamberlain, in the name of the council, has folemnly promifed and

ciborum, et colores, pontes, &c., et vocatur d. magifter pictor frater Johes.— *Storia del Duomo*, docum. B, p. 306.

S

sworn to the same Fra Giovanni, present and accepting for himself and his heirs, and to Benozzo, Giovanni and Jacopo, to give and pay effectually to Fra Giovanni, for his labours, a salary for the four months every year at the rate of 200 ducats of gold, of the value of seven pounds each, for every complete year: that is, the third part of 200 ducats for the four months. Also to Benozzo, every month, seven ducats of the same value, to Giovanni two ducats at the same rate, and to Jacopo one ducat. Also he shall give to the said master-painter all the colours necessary for the pictures, over and above the salary.

" Also for their expences, besides the salaries, bread and wine as much as is sufficient for them, and twenty pounds of pennies every month whilst they are at work.

" Also he shall pay the expences for them up to the present day.

" Also the said master Fra Giovanni, whilst the scaffolding is being put up, shall make the design of the pictures and figures which he is to paint on the vault of the chapel.

" All which the parties have mutually promised to observe, with good faith, etc.   Witnesses, etc."[1]

· [1] Die xiv Junii m cccc xlvii, in Dei noe . . . Amen. Congregatis . . . et habitis inter eos et pictorem multis colloquiis super omnibus et singulis . . . unanimiter . . . Camerarius conduxit ad pingendum cappellam novam versus episcopatum . . . religiosum virum frem. Johem. Petri magrum pictorem ord. Predicatorum observantie Sci Dominici ibid. presentem et acceptantem, et picturas totius dicte cappelle locavit d. mag. fratri Johi. cum pactis quod d. frater Johes . . . serviret ad picturas pred. cum persona sua. Item cum persona Benotii Cesi de Florentia. Item cum persona Johis Antonii de Florentia. Item cum persona Jacobi de Poli, bene et diligenter, et cum ea qua decet solertia et solicitudine.

Item quod faciet et curabit quod d. figure dd. picturar. erunt pulchre et lauda-

Beato Angelico forthwith fet about the work, but a few days after, June 26th, a misfortune occurred which deeply afflicted him. One of his pupils, Antonio Giovanelli, whilft fetting up a fcaffold, was hurt by the falling of a beam, and died of the injury. The *fabbrica* ordered the chamberlain to furnifh all the expences of the illnefs and burial.[1] Beato Angelico fet himfelf to the work, along with Benozzo and Jacopo de Poli. He alfo employed two painters of Orvieto, Pietro di Nicolas and Giacomo di Pietro, who probably executed the ornaments. The work went on until September 28th, and on that day our painter gave an acquittance for 103 florins of gold for himfelf and his pupils.[2] He departed for Rome

biles. Item conductio pred. incipiat cras que eft xv prefentis menfis Junii. Item quolibet anno pinget cum premiffis hoibus, Junio, Julio, Augufto et Settembri quoufque tota cappella fuerit dipincta. Item quod omnia faciet fine fraude, dolo, ad commendationem cujuflibet boni mag. pictoris.

Et pro predictis camerarius . . . promifit folemniter et juravit eidem F. Johi prefenti et acceptanti pro fe et fuis heredibus, et dd. Benotio Johi et Jacobo dare et folvere cum effectu eid. fratri Johi pro fuis laboribus, falario pro dd. iv menfibus quolibet anno quoufque ec. ad rat. cc ducatorum auri valoris vii librar. pro quolibet et pro quolibet anno completo, videlicet pro dd. iv menfibus, tertiam partem cc ducatorum. Item Benotio quolibet menfe feptem ducatos ejufdem valoris, Johi duos ducatos ad d. rat., et Jacobo unum ducatum. Item dabit d. mag. pictori omnes colores incumbentes neceffarios pro d. picturis ultra d. falaria.

Item pro eorum expenfis ultra falaria panem et vinum quantum fufficiet eis, et xx libras denar. quolibet menfe, dum laborabunt.

Item perfolvet eis expenfas ufque ad prefentem diem.

Item quod d. mag. f. Johes, interdum fiunt pontes, faciat defignum picturarum et figurarum quas debet pingere in volta d, cappelle.

Que omnia viciffim . . . promiferunt attendere, bona fide, ec. ec, . . . Acta prefentib . . . teftibus.

[1] Antonius Giovanelli qui (xxvi Junii) dum ftabat ad faciendum pontem in cappella nova, cecidit in ftentu unius trabis cadentis fuper eum. Sed ut tranfeat in bonum exemplum . . . ordinatur quod camerarius poffit ei fubvenire tam in infirmitate ad mortem quam in fepultura ejus, abfque fuo damno et prejudicio. —*Storia del Duomo*, p. 128.

[2] Religiofus vir Fr. Johes Petri mag. picturarum et ordinis obfervantie Frum

again, leaving his work incomplete. The fubject chofen by Beato Angelico for the decoration of the chapel was the Laft Judgment. We have already feen with what fkill and grandeur he treated this fublime fubject of Chriftian art. When we know as yet the paintings of Orvieto only by the publifhed engravings, we dread the neighbourhood of Luca Signorelli for the fweet religious of Fiefole. In his compofitions at Orvieto, that painter, in our opinion, is fuperior to Michael Angelo; he has not his anato-mical exaggerations and gigantic proportions, and his drawing is truer and more diftinguifhed: and to a remarkable elegance he joins a great vigour of ftyle. He feems to have owed thefe qualities to the influence of Beato Angelico. Some figures which our painter has executed on a ground of gold are thofe which moft attract the eye and excite admiration. This unfinifhed work is the one which beft fhows his talent, and what he would have done if he had had great furfaces to paint, like the artifts in the times of Giotto and Raphael. In the three months paffed at Orvieto, Beato Angelico painted the Chrift and the choir of pro-phets above the hell. We can judge from this fragment what the whole compofition would have been. Chrift holds the globe of the world in his mighty hand,

Predicatorum conductus ad pingendum in cappella nova d. mag. Ecclie. cum perfona fua et cum perfonis fuis Benozi Cefi de Florentia, etc. etc., quos fecum habuit ad dictam picturam . . . fecit camerario . . . fuam . . . contentationem abfolutam . . . et pactum de ultra non petendo de centum tribus florenis auri de auro . . . quos debebat habere a d. fabrica tam pro fe quam pro fuprad. Benozzo et pro tribus menfibus, et fe quietum vocabit . . . d. mag. f. Johes juravit ad. S. Dei Evangelia . . . omni tempore attendere obfervare. Infuper ad majorem cautelam liberavit d. fabricam.—*Storia del Duomo,* docum. LXXIV., 28 Sept., 1447.

and with the other curfes the reprobate. Michael
Angelo, they fay, was infpired by it in the Siftine
chapel; he has made only a parody of it by ftripping
the Chrift of its garments and giving it ftrength
without majefty. The group of prophets is perhaps
ftill more admirable. The painters of the Renaiffance
have done nothing of the like, and thefe few figures
will always be the model of religious and monumental
painting, as infpiration, as ftyle, and as execution.

Having returned to Rome, Beato Angelico continued his labours at the Vatican, and perhaps executed
fome of the pictures we have already fpoken of. We
attribute to this period, on account of their beauty,
two pictures we have had the happinefs to find
at Naples in the rooms of the Bourbon Mufeum.
They are numbered 296, 298, and, at the time of our
journey, were attributed to Tommafo di Stephano,
furnamed Giottino (1324-1356). They are certainly
neither of his epoch nor in his manner, and we do not
hefitate to attribute them to Beato Angelico.

The firft (No. 296) is an Affumption. The Bleffed
Virgin is feated in an elliptical glory. Her hands are
joined, and fhe is clothed in a blue mantle fet off with
gold ornaments. On her aureola is written, AVE GRATIA
PLENA. In the upper part of the picture, our Lord
bends towards his mother, and holds out his arms
to her as on the reliquary at Santa Maria Novella.[1]
The choirs of angels furround their Queen. Thofe
who approach her neareft are doubtlefs the Seraphim
and Cherubim, reprefented by a double row of winged
heads; then come, two and two, the other heavenly

[1] Page 173.

ſpirits, with their various attributes: the firſt, clothed in blue robes, hold with both hands an objeĉt ſhaped like an almond, of the ſame colour as their robes. The Thrones are thus repreſented in the moſaics of the Baptiſtry at Florence. The ſecond, clothed in lively red, hold a ſtandard, a globe and a gold rod: theſe are the Dominations. The Principalities carry a a ſtandard creſted with a red croſs; the Powers, a knight's armour, a croſs-bearing buckler and a ſword. The Virtues have golden robes, and hold a banderole, on which is written *Virtutes.*[1] The laſt two orders, the Archangels and Angels, are playing on various muſical inſtruments, like thoſe we have ſeen in the other pictures. This compoſition is executed on a ground of gold; it is worthy of our painter, and can have come only from his thought and pencil.

The piĉture numbered 298 repreſents the miracle of our Lady *ad Nives.* This ſubjeĉt, which brings to mind the foundation of Santa Maria Maggiore, muſt have been choſen and executed at Rome by our painter, who, without doubt, went very often to pray in that church, the moſt charming of the baſilicas in the eternal city. Our Lord and the Holy Virgin appear in the ſky, and preſide over the ſcene paſſing in the lower part. The earth is covered with ſnow, and Pope Liberius traces in it with a ſmall mattock the plan of the church which the patrician John and his wife had received orders to build. The Sovereign Pontiff is mitred and gloved. Behind him, a group of cardinals

---

[1] At the Baptiſtry of Florence, the Virtues are repreſented as driving away the devils and healing the ſick. Beato Angelico has followed the claſſification of S. Bernard rather than that of S. Denis the Areopagite.

and magiftrates is feen ; in the middle, fome clerics
carry the crofs and holy water. The affiftants are
in pious admiration, and look up at the fky. The fun
fhining on the perfonages and buildings in the background, fhow the time of the year at which they then
were. All the figures are drawn and modelled with
the firmnefs which marks the laft years of Beato
Angelico.

It is impoffible for us to explain why Beato Angelico did not finifh his paintings at Orvieto. Certainly
his own will had nothing to do with it ; he muft have
defired to acquit himfelf of his engagement ; but
perhaps the Pope did not let him leave, or his
health hindered his journey. It is pofitive that the
fabbrica of Orvieto hoped for his return up to the
laft moment. Many painters begged to carry on his
work, but they ftill waited, until " envious death broke
his pencil, and his beautiful foul winged its way amongft
the angels, to make paradife more joyous." [1]

[1] La morte invidiofa ruppe il pennello di lui, e la fua bell' anima volò fra gli
Angeli a fare piu ridente il paradifo."—*Storia del Duomo*, p. 132.

CHAPTER XIV.

DEATH OF BEATO ANGELICO.—HIS EULOGY.—HIS PUPILS AND HIS INFLUENCE.

MIDST the magnificent tombs which adorn the church of Santa Maria fopra Minerva, between the facrifty and the apfe, is a fimple tombftone, the fight of which caufes a tender and refpectful emotion. A religious is reprefented there fleeping the bleffed fleep of thofe who die in the Lord. That marble points out the place where the body of Beato Angelico da Fiefole was depofited, who died at Rome, March 18th,[1] 1455, in his fixty-eighth year.

Hiftory has not preferved for us any detail of his laft moments. He difappeared amidft his brethren,

[1 Leandro Alberti, who is the authority for the day of Beato Angelico's death, dates it XII. kal martii, which is Feb. 18th.—TRANSLATOR's note.]

like the autumnal fun athwart the trees of a peaceful
vale whilft fhining on them with its fweeteft rays.
An end full of calmnefs and of hope muft have
crowned a life fo pure and active. From what point
of the paft could trouble come? From his early
youth his intellect had been applied to things divine,
his will had been fubjected to the wholefome yoke
of obedience, and his memory could only offer him
chafte recollections and pious images. He recalled
his pictures as prayers. All the heavenly world he had
reprefented was ftirred, and came to fmile on him:
his agony was an ecftacy; and when, according to the
ceremonial of the Order, the religious of the convent
went to range themfelves around his bed and fing
Salve Regina the laft time for him, the Queen of
heaven doubtlefs heard their prayer. She who had
been the fweetnefs, joy and hope of his life; fhe on
whom he had called with fo many fighs, and whofe
love he had gained by fo many mafterpieces—Mary,
turned eyes full of mercy on her beloved painter,
and fhowed him, on the utmoft verge of his exile,
the bleffed Fruit of her womb. Angels encompaffed
him with their joyous fongs, and when the hour
of his deliverance came, the heavenly fpirit, to
whom his pilgrimage had been entrufted, freed him
from his body in a fraternal embrace, and led him
triumphant into paradife, which he gladdened with his
prefence.

On earth he was bewailed. The fovereign pontiff,
Nicholas V., defired himfelf to compofe his epitaph,
in which he ranked his virtue much above his talent;

for Chrift rewarded lefs the works of his genius **than** the charity of his heart.[1]

People called him The Bleffed, *il Beato*, and pofterity has kept this beautiful name for him. The Church might have decreed him the honours of the altar ; for what has been faid of the writings of S. Thomas can be faid again of the pictures of Beato Angelico : they are fo many miracles. Holinefs beams forth from them, and thofe very perfons whom the errors of the world difable from underftanding them well, experience a charm which gently troubles them and invites them to a better life. Since thefe pictures have been in exiftence, how many fouls have found pure joys and heavenward longings in them! The truth there appears with a beauty victorious over all hefitation and all weaknefs: and fome Proteftants have declared that God had waited for this means to determine their converfion. Many have had copies of thefe mafterpieces made at Florence, in order to carry them into their own country as arguments in

---

[1] HIC. JACET. VEN. PICTOR.
FR. JO. DE FLOR. ORD. P.
M.
C. C. C. C.
L.
V.

Non mihi fit laudi, quod eram velut alter Apelles,
Sed quod lucra tuis omnia, Chrifte, dabam.
Altera nam terris opera exftant, altera cœlo ;
Urbs me Joannem flos tulit Etruriæ.

The word *tuis* indicates the religious of his Order rather than the poor. Beato Angelico belonged to the reform and poffeffed nothing ; ftill his fuperiors could have entrufted him with the diftribution of the money he gained.

[An error in the date given by M. Cartier is here corrected. Marchefe refers *tuis* to the poor. TRANSLATOR'S note.]

favour of the Church alone capable of infpiring and realizing fuch creations.

Now that we have followed the ftream of this bleffed life even into eternity, and admired the riches of its banks, we will caft a laft glance at it, to embrace the whole and refume its inftructions.

One of the merits of our age is the ferious ftudy it is making of the paft. The French revolution had feparated us from it by ruins. All that was great amongft the nations had difappeared under the efforts of an arrogant and depraved reafon; but here are we exploring the fields of hiftory afrefh, and inquiring of tradition our way towards the future. We are ftudying events and their caufes, doctrines and their refults; and if we are ftill awandering, we have, in our perfeverance and good faith, a certainty of life and falvation. One of the happieft fymptoms of this movement is the homage paid to Chriftian art. In the admiration beftowed on the monuments of the middle ages, there is fomething elfe befides the caprice of fafhion; there is a feeling of refpect for the religion which produced fuch wonders. This return towards Chriftian art muft be intelligent: to wifh to copy its outward forms without entering into its fpirit, is to doom ourfelves to a fervility which would be to Chriftian art what hypocrify is to virtue. The ftudy of a painter's works calls for ftill more criticifm and difcernment than in architectural monuments, becaufe beauty is more individualized in them, and it is neceffary to diftinguifh that beauty from whatever defects the nature of the artift may have put into them. In writing the life of Beato Angelico with

love, we have not pretended to bring him forward as
the fole and neceffary mafter of whoever afpires to
produce Chriftian art again: this would be to ferve
badly the caufe which we wifh to defend. On the contrary, we hold to making it known in all truth, without
fearing to tarnifh fo unfullied a glory. We go on
then to examine the place Beato Angelico occupies
in hiftory, what diftinguifhed him from his contemporaries, the charaäter of his genius, his qualities,
his defeäts, and the utility which may be drawn from
the ftudy of his works in our own time.

When Beato Angelico appeared, the great fchool of
Giotto was declining; art was lofing that unity of
doätrine and means, of which Orcagna was the moft
illuftrious reprefentative. The programmes given by
the Church were modified, the traditional types neg-
leäted; architeäture, fculpture and painting were becoming ifolated, and were feeking their particular fortunes
in the progrefs of details. The pofterity of Niccola
of Pifa efpecially, more and more enamoured with the
antique, facrificed the Chriftian thought to the learned
form. Natural beauty unhappily tended to feparate ·
itfelf from moral beauty. The ftream that iffued from
the catacombs faw its courfe divided. Its waves,
which had fatisfied the faith of nations for fo many
ages, were diverted from their confecrated bed to
fatisfy the fenfes, and to be defiled amidft the joys of
the world. Only a feeble part, true to its banks, was
to glide along in folitude for the good of pure fouls.
Two great names perfonify thefe two branches of art,
Ghiberti and Beato Angelico. The fculptor of the
Baptiftry-gates at Florence did works which Greeks

might have admired : the religious of Fiefole painted figures that gladdened angels.

Beato Angelico belonged to the traditional fchool of the fourteenth century. He was the direct heir of the ancient mafters by his faith and works ; and his great compofitions at San Marco, at the Vatican, and at Orvieto prove how well qualified he was to execute great monumental painting ; but the wants of his foul, as well as the deviation of public tafte, gave another direction to his talent.

His piety removed him from the world, and in the peace of the cloifter he fought a fhelter againft the temptations of glory and the rivalries furrounding him. For him art was a fweet and folitary contemplation of the divine goodnefs ; his pictures were prayers at the feet of Chrift and of the Bleffed Virgin ; they iffued from his pencil like ejaculations from his heart. They were not great pages to teach the people ; they were pious images to charm the devotion of his brethren, Madonnas that infpired purity, angels that reflected the joys of heaven, and lives of faints which had the gracefulnefs and fimplicity of the mediæval legends.

He would have wifhed his mafterpieces fhut up in the fanctuary of his religious family, but their fweet perfume attracted the admiration of men. Obedience obliged him to fhow himfelf in broad daylight ; and renown, feduced by his virtue, led him to the eternal city to decorate the auguft palace of the fovereign pontiffs.

What was the principal caufe of his glory, the pedeftal that raifes him above his contemporaries and prefents him to the aftonifhed gaze of pofterity ?

What merit drew on him the eulogies of Michael Angelo and the enthufiafm of his difciple Vafari, the painter who, from the nature of his talent and the prejudices of his fchool, was the moft unfitted to appreciate myftical painting? Beato Angelico had a power before which the world itfelf bows down without underftanding it. Sanctity is a refemblance with God, that places on man, as on the face of Mofes, a light which efcapes from his features and his works. Let it beam forth from the form of a fifter of charity or from the pictures of a painter, that heavenly bright-nefs infpires refpect and captivates the libertine him-felf. Vafari is the echo of a fecular tradition which furrounds Beato Angelico with a divine aureola. The hiftorian of the Renaiffance reprefents him to us as painting his Chrifts and Madonnas on his knees and in ecftacy; all he relates fhows us the meeknefs of his foul, the fimplicity of his obedience, and the humility of his genius. The good fervant had made the talent fructify a hundredfold which his mafter had entrufted to him; in place of burying it in the earth of the world, he had placed it in the bank of religious life. There all his hours had been produc-tive, and his foul had become rich in knowledge and in love. The Sovereign Pontiff judged him worthy of the archbifhopric of Florence, but he avoided the honours by caufing his friend S. Antoninus to be nom-inated in his ftead, and he continued to diffufe his light and charity on his pictures and into the bofom of the poor.

The talent of Beato Angelico was the ornament of his virtue. He knew not the ambition which lengthens the watchings of the artift, and makes him purchafe fuccefs fo painfully. To him labour was without forrow. He cultivated painting as Adam did the earthly paradife; his pictures were the flowers God produced in his foul, and he let them grow in all their freedom, fearing to mar the Mafter's work by a knowing culture. Vafari tells us he never would alter his compofitions, becaufe he looked on his in-fpirations as favours from Heaven.[1] The leaft defire of glory never difturbed his heart: he would make God praifed. To what good fhall we fubfcribe his works? Should a mirror arrogate to itfelf the rays it reflects? He did not pretend to make new compofi-tions. When an image fatisfied his piety, why fhould he not have repeated it, like the prayers we love to fay again? Why not imitate the old mafters when we have no hope to furpafs them? Beato Angelico thought only of loving our Lord and the faints, and of making them loved. He fought the kingdom of heaven before all, and the reft was added unto him.

He had received from Heaven all the qualities that make great artifts: the underftanding and love of the beautiful, an exquifite fenfibility of heart, a fertile imagination, and a hand able and prompt to obey him. If his humility had not removed him from the rivalries of his age, he would have furpaffed Ghiberti in the material progrefs he caufed for art in Italy. More faithful than Ghiberti to tradition, he put a fimpler and more fevere order into his compofitions.

---

[1] Aveva per coftume non ritoccare nè recconciare mai alcuna fua dipintura, ma lafciarle fempre in quel modo che erano venute la prima volta, per credere, fecondo ch' egli diceva, che cosi fuffe la volontà di Dio.

His Laſt Judgments eſpecially ſhow remarkable ſkill in lines and in diſpoſitions of groups. His types are deeply felt; we ſee that he ſtudied them in meditation and prayer. Thoſe of our Lord and our Lady he painted amidſt ſighs and tears.[1] His heads of Chriſt repreſent well the Divinity clothed in fleſh to ſuffer, and his figures of the Madonna make virginity underſtood in what it has moſt ſweet and delicate. But what makes his genius ſhine moſt is his types of angels, which he knew how to vary infinitely. Whilſt looking at the multitude of heavenly ſpirits, who are adoring, ſinging, and performing dances and concerts, how ſhall we not believe that thoſe angels viſited his cell, and that he lived with them in brotherly and ſweet familiarity? The ſaints he has repreſented beſt are thoſe who by their life and youth approach neareſt to the angelic nature.

The drawing of Beato Angelico has not the great charaċter of the ſchool of Giotto. His lines are leſs ſimple, leſs ſevere, and the richneſs of the details ſometimes obſcures the beauty of the whole. Still in his pictures we meet with figures in a high ſtyle, which Raphael would not have diſowned, and with which he even inſpired himſelf. His movements are true, except when they expreſs violent aċtions; he was unable to render the paſſions, ſo oppoſed to the meekneſs of his ſoul, whilſt none equal him when he deals with expreſſing pious and tender emotions; and then the attitudes and geſtures ſuperabound in charming grace and naturalneſs. The feet and hands of his perſonages are ſometimes negleċted: all the life is

[1] Non fece mai Crocifiſſo che non ſi bagnaſſe le gote di lagrime.

concentrated in their countenances. There the artift has difplayed all the perfection and fplendour of his genius. His heads have a delicacy of expreffion, a finenefs of model not fufpected except by trying to copy them. His draperies are noble, full and quiet as in the ancient works. His ornaments are nearly always fober and in good tafte. His contours are of an admirable purity. Beato Angelico's colouring is full of light; its tints are lively and its fhades tranf-parent. The maffes are broadly marked out. We remark efpecially an extreme facility of pencil, and a fimplicity of procedures which particularly agrees with monumental painting. Although no artift's life pre-fents a more perfect unity, a talent more faithful to the fame infpiration, we can ftill diftinguifh three epochs in the unity of the whole, in which the years and means he paffed through are reflected. The firft epoch was that of his youth and ftudies; it began with his exile in Umbria, and was impregnated with the tradition of the primitive fchools, to bloom then in the folitude of Fiefole. To the fimplicity and purity of his foul he added an exuberance, a tendernefs of feeling, an inimitable frefhnefs of expreffion. If he had all the qualities of youth, he had alfo its inex-perience. His compofitions were fometimes too fym-metrical; his figures wanted pliancy; he loved richnefs of ornaments and perfection of details too much. The mafterpiece beft reprefenting this epoch is the Corona-tion of the Virgin, in the Louvre.

The fecond epoch was that of his manhood, which had the convent of San Marco for its theatre. He had corrected his defects, whilft preferving and de-

T

veloping his good qualities. The ftudy of nature completed that of the old mafters; his brufh had more breadth and freedom. He united grace with noblenefs in an admirable fimplicity. His compofitions were more varied and more learned, and it is evident that he placed at the fervice of his fanctity the progrefs wrought in art by the fchool of Ghiberti. This was the moft productive period of his life, and is fittingly reprefented by the Defcent from the Crofs, in the Academy of Fine Arts; by the Adoration of the Magi, in the cell of Cofimo de Medici; and by his Laft Judgments.

Laftly, Rome called Beato Angelico within its walls, and he went to inaugurate Chriftian Art in the Vatican. The fpectacle of the eternal city made a profound impreffion on his foul, and gave frefh power to the maturity of his foul. The chapel of Nicholas V. evinces the ftudy of the antique by the vigour of the drawing, beauty of the draperies, and grandeur of the ftyle. His unfinifhed work at Orvieto indicates the perfection of monumental painting.

Thus, in thefe three epochs, Beato Angelico was always on the progrefs, and demanded the means to give his holy infpirations, in turns, from tradition, nature and the antique. He is and always will be the moft perfect model of Chriftian artifts.

His influence on his contemporaries was not in proportion with his fuperiority. The fovereignty of Giotto, to which he was the worthy fucceffor, ought to have belonged to him; but art had taken another direction, and the patronage of princes had greatly narrowed the domain of religious painting, by replacing the action fo powerful of the church and of the people. Moreover, the humility of Beato Angelico removed him from the movement of his age, and made him prefer the peace of his cell to the diftant journeys which would have fpread his name. Still he had pupils. Vafari names four of them, Gentile da Fabriano, Zanobi Strozzi, Domenico di Michelino, and Benozzo Gozzoli.

Gentile da Fabriano might have known our painter and appreciated his talent; but it feems to us difficult to reckon him in the number of his difciples. He was old, and already the head of a fchool when Beato Angelico was hardly beginning to acquire reputation. We find him at the head of the painters of Orvieto in 1423. Befides, his talent indicates another mafter. He remained a ftranger to the artiftic movement of Florence, and preferved a character and meagrenefs of drawing which recall the fchools of the north. Through Venice, he might have been in contact with German artifts; and the eulogies of Roger of Bruges, who proclaims him to be the firft painter of Italy, are explained by the natural fympathy he muft have had for his ftyle. His inferiority with regard to Beato Angelico is indifputable. It is enough to bring his mafterpiece, which is in the Academy of Fine Arts at Florence and reprefents the Adoration of the Magi, along with the fame fubject treated by Beato Angelico in the Convent of San Marco. We fhould fay that there was more than a century of progrefs between the two pictures. The compofition of Gentile da Fabriano is plain and conftrained; the drawing is feeble, the perfonages badly poftured and over-

T 2

burdened with ornaments, whilft the whole compofition of Beato Angelico is broad, learned and full of
noblenefs and life.

Zanobi Strozzi, Vafari tells us, executed many
paintings for Florence ;[1] but we do not know what
may be now attributed to him. Only a fingle picture
remains to us by Domenico di Michelino, and it is
the one we are all aftonifhment to meet with, to the
left on entering the fombre vaults of Santa Maria dei
Fiori. It reprefents Dante returning to offer his immortal poem to the city of Florence. The illuftrious
exile is crowned with laurels ; but his melancholy
expreffion and lonely fteps remind us how painful glory
was to him. The execution of this picture is firm and
lightfome ; the work is not unworthy of the mafter.

The moft celebrated pupil of Beato Angelico is
Benozzo Gozzoli, who was the faithful companion of
all his labours. The happy influence of fo holy a
direction appears efpecially in the paintings he executed for the churches of Montefalco. But after the
death of the good religious, he gave way to a tendance
which approximated him with Ghiberti. His magnificent paintings at the Campo Santo recall more the
gates of the Baptiftry of Florence than the great
traditions of the primitive fchools. They reprefent
the luxury and elegance of the Italians rather than
the fimple life of the patriarchs. Inferior to Beato
Angelico in the expreffion of Chriftian fentiments, he
is alfo far from equalling him in the purity of the
drawing and in the harmony of colours. [2]

---

[1] Zanobi Strozzi che fece quadri e tavole per tutta Fiorenza, per le case de' cit-
tadini.

[2] Vafari paffes a high encomium on Benozzo Gozzoli, and reprefents him to us

Beato Angelico had other pupils, as the archives of the cathedral of Orvieto prove, which mention Jacopo Poli, and Giovanni Giovanelli, whofe fad death we have feen. His works continued his inftru¢tions, and all thofe who in Italy ftill preferved, for fome time, the veneration of Chriftian art, drew thence ufeful and holy infpirations.[1] Luca Signorelli ftudied them certainly when he had to go on with the chapel of Orvieto. This painter, who is not fufficiently taken into account in the hiftory of art, is fuperior to Michael Angelo in that Laft Judgment. If he is alfo too much prepoffeffed with the fcience of the nude in the Refurreétion of the Dead, at leaft he has not fallen into the anatomical exaggerations and religious inconfiftencies which make the frefco of the Siftine chapel one of the greateft profanations of that fublime fubjeét. His Paradife prefents groups worthy of Raphael, and his angels crowning their eleét fometimes recall thofe of Beato Angelico.[2]

as always Chriftian, and meriting, by a hard and toilfome life, the happinefs of an honoured old age.—Chi cammina con le fatiche per la ftrade della vertù, ancorachè elle sia (come dicono) e faffofa e piena di fpine, alla fine della falita fi ritrova pur finalmente in un largo piano con tutte le bramate felicità. . . . Viffe Benozzo, coftumatiffimamente sempre e da vero criftiano, confumando tutta la vita fua in efercizio onorato · per il che e per la buona maniera e qualità fue lungamente fu ben veduto in quella città.

[1] Let us be permitted to bring together here the name of Menling with that of Beato Angelico. Never had two painters a genius more like in fuch different fchools. The life of the painter of Bruges is unknown to us ; but we may believe that he ftudied the works of Beato Angelico, fince we know that he went into Italy, by the miniatures in the breviary of Grimani which he executed at Venice, and by the portraits he has left at Florence.

[2] Vafari recalls with pride, having feen, when eight years old, the aged Luca Signorelli, who might himfelf have feen Beato Angelico. He ends the fecond part of his work with the eulogy of him, and gives him as the father of the artifts of the Renaiffance.—Porremo fine alla feconda parte di quefte vite, terminando

The school of Sienna, so faithful to its religious
traditions, must have particularly studied the works
of Beato Angelico, and many artists of the fifteenth
century seem to have been his pupils. This idea
has especially struck us as to Giovanni di Paolo
(1403-1482), whose style and grace remind us of the
painter of Fiesole. The imitation is plain in his Last
Judgment, in the public gallery of Sienna.[1] The
composition is the same, and in it we admire the same
groups of angels and blessed embracing.

Sano di Pietro (1406-1481) equally approaches our
painter for the holiness of his virgins and purity of
his angels. His pictures were prayers too, and we
well understand the religious, who ordered of him an
altar-piece for the souls of her father and mother.[2]

The school of Perugino, called the school of
Umbria, is thought to offer the most perfect expression of mystical painting. Mysticism, alike in painting
as in religion, is the higher inspiration of divine love
directing all our thoughts and all our works. Had
Perugino, like Beato Angelico, this inspiration ? We
do not think so. We are far from admitting the
reproaches for atheism Vasari makes against him; but
whilst we quite recognize him as a religious artist, we
do not crown him with the aureola of the saints.
Perugino received from Heaven a happy and sweet
nature, which he cultivated, like Beato Angelico,

in Luca come in quella persona che col fondamento del disegno e degli ignudi
particolarmente, e con la grazia della invenzione e disposizione delle storie, aperse
alla maggior parte degli artefici la via all'ultima perfezione dell' arte.

[1] Stanza terza, No. 11.

[2] Stanza quinta, No. 40. On the frame is read, *Questa tavola afata fare fuoro
Bartholomea di Domenicho di Franciesćho per lanima di suo padre et di sua madre.*

near the tomb of S. Francis of Affifi. The ftudy
of the ancient mafters bound him again to the great
traditions of Chriftian art, and he then went to ripen
his talent in the midft of the material progreffes of
the fchool of Florence. The influence of Andrea
Verrochio over him is indifputable; a fellow difciple
of Leonardo da Vinci, he caught like him, in the
fculptor's workfhop, the love of form, the fweetnefs
of model which is one of his moft remarkable qualities. He preferved his religious tendencies, which
trenched on the paganifm that the patronage of the
Medici was more and more developing; and this was
the principal caufe of his reputation in Italy. He muft
neceffarily have had the favour of all thofe who ftill
had any fenfe of Chriftian art in their foul. Still his
works rarely offer the holy thoughts and the fap of
love we have admired in Beato Angelico's pictures.
The fearch after gracefulnefs and beauty diftracted the
painter from his devotion. His Madonnas are too
pure not to be Chriftian, but they are not divine; and
his angels, with their flying draperies and affected
poftures, do not in anything remind us of thofe that
vifited the Dominican cell.

The two moft celebrated pupils of Perugino, Pinturicchio and Raphael, were faithful to the religious
and poetical tendencies of their mafter. Pinturicchio
alfo approached Beato Angelico by the traditional
character of his compofitions and by the purity of
his talent. Defpite the fad patronage of Alexander
VI., his pencil remained truly Chriftian. His chapels
in Santa Maria del Popolo, and his Hiftory of S.
Bernardine of Sienna at *Ara Cœli*, recall, by the fweet-

nefs of the expreſſions and the quietneſs of the light, the beautiful freſcos in the convent of San Marco.

Raphael had a genius too delicate and too exalted not to love and comprehend that of Beato Angelico. Like Perugino, he perfected his talent at Florence; his intimacy with Fra Bartolomeo lets us difcover him amidſt our painter's maſterpieces. He certainly ſtudied them, and the ſpirit which reflected ſo well the merits it met with, muſt have ſtamped on them the qualities with which he moſt ſympathiſed.

Some Catholic writers ſeem to us to fall into a two-fold exaggeration, by ſetting forth too much the religious ſentiment of his firſt works, and by branding ſo rigorouſly the pagan tendencies of his laſt years. Raphael was neither a ſaint nor an apoſtle. To his lot the happieſt and moſt lofty nature had fallen which an artiſt could, perhaps, poſſeſs. The purity of his underſtanding and tenderneſs of his heart enabled him to comprehend and love the beautiful, and he had the treaſures of a fertile imagination and the reſources of a docile hand for rendering it. No one was more capable of cultivating theſe precious qualities than Perugino. The pupil ſtraightway appropriated the talent of the maſter, but did not, as he, ſtudy the primitive ſchools, and conſequently he ſeparated himſelf from the great traditions of art. He continued to be a religious painter more from taſte than from piety. He choſe Chriſtian ſubjects becauſe they were the moſt beautiful, and he borrowed from the Goſpel ſomewhat of its purity, becauſe he judged nothing more capable of ſetting off the human figure. His Madonnas are amiable and chaſte, but do they preſent that ideal of the Virgin-Mother and of her Divine Son? They are even lefs faintly than thofe of Perugino. To propofe them above all as the moft perfect type of the creature is, it feems to us, to deny all the great traditions of the primitive fchools. Even in the Difpute of the Holy Sacrament, which is often cited as the perfection of Chriftian painting, the fubject leaves much to be defired on the fcore* of religious fentiment; it is, if you will, a thefis on the Real Prefence written in a fine ftyle, but it is not the admirable poem compofed by S. Thomas Aquinas for the feaft of the Holy Sacrament.

By thus raifing Raphael lefs high, his fall will be lefs great; ftill it was real. Senfuality, by degrees, feduced this artift fo loaded with riches and glory; but his hand was never foiled with the exceffes which difgraced Marco Antonio and Giulio Romano.

He abandoned Chriftian fubjects for mythological nudities; but was it not very difficult for him to refift being dragged along by his age? And was he not encouraged and applauded in his defection by the princes of the Roman court? It has been wifhed to make the artiftic patronage of Leo X. a glory of the Church. Yes, it is a glory, for that reign has been one of thofe terrible trials which fhow that the Church has the everlafting promifes, and that the faults of man will never change the doctrine and holinefs of the Spoufe of Chrift.[1]

Leo X. continued the traditions of his family, and completed the ruin of Chriftian art. The world loft

---

[1] The work of M. Audin on Leo X. is deplorable in the point of view of Chriftian art.

the comprehenfion and recollection of it. There were ftill Chriftian artifts, indeed, who, like the faithful Jews of the captivity, offered to God their works, melancholy as the regrets for fatherland around the hearth of the exile. But thefe artifts no longer formed a people : they no more had laws, worfhip, or feftivals. The hoftile conqueror profaned in peace their temples and their altars. What connection have the fchools of Titian, of the Caracci, and of Bernini, with the art of which Chrift is the type and the infpirer? What did thofe idolators of drawing, of colour and of manner feek in realizing the dreams of their grofs fenfuality, if not a little glory and cafh ? They feparated natural from moral beauty ; and their art is merely a body without foul which corruption foon deforms. They pretended to imitate the ancients ; but they are as far from ancient art, as ancient would have been from Chriftian art, had they continued its noble deftinies.

It is not aftonifhing that Beato Angelico has been forgotten during thefe ages of defolation. His name has been buried under the Renaiffance, like the facred tombs which the ruins of a devafted cloifter and the brambles of the defert cover. But amidft the vaft and ferious ftudy we are making of the paft, his glory is beginning to appear to us, like the break of a better day. Weary of its unbelieving and frivolous life, art has feated itfelf on the threfhold of our churches, and architecture, fculpture and painting feem fain to unite again under their fecular vaults to pray to God together.

This archæological labour, not to be barren, muft aid Chriftian art in finding its great infpirations again.

It is not its bufinefs to analyfe forms and to catalogue ruins; it muft profit by the leffons of hiftory Life and not death, the fcalpel ftudies on the inanimate remains. Thefe monuments of the paft have fprung from an idea and a love which are neceffary to continue them. They have a meaning which we muft underftand, a liturgical and fymbolical language which we muft fpeak. Chriftian art is fleeping like Lazarus; it is neceffary to go with Chrift to fet it free.

Beato Angelico is the beft guide to follow in this revival of Chriftian art, and through him the interrupted tradition muft be recovered. After his example, we muft firmly believe the dogmas, meditate the Gofpel, and admire its beauties in the lives of the faints; and we muft alfo ftudy them in the works of the mafters of the old fchools, who are the fathers of Chriftian art, not to imitate the old ftyle, but to follow the types which are the definitions of the truths to be rendered. Art, like religion, has need of a doctrinal authority, which delivers the fame truths to all.

The Chriftian artift muft ftudy nature. Is it not to exprefs the truth that God has made all the wonders of the vifible world? Let him penetrate it then, and reflect them by ftriving with his divine model. Let him employ, as a docile language, the noblenefs of proportions, the pliancy of lines, the magic of light, the harmony of colours, and let him unite them again on the figure of man, that all nature may glorify its Author.

All thefe beauties the artift may ftudy in the works of thofe who have confecrated them to vain idols. Like the people of Ifrael, he may take the precious vales of Egypt, to go and facrifice to the true God in the defert. Ancient art is a rich metal, which his hand may caft to decorate the fanctuary. All that is beautiful is Chriftian. Let him then appropriate the purity of tafte, the perfection of form, the fimplicity, the meafure which fhine in the monuments of Rome and Athens. The paganifm we have to dread is the paganifm of our fouls.

Beato Angelico formed his talent in the three-fold fchool of tradition, nature and the antique. But what will it avail to have his fcience without his love? By holinefs efpecially we muft imitate him. Chriftian art is the art of Chrift, and it has no other law but the Chriftian life. The Chriftian artift then muft hear and follow Chrift : like Him, he muft manifeft the truth, and love God and his neighbour whilft forgetting himfelf. He muft renounce all human glory, and ever repeat, in his attempts as well as in his fuccefs, the device of the monks and knights of the middle ages, " Not unto us, O Lord, not unto us, but unto Thy name give glory : *Non nobis, Domine, non nobis, fed nomine tuo da gloriam.*"

Chapter *XV.*

BEATO ANGELICO DA FIESOLE JUDGED IN ITALY, GERMANY AND FRANCE.

DOUBLE motive engages us to offer a recapitulation of the judgments paſſed on Beato Angelico da Fieſole in Italy, Germany and France. We ſhall thus firſt point out the hiſtorical ſources whence we have drawn, and be able to acknowledge the ſervices rendered us by thoſe authors who have gone before us. What would our labour be without the aid of their reſearches and lights? Then we ſhall reaſſure ourſelves againſt ourſelves. The love we have for our painter neceſſarily influences the appreciation of his work, and perhaps makes our admiration ſuſpected. We will go on after to call in other witneſſes; and we ſhall be happy to ſee Beato Angelico crowned by hands more worthy than own.

Firſt of all, it is eaſy to eſtabliſh the immenſe reputation of Beato Angelico during his life. Facts and texts prove that he was then eſteemed the firſt painter in Italy.

At Florence, Beato Angelico was the painter preferred by Coſimo de Medici. Churches and corporations contended for his pictures; the ſovereign pontiffs entruſted the decoration of their palaces to him; and the magiſtrates of Orvieto, in their deliberation of July 11th, 1447, expreſſed the general opinion when they declared him to be the moſt celebrated painter in Italy: *Et eſt famoſus ultra alios pictores ytalicos.*[1] Pope Nicholas V., in the epitaph he compoſed in his praiſe, proclaimed him another Apelles: *Velut alter Apelles.* Laſtly, the religious of the Order of S. Dominic did not fear to be contradicted by their contemporaries when they alſo placed him in the firſt rank in their necrological notices. The chronicle of San Domenico of Fieſole names him eminently the painter: *F. Joannes Petri de Mugello juxta Vichium, optimus pictor.*[2] The annals of the convent of San Marco, in ſpeaking of Fra Benedetto, ſay he was brother of Beato Angelico, " that admirable painter: *Germanus fratris Joannis, illius tam mirandi pictoris.*"[3] In another place, they declare " that he paſſed for the great maſter of painting in Italy: *Qui habebatur pro ſummo magiſtro in arte pictoria, in Italia.*"[4]

Two poets contemporary with Beato Angelico

---

[1] See page 256.
[2] *Cronica conv. S. D. de Feſulis,* fol. 97.—1407.
[3] *Annalia conv. S. M. de Florentia, A,* fol. 211.—1448.
[4] *Annalia conv. S. M. de Florentia,* fol. 6.—1449.

equally prove his great reputation. The firft is Padre Domenico Corella, of the Order of Friar-Preachers, prior of Santa Maria Novella, who died in 1483. In his poem entitled *De Origine urbis Florentiæ*, he has not placed our painter below Giotto and Cimabue.

> *Angelicus pictor quam finxerat ante, Johannes*
> *Nomine, non Jotto, non Cimabove minor.*

The fecond is Giovanni di Santi of Urbino, father of the great Raphael, who, in his poem, *Dei fatti ed imprefe di Fedrico duca di Urbino*, fpeaks of Beato Angelico as a glory of Italy:

> *Ma nell'Italia, in quefta eta prefente*
> *Vi fu il degno gentil da Fabriano*
> *Giovan da Fiefole al bene ardente.*

Pofterity has not difavowed thefe encomiums, and three authors repeated them before Vafari. Thefe were,

1. Pere Jean de Touloufe, who wrote the chronicle of Fiefole in 1516. His notice on Beato Angelico and his works is very incomplete.

2. Padre Roberto Ubaldini, annalift of the convent of San Marco, who died at Siena in 1534, has not made known, too, any important fact.

3. Padre Leandro Alberti, the celebrated hiftorian and geographer of Bologna, in his Latin Eulogies on the illuftrious men of the Order of Friar-Preachers, has written on Beato Angelico. This is the eulogy which gives us the exact date of his death, and relates, with fome variations, his fcruples on the occafion of his invitation to dine by Nicholas V.[1]

---

[1] V. *Marchefe*, vol. i. p. 294.

B. JO. Fesulanus.—" Joannes Fefulanus. He-
trufcus, vir fanctitate confpicuus, et pingendi arte
peritiffimus, anno Domini mcccclv . xii. Kalend.
Martii, Romæ vitâ functus eft, et in bafilicâ S. Mariæ
ad Minervam in fepulchro lapideo tanto viro digno
tumulatus, quod Nicholaus V, Pont. Max. duobus
epitaphiis graphice exornari curavit. Fuit hic vene-
randus vir tantæ obfervantiæ inftitutionum fuarum,
ut in palatio Pont. Max. confiftens, minimam earum
partem haudquaquam omiferit. Nam cùm Nicholaus
Pontifex ei facellum in palatio, quod adhuc cernitur, picturis exornandum tradidiffet, et eum aliquandò viferet,
ac diceret : Hodiè, Joannes, volo ut carnibus vefcaris,
nimis enim laboribus indulfifti, refpondiffe ferunt :
Pater fanĉte, hoc mihi præfectus cœnobii non indulfit.
Et Pontifex : Ipfe qui omnibus præfum, tibi hoc in-
dulgeo. Ex hoc enim conjici poteft quanta fuerit cum
ifto fanĉto viro patrum noftrorum obfervantia inftitutionum, qui fibi non indultum a cœnobii fui præfidente
hoc Pontifici objecerit. Apprimè Nicholaus tantum
vivum coluit, ac veneratus eft, ob ejus vitæ integri-
tatem ac morum excellentiam.''[1]

Notwithftanding his imperfeĉtions, Vafari is the hiftorian who gives us the beft information on the painters
anterior to the Renaiffance. He publifhed two editions
of his work, the firft in 1550, and the fecond in 1568 ;
and from this laft all the other editions have been
taken fince his death. The author correĉted his
labour with care, threw it into better order, and made
numerous and important additions. Thefe changes

---

[1] *De viris illuſt. Ord. Prœdicatorum libri ſex in unum congeſti, auĉtore Leandro Alberti Bononienſi;* 1 vol. in fol. ; Bononiæ, 1517, fol. 5, f. 252 a tergo.

are perceived efpecially in the Life of Beato Angelico, which has gained much both as to form and extent. It is natural to feek how the facts given by Vafari came to him. The tradition of a painter's life is eafily preferved by the ftudy of his works ; and Vafari dwelt in the two cities, where the memory of Beato Angelico would be beft perpetuated. He would get at it through three artifts, with whom he was con-nected.

Luca Signorelli was contemporary with Beato An-gelico, as he was born in 1440 or 1441. He muft have been particularly interefted in everything that concerned the celebrated painter, whofe works he continued in the cathedral of Orvieto. He was a rela-tive of Vafari, who perfectly well recollected having feen and heard him in his youth ; and the good octogenarian, who loved chatting very dearly, muft have told many a ftory of old times, when he went to paint a picture for the nuns of Santa Marghereta at Arezzo. Then he became acquainted with the young Vafari, perfuaded him to work, foretold a brilliant future for him, and faved him from death by ftopping a bleeding at the nofe. Vafari declares that he retained an everlafting recollection of him.[1]

Vafari's drawing-mafter alfo was a French Do-minican, Guillaume de Marcillat, who, at that time, was executing the ftained glafs for the cathedral of Arezzo. Luca Signorelli muft naturally have fpoken

---

[1] Et perchè egli intefe, ficcome era vero, che il fangue in fi grand copia, m' ufciva in quell' età dal nafo, che mi lafciava alcuna volta tramortito, mi pofe di fua mano, un diafpro al collo, con infinita amorevolezza, la qual memoria di Luca mi ftarà in eterno fiffa nell' animo.—VASARI, *Life of Luca Signorelli.*

of Beato Angelico with this religious, who had been able to admire his works in the convents of his Order.

When Vafari ftudied at Florence under the direction of Michael Angelo, his mafter made him fhare his admiration for the wonders of Santa Maria Novella and of San Marco. Laftly we know pofitively that he was very thick with an old miniature-painter, who received the religious habit from the hand of Savonarola in 1496, only forty years after the death of Beato Angelico. Fra Euftachio had a prodigious memory, and his contemporary Padre Timoteo Bottonio tells us that Vafari obtained very valuable information from him, when he made his firft edition of the Lives of the Painters.[1] We fee how tradition might eafily have reached Vafari.

The Life of Beato Angelico by Vafari is wanting in judgment, and offers us but little except a confufed and incomplete enumeration of his works. What it prefents moft remarkable, is the fincere enthufiafm of the author for an artift whofe genius muft have been fo little underftood at the epoch of the Renaiffance. The merit and holinefs of the painter put Vafari out and fubdued him. Ideas clafhed in his mind, as is feen

---

[1] Fra Euftachio Fiorentino, converfo di San Marco, fu un belliffimo fpirito et di raro ingegno. Era miniatore eccellente, et fece belliffime opere, in quefto genere; fpecialmente un faltero grande belliffimo che fi adopera nel choro di San Marco. Hebbe gran memoria, et tutto che foffe decrepito, recitava a mente infiniti luoghi di Dante, nel quale egli haveva gran pratica. Quando il Vafari fcriffe la prima volta le Vite de' pittori, veniva fpeffo a ragionare con quefto vecchio, dal quale cavò molti et belliffimi particolari di quegli antichi et illuftri artefici. Andava per il convento con un baftone al quale fi appoggiava, et mi ricordo che affai temeva il punto della morte, la quale poi gli avvenne dolciffima et placidiffima, ficcome io proprio vidi. Haveva 83 anni, et morì a 25 fettembre. *Annal. mfs.*, vol. ii., p. 301; 1555.—V. MARCHESE, vol. i., p. 175.

in the reflections which commence the Life of Beato Angelico in the edition of 1550 and clofe it in that of 1568.

He certainly acknowledged that " he who does religious and holy fubjeҫts ſhould himſelf be religious. For we know that when theſe fubjeҫts are treated by perſons who have little faith and little reſpeҫt for religion, they often inſpire unbecoming and licentious thoughts. We then blame the work as immoral, even whilſt we praiſe the talent of the artiſt." Still he would not wiſh " that what is only ill-made and fooliſh ſhould be found pious, and what is beautiful and good licentious, as they do who condemn as profane the figures of females or of young perſons a little more beautiful than ordinary. They do not ſee that they are in the wrong to blame the painter who has reaſon to believe that the ſaints of both ſexes in heaven ſhould have a greater beauty than on earth. They ſhow all the perverſity of their heart by criticizing like things with a ſtupid zeal ; for if they were as chaſte as they would fain appear, they would ſee there only the love of heaven and a homage paid to God, the ſupreme perfeҫtion, from whom all the beauty of His creatures comes."

The writer of the Renaiſſance here confounds two very diftinҫt beauties, the beauty that pleaſes the ſenſes, and the beauty that pleaſes the ſoul. The figures of females and of young people of whom he ſpeaks are not more beautiful, but more nude than ordinary.

In the ſecond edition of his work, he adds to theſe refleҫtions an argument which he thinks triumphant. " What would theſe ſcrupulous people then do," ſays

he, " if they found themfelves in the prefence of living
beauties, with voluptuous manners, fweet words, graceful movements, and looks which ravifh feeble hearts?
What would they become, if the image alone, the
fhadow of beauty, fo overturns them?" We clearly
fee of what beauty Vafari fpeaks, and we need not
decide if the image offers lefs danger than the reality.
Still Vafari makes his refervations, and declares, " that
he would not have it fuppofed that he approved of the
almoft entirely nude figures which are depicted in
churches. The painter ought to refpect the fanctity
of the place." Did Vafari apply this reproach to the
Laft Judgment in the Siftine chapel?

Whilft ftudying the works of Beato Angelico, we
have liked to quote an admirer fo little fufpected.
Vafari feems to have been very well informed on the
virtues of Beato Angelico. "Would to God," he
cries, " that all religious men would employ their life
as this truly Angelic father did! for he confecrated
every moment of his to the fervice of God and to the
good of the world and of his neighbour. What more
can or ought to be defired than to gain the kingdom
of heaven by living holily, and an everlafting fame on
earth by making mafterpieces? Befides, a talent fo
fuperior, fo extraordinary, as that of Fra Giovanni
could belong only to a man of great fanctity. He
avoided all the works of the world, and his life was fo
pure, he loved the poor in fuch a manner, that I believe
his foul is now in heaven. He continually laboured
at painting, and would reprefent only faints. He
might have been rich, but he thought not of it, and
he was accuftomed to fay that true riches confift in

being contented with a little. He might have commanded many, and would not do fo, faying that it is lefs
troublefome and fafer to obey. He was free to have
honours in his Order and elfewhere ; he refufed, reply-
ing that he fought no other honour but that of avoiding hell and reaching heaven. He was extremely
meek and temperate. He was always chafte, and
avoided the fnares of the world. He was accuftomed
to fay that an artift needed quiet and a peaceful
life, and that *he who does the works of Chrift, with
Chrift muft always be.* He was never feen to be angry
amongft his brethren, a thing which feems very aftonifhing and hardly to be believed. He was contented
to admonifh his friends mildly and with a fmiling
face. He replied with the utmoft kindnefs to thofe
who afked any painting of him, to obtain the prior's
confent, and he would fatisfy him. In fine, this Father
will never be too much praifed for his works. His
words were full of humility and modefty, his pictures,
of grace and devotion. The faints he has reprefented
refemble faints more than all the others. He never
would retouch his works or begin them again. He
left them as he had done them at firft, for he faid that
it was the will of God. We are affured that Fra
Giovanni never touched his pencil without having
firft faid a prayer. He never painted a Crucifixion
without watering it with his tears. Thus, in the heads
and attitudes of his figures, we fee all the goodnefs,
faith and greatnefs of his Chriftian foul."

Vafari has been pleafed to give a portrait of Beato
Angelico ; but this portrait anfwers badly to the
ideal we have formed of him from his life and works.

The moſt authentic portrait of Beato Angelico is the one on his tomb. The ſculptor might have executed it from memory, or even from a plaſter mould. Unfortunately, this bas-relief, which is well preſerved, is very coarſely done, and can ſerve but little to make up again the principal features of our Beato. According to tradition, Luca Signorelli, in his freſco at Orvieto, has repreſented Beato Angelico in one of the religious preſent at the puniſhment of the martyrs of Antichriſt. The head of that religious has not been drawn from life; it is too young, and Luca Signorelli was not yet ſixteen years old when our *young* painter died, in 1455, at the age of ſixty-eight. We cannot then receive this tradition.

Vaſari's portrait may be more valuable, although it is deteriorated by the pencil of the drawer and by the wood-engraver's execution. This portrait has been copied from the one which Fra Bartolomeo put, they ſay, in the Laſt Judgment executed for the hoſpital of Santa Maria Nuova, at Florence. Fra Bartolomeo, in faͨt, might have copied the authentic portraits which exiſted in his time in the convents of Fieſole and San Marco. The portraits of the celebrated Dominicans of the reform had been placed in the cell of S. Antoninus, and one of Beato Angelico figured there : another exiſted alſo in the refeͨtory of Fieſole, and at the bottom was written,

> *Beatus Ioannes piͨtor, moribus et penicillo*
> *Angelici cognomen jure merito H. C. F.*
> (hujus conventus filius).

The moſt important hiſtorian of painting, in Italy, ſince the Renaiſſance, is the learned Jeſuit Lanzi. But he fpeaks very briefly of Beato Angelico, whom he feems to have little ftudied and little underftood.[1] Still he marks out his relations with the fchool of Giotto, and highly extols the Coronation in the gallery at Florence. He fays nothing of the frefcoes at the convent of San Marco, and only cites the paintings at Orvieto and Rome from authors, *Opera lodatiſſima dagli ſcrittori.* He thought to praife our painter vaftly by calling him the Guido of his epoch, *Vero Guido per quella età.* Although this comparifon is injurious to Beato Angelico, fome truth may ftill be found in it. There certainly are fome material relations between the two painters. Guido reminds us of Beato Angelico by the extreme facility of his pencil, by a certain elegance of proportion, and certain fweetnefs of colouring : but what have thefe natural qualities become with the two painters? Beato Angelico developed and perfected them in pure and faintly works, whilft the artift of the decline lavifhed and diffipated them in vulgar ones. Beato Angelico was always progreffing up to his laft day, whilft Guido atoned for his eafy triumphs in a flighted old age.

The firft and real hiftorian of Beato Angelico is Padre Vincenzo Marchefe, of the Order of Friar-Preachers. His *Memoirs of the moſt eminent Dominican Painters, Sculptors and Architects,* is a glory for Italy and for the church.[2] The author explains, with

---

[1] LANZI, *Storia pittorica della Italia ;* Scuola Fiorentina, Epoca prima.

[2] *Memorie dei più inſigni pittori, ſcultori e architetti domenicani* del P. Vincenzo MARCHESE, 2e edition, 2 vol., in 12mo ; Florence, Felix Le Monnier, 1854. The fecond edition is much fuperior to the firft. We hope that this excellent work will be tranflated and publifhed in the *Bibliothèque dominicaine.* [The firft edition has already appeared in Englifh, by the Rev. C. P. Meehan, 2 vols., Dublin 1852. TRANSLATOR'S Note.]

great talent, the various merits of the artifts of whom
he fpeaks and developes general ideas, which denote a
deep infight into Chriftian art. Beato Angelico is
naturally his favourite artift, and he has written his life
at the greateft length and with the moft love. We
are happy to pay our debt of gratitude here, by
declaring that Padre Marchefe has been our guide
throughout all our labour. His refearches into the
archives of his Order procured new documents for
him, which make known the principal phafes of
Beato Angelico's life. He explains, by his refidence
in Umbria, his relations with the primitive fchools,
and thus marks his progrefs in Chriftian art. " It is
faid that Dante, in his Paradifo, mated the harmony
of verfe with the doctrine of S. Thomas Aquinas;
I will freely add that Beato Angelico depicted the
works of both. There are fo many connections
between the manner in which thefe three great Italians
explain the fupernatural world and clothe it with
images, that we may unceafingly compare the words
of the writers with the paintings of the artift. The
old myftical fchool of Bologna had confined itfelf to
the reprefentations of certain fubjects. Simone painted
Crucifixions, and Vitale, Madonnas. Brought up in
the poetical and fruitful fchool of Giotto, Spinello
and Memmi, Beato Angelico embraced the whole
hiftory of the New Teftament, and to it added, from
time to time, fubjects of legendary painting, in which,
in my judgment, he furpaffed all who had preceded
him. He had confecrated his life and genius to
religion ; he refolved to follow faithfully the ftrict
canons of Chriftian art, and all the traditions of the

fchool of Giotto, of which he may be faid to have
been the laft off-fhoot. He never fullied his pencil
with profane fubjects, and he made it, like the Gofpel-
word, a means of moral and religious perfection."[1]

The refidence of Beato Angelico at Fiefole feems
alfo to Padre Marchefe to be the moft charming and
richeft period of his talent. "In all the places were
he ftayed," fays he, "he ftrewed the flowers of art
abundantly, and thofe flowers feem to have been culled
in heaven. He fcattered them on the mountains of
Umbria and of Tufcany, on the banks of the Arno
and of the Tiber; but the faireft and moft fragrant
were referved for his beloved hill of Fiefole."[2]

Padre Marchefe equally proves the progrefs of Beato
Angelico in the pictures at San Marco. "In thefe
works," fays he, "the progrefs of art at Florence
became fenfible, in the play of the draperies, the ftyle of
his figures, and particularly in the improvement of his
manner, by more vigour in the drawing and model."
Laftly, he gives the chapel of the Vatican as the
apogee of the artift's talent. "We will clofe by faying
with Profeffor Rofini, that in this work more than in
all the others, Beato Angelico improved his manner,
and arrived at fuch a perfection, that he may difpute
the palm with the nobleft geniufes of his age."[3]

If the want of fome practical and fecondary knowledge hinders Padre Marchefe from feparating the
works of Beato Angelico from thofe of his brother
Fra Benedetto, he lays down at leaft the true principles
of the diftinction. After having refuted Profeffor

[1] MARCHESE, vol. i., l. II., ch. 4.
[2] *Id.*, ch. 5.
[3] *Id.*, ch. 8.

Rofini, who wifhed to recognize the work of each painter by the greater or lefs richnefs of their pictures, he adds, " If Fra Benedetto has really painted pictures and frefcoes, we muft rather feek his works amongft the feebleft paintings we have been accuftomed to attribute to Beato Angelico, and efpecially amongft fome frefcoes of the convent of San Marco, which are evidently inferior to thofe of Fra Giovanni."[1]

With the foul of a Chriftian and a religious efpecially, does Padre Marchefe judge Beato Angelico, and we fhould not end if we were to tranflate all the paffages in which he has expreffed his pious enthufiafm. After defcribing the Coronation of the Bleffed Virgin, in the Gallery of Florence, the author adds, " To give the impreffion this picture caufes, is impoffible for the moft fkilful eloquence. The heart has a language which words cannot always exprefs, and we are unable ever to contemplate that picture without feeling ourfelves ardent for heaven. Oh! if all thofe made for the Catholic Church were like it, the unfortunate ones who are feparated from our creed would not be able to flander the worfhip of images; for images, like fpeech, would be a means of making virtue loved."[2]

Padre Marchefe's work will powerfully contribute to give art that fublime miffion. The ftrong and independent truths which he has made heard in the country of the Medici will re-echo far away; and we hope that his work will be foon tranflated into French. In the meantime, we fhall be allowed to make a laft

---

[1] MARCHESE, vol. i., l. I., ch. 18.
[2] *Id.*, vol. i., l. II., ch. 5.

quotation, which will give an idea of our author's manner of looking on art. After sketching with masterly strokes, in the chapter serving as an introduction to the Life of Beato Angelico, the history of art in ancient and modern times, Padre Marchese shows that Christian art has varied its means according to times and nations, without changing for all that its invariable principles. The principles are these : "To have always for its aim, not to please, but to move and instruct ; pleasure should be the means and not the end. The thought should be given with all simplicity and clearness. Accessories which would disturb the moral and religious effect of the subject, must be rejected. The artist ought to have full liberty in his work ; he may use all the means he judges best to gain his end. All ought to speak to the soul and heart of the spectator, and where painting is not enough, he must resort to clear and easily understood symbols, and if symbols do not suffice he must aid himself by speech, and choose texts out of the Bible that give the artistic thought best, and put them in the most convenient place. In pictures exposed to the veneration of the faithful, he must pourtray the saints, not in their pilgrimage, but in heavenly light and glory ; and in these representations, especially of Christ and of the Holy Virgin, he must guard well against giving portraits of living persons, for the portrait awakens in the mind of the spectator recollections of the original and of relations with him, and public devotion will certainly be only lost. Decency ought to be severely observed. Lastly, he must dread every immoral subject, and bear in mind that Christian art is a divine inspiration,

and that the images of the blefled and the holy joys of
Paradife cannot be properly and worthily reprefented
without a pure heart, lively faith, ardent charity and
fervent prayer."

Germany is perhaps the country of Europe given
up to the greateft conflicts between error and truth.
Whilft Proteftantifm is attacking reafon, both divine
and human, by denying with Dr. Straufs the divinity
of Chrift and by falling with Hegel and his difciples
into contradiction of terms, Catholicifm is publifhing
admirable works, which it fuffices to tranflate to refute
all the falfe fyftems that French eclectics go to feek
beyond the Rhine. Hiftorical fcience in particular is
on the advance in Germany. The ftudy of the paft
is the great work of our age ; its extent affrights. All
peoples, all languages, all points of time and of fpace
are interrogated with unheard-of ardour and perfeverance. God feems to have given the order for uniting
the teftimonies of all ages together, to affure to the
world a laft and fupreme manifeftation of the truth.

This effort towards the True muft naturally be a
progrefs towards the Beautiful ; and in fact we fee
Germany taking an immenfe ftride towards Chriftian
art. When the French Revolution and the conquefts
of the Empire had re-awakened the national fpirit of
the Germanic races, they found, in tracing back their
origins, a literature and monuments, the infpiration of
which was neceffarily religious, for religion is the
principal and fap of the people. In the ftudy of
their ancient poems, the architecture, fculpture and
painting of the middle ages foon recovered favour.
The brothers Sulpice and Melchior Boifferée made a

collection of old German mafters, which attracted the
attention of the public, and was purchafed in 1817 by
the King of Bavaria.   The brothers Schlegel, in particular, aided very much in this national reaction againft
the academical and pagan fchool then reigning. By their
writings and lectures, they became the guides of tafte.
In 1817, Auguftus William Schlegel publifhed, at
Paris, a notice on Beato Angelico and his picture in
the Mufeum of the Louvre: a very remarkable work
for that time.[1] The author affigns to our painter " a
diftinguifhed rank amongft the reftorers and promoters
of art who went before the celebrated mafters of the
fixteenth century." After having given an abridg-
ment of his life from Vafari's incomplete authorities,
he examines and analyfes with tafte the principal
fubject and the gradino accompanying it.   He praifes
the difpofition, " which is," he fays, " very well ordered,
and the fymmetry, which reminds the fpectator that
he is affifting at a folemn act ; it unites richnefs and
variety, which diffufe life.   The painter has fhown
befides, in that part, a deep knowledge of lineal perfpective. . . .   If we then occupy ourfelves with each
figure in particular, we directly admire the imagination of the painter, who, in a fubject wherein oppofition of characters cannot properly find a place, and
wherein it is neceffary for the uniform expreffion of
affectionate joy and calm happinefs to be fhown
in every countenance, has known how to create fo
great a variety, whilft keeping himfelf within the
limits of gravity and beauty.   It cannot be faid that

[1] *Le Couronnement de la fainte Vierge et les Miracles de faint Dominique,* in
folio ; 15 plates. Paris: 1817.

one fingle head is the repetition of another; and this variety is extended, not only to features and looks full of foul, but alfo to the cut and arrangement of the hair and beard, which is ufually of uncommon beauty, and laftly to the movements and attitudes."

He praifes, above all, the two principal figures. "The Virgin is kneeling upon the topmoft ftep before the throne, a little bent forwards, her beautiful hands croffed on her bofom, which is but flightly marked. Nothing exceeds the elegance, the gracefulnefs of this almoft unmaterial figure, and the virginal purity of her head. There is fomething paternal in the whole of our Lord's body, and it is difficult to imagine that he is the Son of her whom he is crowning. He holds the crown with both hands, in order to place it as gently as poffible on a beloved head. The angels are figures of young perfons full of amiable franknefs and happy innocence ; they touch the cords with a graceful negligence, as if harmony were their nature. The laft one, who plays a fort of viol, and turns afide, has the air of one inebriated with joy and ravifhed with the founds he is drawing from his inftrument."

After having examined the other figures and the compofitions reprefenting the Life of S. Dominic, Schlegel refumes, and ends with an accommodation between the arts of the ancients and moderns, in which fome ufeful truths are found.

"The work we are examining places us in a perfect condition for paffing a general judgment on Giovanni of Fiefole, without the need of prefenting any other ones. This artift fhares the qualities and defects of his contemporaries. Through a refpectful attachment

for the ancient manner, perhaps, he will be left, in fome
way, in the background, in regard to the fkill in the
effect of the painting, and to many other parts of the
art. His principal qualities are fweetnefs, delicacy
and gracefulnefs. . . . His talent is like a copious
fpring, which glides evenly along, without impetuofity
and without reftraint, from a lovely foul purified by
piety and contemplation.

"The gracefulnefs of Giovanni of Fiefole has made
Lanzi give him the name of the Guido of ancient
painting. Lanzi, no doubt, wifhed thereby to pafs a
grand eulogy on Giovanni of Fiefole, and the admirers
of Guido's agreeable and fuperficial manner will perhaps find the comparifon not very flattering to their
favourite mafter; but whofoever feeks originality and
depth in art will not regard it either as juft or as fatif-
factory.

"Although gracefulnefs and fweetnefs particularly
diftinguifh Giovanni of Fiefole, ftill thefe qualities are
not generally foreign to the genius of the Florentine
fchool. On this occafion, we will take up an affertion
of Winkelman, who pretends that the Tufcan artifts
inherited a harfh, forced and over-done ftyle from the
ancient Etrufcans. . . The comparifon is exceedingly
defective, and all comparifons will be more or lefs fo
which anyone would defire to eftablifh between the arts of
the ancients and of the moderns; for not only do they
differ, but they are even completely oppofed in their
intimate effence, and cannot, therefore, be fubmitted to
a common meafure. With the Greeks, art began with
the imitation of the human form; with the moderns,
it is attached, from the firft, to exprefs the affections

of the foul. In the works of the Greeks, the human body was already reprefented in all the perfection of its ftruclosure. All its movements, all the developments of phyfical power, had been imitated with the greateft vigour, before the foul was manifefted on the countenance. Even the beauty of the heads, which confifts in the proportions and regularity of the features independently of the expreffion, was difcovered only very flowly with the Greeks, comparatively with the progrefs of art in all the reft. With the ancient Chriftian painters, on the contrary, the body is drawn in a very imperfect manner; it is added to the head, in fome fort, as a neceffary evil, whilft, in the variety of phyfiognomies, thefe artifts already fhow gradations of feeling with an exquifite delicacy, and that they fucceeded in painting what we may call the beauty of the foul. They took a more intellectual view of the world, and alfo had under their eyes quite another generation. By imitating the ancients only, have the moderns perfected themfelves in drawing the body. It belongs to the hiftory of art to fhow how difference of religion produced thefe oppofite directions. The farther we go back towards the beginnings of art with the ancients and with the moderns, the more do we find it exclufively confecrated to worfhip, and fixed by religious ideas. With the progrefs of time, art always became more and more worldly, and there is properly its laft epoch. In our days, they have fought to reanimate it by purely temporal reforts and with worldly views ; but this means never can fucceed. All fcience, all obfervation of real things, is infufficient to infpire talent with truly original creations. The

artift muft be initiated into myfteries of a higher order;
whether it be, as with the Greeks, in the fphere of the
creatrix-powers of nature, or, as with the ancient
Chriftian painters, in the fpiritual kingdom of man
regenerated by faith. Art, deftined to fhow us a
reflection of the divine perfections in the vifible
world, is a fublime want of man, but he will not know
how to fulfil his end unlefs heaven and earth engage
in the work."

In Pruffia, an Englifh amateur, Mr. Solly, formed a
collection of the old Italian mafters, and was guided
in his fearches by the learned M. Hirt. This collection was fold to the king in 1820, and began the
Mufeum of Berlin. Thefe pictures, purer in ftyle
than thofe of the ancient fchools of Germany, aided
the return towards Chriftian art. The government
favoured this movement by the miffion which it
entrufted to the learned Rumohr, and to the two
brothers Tieck, poets and fculptors. Rumohr ex-
plored Italy without following the beaten paths; he
ftudied the artifts in their works, lives, and mutual
relations, rummaged archives, rectified Vafari, and
threw great light on the hiftory of the primitive
fchools. M. Rio renders juftice to the value of his
work, which was often ferviceable to him in his refearches. Rumohr naturally gives an honourable
place to Beato Angelico, and we regret that we cannot
give here the tranflation of the pages which he dedi-
cates to him.[1]

The happieft event for the Renaiffance of Chriftian
art in Germany has been the fchool founded at Rome

---

[1] RUMOHR, *Italienifche Forfchungen*, vol. ii., p. 251.

by Frederick Overbeck. The date of this new era is 1809. The young Proteftant of Lubeck was obliged to fly from Vienna before the intolerance and far-cafms of the partifans of Raphael Mengs and David. His Chriftian and national ideas clafhed with the academical routine, and he went to feek at Rome a freer air and purer doctrines. Whilft ftudying beauty he found truth; he recognized the faith of his forefathers in the paintings of the catacombs and of the bafilicas. Overbeck became a Catholic, and God fixed him in the eternal city, there to win back the traditions of Chriftian art, and to give to all the artifts who went there the great inftruction of his life and works.

The whole world knows the touching hiftory of the new German fchool, its humble and courageous beginnings, the ftruggle of a few young people againft privations of every kind, the rare friendfhip which fhared both toils and crowns. From the poor convent which gave them an afylum has gone forth the generation of artifts that now covers Germany. Rationalifm, without doubt, finds fome partifans there; but Catholicifm is ever truly the infpirer of the progrefs and the mafter of the work. We cannot here appreciate the character of the German fchool, and fay how beautiful it is in its whole, how happy in its independence. We will only long to fee our own French fchool follow a like path, and repeat the beautiful words of M. Hallez, in his letter to M. Claudius Lavergne, on the fubject of the univerfal expofition of 1855. "What we have to do, is to ftudy with brotherly fympathy what our elders have done in the career, and to fupport them. Chriftians of different nations, that is to fay, different companies of the fame army, let us endeavour, in good .time, to outftrip one another; but let us never forget that the victory of the one is the victory of all." [1]

We regret that we cannot do homage here to the German fchools, particularly to that of Duffeldorf, which is rendering, through its Society, fo great fervices for the propagation of religious prints; [2] but we hail them all in the perfon of Frederick Overbeck, their chief, the moft worthy fucceffor of Beato Angelico. During our laft ftay at Rome, one of our devotions on the Sunday was to vifit his ftudio, where he received everyone with fo touching a fimplicity; and we own that no preacher has made us underftand virtue better and love it more. His words fhed a heavenly brightnefs over his works, whether he was explaining his picture, in which Mary, Queen of the arts, fings her everlafting *Magnificat* amidft the angels, or was making admirable homilies whilft explaining his beautiful compofitions of the Sacraments: and when he humbly fhunned our hearty homage, we afked God to delay his reward ftill longer and to give him many imitators.

Catholic France could not remain a ftranger to the

---

[1] *Expofition univerfelle de* 1855: BEAUX ARTS, par Claudius Lavergne; Paris, Ve Pouffielgue, page 124.

[2] The Society of Duffeldorf is reprefented at Paris by the houfe of A. W. Schulgen, Rue St. Sulpice, No. 25. From the catalogue of this house, M. Bathil Bouniol has written an excellent pamphlet on Chriftian art and the German fchool.

[In England, too, the Society of Duffeldorf is reprefented by an eftablifhment, which is not a fimple agency, but alfo energetically co-operates in the great work of the German affociation. This is " THE ESTABLISHMENT FOR PROMOTING CHRISTIAN ART" of Mr. John Philp, 7, Orchard Street, Portman Square, London, W.—TRANSLATOR'S Note.]

Renaiſſance of Chriſtian art, and Overbeck's little
colony at Rome found ardent ſympathy in ſome
French artiſts. Orſel eſpecially was worthy to ſtretch
out a brotherly hand to him; for he too was there,
far from noiſe and favour, dreaming and preparing a
better future for his country. He is ſcarcely dead,
and glory has placed a very tardy crown upon his
brow; but his example will live, and his tomb will
be one of the ſolid baſes of the new temple art
muſt raiſe to the Creator in France. There is an
eloquent inſtruction in that laborious and diſintereſted
life, in thoſe perſevering efforts and progreſſes, in that
generous ſacrifice of his years and fortune, amidſt an
age when talent even is only prized by what it brings
in. There is a great example, too, in the touching
friendſhip which united Orſel with M. Perrin, his other
ſelf, whoſe eulogy is inſeparable from his. The holy
brotherhood ſo common in Germany is very rare
in France; yet it would be worth more than the
gay companionſhip of our artizans. Amongſt us,
Chriſtian artiſts would need to be united for ſtruggling
againſt the difficulties of their poſition; and what we
wiſh moſt for our country is a religious aſſociation,
having a centre and unity of action by inſtruction.
The State gives only an incomplete artiſtic education,
and encouragements which lead young perſons aſtray
in the routine. In the midſt of the groſs life of our
artizans, what can they learn who feel a vocation for
the fine arts? Their intellect is deprived of all culture,
and their heart ſoon loſes all moral feeling. This is
to pay dear indeed for ſome procedures in colouring
and drawing.

A religious affociation may alfo protect Chriftian artifts by its connection with the clergy. It would defend them againft the injuftices of cabal, againft the omnipotence of adminiftrations, and particularly againft that lying criticifm which makes reputations and diftributes orders. Criticifm of works of art is one which requires the moft fpecial knowledge and varied ftudies, and yet all the world thinks itfelf capable of writing on this fubject. It is the theme chofen by all our literary beginners. But what do we moftly have ? Pamphleteers who repeat, in the jargon of the artizan, the common-places and prejudices of the hiftory of art.[1]

The ferious ftudy of the hiftory of art will be very ferviceable for the revival of Chriftian art. Catholicifm defires only the truth, and monuments are witneffes from which it has nothing to fear; for let them be . proofs of greatnefs or of decay, all muft turn to its glory. Since Montfaucon until our own days, arch-æology has done immenfe work. Its learned analyfis has claffified and catalogued all the ruins of paft ages ; but hiftory muft now, by fynthefis, make their origin and laws known, and find therein useful leffons for the future.

France has gone before Germany in this juftice rendered to the middle ages. Seroux d'Agincourt be-

---

[1] There are, without doubt, fome happy exceptions, and we place at the head of thefe exceptions the articles on art publifhed by M. Claudius Lavergne in the *Annales Archéologiques* and in the *Univers.* We do not know a jufter, firmer and more Chriftian critic. For depth as well as for form, his account of the Expofi-tion of 1855 is a model. Would that artifts thus raifed their pen to the height of their talent, and did not fubmit to the fhameful flavery of all thofe frivolous and lying babblers !

longed to the laſt century (1730-1814). His *Hiſtoire de l'art ſur les Monuments* is very remarkable for the period at which it appeared. We have always revolted againſt ſcorn for authors whoſe knowledge the natural progreſs of ſcience has outſtripped. Why not, on the contrary, honour their memory? Their merit ought to be meaſured by ſervices rendered; if our fortune has been increaſed, is it a reaſon for deſpiſing thoſe who left it to us? Muſt not that young gentleman be admired who was ſmitten with mediæval art in the midſt of the frivolities and debaucheries of Louis XV's reign, and purſued his ſtudies throughout the bloody horrors of the French Revolution, ſpending life and fortune in reſearches and travels? D'Agincourt ruined himſelf in publiſhing his work. His plates are engraved as they then engraved; but, in ſpite of their imperfections, they preſent an unique whole of monuments. As for ourſelves, we declare that we prefer D'Agincourt to Winkelman, that fanatical antiquary, who never had the true knowledge of art, and in his factitious enthuſiaſm exalted himſelf in ſuch a manner that it was impoſſible for him to ſupport the ſky and ſcenery of his own country. He died whilſt returning to his Italian collections, the victim of his paſſion for medals.

D'Agincourt has ſome very remarkable and bold perceptions for the time in which he lived. He recognized the influence of Catholiciſm on the arts, and the ſervice rendered them by popes and religious orders. He preſents the reign of Nicholas V. as the preparation for thoſe of Julius II. and Leo X. He has particularly ſtudied Beato Angelico in the chapel of the Vatican, and renders full juftice to our painter. He is perhaps the firft who praifed him in France.

After having faid that he was diftinguifhed in miniature-painting, he adds: "Fra Giovanni of Fiefole fhowed himfelf able to execute great compofitions in frefco, and in this manner he adorned the church of his convent at Florence, and amongft many others, that of San Marco, which he painted by order of Cofimo de Medici called the Father of his country. His paintings are admired even at this day, and ferve always for the edification of the Faithful, by the truthfulnefs of the attitudes, by the fweetnefs and livelinefs of the expreffion, and particularly on account of the beautiful heads of angels and faints. The noble character agreeing with thefe figures is fo well rendered, that according to Vafari's words, *non poffono effere altrimenti in cielo.* This beauty earned for the author the title of *Angelico*, which he, moreover, merited for his virtues.

"Pope Nicholas V., who cherifhed men of talent, called him about him from the earlieft years of his pontificate, and charged him to paint his private chapel in the palace of the Vatican.

"The ability with which thefe frefcoes have been finifhed is truly prodigious: nothing is fweeter to the eye than the colouring of them; little of deep fhades, an harmonious chiar-ofcuro. Near, thefe pictures have all charms of miniature; at a diftance, they produce, by the vigour of the tints, all the effects of a broad and free pencil.

"His drawing does not want correction. Neverthelefs his figures are fhort, which might have happened from a habit contracted in the miniatures of

books, or from the obligation of painting on the contracted borders, and on the tranfverfe ftrip at the
bottom of the pictures called the *predella*, where it
was ufual to treat fubjects and little *iftoriette*. The
modeft attitudes, the air of attention and expreffion of
piety which feem to animate the perfonages, have
fomething touching, for we fee there the imitation of
nature. In thefe works there is another very remarkable peculiarity, which likewife fprings from the attention of the artift to give all the circumftances of the
fubject faithfully, and it is that the difpofing, wife in
this regard, fhows it without uncertainty. The religious artift certainly owed the juftnefs of the expreffion
to the fenfe of his own virtues, and to the models
which his pious brethren daily afforded him; and he
drew the talent to feize thefe beauties from the fchool,
which, for more than a century, fought perfection by
attaching itfelf to the fimple truth." No one could
better judge and more highly praife the great fchool
of Giotto.

The work of M. Rio on Chriftian painting in Italy,
has been one of the happieft events for the regenera-
tion of art in France, and whilft recalling here the
eulogies which have welcomed and the fuccefs that
has crowned it, we love to pay our debt of gratitude
to our author. Our firft ftudies in art were wholly
directed towards the antique;[1] but afterwards, whilft

---

[1] Let us be allowed to pay homage here to the memory of our good mafter and
friend, M. Paulin Guérin. For all who ferioufly ftudy the hiftory of art in France,
his picture of Cain curfed will be a glorious date. Diverted from his natural
method by the courfe of the fchool of David, and detained by an interefted direction in a fecondary rank, M. Paulin Guérin efcaped from the ftudio of Gerard, to
take in the Bible, our hiftory for all, a religious fubject outfide the antique and

vifiting the monuments of the middle ages, the galleries of the catacombs and the mofaics of the Roman
bafilicas, art appeared to us intimately knitted with our
faith, and we fought to know its true principles. The
work of M. Rio then offered itfelf to us as a friend,
and ferved to guide us in our new impreffions. To
how many others has it not rendered the fame fervice!
We have not to praife it, after the juftice done it
by Comte de Montalembert;[1] but we cannot help
regretting that M. Rio has not carried out the magnificent plan, of which he has let us have a glimpfe.
The beautiful fragments he has publifhed fhow us
that he has all the qualifications for doing it. To the
deep faith of a fervent Catholic, he unites the accom-
plifhments of the happieft writer, and to very extenfive
knowledge of hiftory, joins a clearnefs of ftatement, a
livelinefs of expreffion, a fobernefs of ftyle and a purity
of imagery, which charm at once the mind and heart.
Why may we not ftill hope? Some years would fuffice
for M. Rio to write the æfthetic Sum of Chriftian art.

M. Rio promifes us a new edition of the firft volume
of his work. We are defirous that he foften his feve-
rity in regard to the Byzantine fchool, and that he
carry back to the Siennefe fchool his predilection for
that of Perugino, one much lefs Chriftian and lefs
myftical, in our opinion, than the fchools of Giotto
and Simone Memmi. We hope alfo that he will give

mythology. This picture was admired by all Europe. In his laft years, M.
Paulin Guérin did not enjoy public favour, but there are fometimes conditions for
obtaining it that render oblivion glorious. What do the crowns of men fignify
to him now? We know what joy he had to receive the one which awaited him
in heaven.

[1] *Univerfité catholique*, Août 1837.

a ftill more glorious place to Beato Angelico, whofe artiftic merit he does not perhaps fufficiently appreciate. Beato Angelico is not only a faint, he is a great painter too; and the faults he reproaches him with muft be now attributed to his brother Fra Benedetto.

Here is the fine encomium paffed by M. Rio on our painter.

"A very remarkable fact in the hiftory of this incomparable artift, is the influence he exercifed over his biographer Vafari, who lived in an age when enthufiafm for myftical paintings was very much enfeebled, and who, neverthelefs, in his account of thofe of Beato Angelico, feems to have been difengaged from all the prejudices of his time, to célebrate, with the accent of admiration, the moft fenfible and fublime virtues embellifhing his foul, and the numberlefs marvels iffuing from his pencil. In the fervour of his momentary converfion, he has gone as far as to fay, that fo fuperior and fo extraordinary a talent as Beato Angelico's can and muft have been only the inheritance of the higheft fanctity, and that, to fucceed well in the reprefentation of religious and holy subjects, the artift muft be religious and holy himfelf.

"This fuperiority, to which Vafari pays fo fine a tribute, does not confift, neverthelefs, in the perfection of the drawing, nor in the relief of the figures, or in the truthfulnefs of the details: pictorial order is never maintained by a clever diftribution of fhades and lights, as in the frefcoes of Maffaccio; and what muft appear ftill more offenfive to certain obfervers, the life superabounding in the heads and fufficient in the upper parts of the body, becomes weakened in the

lower members, fo far as to give them the ftiffnefs
of artificial fupports. But they muft need be very
inacceffible to all the moft delicate emotions to which
Chriftian art can give rife in a foul properly prepared,
to take up minutely all the technical imperfections in
the productions of this truly divine pencil, imperfections which, befides, are a matter far lefs of inability
of execution in the artift, than of his indifference for
everything foreign to the tranfcendental aim of his
pious imagination.

"Compunction of heart, ejaculations to God,
ecftatic rapture, foretafte of heavenly beatitude, all
that order of profound and exalted emotions which no
artift can render without having firft proved them,
were as the myfterious-cycle through which the genius
of Beato Angelico was pleafed to travel, and when he
had finifhed it he began it again with the fame love.
In this kind, he feems to have exhaufted all combinations and fhadings, at leaft relatively to the quality and quantity of expreffion ; and if we ever fo little
examine certain pictures clofely, where a fatiguing
monotony feems to reign, we fhall difcover a prodigious variety embracing all the degrees of poetry which
can exprefs the human phyfiognomy. It is particularly
in the Crowning of the Bleffed Virgin amidft angels
and the heavenly hierarchy, in the reprefentation of
the Laft Judgment at leaft in what concerns the elect,
and in that of Paradife, the higheft limits of all the art
of imitation : it is in thefe myftical fubjects fo perfectly
in harmony with the vague but infallible forefight of
our foul, that he has difplayed with profufion the inexhauftible riches of his imagination. We may fay of

him, that painting was nothing elſe but his favourite
ſet-form for acts of faith, hope and charity." [1]

What Count de Montalembert has done for Chriſtian
art is not one of his leaſt titles to glory. The illuſtri-
ous defender of religious liberty in France muſt ſerve
beauty as well as truth with all the power of his
talent. His *Hiſtoire de S. Elizabeth* is a maſterpiece
which has cauſed mediæval art to be better underſtood
and more loved than the moſt learned archæological
diſſertations have done. In making his *dear Saint*
live again in thoſe pages ſo full of poetry and piety,
Count de Montalembert has given to artiſts a ſweet
patroneſs who may lead them acroſs the fields of the
paſt, even into the preſence of God Himſelf. S.
Elizabeth has well .rewarded her noble hiſtorian; ſhe
has armed him as a chevalier for the defence of Christian art, and no one has forgotten the brilliant victories
over vandaliſm brought back by him at the tribune
and in the preſs. To him, how many monuments owe
their preſervation, and truths their glorification!

Beato Angelico is the beloved painter of Count
de Montalembert. He has placed him again in his
rank, in his examination of M. Rio's work, and he has
devoted a ſpecial article to him in the introduction to
the monuments of the *Hiſtoire de S. Elizabeth*. We
have already quoted the fine deſcription he has given
of the Laſt Judgment in the Academy of the Fine
Arts at Florence; let us be allowed to give again ſome
pages of the Count de Montalembert: it will be the
laſt and moſt beautiful crown we can offer to the
memory of the painter whoſe Life we have written.

[1] *De l' Art chrétien,* vol. I., p. 191.

After having fpoken of the monks who painted manufcripts, Montalembert adds :

" All thefe painter-monks were forerunners of him whom we do not hefitate to call the greateft, as he was the holieft, of Chriftian painters, the Bleffed Fra Giovanni of Fiefole, surnamed *Angelico,* on account of his angelic piety, and at this day ftill called at Florence eminently, *il Beato.* This incomparable artift, who hardly begins to be known by name in France, although we have one of his mafterpieces, triumphed even over the claffical prejudices and repugnances of Vafari, and finds a worthy and eloquent panegyrift in M. Rio. It was he who fet himfelf in prayer, every day, before he began to paint, for he laboured only to express his faith, hope and love to God ; it was he who fhed warm tears every time he had to paint a Crucifixion, fo greatly did he fuffer with his Saviour dead to redeem him. Every Catholic fhould experience an unfpeakable happinefs in contemplating his marvellous works, wherein God permitted the perfection of the expreffion to anfwer to the holinefs of the intention, and which are, we may boldly fay, the *ne plus ultra* of Chriftian art. What proves it better than all, is the feeling of piety and compunction which ftraightway feize everyone at the fight of our Beato's pictures. We acknowledge religion with all its power, which fpeaks to us under the veil of the pureft beauty." [1]

Montalembert thus begins his notice on the Bleffed Fra Angelico of Fiefole.[2]

"The name of the monk Giovanni of Fiefole, a

---

[1] *Du Vandalifme et du Catholicifme dans l'art,* p. 96.

[2] *Id.* p. 245.

painter of the Catholic fchool of Florence (Fra Giovanni
Angelico da Fiefole), furnamed the Angelic, and in
Italy commonly called Il Beato, is fcarcely found in
any of the works treating on art during the laft three
centuries.   But we cannot be aftonifhed nor complain
of it.   His glory who has reached the ideal of Chriftian
art deferves not be confounded with that decreed to
fuch artifts as Giulio Romano, Dominichino, the
Carracci, and others of that clafs : it was much better
for him to be totally forgotten than to be placed in
the fame line with them.   A fhort time after his death,
paganism broke in upon all branches of Chriftian
fociety : in politics, by the eftablifhment of abfolute
monarchies ; in literature, by the exclufive ftudy of the
claffical authors ; in art, by the cultivation of mythology, of nudity, and of the naturalifm characterizing
the epoch of the Renaiffance.   Having rapidly become
conqueror and mafter, it took care to difcredit men
and things that bore the ineffable impreffion of
Chriftian genius.   Beato Angelico had the honour of
being mixed up in the profcription, which enveloped
at once the focial conftitutions of the middle ages and
the pious and chivalrous poetry that had fo long
charmed Europe, and laftly the art fo glorioufly and
happily infpired by the myfteries and traditions of the
Catholic faith.   That was all declared *barbarous*, and
deferving of oblivion and contempt ; and conformably
with the decree of the mafters, they have been forgotten and defpifed for three centuries.   Now that the
human mind, arrived, perhaps, at the limits of its long
wanderings, ftops uncertain, and feems to caft a look
of envy and admiration towards Catholic ages, we

begin again the ſtudy of the art, which was ſo completely the ſet-off of that epoch, and the beatified
painter has reſumed, by degrees, the place aſſigned
him by the judgment of his contemporaries. Still
ſtrangely unknown in Italy, he is admired with enthuſiaſm in Germany; and France, poſſeſſed of one of his
maſterpieces, becomes accuſtomed, in its turn, to ſee
him always counted amongſt the great maſters."

May our efforts, too, have contributed to make
known, loved and imitated Beato Fra Angelico of
Fieſole, the model of Chriſtian artiſts!

CATALOGUE OF THE WORKS OF

BEATO ANGELICO

DA FIESOLE.

 E have not neglected anything for making this catalogue as complete as poffible. Still if any other pictures and drawings by Beato Angelico exift, we beg that they may be made known to us. All communications will reach us fafely through the medium of our Publifher.

We have followed a geographical order, fo as to render this catalogue convenient for travellers; and when we have deemed it ufeful, we have added fome notes on the execution, prefervation, dimenfions and hiftory of each picture. We have pointed out thofe which, it feems to us, ought to be attributed to Fra Benedetto; and have marked (?) fuch as we have not feen, or are, to us, of dubious authenticity.

Laftly, we have indicated authors who have fpoken of them, and engravings of them. Thefe engravings may certainly give fome idea of the pictures; but Beato Angelico is an untranflatable painter: to render him, it is neceffary to have his foul and the flexible and fine graver of Lucas van Leyden.

PERUGIA.

Church of S. Domenico.—Chapel of S. Orfola.

I.—1. A Madonna with the Child Jefus. On the acceffory fhutters: 2. S. John Baptift, and S. Catherine Virgin and Martyr.

Y

3. S. Dominic and S. Nicholas of Bari.—See page 56. V. Marchese, t. 1, p. 214.

Sacrifty of the Convent.

II.—Twelve fmall pictures, which ferved as a frame for the preceding picture.   The firft eight are twelve inches in height; the other
four only eight inches.

1. S. Peter Martyr. 2. S. Jerome. 3. S. Benedict. 4. A Bifhop-
faint. 5. S. Mary Magdalen. 6. S. Thomas Aquinas. 7. S. Lawrence
Martyr. 8. S. Catherine of Sienna, or Bleffed Villana. 9. S. Peter
Apoftle. 10. S. Agatha holding the pincers. 11. S. Paul Apoftle. 12.
A Prophet. 13. A compartment of the gradino which reprefented the
legend of S. Nicholas.   The other two are in the Gallery of the
Vatican. 14. The B. Virgin and the angel Gabriel, in two panels which
probably ferved as a crown for the fame altarpiece.—This altarpiece
was made for the chapel of S. Niccolo dei Guidalotti.   Padre Bottonio
fays that it was executed at Florence in 1437; to us, it feems older.
At the time of the French invafion of Italy, it was carried away to
Paris, but it was reftored at the general peace.

CORTONA.

Church of S. Domenico

III.—At the entrance-door of the façade, in the tympan, a Madonna
and the Child Jefus holding a globe, with S. Dominic and S. Peter Martyr.
A mural painting damaged.   On the arch, the four Evangelifts better
preferved.   In the fecond edition of his work, Padre Marchefe thinks that
this painting is later than the date he at firft affigned to it, becaufe a
bull of Eugenius IV., Feb. 13th, 1438, grants to the prior of the convent
of S. Domenico at Cortona faculty to commute vows of pilgrimages and
of holy images *(del far dipingere facre immagini)* into alms for the con-
ftruction and building of his church *(pro conftructione et fabbrica).*
Thefe words may be applied to the completion of the church.—See
page 60. V. Marchese, t. 1, p. 218.

IV.—In the church, on the right of the high altar, a Madonna and the
Child Jefus furrounded with angels.   In the compartments, S. John and

S. Mary Magdalen. This picture is in the form of a pointed triptich. In the two acceffory compartments, on the right, S. John and S. Mary Magdalen, S. John Baptift and S. Mark. In the angle of the crowning, in the centre, Jefus on the Crofs with the B. Virgin and S. John Evangelift; and on each fide, the B. Virgin and the angel of the Annunciation.

In the church of the Gefû, near the Cathedral.

V.—Legend of S. Dominic. It formed the gradino to the preceding picture.

1. Vifion of pope Innocent III. 2. Kifs of S. Dominic and S. Francis. 3. Apparition of S. Peter and S. Paul. 4. Refurrection of the young Napoleon. 5. Ordeal of the book. 6. The angels ferving the Dominicans in the refectory. 7. Death of S. Dominic.

Thefe fubjects are framed and feparated by four figures: S. Peter Martyr, S. Michael, S. Vincent Deacon and Martyr, S. Thomas Aquinas.

VI.—Great Annunciation. In a corner of the compofition, are feen Adam and Eve driven out of the earthly paradife.—Page 63. V. MARCHESE, t. 1, p. 222.

VII.—Legend of the B. Virgin.

Gradino of the preceding picture:

1. Birth of the B. Virgin. 2. Marriage of the B. Virgin. 3. Vifitation. 4. Adoration of the Magi. 5. Prefentation. 6. Burial. 7. The B. Virgin gives the habit of his Order to Bleffed Reginald of Orleans.

FIESOLE.

Church of S. Domenico.

VIII.—Behind the high altar, the Madonna on a throne furrounded with angels and faints: S. Peter Apoftle, S. Thomas Aquinas, S. Dominic and S. Peter Martyr. (This picture was reftored by Lorenzo di Credi in 1501.) At the bottom, is a copy of the gradino actually at Rome reprefenting our Lord triumphant amidft angels and faints.—Page 77. V. MARCHESE, t. 1, p. 228.

IX.—In the old refectory, now private property, our Lord on the Crofs, accompanied by the B. Virgin and S. John Evangelift. A mural painting damaged.

X.—In the old ſtrangers' hoſpice, and now at the top of a ſtair-caſe in a neighbouring dwelling, the B. Virgin and the Child Jeſus, accompanied by S. Dominic and S. Thomas Aquinas. This painting appears retouched by Lorenzo di Credi.

Church of S. Geronimo.

XI.—The B. Virgin, S. Jerome and other ſaints (?). A painting which may have been by Fra Benedetto. Reſtored.

FLORENCE.

Convent of S. Marco.

The paintings at the convent of San Marco have been publiſhed *in* the fine work, entitled, *S. Marco, Convento dei Padri Prædicatori; Firenze*, 1852. The text is Padre Marcheſe's, and includes the Life of Beato Angelico and the hiſtory of the convent. The engravings were executed by the Artiſtic Society, under the direction of Profeſſor Perfetti. They are unqueſtionably the beſt engravings after Beato Angelico. In England, this work is to be had at Mr. John Philp's Eſtabliſhment for Promoting Chriſtian Fine Arts, 7, Orchard Street, Portman Square, W.

In indicating the pictures at S. Marco's, we follow the order of our text, ch. xi., p. 204; we will give only the number of the engraved plate.

In the firſt cloiſter, called the cloiſter of S. Antoninus :

XII.—Our Lord on the Croſs and S. Dominic at his feet. Pl. xxxvii.

XIII.—Above the door of the ſacriſty, S. Peter Martyr. Pl. ii.

XIV.—Above the door of the chapter, S. Dominic holding the Book of the Rule and a diſcipline.

XV.—At the end, going to the right, a *Pietà*. Pl. iii.

XVI.—Above the door of the ſtrangers' hoſpice, our Lord as a pilgrim received by two Friar-preachers. Pl. xxxii.

XVII.—Same ſide, S. Thomas Aquinas. Very much injured.

XVIII.—Chapter-room. A great mural painting, twenty-ſix feet ſix inches in breadth by twenty-three feet in height. (We do not guarantee the exactneſs of theſe numbers.) It repreſents our Lord on the Croſs, with the B. Virgin, the founders of orders, and the protectors of the convent. We attribute the figure of S. Mark to Fra Benedetto. In the border of the frame are figures of prophets holding texts.

XIX.—At the bafe, in the foliage of a tree fpringing from S. Dominic, the faints and bleffed of his Order. The names of them have been changed fince Beato Angelico's time.

The background of all this picture has been unhappily injured. The figures are well preferved. Pl. v.

This compofition has been brought out in colours in *Moyen Age et Renaiſſance*, after a drawing by M. Victor Gay, architect. The beautiful head of S. Bernard was copied for Count de Montalembert, by M. Claudius Lavergne. Many fmall engravings have been made from this copy.

XX.—In the upper corridor of the cells, an Annunciation. Pl. x.

XXI.—In the cells, another Annunciation. Pl. xi.

XXII.—Nativity of our Lord. Pl. xii. By Fra Benedetto (?)

XXIII.—Prefentation in the Temple. Pl. xiv.

XXIV.—Adoration of the Magi. In the cell of Cofimo de Medici. Pl. xiii.

XXV.—Baptifm of our Lord. Pl. xv. By Fra Benedetto.

XXVI.—In two cells removed fo as to open the door into the library the Temptation in the Wildernefs and the Entering into Jerufalem. There remains but little of them. The figure of our Lord praying in the Defert. Pl. xvi.

XXVII.—Sermon on the Mount. Pl. xvii. (Fra Benedetto.)

XXVIII.—Transfiguration. Pl. xviii. This picture has been publifhed in colours by Curmer, in the firft part of the *Convent de Saint Marc*, by Henri de Laborde. (This publication has not been continued.

XXIX.—Inftitution of the holy Euchariſt. Pl. xix. (Fra Benedetto.)

XXX.—Prayer in the Garden of Olives.—Pl. xx.

XXXI.—Treafon of Judas. Pl. xxi. Fra Benedetto (?)

XXXII.—Jefus in the Prætorium. Pl. xxii.

XXXIII.—Chrift bearing his Crofs. Pl. xxiii.

XXXIV. The Crucifixion. Pl. xxiv.

XXXV.—Chrift on the Crofs. Pl. xxvi. (Fra Benedetto.)

XXXVI.—Longinus piercing the fide of our Lord. Pl. xxxv.

XXXVII.—Burial of our Lord. Pl. xxviii. (Fra Benedetto.)

XXXVIII.—Defcent into Hell. Cell of S. Antoninus. Pl. xxix. (Fra Benedetto.)

XXXIX.—The Holy Women at the Tomb. Pl. xxx.

XL.—*Noli me tangere.* Pl. xxxi.

XLI.—Our Lord on the Crofs, furrounded by the B. Virgin, S. John, S. Dominic and S. Jerome. Pl. iv.

XLII.—Crowning of the B. Virgin. Pl. xxxiii. This painting has been publifhed by Curmer, after M. Henri de Laborde.

XLIII.—Madonna and her Son, with S. Auguftine and S. Thomas Aquinas.

XLIV.—On the wall of the corridor, Madonna, having on her right, S. Mark, SS. Cofmas and Damian and S. Dominic, and on her left, S. Paul, S. Thomas Aquinas, S. Lawrence and S. Peter Martyr. In the cells occupied by the ftudents, are many Crucifixions, which approach the ftyle of Beato Angelico, but cannot be attributed to him.

XLV.—The convent of S. Marco poffeffes the choir-books executed by Fra Benedetto; and his brother, Beato Angelico, may have painted fome of the miniatures, but we do not know what may be attributed to him with certainty. Thefe are the principal fubjeƈts of his miniatures.

Volume A.   1. Vocation of S. Peter.   2. Martyrdom of S. Stephen.   3. S. John Evangelift.   4. Maffacre of the Innocents.   5. S. Agnes, engraved pl. vi.

6. Converfion of S. Paul.   7. Prefentation.   8. Annunciation.   9. Jefus in the midft of the apoftles.   10. Apparition of our Lord to a female faint.   11. Chrift bleffing martyrs.   12. Chrift before a bifhop.   13. Virgins finging, engraved pl. viii.

14. Our Lord on the Crofs, perhaps by Beato Angelico.

Volume B.   15. Annunciation.   16. S. Peter Martyr receiving three crowns.   17. S. Peter opening Heaven.   18. S. Mary Magdalen carried to Heaven.   19. S. Dominic receiving his miffion from SS. Peter and Paul.   20. Affumption.   21. Birth of the B. Virgin.   22. S. Michael.   23. All-Saints.   24. Jefus in the midft of the apoftles.   25. Jefus putting his hand upon the head of a martyr.   26. Chrift bleffing two martyrs.   27. Chrift giving back a crofs to a bifhop.   28. Virgin finging.   29. Chrift bleffing virgins, engraved pl. vii.

Volume G.   30. A faint reading in a garden.   31. An angel holding three flowers.

Antiph. A.   32. Chrift carrying a book.   33. Nativity. Page 272. V. MARCHESE, t. 1, p. 164.

The painting by Beato Angelico in the refeƈtory of S. Marco, has been deftroyed, others have been covered with whitewafh. It would feem that fome are to be reftored.

Academy of Fine Arts; Gallery of large pictures.

XLVI.—Defcent from the Crofs, No. 14 in the catalogue. A picture from the facrifty of Santa Trinità, Florence, cited by Vafari. Height, five feet five inches; breadth, fix feet eight inches. See page 160. V. MARCHESE, t. 1, p. 273. This picture has been engraved in the Convent of S. Marco, pl. xxvii.

XLVII.—The frame is formed of fixteen fmall pictures by Beato Angelico.

On the left of the fpectator: S. Benedict with the rod of his rule. 2. S. Lawrence. 3. Head with a capuce (?) 4. S. John Baptift. 5. S. Bernardine. 6. S. Andrew. 7. S. Francis. 8. S. Michael.

On the right: 1. S. Jerome. 2. S. Auguftine (?). 3. A faint holding a ftaff (?). 4. S. Stephen. 5. S. Dominic. 6. S. Paul. 7. S. Peter Martyr. 8. S. Peter Apoftle. Six of thefe figures have been engraved in the fine publication of M. Perfetti, *Galleria dell' i. e Reale accademia delle Belle Arti di Firenze;* 1847: thefe are, S. Andrew and S. Paul, S. Michael and S. Peter, S. Dominic and S. Bernardine.

The three pictures of the Crowning, the *Noli me tangere*, the Refurrection and the Holy Women at the Tomb, are attributed to Lorenzo Monaco.

Gallery of fmall pictures.

XLVIII.—Life of our Lord. This great poem, ordered by Cofimo de Medici, is divided into eight panels and thirty-five compartments. We cannot give an account how thefe panels were arranged, when they formed part of a prefs in the chapel of the Nunciata. The Life of our Lord has been entirely engraved by Giov. Bat. Nocchi, *La Vita di Gefù Crifto, dipinta da Fra Giovanni da Fiefole,* engr. in folio; Florence, 1843. Thefe engravings are not without merit, particularly as they are executed on chalks of the originals. They are preceded by the Life of Beato Angelico by Vafari, and by a remarkable preface by P. Tanzini.

We go on to enumerate the fubjects, whilft pointing out thofe which we do not think were executed by Beato Angelico.

1. The Vifion of Ezechiel.
2. The Annunciation.
3. The Nativity.
4. The Circumcifion.
5. The Adoration of the Magi.
6. The Prefentation in the Temple.
7. The Flight into Egypt.
8. The Maffacre of the Innocents.
9. Jefus amongft the Doctors.
10. The Baptifm of our Lord.
11. The Marriage at Cana.
12. The Transfiguration.

Thefe laft three fubjects united together in one panel, do not appear to me to be painted even by Fra Benedetto, fo feeble are they in ftyle and execution.

13. The Refurrection of Lazarus.   (Fra Benedetto.)
14. The triumphal Entry into Jerufalem.   (Fra Benedetto.)
15. The Bargain of Judas.
16. The Laft Supper.   (Fra Benedetto.)
17. The Wafhing of the feet.   Fra Benedetto (?).
18. The Eucharift.   (Fra Benedetto.)
19. The Prayer in the Garden of Olives.
20. The Kifs of Judas.   Fra Benedetto (?).
21. Arreft of our Lord.
22. Our Lord mocked.
23. Chrift before Pilate.
24. The Scourging.
25. Jefus carrying his Crofs.
26. Jefus ftripped of his garments.
27. Jefus on the Crofs.
28. Burial.   (Fra Benedetto.)
29. Defcent into Hell.   (Fra Benedetto.)
30. The Holy Women at the Tomb.   Fra Benedetto (?)
31. The Afcenfion.   (Fra Benedetto.)
32. Pentecoft.
33. The Communion of Saints.
34. The Law of Love.   (Fra Benedetto.)
35. The Laft Judgment.

Numbers 1, 5, 7, 13-15-19, 24-28, have been engraved in the *Galleria dell' i. e reale accademia delle Belle Arte.*

The *Gallery of small paintings* also contains other works by Beato Angelico.

XLIX. Burial of our Lord, No. 4 in the catalogue. This picture was made for the confraternity of the Crofs of the Temple. Cited by Vafari.—See page 165. V. MARCHESE, t. 1, p. 239.

L. The Laft Judgment. (No. 18.) Executed for the monaftery of the Angels at Florence. The upper part is by Beato Angelico, the lower part by Fra Benedetto. Cited by Vafari.—See page 150. V. MARCHESE, t. 1, p. 279.

The upper part has been engraved in outline, in Rofini's work, *Storia della Pittura.* Pl. xxxvi.

A fragment of the lower part, fide of the elect, has been lithographed at Florence; but this is not on fale.

LI.—Two fragments of the legend of SS. Cofmas and Damian. Nos. 13, 22 (?).

LII.—Picture in two parts. *Pietà* and Adoration of the Magi (No. 27.)

LIII.—Madonna and the Child Jefus. Above, the Holy Trinity. (No. 31.)

LIV.—S. Thomas Aquinas teaching theology. (No. 46.)

LV.—Albert the Great teaching the natural fciences. (No. 53.)

Thefe two wainfcot panels, from the convent of S. Marco, may be copies of Beato Angelico, or paintings by Fra Benedetto.

LVI.—Crucifixion. (No. 47.) Crowning of the B. Virgin. (No. 54.) After Beato Angelico (?).

LVII.—The Legend of SS. Cofmas and Damian. (No. 51.)

A gradino of the altar of the chapel of S. Luca, in the cloifter of the Annunciation at Florence. Six fubjects. 1. The faints refufing money. 2. SS. Cofmas and Damian before the judge. 3. The two faints caft into the fea. 4. They are condemned, without avail, to the flames. 5. They are faftened on a crofs, the arrows aimed at them rebound on the executioners. 6. They are beheaded.

Expofition Room.

LVIII.—Madonna with the Child Jefus, between two angels.

(No. 13.)   On one fide, S. Peter Martyr, SS. Cofmas and Damian; on the other, S. Francis, S. Anthony, S. Auguftine (?).

The gradino, not fo well preferved, reprefents a *Pietà*, S. Dominic, S. Peter, S. Paul, S. Bernardine, S. Benedict, S. Peter Martyr.   This picture came from the convent called *il Bofco à Fratri*, in the province of Mugello.

LIX.—Madonna with the Child Jefus furrounded with angels.   (No. 16.)   SS. Cofmas and Damian kneeling before the throne.   On the left, S. Dominic, S. Francis, S. Peter Martyr; on the right, S. Mark, S. John Evangelift, and S. Stephen.

This picture came from the church of S. Marco.   Cited by Vafari. —See p. 166.   V. MARCHESE, t. 1, p. 247.

LX.—Madonna with the Child Jefus, S. Dominic, S. Francis, SS. Cofmas and Damian, S. John Evangelift and S. Lawrence.

This picture came from the monaftery of *Annalena* at Florence.

Gallery at Florence, called degli Uffizi.

LXI.—Corridor on entering.   Altarpiece with fhutters, executed, in 1433, for the Guild of Joiners.   Madonna holding the Child Jefus.   In the breadth of the frame, twelve figures of angels playing on various inftruments.   On the fhutters, infide, S. John Baptift and S. Mark; outfide, S. Peter and S. Mark.   Cited by Vafari.—See page 167.   V. MARCHESE, t. 1, p. 235.

Catalogue of the Gallery, 18th edit., page 55.

Height, four feet ten inches; breadth, two feet one inch.

LXII.—Gradino of the preceding picture, in three fubjects: Adoration of the Magi; Preaching of S. Peter; Martyrdom of S. Mark.

LXIII.—*Tufcan fchool.*—Crowning of the B. Virgin.

This beautiful picture has been engraved by Domenico Choffione, at Florence.   A good copy, by Antoine Saffo, was brought out at Paris in 1855.   (Catalogue, page 234.)—See page 169.   V. MARCHESE, t. 1, p. 237.

LXIV.—Nativity of S. John Baptift.

LXV.—Marriage of the B. Virgin.   Engraved in outline, in Rofini's work, *Storia del Pitt.* Pl. xxxiii.

LXVI.—Death of the B. Virgin.

In the collection of original drawings, in the fame gallery, are the following drawings attributed to Beato Angelico. (V. MARCHESE, t. 1, p. 278.)

LXVII.—1st drawer. 2nd Cartoon. The four evangelists and two doctors of the church. On a sheet of parchment.

LXVIII.—A demi-figure of a saint holding a book in his left hand. On parchment.

LXIX.—Figure of a man breaking a wand. Study for the Marriage of the B. Virgin. On paper tinted red.

LXX.—S. Dominic disputing with other persons. On like paper.

LXXI.—Two figures seated side by side. A religious standing and in profile. White paper, with the pen and washed (?)

LXXII.—Monk seated disputing with three religious of the same order (?).

LXXIII.—B. Virgin with the Child Jesus upon her knees. White paper, with the pen and washed (?).

In the cartoon following:

LXXIV.—B. Virgin and the Child Jesus in a glory supported by angels and seraphim. Parchment, with the pen and washed.

LXXV.—An angel flying crowned with roses. Study for a Last Judgment. At the bottom of the sheet, in the right-hand corner, are seen lightly marked out, the gate of hell and some devils. White paper, with the pen and washed.

Pitti Gallery. Hall of Justice, No. 399.

LXXVI.—Madonna with the Child Jesus, having on her right S. Dominic and S. John Baptist, on the left, S. Peter and S. Thomas. In the upper angles of the frame : Christ blessing ; the Annunciation ; the Preaching and Martyrdom of S. Peter of Verona. By Fra Benedetto (?).

Santa Maria Novella. Sacristy.—Three reliquaries.

LXXVII.—Madonna standing, carrying the Child Jesus. At the top, our Lord letting a crown fall upon the head of his mother. Around the frame, eight angels adoring ; at the bottom, two other angels seated and playing the organ. On the pedestal, three medallions : S. Dominic, S. Peter Martyr and S. Thomas Aquinas.

LXXVIII.—The Annunciation, and the Adoration of the Magi, in two pictures. On the pedeftal, Bleffed Catherine of Sienna; S. Apollonia; S. Margaret; S. Lucy; S. Mary Magdalen; the Holy Virgin; S. Catherine of Alexandria; S. Agnes; S. Cecilia; S. Dorothy; S. Urfula.

LXXIX.—Crowning of the B. Virgin. (Fra Benedetto.)

In the lower part: The Nativity. Four fmall angels dancing and two others playing the timbrel.—See page 175. V. MARCHESE, t. 1, p. 270.

Thefe three reliquaries have been publifhed by Luigi Bardi, and engraved in five plates folio by R. Redetti; Florence, 1854.

Abbey of Florence.

LXXX.—On an arch of the cloifter, S. Benedict recommending filence (?). Painting injured.

Collection of the Brothers Metzger.

LXXXI.—S. Thomas Aquinas receiving the angelic cord (?).

Gallery of F. Lombardi and V. Baldi.

LXXXII.—Martyrdom of SS. Cofmas and Damian. Well preferved.

LXXXIII.—Adoration of the Magi. Injured (?).

ROME.

Vatican.—Chapel of Nicholas V.

This chapel is attached to the apartments of Mgr. de Merode, who kindly facilitated our ftudy of it. It ftands on the fecond ftory of the pontifical palace, and the entrance into it is in the left-hand angle of the antechamber of Conftantine's hall. It is twenty-one feet ten inches in length, by thirteen feet eight inches in breadth. Although it has been many times reftored, the prefervation of it is ftill very fatisfactory. The weft wall has fuffered moft from damp. The part neareft the altar has been taken off on canvas: an operation in which Italians fucceed to a marvel. The chapel of Nicholas V. has been engraved and publifhed at Rome *(Calcographie pontificale)* in 1810, by Francefco Giangiacomo, fix plates folio. D'Agincourt has alfo given a little outline of it in his *Hiftoire de l'Art*, vol. 6. Pl. CXLV. Some fragments have been given in other works, which we will point out, whilst enumerating the fubjects.—See page 236. V. MARCHESE, t. 1, p. 292.

LXXXIV.—Hiftory of S. Stephen.

1. S. Stephen receiving deaconfhip.

2. Diftribution of alms.

3. Preaching of S. Stephen. Engraved by Piroli, publifhed in London by W. Ottley. *Florentine fchools.* Pl. XL.

4. S. Stephen before the high-prieft.

5. S. Stephen led to execution.

6. S. Stephen ftoned.

LXXXV.—Hiftory of S. Lawrence.

1. S. Lawrence receiving deaconfhip.

2. Farewell of S. Sixtus and S. Lawrence.

3. Diftribution of alms. Engraved by Piroli. *Florentine fchools.* Pl. XLI.—By Gatti. *Storia della Pitt. de Rofini.* Pl. LXII.

4. Condemnation of S. Lawrence.

5. His Martyrdom.

LXXXVI.—The figures decorating the corners are: S. John Chryfoftom, S. Leo, S. Athanafius, S. Gregory, S. Auguftine, S. Ambrofe, S. Bonaventure, S. Thomas Aquinas.

LXXXVII.—On the arched ceiling. The four Evangelifts.

Gallery of the Vatican.

LXXXVIII.—Pictures of the gradino at Perugia, in two compartments.

1. Birth of S. Nicholas. S. Nicholas, a child, hearing a fermon. S. Nicholas giving doweries to the young daughters of a gentlemen. S. Nicholas provifioning the town of Myra and faving a veffel in danger.

LXXXIX.—In the Chriftian Mufeum attached to the Vatican Library, are three pictures which may be attributed to Beato Angelico, or rather to his brother or to his pupils.

1. The Entering into Jerufalem. Drawing heavy, extremities defective.

2. Adoration of the Magi. Here are again found the fame figures as in the compofitions of Beato Angelico.

3. Picture above the two preceding ones. It is divided into two subjects: Jesus in the midst of the doctors, and the Transfiguration. The figure of Christ is fine, but very youthful. What does this connection signify? Dogmatic theology and mystical theology?

Corsini Gallery.—Seventh room, Nos. 22, 23, 24.

XC.—Pentecost. A picture restored.

XCI.—The Ascension.

XCII.—Last Judgment. In fine preservation.

These pictures came from a chapel in the neighbourhood of Florence, belonging to the family of Corsini. See page 155.

Valentini Gallery (?).

XCIII.—Fragment of the gradino of the picture of S. Dominic at Fiesole. See page 77.

Gallery of Count Guido di Bisenzio.

No. 44 in the catalogue (?).

XCIV.—A Madonna surrounded with angels and saints.

The two pictures in the church of Santa Maria sopra Minerva, cited by Vasari as being by Beato Angelico, are not by him. The Triumph of S. Thomas is attributed to Filippino Lippi, and the Annunciation to Benozzo Gozzoli (?).

Count de Montalembert cites two other pictures by Beato Angelico at Rome, one in the church of Santa Cecilia, the other in the church of Santa Maria Maddalena (?).

NAPLES.

Bourbon Museum.

Two pictures attributed to Tommaso di Stefanno, and catalogued under the Nos. 296, 298.

XCV.—The first (296) represents the Assumption of the B. Virgin; on wood, and ground of gold.

XCVI.—The second (298) represents the Miracle of our Lady at Nives, or the foundation of Santa Maria Maggiore. See page 261.

ORVIETO.

Chapel of the Bleſſed Virgin.

Great mural painting, on a gold ground.

XCVII.—Chriſt and a choir of prophets, for the Laſt Judgment; finiſhed by Luca Signorelli.

The figures of Chriſt and of Moſes have been engraved by Ales. Mochetti, in the *Storia del Duomo.* Pl. xxxii.—See page 260. V. MARCHESE, t. I, p. 299.

MONTEFALCO.

Church of the Franciſcan Fathers.

XCVIII.—A Crowning of the B. Virgin. A gradino of five piĉtures, which Profeſſor Roſini attributes to Beato Angelico, and which Marquis Selvatico believes to be by Benozzo Gozzoli, or by ſome other painter.

TURIN.

Royal Muſeum.

XCIX.—Two figures of angels. From the colleĉtion of the Brothers Metzger of Florence.

C.—A Madonna and the Child Jeſus. Sold by Achille Sandrini.

BRESCIA.

Church of S. Aleſſandro.

CI.—An Annunciation. Figures of natural ſize, painted on wood in two panels.

This piĉture was executed by Beato Angelico in 1432, as a curious document proves, found in the chronicle of the convent of S. Aleſſandro at Breſcia, of the order of Servites, taken from the archives of the monaſtery by Maéſtro Fra Giovanni Paolo Villa, in 1630. This is the document, which relates all the expences incurred for the piĉture.

1. 1432. " *Item* la tavola della Nunziata fatta in Fiorenza, la quale depinſe fra Giovanni, ducatti nove.

Item ducatti ij fono per oro per detta tavola, quali hebbe **Fra** Giovanni de' Predicatori da Fiefole per dipingere la taola.

1444. Gennaro. Spefa fatta per me et frate Gioſeffe col **Prior di** San-Salvatore quando andaſſimo a Vicenza per la Nonziata.

Febbraio, primo per fpeſſe fatte in far portar la Nonziata da Vicenza a Brefcia. L. iii, foldi 19.

Item per parte di pagamento alli maeſtri, che fecero la bradella della Nonziata.

Marzo. *Item* per alquante taole per far la caſſa dell'ancona della Nonziata. L. i., foldi 2."

See V. Marchese, vol. 1, pp. 284, 401.

PARIS.

Mufeum of the Louvre.

Italian Schools, No. 214 in the excellent catalogue of M. Frederic Villot, confervator of the paintings.

CII. The Crowning of the B. Virgin. Height, ſeven feet; breadth, ſix feet eleven inches.

CIII. The gradino includes ſeven ſmall pictures, all eight-and-a-half inches high, and from nine to twelve inches broad. The ſubjects are:

1. In the centre, a *Pietà*.
2. Viſion of Innocent III.
3. Apoſtolate of S. Dominic.
4. Refurrection of the young Napoleon.
5. The Ordeal of the Book.
6. The Miraculous Repaſt.
7. Death of S. Dominic.

Picture executed for the church of Fiefole, and very highly praiſed by Vaſari.—See page 79.

It was publiſhed in 1817 by A. G. de Schlegel, and engraved in fifteen plates in outline by Guillaume Ternite.

Some of the beautiful heads were publiſhed in lithograph by Rev. Père Arthur Martin, whoſe loſs is ſo great for Chriſtian art.

A large chromo-lithograph in folio has been recently publiſhed by M. Alcan.

At this preſent time, the imperial calcograph is employed in executing a new engraving.

Muſeum of Sketches.

CIV.—A drawing on paper tinted yellow, raiſe with white. A S. Francis in a glory (?) On the reverſe, a little ſtag after nature.

Colleƈtion of M. Frederic de Reiſet.

CV.—Two figures of Apoſtles (?).

CVI. Two beautiful drawings. (Nos. 5 and 6 in the catalogue.)

1. Studies of various figures for the compoſition of the Laſt Judgment. At the top, ſtudy of a hand taken from nature. With the pen and in biſtre. On the reverſe, head of a monk ſeen in front. Waſhed and raiſed with white. On paper tinted yellow.

CVII.—An Evangeliſt ſitting and reading an open book, which he holds with both hands on his right knee. Waſhed and raiſed with white. On paper tinted green.

On the reverſe, another Evangeliſt ſitting. He holds a pen in his right hand, and a cloſed book in his left. With the pen and waſhed with biſtre. On white paper. See page 53.

Colleƈtion of M. Gatteaux, member of the Inſtitut.

CVIII.—A charming little piƈture, eight inches broad by four inches high. Six perſonages are there repreſented half-length. In the middle, Moſes holding the tables of the law; they are pierced like a painter's pallet. On the one which Moſes raiſes up, are the words,· NON ABEBIS DEOS ALIENOS. On the right of the legiſlator, is placed Abraham, the father of believers, holding the knife of ſacrifice, ſymbol of his faith. On his left, Aaron with the rod and in ſacerdotal coſtume. Behind Moſes, are two perſonages, whom no attribute diſtinguiſhes; their looks and poſition expreſs adoration. They are perhaps the patriarchs Iſaac and Jacob, whom Scripture unites with their father in ſpeaking of the God of Abraham, of Iſaac and of Iacob. Behind Aaron is an angel, as our painter knew ſo well how to do.

This piƈture, doubtleſs, belonged to a gradino, and may repreſent the Law of Fear. All the figures are turned to the right, as to a common centre, where there was perhaps a Chriſt, the union of the Old and New Teſtament. On the other ſide, doubtleſs, were S. Peter and S. Paul, and ſome ſaints of the Law of Grace.

z

This picture is painted on a gold ground. The colouring is very soft; the heads are admirable for character and execution. The hands are neglected.

BERLIN.

Royal Museum.

CIX.—Last Judgment, recalling very much by the composition the one in the Gallery of small pictures in the Academy of Fine Arts at Florence. But the execution is very feeble, and makes it thought to be a copy.

CX.—Madonna with the Child Jesus. Ground of damask of gold. On the two sides, are seen, but in very small proportions, S. Dominic and S. Peter Martyr. This picture has been badly restored (?).

CXI.—The kiss of S. Dominic and S. Francis.

CXII.—Appearance of S. Francis to his disciples.

CXIII.—Small pictures badly restored. Of dubious attribution.

MUNICH.

Pinacotheca. (¹)

CXIV.—Three pictures from the convent of S. Marco, representing the legend of SS. Cosmas and Damian.

   1. SS. Cosmas and Damian before the proconsul.

   2. SS. Cosmas and Damian placed on a Cross.

   3. SS. Cosmas and Damian thrown into the sea and saved by angels.

CXV.—The Eternal Father in a glory, surrounded with the choir of angels.

CXVI.—Burial of our Lord. See the *Musées d' Allemagne*, by L. Viardot, p. 103.

---

¹) In 1860, we remember seeing a small Tableau of Beato Angelico in the Pinacotheca at Munich, of the Assumption of the Blessed Virgin, accompanied by numerous angels. The painting measured about fourteen inches high, by about eleven inches wide (as well as we can remember). This does not appear in the Catalogue of the Pinacotheca of 1858 now before us. —*Publisher's Note.*

BRUSSELS.

Collection of King Leopold.

CXVII.—A Madonna with the Child Jefus. Two angels are holding up a drapery, three others fitting at the B. Virgin's feet. This picture belonged to the family of Gondi, at Florence.

ENGLAND.

Prince Albert's Collection.

CXVIII.—S. Peter Martyr.

CXIX.—A Madonna with the Child Jefus (?).

CXX.—A Nativity, with a choir of angels above the cot.

Thefe pictures are from the collection of the Brothers Metzger, at Florence.

National Gallery.

CXXI.—The Adoration of the Magi. In tempera, on wood, feven-and-a-half inches high, by one foot fix-and-a-half inches wide. Formerly in the collection of Profeffor Rofini, at Pifa. Purchafed from the Lombardi-Baldi Collection at Florence, in 1857.

CXXII.—Chrift Triumphant, with the ufual banner of triumph in his left hand, in the midft of a choir of angels, fome blowing trumpets others playing various mufical inftruments. On the two fides are kneeling a great crowd of the Bleffed :—the Patriarchs ; the Prophets ; the Madonna ; the Apoftles ; and the Saints and Martyrs of both fexes : at the extreme ends are the faints of the Dominican Order, in their white robes and black cappas. Altogether two hundred and fixty-fix figures, or portions of figures ; many with their names attached, " So beautiful," fays Vafari, " that they appear to be truly beings of Para-dife."

In tempera, on wood, in five compartments, each twelve-and-a-half inches high by eight-and-a-half inches—two feet one inch wide the fides refpectively, and two feet four-and-a-half inches wide the centre picture. Formerly the Predella of an altar in San Domenico, at Fiefole, and fold by the friars about fifty years fince to Signor Valentini, Pruffian

Conful at Rome.   Purchafed from his nephew, Signor Gioacchino Valentini, at Rome, in 1860.

W. Young Ottley's Collection.

CXXIII.—The B. Virgin carried to the tomb by the apoftles. Little picture from the church of Ogniffanti at Florence. Attributed to Giotto by Vafari, and to Beato Angelico by modern critics.—See VASARI, edit. Lemonnier, vol. 1. p. 332.

In the Life of our Lord publifhed by G. B. Nocchi, the fame fubject is marked as being in Rev. J. Sanfort's Gallery.

CXXIV.—In the houfe of a private perfon (?). Two fhutters of a tryptich reprefenting, the Elect afcending into Heaven and the Reprobate caft down into Hell.

From the Gallery of Cardinal Fefch.

CXXV.—The Laft Judgment.

Padre Marchefe (vol. 1, p. 302) fays that this picture became the property of the Prince of Canino, but it does not belong to him any more; and we are affured that it is now in England, in the collection of Lord Ward.

ANALYTICAL TABLE.

Vidit FR. V. H. FERRERI, O.P., Conv. Annun. Supprior,
 S. Th. Lector, et Libr. Revisor.

Vidit FR. VINCENTIUS KING, O.P., S. Th. Lector, et Libr.
 Revisor.

> Attentâ relatione revisorum nostri Ordinis à nobis designa-
> torum super operâ cui titulus, *Life of Beato Angelico
> da Fiesole, of the Order of Friar-Preachers. Trans-
> lated, &c., &c.,* eandem typis mandari permittimus.

F. THOMAS NICKOLDS,
 S. Th. Lector, Præd. Gen., et Prior Provinc. Ord. Præd. in Angliâ.

TABLE OF CHAPTERS.